The Last G

by

John Behardien

Duncurin
Publishing

Duncurin.com

This is a work of Fiction. Also available in hard copy.

First Published in England MMXI

Duncurin Publishing
Monton
England

Duncurin.com

ISBN : 978-09570982-1-3

Book Design : Sheepie

DEDICATION

For Mum and Dad. Dad, it's been almost thirty years, you both remain forever in our thoughts, our dreams and our prayers. What delights you would have seen!
We strive each day to be worthy of the pride in us, you always held.

WITH THANKS

With sincere thanks to my friend Eva Jacobs, the original 'Superdoc', to whom, as always, I am indebted for her unstinting efforts, endless patience and a wonderful command of English that I aspire to.

With thanks also to Roger Ellis for allowing me to use another fantastic photograph from his amazing collection. www.theplacephoto.com

And to Howard Evans whose artistic flair and skills with everything and anything that can be printed, knows no bounds, of which I am in constant awe and admiration.
howarde@kingfisher-graphics.co.uk

CONTENTS

CHAPTER 1

"FUTURE FORETOLD"

Shiplake Manor had been associated with the village of Little Dunham for as far back as any of the inhabitants could remember. There it lay, on the edge of the village, like an imposing cruise liner, at anchor amidst a sea of green rolling fields, manicured gardens and structured woodland. Those who saw its awe-inspiring mass were invariably of the view that it was also a thing of beauty: the builders and craftsmen having all worked closely to achieve the desired result from unyielding brick, stone and timber. Though the Scottish architect had chosen an Edwardian butterfly plan, he had avoided a complicated roof-line by the simple expedient of placing the highest and most dominant section of roof over the central body of the house, to form the imposing hall. Overlooking the central, circular courtyard, nestling between the two wings, was a majestic window set into the wall to illuminate the vast hallway with its mosaic floor of Carrara marble.

Time had served only to enhance the charm of the manor, as weathering had carefully caressed the brick and mellow stone. The lie of the land had been harnessed, all those years ago, to complement the grand house, and the grounds planted with woodland and gardens, to give colour and vibrancy with each passing month. Regardless of sun or season, the rooms would collect and distribute the available light to create a bright airy feeling, which seemed to permeate through the entire building from the lofty attic rooms to the deepest cellar.

Those who had been fortunate to live within its calm, friendly walls over the years had been witness to happy, contented times almost as though the house imbued a benign, vital essence coupled to its pleasing ambience. Some years earlier the house had changed hands and the new owners, too, at first, drew benefit from this unseen and unquantifiable substance. Perhaps no-one could have foreseen that things were to alter in a violent and cruel way. The preceding twelve months however, had been accompanied by considerable change. Where there had been brightness, now lay darkness. Any trace of happiness was now besieged by total despair. Open, once glorious gardens, now reflected a lonely and frightening wilderness, and large expanses now resembled a prison, as if a lifelong sentence was to run concurrently with abject misery. Today was to signal another transposition, one final unalterable change to deny the ongoing gloom its remaining victim.

She had been sitting on the edge of her bed since well before the dawn chorus had announced the arrival of yet another day. Her deep catatonia had ensured that her brain understood there was little point in rising, in moving, or even in gazing at the photograph that her right hand had been holding for well over two hours. She remembered only that there had been a reason for her to take it from her bedside table, but the brain would go no further, as it instructed the body to remain motionless apart from fundamental respiration that it had not managed to shut down. Slowly, the reason why she had been holding the photograph drifted back into her mind. She now knew that this day was to be different from each preceding one. She crossed to the window and drew back the curtains. It was a bright May morning with the sun coming up over the south lawn, but her brain no longer registered such irrelevancies. She no longer noticed the magnificent view, the ornate, well-tended gardens and beautiful grounds that her staff worked on with a passion totally missing within herself. It was as if the all-pervading despondency had replaced all other emotions like some malignant cancer spreading inexorably through her whole being.

She almost smiled to herself as she grasped the top of the container. '*Lydia Jardine*' could still be clearly read on the peeling label and just above, the words - *'Dothiepin 75mgs. One to be taken at night. It is dangerous to exceed the stated dose.'* She had counted the shiny, red tablets weeks before. 'Fifty should be more than enough,' she had decided. It was a perfect irony that she would use, as the instrument of her demise. the tablets that had been prescribed for her mother two weeks before, in the soundless despair of depression, she had killed herself.

Twelve months had passed since then, with one day of quiet torment being much the same as the one before. Friends had told her that she would feel better with time. One by one they had all prophesised that within six months she would have recovered from her grief. One by one they had been wrong, and the illness that now filled her, had shown itself to be more persistent than her friends, and ultimately stronger than herself. Today she would acknowledge its strength, its inalterability and also her total and irrevocable capitulation. All she could see was the despair, which no doubt had faced her mother, and it seemed fitting that she too should choose to exit rather than remain feeling wretched and alone.

Only the gypsy had been right. That caused the smile to break through, though fleetingly. What had begun as a bit of fun on a wet Saturday in Manchester, as she and a friend had found themselves visiting Madam Orrah whose rusting sign in a back street of the Northern quarter advertised *Futures Told and Destiny Announced*, had ended with a sinister and terrifying prophecy.

The gypsy's adaptation to her native Eastern European steppe had been comprehensive. The weather-beaten face was smooth, red and shiny from exposure to scorching sun, biting wind and severe winters. The thick, greying hair had been tied back, serving only to enhance the rounded face: the squat, powerful figure and those large, square-shaped hands, covered in material more reminiscent of leather than human skin. The skin as a whole had a texture more grained than wrinkled. Only the bent spine had developed since her arrival in England; the product of weakening bones, and her tendency to stoop over the baize of the table. The one feature which held Melanie's attention despite her efforts to look elsewhere was the left, opaque-white eye, blinded by the intrusion of a foreign body some years earlier. It drifted asynchronously from the right one, which remained keen and alert.

A leathery grasp had taken Melanie's soft palm. The single cognisant eye peered carefully as if looking straight into the steaming cauldron, like some alchemist about to summon pure gold from the mix before them. She began with her usual preamble to underline her authenticity. At first geniality had shone from the round face with its well-practised ease, then things began to change. Madam Orrah had gripped her palm as if frightened to let go. The stare was transmuted from fascination, to incredulity, to alarm. She hesitated before speaking, as if struggling with the enormity of revealing even a little of what she had seen. Then, unable to represent her vision in more favourable terms, and with a mixture of horror and strange magnetism, she unleashed the words still ringing in the young woman's ears.

"I see nothing but death and misery all around. All you shall know, and see, and feel will end with violence and with pain. Your future is foretold and holds nothing but unhappiness from this day forth. Those who try to help you, shall be the first to die."

Initially it had seemed like a joke, then like the curse that it undoubtedly was. Melanie felt her head throb with the strain of attempting to rationalise what she had heard. She had begged the gypsy to tell her the truth, but the older woman remained transfixed as if a protective torpor would be the only thing to prevent her too from being affected by the pain of what she had seen; further speech, long since impossible. The gypsy refused to say more and bade her farewell with an impassive look that pierced, as if she had been already looking at a cold corpse.

Stephanie, who had come with her, awoke from her trance-like state and tugged at her arm. "Melanie, lets go, there's nothing more here. Let's grab a drink." Her voice quivered as the terror rose within her. In the bar across the street, they both reassured each other that the gypsy was lying, that all the mystery held no substance. They did their best to replace clairvoyance with sound reasoning and bravado: a strategy that was bound to fail before first utterance.

An hour later they left the bar and parted with a hug. Melanie caught a taxi and returned to her penthouse on the 47th floor of the Beetham tower. The concierge gave his usual jovial greeting as he opened the entrance door. "Afternoon Miss Jardine, are you well?" Melanie responded affirmatively to the polite enquiry and rushed up to her apartment to pour herself another stiff drink. Her hands were still shaking with an uneasy fear, that had enveloped her like a summer smog. She spent the afternoon phoning her family and friends. Only her elder sister, Patricia, sensed the panic.
"Melanie what's wrong. Why do you sound so tense?"
She told her of the visit and the cruel words that had been unleashed.
"Melanie, don't be silly, how could she possibly know what your future holds? She doesn't know you, and it's a load of mumbo jumbo. I'm surprised at you. MBA Harvard and you listen to a load of guff. How could she possibly know anything?"
"Trish, she told me that it's your birthday next week - how could she know that?"
Silence followed, but Patricia was unwavering.
"Simple guesswork, sis, nothing else. These people are all con artists to get money from you. Why not come home at weekend and let's talk."
"I have a holiday next week - I'll drive up to see you," Melanie suggested.

That night sleep brought no release from the horror now coursing through her veins. Melanie seemed to sense, as the early hours ushered the coming sun, that she would never sleep again. The relaxing holiday never arrived. As the phone rang the following day, she picked up the receiver with the uneasy calm of a bomb disposal expert, uncertain whether her next move would be the last. At first she heard nothing but sobbing, then her mother's voice.

The terrible accident echoed in her ears and shivered down through her body. A motorway pileup in dry, bright conditions. Trish and her father had been killed outright. The police were at a loss to explain why the Bentley had left the road and collided with a bridge support on the M6. Death had been instant. Eye witness reports said that the car suddenly swerved and continued at speed until it hit the concrete support, head on. For moments Melanie stood stupefied, and then slowly replaced the receiver. She remembered only telling her mother that she would be home that night. First, she had a call to make.

Only the gypsy could make sense of the madness unfolding through her life. She found the back street. Once again she pushed back the dirty, creaking door with filthy windows through which light struggled to penetrate. At first Madam Orrah refused to say anything, almost as if Melanie's very presence signalled doom to all who might look at her.
"I can tell you no more, than this. The hand of fate shall reach out to you, and you shall turn it away. Nothing can protect you then, mark my words well." Suddenly her expression softened in the warm glow of the lamp. "Take this, child, and go in peace." A silver necklace was pressed into her hand, with the patina of age and careful wear; the inscription no longer decipherable.

Her mother was devastated by the enormity of her loss. Melanie knew that her grieving would never end. Melanie's own energies were diverted into supporting her mother and struggling to add meaning and the will to continue. The battle was already lost. Dr Michaels visited from the nearby village and prescribed more and more tablets. Consultants came and went, as did counsellors and numerous others. All did their best to reassure and advise that it would take time. Only Melanie could see that time was running out. Even as the housekeeper ran from the fume-filled garage, Melanie had found the note on her mother's dressing table. Her eyes scanned the words but her brain had already registered the message. ‘No point to life, nothing to live for, forgive me....’ The beautiful, flowing script had ended simply, like life itself. 'I love you.'

The tears had not flowed then, nor thereafter. Why they should appear now, twelve months later, Melanie neither knew nor cared. She carefully placed the photograph on the dressing table. Her brain was only aware that it had somehow triggered instructions that it, too, was compelled to obey. It did so with a purpose that the wasted body had not seen for months. She moved to unscrew the cap to release the tablets that would also now release her.

Then fierce pain diverted her with an immediacy all of its own. She rushed to the en-suite bathroom as the nausea welled up. The searing pain drove away, at once, her view of the black abyss of utter misery. She rolled with agony on the bathroom floor clutching her side. Mrs Perkins the housekeeper, came rushing in.
"Are you alright Miss?" Her concern was as thoughtful and genuine as her comment redundant. The pain wracked Melanie's body once again as the writhing continued, she clutched her abdomen as beads of sweat appeared across her face.
The next words were more constructive. "I'll phone Doctor Michaels." As Melanie motioned her dissent, the wave of pain and vomiting crashed through her body once again.

Dr Michaels sat behind his large desk, pulling down his waistcoat over his increasingly ponderous abdomen. As he did so he thought, as so often, about a diet. Such thoughts would last usually for moments only, or at least until the next urgent request was generated from his overworked schedule. He was about to start his morning surgery when the call came through. Janice, one of the junior receptionists, rushed in after a quiet and respectful knock on the panelled door.
"Sorry to trouble you Dr Michaels we've just received an urgent call from Shiplake, Melanie Jardine is in a lot of pain."
"Gosh that family," Dr Michaels thought aloud, "talk about star crossed." His awkward dilemma of whether to rush out now or,

hopefully, visit later, was shattered by the roar of an engine outside.
'Ah, Smith,' he thought, with relief already breaking through his concern. "Janice, tell Smith to go. I'll see his first few patients, but tell him not to be away too long."

He nodded to himself with sheer relief, as he remembered the advice given by Mrs Farnell, his practice manager, about cutting down some of his workload, by taking on a junior partner. He continued to deliberate in his relaxed mood, that she had been correct, as usual. What a wise move he had made appointing her, now nearly forty years ago. He was grinning to himself as Dr. James Smith peeped uncertainly round the door, followed quickly by Mrs Farnell and Janice trotting in her wake.
"Sorry Dr Michaels, about being late," offered the young doctor uneasily. "The car wouldn't start," everyone mouthed the words, as Smith uttered them, with well-rehearsed unison.

"Get back into that old banger of yours, Smith and get up to the Manor, Melanie Jardine; never really seen her as a patient. Sole surviving member of her family. Poor buggers."
Dr Michaels spoke just as he consulted, in short bursts which were usually straight to the point. He had a loyal following and, despite the recent arrival of the young Dr Smith, patients would happily wait for his no-holds-barred philosophy and direct approach. He looked over the half-moon glasses, as usual, on the very edge of his nose, as he gazed expectantly at Smith. Mrs Farnell, as efficient as ever, held out the patient notes. She looked at Dr Michaels; his greying hair had become just a little curly, as it always did when he needed a trim. He caught her gaze, just as Dr Smith disappeared with the notes and his bag. After what seemed like an age the car finally started and the battered Maestro made its brisk but choppy way through the village and up the long, tortuous lane to the Manor.
"Mrs Farnell, would you phone Albert and ask him if he can fit me in for a trim this lunch?" asked Dr Michaels as he looked through the window at the clouds of smoke belching through the exhaust.

"Must take a gallon of petrol just to start that thing," he mused as he called his first patient.

Mrs Perkins had managed to get Melanie onto the bed where she was sweating vigorously with short, shallow breaths and obviously in pain. It was not the deep brown eyes that she noticed first, it was the calm steady voice and the soft but firm hand which shook hers with a keenness and vitality echoed by their owner. 'Not working hands, those', as her father would have said, yet nevertheless elegant, precise hands which had been carefully nurtured, directed to study rather than to performing manual work. Fleetingly, through her agony, she gazed into those shining, vital eyes, so perceptive and yet so warm and so comforting, as Smith smiled nervously.

"Hello Miss Jardine, I'm Dr. Smith, Dr. Michaels' new partner."

"Smith – that's not very original, Doctor, or is it a cover to hide your real identity?"

"Well, I thought of changing it to something a bit more exotic, but I couldn't come up with anything suitable, so I stuck with 'Smith'; something plain and ordinary, a bit like me!"

Despite her misery and her pain Melanie couldn't see that either 'plain' or 'ordinary' would apply to the young doctor, as he stood a little uncertainly by the side of her bed, carrying his large case.

"Perhaps we could have a competition and invite suitable suggestions on the back of a postcard?" she asked, as she winced once again with pain.

"Well, Miss Jardine, I thought of that, but I was a bit frightened they'd all come up with rude names."

"No, don't you worry doctor, I'll screen all the answers and destroy the rude ones unless they're really funny. Until then, how about 'Superdoc'?"

"Well, Miss Jardine, let's see if we can get you better first; until then I'll be plain Smith?"

Once again another sharp pang of pain crashed across her abdomen causing her to wince under its severity.

"Tell me what's the problem?" he asked, aware that something was in progress that would need his undivided attention.

Melanie noted the dark brown hair and the bright eyes - almost like shiny conkers, newly fallen from the tree on a sunny autumnal afternoon. Honest, open eyes, capable of perceiving so much, yet also able to give so much away. More than a momentary contact, she could no longer trust. Mrs Perkins could contain herself no longer.
“I knew doctor, she hasn't been eating for months and months, and she's been going downhill steadily. Good job I came early today, I don’t think Miss would have phoned.”
Melanie silenced the interruption with a pant and a wince. “I've had this pain in my stomach all morning, though now it’s moved to my right groin.”

The patient was talking in short bursts, as if the inflamed tissues could no longer sanction movement from the abdominal musculature, even for the purpose of breathing. He in turn had noted her striking hazel eyes with tiny flecks of pale amber, arranged radially, around their rim. Eyes that could make contact for the shortest of instants, preferring either the corner of the ceiling, or better still the warm, familiar pattern on the duvet. The lank, greasy hair could not detract from her fine-featured face, though the cheeks had turned sallow, the lips pale and the body wasted with self-neglect.
“Are the bowels and waterworks all right?”
She nodded enthusiastically at first, but this too was checked by pain.
“Have you been feeling sick, Miss Jardine?”
“Please call me Melanie, Doctor. Yes with vomiting.”
Smith took her blood pressure as they talked, and motioned to feel her abdomen.
Carefully and thoughtfully the hands were applied with gentle yet revealing skill.
“Appendicitis, if I'm not mistaken. How old are you Melanie?”
“Twenty six next, Dr Smith.”
“Are you on any tablets?”
Their eyes engaged for the second fleeting moment.

“No, nothing.”

She glanced over to the dressing table where the tablets had been left in the flurry of pain. The quick glance was noted in a blink from the chestnut eyes which for some years now, had taught him the power of observation in the most simple or complex consultations. Dr Smith rose to his feet and asked to use the phone after apologising that his mobile’s battery had gone flat. Respectfully, Mrs Perkins led him to an extension where he was assured of privacy. Within seconds he was through to the hospital switchboard.
"Could I have the Resident Surgical Officer please? Hello, are you the surgeon on call? I have a young patient here with right iliac fossa pain, with rebound and guarding. I'm sure it’s an appendix.”
The RSO accepted his assessment without dispute and asked for the patient's details. Smith sat at the small table on the first floor landing and produced a sheet of notepaper upon which he summarised his examination.

Moments later the Ambulance was on its way. Melanie managed another painful smile.
"Thanks for coming, Dr Smith, Superdoc, I won’t give your true identity away; your secret is safe with me."
“All part of the service ma’am,” as he feigned a serious salute. He handed Mrs Perkins the letter, “Please give this to the ambulance men, they'll pass it on to the surgeon on call, who'll see Melanie in Casualty.”
Turning back to his patient, "I'll come and see you when you get home, if I may?” He walked across the room to pick up his case. At this point he feigned chancing upon the tablets that he had deliberately sought as he crossed the room. He picked up the tiny bottle that he’d noted from her fleeting, stray glance.
" ‘Dothiepin’ - these are not yours, Melanie, are they?" As he deciphered the label,
"They are rather dangerous to leave around, may I take them?"

Melanie nodded as the gloom enveloped her again. She would find some other way when she got home. Mrs Perkins walked with Dr Smith down the magnificent oak staircase, past the large stained glass panels filtering the morning sunshine into the hall. He remarked on how beautiful the grand house was.
“This is no happy house Doctor," Mrs Perkins countered with a passive despair. She bit her lower lip firmly so as to prevent it quivering with the unleashed memories, and changed the subject quickly. “I've been so worried about her. She hasn't been eating for months. Some nights, when I sleep in, I can hear her pacing in the early hours, night after night.”
“We'll be admitting her to hospital for a few days. Hopefully she'll feel better soon. Don't worry, she’ll be fine.” He deliberately understated, to gauge more accurately her worry and hopefully gain more insight.
“She just isn’t well Doctor, even before this. I can see her going the same way as her dear mother. Gassed herself, she did.”
"My goodness, I see! I'm so sorry to hear that. She seems so young to have faced such a traumatic event. May I ask what happened to her father?”
“Never been ill in his life. They say he must have had a heart attack whilst driving. The car came off the road at speed, clear as day, it was, and smashed into a concrete wall. He and Trish, that’s Melanie’s older sister, were killed in an instant.”
Smith wasn’t sure that his mind could compass so much bad news so quickly. He knew he needed time and some more thought on the matter. His instinct was to withdraw, for now, and it looked as though appendicitis had bought him at least a few days.

The GP knew in that moment that he was dealing with a serious case of depression. The wasted body could only have come from months of self-neglect, the hollow, sickly complexion with the lustreless eyes, helpless expression and the look on her face as each breath came as if, only, to defy her. Doctors would talk of the efficacy of modern antidepressants but Smith knew that in serious cases, they could fail. Psychiatrists who had been brought in to manage such cases would sometimes fall back on the treatment of last resort: a treatment known as Electro-Convulsive Therapy or ECT, which had been in use for over one hundred years and offered some, but by no means every, chance of success.

“Thanks for that Mrs Perkins. I will keep my eye on things. Please phone me when she gets home and I'll make another house-call."

As they crossed the marble floor Mrs Perkins became engrossed in her own thoughts. She had heard the assurances before. Dr Michaels said the same words more than a year ago, but still could do little to change the outcome. Perhaps the new doctor could do what his more senior colleague could not. He seemed ever so young: too young to be a doctor. People always said that about policemen, but this young man looked as if he should still be in college. He seemed much too young to be responsible for his own life, let alone others’. At least for the time being, she was going into hospital. Maybe they would encourage her to eat and look after herself a little better. One thing intrigued the elderly housekeeper and that was how quickly the handsome young doctor had sparked just a little of the former happy and carefree person in her boss; the one she had known before the dreadful events had overtaken her. What a shame about that horrible bushy beard that didn't seem to suit him at all.

"Thank you doctor, I will."

Dr Smith left to coax the Maestro, once more, into life as Mrs Perkins went back upstairs, to sit with Melanie until the Ambulance came.

“That nice doctor said he'll come back and see you when you get home, Miss.”

Melanie's black mood continued apace as she thought only of her own means of escape. She knew that it would make no difference and that Carbon Monoxide was perhaps her best way after all. Another bout of pain shot through her stomach to distract her, only for a few moments. Her admission would mean only the shortest of delays to her plans. With luck she might get there too late or, better still, die under the anaesthetic, never to have to face her private hell ever again. An escape was just that, regardless from whence it came.

Dr Smith drove down the tree-lined drive, the long way back to the main road. He had just reached the gate as the Ambulance crew passed him at speed. He took the tablets from his pocket and placed them in the ash-tray, with a gentle tap on the loose cap.

Back at the surgery, Dr Michaels supplied more detail about the unhappy events of the past year. Thoughtfully, and with a certain prescience, the younger man asked Dr Michaels if he thought Melanie was a suicide risk.
"I pulled all the stops out with the mother. We had specialists going in. I tried everything I knew. I even admitted her to the Psychiatric ward at The Priory for a couple of weeks." Michaels was strangely defensive as if the memories had woken feelings of guilt, that he had hoped that time would submerge. "I tell you. You try your best, but it won't make any difference. Once these Jardines get an idea into their heads, that's it. You might as well call the Coroner now," he said, attempting to disguise his discomfort with his usual abrupt manner.

Smith was deep in thought as he stared intently at the steaming coffee mug that Janice had offered, with her usual deference. He did not doubt Dr Michaels' word, but was not going to accept it as a *fait accompli*, nor was he used to accepting failure. "Possibly." was all Smith could counter as the receptionist brought in the notes for his morning surgery. He placed Melanie's notes in his bag so that he could study them in more detail for any clues that might help him in his undertaking.

CHAPTER II

"MISDIAGNOSES"

A week later as Doctor Smith began his early surgery just after eight a.m. Molly Fay, a middle aged woman he had never met before, came in and sat down.

"I'm so sorry to trouble you doctor and I do hope I'm not wasting your time. I'm a nurse at Macclesfield General and I usually work nights so I've just finished my shift. I've noticed for the past four weeks that I've been getting breathless. I'm sure it's nothing but I wonder if you have any ideas?"

"In what way have you been getting more breathless, Molly?"

"Well, I like to swim at least once a week and I can usually manage fifty lengths. Last week I had to get out of the water because I just couldn't breathe, at well under fifty lengths."

Smith's interest picked up. He knew there were a thousand-and-one reasons why a forty-five year old person could become more breathless, but this sounded like something more acute, and also something dangerous.

"Would you mind if I took your blood pressure?"

He was alarmed to find that the blood pressure was very high where the heart made its beat, but very low where it filled. The wide range was very unusual for someone who was still fairly young. More worryingly, the heart seemed to be beating very slowly. He knew that a slow pulse was not unusual in athletic people who did a lot of training, but this would never be accompanied by such a high blood pressure. He listened to her heart and his worry intensified. The heart was beating so slowly that the only way it could maintain sufficient output was with massive, forceful beats that would have been beyond the capacity of an older, or less fit person. He placed his little Oximeter on her finger, which would test her lungs and heart. The oxygen level in her blood was good but the pulse showed 42, about half the normal rate. The little light blinked ever so slowly. He looked at Molly and spoke carefully. "I'm afraid I'm going to have to admit you to

hospital, Molly."
She looked incredulous. "But you can't, I'm working tonight and I'm the most senior nurse on the ward, and besides at weekend I'm flying to Spain for two weeks' holiday."
"Forgive me, Molly, but I can't promise you that you'll be doing either of those things."
She looked at him as if he had taken leave of his senses.
"I think it's necessary to phone an Ambulance and get you seen in casualty now?"
"I drove here, Doctor, my car is outside; can I not go home and change?"
"Sorry Molly, I need to organise an Ambulance for you, and I'll get you seen straight away. I think your heart is beating too slowly, and although you are young for such a thing, I'm worried that you may be in complete heart block."
He left the room to request an urgent ambulance.

She knew seeing a young, inexperienced doctor was a mistake. If only she'd gone with her instinct and requested Dr Michaels. He would have her sorted by now without all this palaver. She knew that complete heart block sounded serious. She supposed she had better go along with what he'd said, and in any case, she knew that Casualty would discharge her as soon as they set eyes on her. For the life of her she couldn't think why he didn't let her drive herself there. The ambulance staff were always going on about how people abused the service for trivial things.

The ambulance came. Dr Smith went out to meet them and give them the letter.
"Where's the patient, Doctor?" the ambulance driver said with urgency, as his colleague unloaded the stretcher. Incredibly, Molly walked out to the Ambulance, not far behind Smith.
"Many thanks for coming lads," Smith said, "straight to Casualty please and here's the letter. I'll phone ahead."
He went inside to continue his surgery. The waiting room was full of patients who couldn't help but hear the comments made by the ambulance men as soon as Smith had gone. Unfortunately Dr

Michaels had just arrived and was sitting behind his desk, his window, next to the car park, open in the warm day.

The younger driver who had wrestled with the superfluous trolley looked puzzled but his more senior colleague, Bill Weston, seethed with anger. Anger which bubbled up as soon as the ambulance door closed behind their patient.
"What's he up to, there's nowt wrong with her. He says he's going to phone ahead, indeed! What a joke, and he goes 'n books an urgent Ambulance for this. Get this, her car's over there. These bloody young doctors don't know their elbows from an Aspidistra. I don't know where old Michaels 'as dug him up from, but he won't last two minutes 'ere. Michaels never wastes our time like this. You wait, I'm gonna tell the super. about this, she'll av 'is guts for a new washing line. 'E'd better get used to them flowers: 'e'll be working in a flower shop by the time she's got 'old of him."
The younger driver grinned. "What shall we do with 'er, Bill?"
"S'pose we'd better take her. Urgent ambulance 'n'all. You just wait till the super. 'ears about this. Must tell the wife to make sure she always sees Michaels," confirmed Bill, who was unable to match the lighter mood of his colleague. "That beard knows more medicine than 'im I'll wager," he continued as they both entered the ambulance and switched off the flashing lights.

Michaels looked crestfallen. He poured an extra measure of whisky into his mug of tea with less guilt than usual. Smith had interviewed well, he seemed so young, so keen and so full of energy. He had arrived with some wonderful references. Maybe it just wasn't enough to make up for the fact that he seemed to be a poor clinician unsuited to life as a General Practitioner or to village medicine. Of course Dr Michaels remembered a time when he, himself, was still learning, but he'd never made a mistake like the one that seemed in progress now. To make matters worse, Mrs Farnell had endorsed his choice, and it was very unusual for her to be wrong. Perhaps they had both made a mistake and should have chosen another. How to tell Smith? That was the next dilemma. He would have to choose his moment carefully but do it fairly soon; perhaps he could simply wait for the complaint to come in and use this as a prompt. He sipped his slightly more than usually potent tea, and decided with another weary sigh that he had better start his own surgery; someone had to keep the ship afloat.

Later that morning, Dr Smith received a call from Mrs Perkins at the manor. Melanie was home and could he pop in. He found himself ascending the oak staircase with its panelled walls, and staring at that stained glass window, reflecting on its beauty, which seemed strangely at variance with the mission he now faced. He could see, through the antique glass, the beautiful gardens in front of the grand house, and beyond them the fields of the Cheshire plain. Michaels had all but written her off, no doubt still smarting from his failure twelve months earlier. He tapped on the bedroom door and walked in followed quickly by Mrs Perkins.
"Ah 'Superdoc'. As you can see, another mere mortal saved," she offered a little accusingly. "We'll have to get you a uniform, in case people learn who you really are," she continued.
"I thought plain clothes today, as you already know my true identity."
She looked carefully at him, sensing that something seemed a little out of place.
"Is that beard part of your disguise?"
He stroked it meditatively, but looked a little embarrassed by the attention. "Actually it's a stick-on one. It comes off when I go in the bath," he offered unwarily.
" I thought so. It looks like one of those pads I scrub my back with," she ventured, and couldn't help but think how little it suited him. "You lost a bet didn't you and you've had to grow that?"

Her father was always suspicious of men with bushy beards, just like the one sported by Smith. This image seemed at complete variance with the person she thought she'd seen at their first meeting, which was probably why she couldn't quite hide her dislike of it. Even Smith's ears blushed. He decided to change the conversation quickly and to more professional matters.

“How are you Melanie?”

The eager, chestnut eyes met, briefly, those intense hazel ones with the little flecks, but this time it was as a stormy day where the sun had been eclipsed by a total black cloud, and made all dark and uninviting.
“I'm fine,” she said, without conviction, as eye contact broke in an instant.
“May I feel your tummy,” he said, whilst shifting ground quickly as he felt himself growing nervous. “A first rate job if ever I saw one. Are your waterworks and bowels OK?”
“Yes, fine doctor,” she confirmed.
“Have you lost weight or have you always been this thin?” The question hung unanswered. “What about your sleep, Melanie, how is that?” The silence, once again, supplied the answers without further enquiry.

Smith was thinking furiously. There was a lot more here than met the eye. He continued to survey the situation as he spoke. “The suture line will heal in no time, and you'll be left with a tiny scar about an inch long. I don't know if you're a sunbather at all, but it should be hidden by the average sort of swimsuit.” For a moment he looked slightly embarrassed. He looked briefly at her thin almost emaciated abdomen; in an otherwise healthy person this could only be the result of self-neglect. This would fit with the picture that was forming quickly in his mind. “Should be back to your old self in no time.” His calm demeanour was an attempt to reassure her, but of much more importance were the words that came next. “Melanie, will you pop into the surgery some time for a chat?”
“Why is that doctor?”
“Just so I can see how you're getting on. Sometimes people can be very run down after something like this,” he suggested.

Though the appendicitis was mild and caught nicely before peritonitis supervened, he knew that if he was to be any help to her at all, he had to keep her under review. He hoped that she would

not see straight through his subterfuge. He knew also that if he declared his hand too soon, she would never attend.
“I'm sure you're much too busy, Dr Smith. I’ll be fine now.”
“No, actually everyone wants to see Dr Michaels.”
“Come now, Superdoc? That can't be possibly true.”
“Well, in point of fact it’s true,” he lied once again, but more convincingly this time.
“I could do with one or two turning up, asking specifically for me, even if only to complain.”
“OK. I'll come and complain. I wanted a longer scar. Also, I am not sure you're tall enough for a superhero. You aren’t an imposter are you, and are not really here to save the world? I bet you're no taller than five feet, nine inches.”
“Five foot nine and three quarters actually,” he offered after feigning a little hurt, “five ten if I wear woolly socks.”
Melanie smiled again. "I’ll be as tall as you if I stand next to you in my Laboutins.”
“Melanie, you can stand next to me any time in your ‘labby tootins’,” he replied, without quite knowing what she meant.

The cloud parted again as she found herself staring at this bright, unassuming youthful doctor who seemed to combine the eagerness of a young puppy greeting his master, the energy of a sheep dog on a Welsh mountain, and the warmth of a Golden Retriever curled up in front of the fire. She smiled again at the thought of what he would say if she had revealed some of this imagery floating in her brain. In any event, his calm self-effacing manner had banished the irritability that she somehow couldn't hide.
“How about next Tuesday?” he offered, as inevitably he re-focussed on the business in hand.
“You must be desperate for custom, Dr Smith.”
He smiled. “Melanie I’m out on a bit of a limb here, but I’m going to take that as a ‘yes’. It’s a deal?”

Mrs Perkins beamed with delight. The delicate interplay was not lost on her, nor was the vital concession that had been won. She almost skipped down the stairs as she showed him out. May be this young man was to be the one who would peer into the accumulating gloom and see a way out of her employer's private misery. His enthusiasm and keen edge were certainly there for all to see, and she noticed that Melanie had responded to him better than to anyone else of late. Young or not, Dr Smith was sticking by his promise. People had been and gone, even good friends, all failed to break through that all-pervading misery, which seemed to envelope the onlooker, so that it could be borne no longer.

"Many thanks doctor. Can you make her well again?"

"It won't be for the lack of trying, Mrs Perkins."

His eyes were wide and open with sincerity. He had a calm steady gaze that seemed to lock onto the person with whom he was conversing in a warm, friendly way, as if his thoughts had been concentrated exclusively on that person. Despite being in her sixth decade, even she found herself a little lighter of heart and of step.

Melanie gently caressed her silver necklace as the blackness descended once again. Maybe this was to be the hand of fate that she was about to ignore. She knew that she no longer cared one way or another, but perhaps she would keep the appointment although any hint of optimism still lay swamped by a hopelessness that filled her.

Mrs Perkins returned, a little more breathless from excitement, rather than exertion.

"What a nice young man. You're so lucky to have such a dashing young doctor. In fact, he doesn't look old enough to be a doctor. I've never noticed him before at old Michaels' surgery. Things are looking up. Not keen on that beard though, Miss are you? You are naughty, you know, embarrassing him like that, and him being a doctor n'all. Still, he took it in good part I expect."

Melanie let her continue for some time, without saying a word. Mrs Perkins was always doing her best to stimulate and motivate. She was certainly no-one's fool. Perhaps she had already recognised the terminal slope down which her poor mother had descended in the weeks before she died. She was sure that Mrs

Perkins would have done her utmost then, just as now, but like all the doctors and specialists had also failed to derail the gypsy's prophecy. It was almost that it had gathered such momentum that it was now impossible to divert. It seemed far easier to go along with it, than attempt to stay and fight in a lonely depression.

Brilliant sunshine greeted the Tuesday and the silver Jaguar XKR, Convertible flowed, almost noiselessly, into the surgery car park. She parked next to Dr Smith's reserved space in which sat a rusting, old Maestro, and pressed the button to close the electric roof. The village was small enough so that even unexceptional events triggered a wave of inquisitiveness. Melanie walked slowly and hesitantly into the modest waiting room and approached the Reception window. Her appearance was heavily modified by self-neglect. The flat shoes, chosen, neither for comfort, nor practicality but simply the first pair she had chanced across. The normal erect posture, bowed as if it had been directly worn down by events. The slim figure, just a little too slim as neglect damaged the appetite, to reveal more of a wasted appearance. Her clothes seemed ill-fitting as they hung from the waist, their style and colour oddly at variance with what a young woman would usually choose to wear, and the overall picture: one that made her look dishevelled and uncared for. Heads turned as this emaciated and ill-looking young woman engaged as briefly as possible with the receptionist behind the glass louvred window. More heads turned as she gave her name. Some of those who had made her acquaintance under happier times, simply did not recognise her, her lethargic and purposeless gait making barely a sound on the hard floor, as her feet made slow and uncertain contact. She spoke very quietly and indistinctly in the hope of attracting as little attention as possible. Unfortunately this strategy was swept away, as all those who were present were impelled by unremitting curiosity. More heads turned as she remained standing rather than look for a vacant seat and attract more attention than her depleted state could withstand at that time.

Mrs Farnell studied the young woman carefully, her powers of observation, as always, carefully tuned to see much more than the obvious and a person's outward appearance, which she had learned could often deceive. The skin had a slight olive appearance that lack of sunshine had been unable to dull. The cheekbones, high and well formed, had not suffered from the more general wasting of the rest of her body and the eyes shone like beacons, projecting through flawless crystal, that even her averted gaze could somehow not diminish. Despite her somewhat flaccid posture, some had also noted the athletic poise that was more than hinted at, the beautiful, clear skin that needed no makeup to embellish, and the glorious hair, the colour of a creamy caramel, that had simply been washed, combed through and allowed to dry in the warm day, its informal style seeming only to enhance her uncommon looks.

She waited patiently, doing as little as possible to attract attention to herself, which only served to rouse more curiosity in others who were present that day. The reception staff informed Dr Smith that his patient was waiting. Her attempt to simply blend in and do her best to look like one of the supporting pillars of the divide that separated the Reception office from the waiting room, was doomed to fail as soon as Smith entered. He bounded forward, as would a collie on finding a lost sheep to return to the fold. He shook her hand warmly, his style just a little more effusive than her fragile state could bear. He grabbed her hand and supported it with his free one and shook it with more enthusiasm. The people in the waiting room looked aghast, some 'tutted' with thinly veiled disgust. Old Michaels was never like this, the poor girl looked stunned.

"Oh, Miss Jardine, thank you for coming, so nice to see you."

Melanie paused, realising that no words would come at that point, and elected simply to follow him, as he led the way into his consulting room. Nevertheless, as she did so, a tiny flicker of a smile had formed momentarily upon her face, though like some rare isotope, it existed only fleetingly. The delicate nuances of emotion that crossed her face were not missed by Mrs Farnell, nor were the more transparent emotions, that existed in force, on the doctor's face.

Neither Melanie nor Dr Smith were concerned with physical appearance. Her priority was simply to stop the wretched feelings that existed within, even if that meant departing from this world, and his to show that there was a future and a way out of the dark despair if he could only persuade her to follow, in her helpless and weary state. Dr Smith ushered her into a small but comfortable consulting room. His open and friendly countenance seemed to permeate every aspect of his being. The beaming smile gave way to one of measured concern as the empathic mood became dominant.

"Not very big for a superhero?" she queried, as she glanced around the room.

"This is all part of my disguise," he countered.

The fleeting smile brought about the transient parting of the deepest, black, clouds once again.

"Is that Maestro also part of the disguise?" she continued.

"MG Maestro, if you please. And can you think of more appropriate transport for today's superhero," he corrected, with mock tone more befitting a headmaster.

"No, no of course not," she mused, only for an instant, as the black clouds regrouped.

"How are you Melanie?" he asked quickly, as if hoping to extract an unguarded reply

"Fine."

Eye contact vanished once again as the floor seemed safer.

“Are you sure?” his eyes narrowing a little, as he tried to pierce, what he detected, was a hastily erected defence.

“Yes,” she replied, as she hoped that simple, short answers would quickly terminate any further enquiries and disrupt the attention that he had focussed unequivocally upon her.

“I don't believe you.”

“I'm not sure why I came. Why did I come?” as if she were really asking him to confirm what she already knew to be a hopeless situation. “I think I should go,” she concluded.

"No, please stay. Dr Michaels will come in and beat me. You'd be my fifth 'walk out' this morning. Any more and Dr Michaels says he'll dock my pay."
"You mean all this and you get paid too?" As the dying embers of what had been a temporary flash of confidence ebbed away, "I'm sorry," she said, as she rose to go. There was an urgency in her need to escape, almost as if she suddenly feared being trapped.
"Please stay, Melanie. I can help you."

The calm but assertive voice seemed to reassure, just when everything seemed to be coming apart. Suddenly the tears began to flow as the immense efforts she had applied into keeping her outward appearance calm and unruffled, failed. He shot to his feet, as if her life depended directly on his next action. He quickly offered a box of tissues, which were near at hand. Of more significance, was the firm grasp applied to her arm which served to supply reassurance that she would no longer face her ordeal alone.
"I can help you through this, Melanie. If you will let me, I can make you better," he said with conviction.
"Can you bring people back from the dead, then, Doctor?"
"No-one can do that, Melanie, as you know; but at least we can make their loss bearable and not quite so desolate. It's not a case of if you will get better, it's just a matter of when," he offered with as much confidence as his worry for her would allow. "It's all a question of time."
"Everyone keeps telling me that, but I'm not sure about any of it."
"'Everyone' is not me, and I'm not about to give up, of that I'm very sure. If your family were still here, what would they want for you?"

The very mention of her family brought back a vivid reminder and an accompaniment of yet more tears. Smith was thinking furiously. He would only get one chance and had to make each word count. He could see that she was poised in the agony of indecision as to whether to depart or not. Seconds only, seemed to remain, in the hour-glass that was measuring her life.

"I really need to go."
The concern deepened still further on his face as he gazed at her, now not daring to breathe, let alone blink.
"No, I am fine," she offered, as if this would decouple his interest in her and allow her to slip away in the noiseless despair of depression. The closer he came to the truth, the harder it became to look him in the eye and to confront her innermost feelings.
"With respect, Melanie, I think you are a long way from 'fine'."
It was now or never. The direct approach was, perhaps, his best chance.
"Not sleeping Melanie, early morning waking, poor appetite, weight loss. Do you think you could be depressed?"
"No; I am fine, Dr Smith," she said with finality, and once again rose to go.
Smith rose too, acutely aware that this might well be his last chance to stage a rescue.
"What about these Melanie?" He produced the bottle of tablets, he had taken from the dressing table.
"Those were my mother's."
"You know, in overdose they would kill you? It's a horrible, painful death too."
She barely resisted the temptation to say that she didn't care, but the defiant look said much more. She turned to go.
"I can help you, Melanie," he offered again as desperation caused him to repeat the words he clung to.
"They told my mother that, yet an army of specialists made no difference."
"There is no army here, Melanie, just me; and I've never failed yet," he said with some truth. What he didn't say was that he had never managed a serious case of depression before!
"I don't need any help." She wanted him to see that she just wanted to be left alone. He wanted her to know that he understood that if he left her alone she would succeed at her next attempt.
"Please, Melanie," he half pleaded, half shouted, "I think that you do need help. Give me four weeks, and if you don't see any reason to continue, we won't."
"Will you leave me alone then?" she said, with finality.

The tears burst through the hastily erected defence and flowed and flowed. He showed her back to her seat and sat her down with yet another tissue from the rapidly diminishing store. A pause followed, in which she composed herself but also gave just a little consideration to his words. Only the slight nod of her head gave a clue to the fact that a tiny ember had begun to glow once again in the storm that continued to force its way through every aspect of her life.

"May I go now, doctor ?"
Disarmingly, Smith said, "will you come again?"
He realised that the first round had been lost. He knew that he could not make her stay, any more than he could insist that she return, but his instinct detected that weakest of glowing embers that might just be kindled back to life, and he decided to pursue that tiny glow in the darkest of nights and fiercest of storms. Little more could be done to break through her defences which contained, but also sustained, her grief and depression. He knew he had to persuade her to come back.
"Even superheroes need supporters. Next Tuesday?"
"Perhaps."
"How about 11.00? I'll have finished my surgery by then."
"I thought I was your only patient," she teased with a little more composure.
"Well I'm trying to encourage one or two more."
At this point the receptionist interrupted with a purposeful knock on the door. "Dr Smith, the other patients have been waiting for half an hour."
"Lies, Dr Smith?" she enquired.
"No, I pay her to say that," he defended, with only the slightest of pauses as he thought quickly.
Her smile returned only for an instant, and she was gone. She hurried on past the receptionists' window and out into the summer sun. She had quickly found her sunglasses, in her bag, so as to hide the tear-stained face. Judging by the speed of her exit, few were in doubt as to her emotional state, as she reached the safety of the car park. The ever-present, ever-watchful Mrs Farnell watched

impassively as the young woman made her exit. She waited for her opportunity to slip in between patients and brief Dr Michaels.

The Jaguar purred into life as she carefully guided the Cabriolet past the rusting Maestro. As she looked in her rear view mirror she noticed the MG graphics, still visible despite the expanding rust along the tailgate margins.

Smith finished the surgery and was relaxing in the common room upstairs. He peeped his head over the banister rail. The patient, Ruby Jones, an elderly lady was hard of hearing and voices had had to be raised slightly to allow effective communication. Smith was able to hear a few words from Janice, who was repeating the old lady's words, just to make sure that she had not missed the nature of the request.

"You say you have a sore tongue and you want to be seen today? I can offer you an appointment tomorrow morning with Dr Michaels, is that any use to you?" The old lady was about to accept the appointment gratefully. Smith deduced that it was unlikely to be anything serious, most likely a bit of thrush in her mouth, and would easily wait until the morning. It was only when she gave a little rub to her temple that he knew he would have to act, and quickly.

Later that day, Mrs Farnell was telling Dr Michaels what happened next.

"He came rushing down those stairs and nearly knocked poor Ruby off her feet. He grabbed her by the arm as she hung on to her walker and whisked her into his consulting room before I had a chance to get to the window. Minutes later he came rushing out with some blood tests and asked me if I could organise an urgent taxi to take the samples to the laboratory. What could I say but 'yes'. Dr Smith then appeared, walking the patient to the door, telling her that she must start the treatment today and must not wait for the blood tests. All for a sore tongue, Dr Michaels. Apparently he'd given her steroid tablets, told her to take eight a day until coming back to see him next week. All for a sore tongue," she repeated, as if she couldn't quite believe what she had seen herself.

"Thank you Mrs F., I will have a word with young Smith. I can't imagine what he thinks he's doing. Do you think I've made a mistake in taking him on? He's so kind and so keen, but I just wonder if this is not the right place for him." He spoke the words as might an old lady, with arthritis, on hearing the news that the large dog she had just been sold needed a five mile walk each day! Mrs Farnell's silence could only mean reluctant agreement.

"I'm going to wait for the complaint to come in about the Fay woman; you heard what happened just this morning, eh Mrs F? As you know he's still on his trial period, and I suppose we need to tell him that we've decided not to go ahead. Shame, but we can't have all the patients being upset like this, and I can see how hard he's trying with the 'Jardine heiress'," as he insisted on referring to her. Mrs Farnell left the room quietly. Both were deep in thought, but both could see that Dr Smith did not seem to fit the ethos of the quiet surgery. Dr Michaels had seemed so keen on the young doctor and she had to admit that she too had supported his choice. Perhaps they were getting old.

CHAPTER III

"DISCONNECT"

The week passed quickly, though Melanie greeted the day impassively when Tuesday arrived. Hopelessness and helplessness went hand in hand with her depressed mood, and like all unwelcome guests would remain until actively displaced. She knew that even the enthusiastic and persistent Dr Smith would not save her from her destiny. The course had been planned and plotted, deviation was surely futile. Another night's disturbed sleep with strange visions and nightmares only served to reinforce her view. Her conclusions formed on the morning of her appointment. Smith was wasting his time and a further meeting was futile. She picked up the phone.
"May I cancel my appointment with Dr Smith?" she asked the receptionist who
was polite and courteous. She thanked the patient for notifying her and cheerfully blanked off the appointment space, so created. Mrs Farnell pacing the office like a captain on the quarterdeck, looked over the girl's shoulder and in her calm authoritative manner advised the junior to notify Dr Smith at once.

Smith greeted the news with alarm. He knew that her cancellation might well sever the delicate links he was desperately attempting to forge. To lose his patient now from follow-up would mean almost certainly an attempt to take her own life. He knew that she was both intelligent and determined enough to bring it about if she so chose. Within minutes he was making a call.

Mrs Perkins had somehow detected that the hall table needed dusting at the very moment the phone rang.
"I hear you've cancelled, Melanie. What about all the patients I put off just for your appointment?"
"What patients?" she challenged.

"Come and see for yourself, there's a queue into the car-park. I thought you'd started your competition and they were all here to post their entries."
"No, Doctor, they're there just to see if that car of yours will start."
He couldn't resist the laugh. "Well, if you come now you'll be able to sneak in past them, whilst they have a look at my classic car."
Mrs Perkins had not failed to detect her boss's lighter mood, and could have sworn she saw a small glimmer exist fleetingly across her face; she nearly knocked the lamp off the table as curiosity and distraction appeared in equal measure.
"Classic, that's a good word. You'd be good selling second hand cars, I think"
"Dr Michaels will have me doing that, if you don't turn up."
"I can't come."
"I've been sitting here all morning, just waiting for your appointment. Please."
"I'm waiting for the electricity man," she lied.
"And Mrs Perkins?"
"It needs two of us, he's so hunky," she volunteered quickly.
"And I thought I was a bad liar. Please come. I need your opinion about having shaved my beard off. My chin is so cold, I dread to think how it will feel, come winter."
In the slight pause, he wondered if her curiosity was being awakened.
"You mean the bet's over now, don't you? Some bet you must have lost to grow that thing: was it either grow that, or take all your clothes off, on the Christmas night out."
"Well actually both. I feel much lighter without it. Why not pop in and tell me what you think?"

As a last resort, Smith was hoping that curiosity and intrigue might just trigger her attendance, though he had absolutely no idea why his instinct had led him along this route.
"I'll come in that case, if I can have an invite to your Christmas party, and I won't stay long."
"I usually knock off for lunch at eleven thirty and then spend the afternoon on the golf-course."

"Yes I know, I read all the newspapers about you GPs. That's why I can never get an appointment."
Mrs Perkins tittered to herself before she realised that the table had probably been polished enough for some time to come.
"I suppose I will have to turn up then; no doubt it'll take weeks before I can get another appointment with my GP."
"You obviously haven't been reading your newspaper; as they all carry stories about how GPs are always on the golf-course, and have time neither for work nor for patients. You wouldn't want me to start trying to disprove the image that they've painted, and start going against type?"
"No; that will never do, especially as I know they're always right. OK you win, as you seem desperate to do at least a little work today. I'm on my way."

Smith had successfully interwoven the serious business in hand with his natural, effusive style. Melanie found it refreshing as well as intriguing. His instinct had paid off, at least for now, though he suspected it was a close contest: it was just enough to stimulate her out of her tortured reverie.
"I'll be waiting for you. I'll polish your chair, and don't hit my classic car will you."
Smith smiled, more with relief than delight. She seemed to be making the effort to break out of her depressed state, and with encouragement the tiny flicker could grow to brighten the darkness.

Once again, her silver Jaguar negotiated the tiny car park and once again found the spot next to the battered red Maestro. The batch of patients waiting, were no less curious than the ones of a week before. All heads turned as she walked up to Reception.
"Melanie Jardine for Dr Smith."
"Please take a seat Miss Jardine, he'll be right with you," offered Janice, as she couldn't quite help but stare at the young woman.
The eager Dr Smith appeared and ushered her into his tiny room.
"How are you, Melanie?"

Once again, her confidence had deflated like a balloon exploding; the view of the floor seemed safer than meeting him eye to eye. However, she found herself staring more and more at his new-shaven look, as curiosity buoyed up. The absence of the beard had brought out those high cheek bones and also the array of strong, white teeth that appeared reflexly with each smile, and certainly with every laugh. Lack of facial hair in the lower half of his face had also emphasised the shock of lustrous brown hair which gave off a glossy sheen in the surgery lighting, despite having been hastily and imperfectly cut. He detected her interest.
"Well, what do you think?"
She looked carefully for a few seconds before framing her reply. The handsome face had been liberated, and some really fine features like the strong jaw line and, as ever, those vital, shining eyes that seemed to carry his unabridged interest to everything and everyone that came within their gaze. His mounting impatience under her deliberative gaze, could bear it no longer.
"Well! Go on tell me. I can take it!"
"Actually," she paused deliberately and mischievously as if genuinely uncertain as to the wisdom of such a change. "Not bad I suppose, no, no I'm wrong: sorry, I preferred you the way you looked before."
Suddenly, he looked crushed, as he failed to detect her nascent playful mood.
"Well, I suppose I could grow it back," he offered as he reflected on how long it would take to re-grow, whilst rubbing the denuded chin.

Then it happened. She laughed. She laughed out loud for probably the first time in twelve months. Her head came back and suddenly her own array of shining white teeth in the pale olive skin were visible.
"I suppose you could grow it back if you wanted to look, older, less handsome, more creepy: a bit pervy perhaps."
"Pervy? Surely no."
"I just have to tell you. Pervy!"

"OK then, in that case it's gone for good and I'll save the beard in future, for when I dress up as Santa."
"Look, what you do in private is up to you."
"Well, you seem much better already," he opined a little prematurely.

Suddenly the reminder of what she had been feeling better from, was enough to shatter her temporary light-heartedness. The change on her face was as sudden as it was brutal. She looked down at the floor again and away from his gaze, that had changed from a smile to one of concern.
"Look, Melanie, I can't tell you that I know how you feel. I'm not you and, clearly, I haven't been through what you have." She was about to speak, but he knew he had to keep talking. "What I do know, is that we can get through this."
"We?"
"You and me. This is a serious depression. I have a feeling I don't need to tell you that, and who can blame you after what you've been through. You are flesh and blood, not some refrigerator in the corner."
"Not the last time I looked."
"So, how about it: you and me, suppose we tackle this head on?"
"What have you in mind?"

He had played the curiosity card for all it was worth; he was now trying the bargain. He knew that if he could get his patient to agree a strategy with him, it would buy him time: by attempting to place himself within the framework of her illness, he hoped she might just be more inclined to go along.
"I need four weeks, four weeks of tablets a bit like these. Here, Melanie: I want you to try the same as mine."
He produced a small box of tablets. "These are very safe and not addictive. We need to tackle your sleep disturbance and see if we can get you feeling stronger." He held up the little box for her inspection. "You'll have to pay for your own prescriptions" he said mischievously. "If I may I'll give you a prescription for a box, just

like mine? Please take one every morning with breakfast. Now how does that sound?”
The bargain was offered for her scrutiny.
“Four weeks and if it doesn’t work, then..,” he repeated as nervousness intruded unequivocally.
“Then what?” she asked as she placed his offer under consideration.
“Then, then, I don’t know what I’ll do. I've never failed before,” he offered, as some recompense for his inability to consider any other strategy. He decided that he had just better keep talking as he sensed she was about to turn and depart.
“Depression is like an illness," he said, "a bit like a broken leg that you can't see or touch but you can still feel. But like an illnesses it can be cured. We can cure this but it takes time. The big problem is that it takes at least three weeks for any tablets to have any impact at all, and in that time you will continue to feel very low. Not only that, depression tends to alter the way you think. The half-full glass becomes a half-empty one.”
He gave her the prescription he had written out for her.
“The cost of prescriptions! I may have to increase the mortgage now,” she retorted sportingly, but more significant was that she accepted it from him. She rose to go and held out her hand, her thoughts at that point of more significance than any words. He grabbed it firmly, as one might a rope thrown from a lifeboat. She noted that his grip was firm but dry, secure yet not too tight. Why did all her friends seem to have had weak and cold, almost damp handshakes? Perhaps that was why they had deserted her one by one, as her crisis unfolded.
“Four weeks then, Dr Smith, let’s give it a try.”
The tension eased in his shoulders, as he stifled an urge to sigh with relief.

Mrs Farnell knocked, then entered, carrying a set of notes. “I am afraid this patient Miss 'A' is here to see you again, Dr Smith,” as she carefully showed him the notes.
“Third time this week,” Smith said, with concern tinged with weariness.

“Shall I tell her that you're otherwise engaged, and ask Dr Michaels if he'll see her?” suggested the Practice Manager, as she moved to recover the set of notes. Smith looked very relieved as the practice manager’s suggestion sank in and his bright smile returned.

"An admirer Dr Smith?" Melanie asked.

“More of a teenager with a hormonal crush, Melanie, but we can cope."

She glanced round the room, looking for photos.

"You could do with a few photos of the wife and kids; that would discourage these weak willed women panting for you.”

“We superheroes are pledged to fight illness and have no time for mortal pursuits.”

“Yes,” she said thoughtfully, “I thought you might say that. You wait until she sees you without that beard, she won’t recognise you.”

“Well in truth no-one has been able to see past the plain and ordinary bit, as my disguise is usually so effective.”

“Mm, can see why,” was unleashed carefully, with the playful smile that was starting to break through with increasing frequency. As she left the room and slipped into the soft leather of the Jaguar, only the manager, Mrs Farnell, noted that the step had a gentle spring, where before there had been nothing but a flat-footed slog.

“Lovely girl, Dr Smith," she could not help volunteering, as they both watched her cross the car-park.

Dr Smith's thoughts were elsewhere. He couldn’t afford to squander the four weeks he had bargained for, and was determined to give it his very best shot. He hoped that he had played for enough time to re-establish a more balanced thought pattern. A shorter period would almost certainly have failed, yet a longer follow up might have seen her depart and not return. He was only certain of one thing at this point, that he was going to use every ounce of resource at his disposal to get her better, whatever it took. Mrs Farnell handed him his visits. “Off to see your mother this afternoon?” she asked gently, as if aware of his uncertainties.

"Yes Mrs F, my usual half day routine, you know. Thank-you."

He grabbed his case and carefully slipped out of the building before the teenager caught sight of him, as she waited miserably for the senior partner rather than the ever-so-dishy, Dr Smith. He eventually summoned the Maestro to life and then disappeared in a cloud of dust and smoke as the twin carburettors did their best to keep the engine supplied with the right amount of air and fuel; failing in their usual mismatched and inefficient way. He continued to think about his patient. His basic rule about clearing his mind between cases shattered, as he relived the consultation over and over.

Melanie drove briskly home and found, as usual, Mrs Perkins waiting to fuss over her and tempt her with a snack or afternoon tea depending upon what time of day it was. For months the housekeeper had noted the declining appetite and disdain for food, any food. She had correctly surmised that this was a useful barometer to the young woman's condition, and if she could influence this she might, just might be able to bring about other positive changes too. Stella, Melanie's personal assistant, had arrived to give her the usual weekly bulletin, about the family business. Melanie hated getting news from the factory, it reminded her so vividly of her father and Trish who had transformed what had initially been little more than a hobby, into a successful business, that had grown with each passing year.

Stella asked her how she was, and as usual couldn't wait to pass on the gossip from work. Melanie did her best to look interested and attentive but really couldn't wait for her to finish. Concentration had long since been a casualty in the war she had already taken as lost. Her thoughts had returned to her consultation with Dr Smith. Perhaps he was right and the illness could be cured. He had sensed that she didn't really care one way or another, and suicide remained the least unattractive of the options; to stay in misery, or exit to oblivion. Her thoughts returned to focus more on her guest. Stella was still talking and hadn't noticed the glassy look from the hazel eyes as her thoughts were tossed on the stormy sea.

“The 3D Games chip will be ready by the end of August and the new solid state Lightdrive by the autumn.” Stella could barely contain her enthusiasm. A strategy Melanie had found useful was simply to repeat the last couple of words that had been said. “By the autumn?” Melanie tried to look interested and did her best to also nod and grunt in the right places. It was only when Stella told her of her suspicions about Newman, the Finance director, with meetings after work and his unusually secretive conduct that Melanie’s subterfuge to hide her wandering mind, was exposed. She continued the look of delight when it should have been replaced by one of worry. Stella stopped and apologised for boring her.
“No, Stella, I'm the one who should be apologising. You must forgive me, I just don't seem to be able to concentrate on anything. I want to thank you for all your efforts in keeping the place afloat through the months and months of my absence, and for coming here, to keep me in touch.”

“I know it can't have been easy for you. Have you tried counselling or treatment of any kind?” Stella queried gently.
"I have a new doctor. Dr Smith is the new partner to Dr Michaels at Lorne Street. He's young, good looking, drives an old banger, what more can I say?"
Stella could think of one or two more things.
“Married?”
“I couldn’t say.”
“Come on,” Stella challenged.
“He's not your type.”
“Let me be the judge of that. Is he yours?”
“I'm not at all interested. Besides, he'd get struck off if he so much as laid a finger on me.”
“That hasn't stopped plenty of other GPs.”
“I'm told so!” Melanie said with a giggle.
It had been months since Stella had last heard that laugh.
“Well, he seems to be doing you good already.”

Stella knew her friend too well not to detect a tiny flicker, something that had not been there before, or at least for many a month. It could only have something to do with her new doctor.

Mrs Perkins brought tea and as many tasty treats as she could think of. Stella pitched in with a gusto complaining, as she did so, about how Mrs Perkins was guilty of wrecking her diet. Melanie became quiet and thoughtful again as she picked at the Danish pastry that her eyes told her she could eat, but her stomach decidedly thought otherwise. They chatted on for a while before Stella returned to the factory to look out for her employer's interests, despite the fact that it was obviously futile to attempt to stimulate her with something that held too many painful associations.

Another week came round with the same monotony. Melanie took her tablet each morning as she had promised, but did not really notice any improvement. She was awake before dawn each day and the hour or two she did manage to sleep revealed more vivid and disturbing images, fantastic enough to stimulate, yet horrible enough to distress.

Smith was watching at the end of his surgery as she drove the shining 4x4 into the tiny car park. He wondered if it would fit in there at all. He couldn't help but notice the long shapely legs that seemed to be extruded from the open door until they finally met up with the sidestep, to be closely followed by the skirt. She jumped from the step to the ground with well practised ease. He met her in the corridor between the reception desk and the open plan waiting room. Both were oblivious to the patients waiting for Dr Michael's surgery to begin.
"Ash tray full, Miss Jardine?" he said, doing his best to look disinterested while his curiosity bubbled to the surface.
"Sorry, the Jag. is in for a service," she offered defensively.
"I'm only jealous," he said, "still you haven't got a Maestro like mine."

"No, no you're quite right there Doctor. Cars like yours are a bit thin on the ground, I should imagine. I don't suppose I could talk you into a straight swap, as long as I get it serviced first?"
"I might think about it, if you throw a full tank of fuel in as well," he offered and continued, "come to think of it, my car is probably only worth as much as a full tank on that thing," as he looked at the massive Range Rover which seemed to dwarf everything else in the car park.

The patients were becoming more and more curious, as they listened to this conversation. Some had started peering over their newspapers in order to gain more information from the scene unfolding. Aware of eyes upon them both, he led her quickly, into the consulting room so as to avoid the quizzical looks now coming their way from the assembled patients. He heard one patient asking another, "where has Michaels found him?"

She sat more comfortably in the chair, as Dr Smith offered her a cup of coffee.
"Do all your patients get offered coffee Dr Smith?" she asked, with a deliberate hint of tease.
"Oh yes, both of you," he retorted, his face held so as to suppress his grin perfectly.
He caught her gaze at the photo on the shelf.
"I took your advice."
"An old case you were working on? - She's very pretty."
"Went off with my best friend."
"What, left the Maestro? Must have been mad. Obviously she couldn't see the "Superdoc" in you."
"That's what I've been telling myself ever since."
"Never mind, a go-ahead guy like yourself is bound to have women falling at his feet wherever he goes - even if some of them are spotty teenagers."
"I don't know what Dr Michaels said to the poor girl, but she's not been back since. How are you Melanie?"
"I'm here and I'm coping. By the way does this count as week one or week two?"

“Week one?” he suggested.
“OK,” as she sat down, “I'll give it a try. I even took your tablets. One, each morning. What happens if I take the lot?” she teased.
“Not very much, Melanie, you just sleep for a couple of days. Those tablets are much safer than some of the older tablets we used to use and, see, no expense spared to get you better, very pricey. Keep on with them, if you would.”

Hoping to capitalise on the pleasant preamble, he changed the subject. "Tell me about yourself?"
“Is this to get me off my guard, or to get me to talk, or is it ‘Truth or Dare’?”
“Both,” he admitted, “and also because I'm nosy.” The steady brown eyes were levelled at her for inspection and so that she could detect any trace of deceit. Whilst her own eyes, too, were capable of receiving such information, they were also far too likely to give out more than she could permit, and contact broke within a second.
“What’s ‘Truth or Dare’?” he just had to ask at this point.
She was surprised, having to explain what this common party game was, to someone of his age, when any schoolchild would know, and it caused her to wonder just what sort of upbringing he'd had.

Using his new-found knowledge he said, “OK then, I dare you to tell me about Melanie Jardine.”
She smiled, she wasn’t quite sure that he had grasped the nature of the game but she complied with the ‘dare’ anyway. He listened intently as, for a few moments, the care-worn adult, with the worries of the world on her shoulders came out of her pit of despair and became the happy little girl again.

“We moved down from the North. My father's family had built their wealth on cotton, and my mother's on coal. Dad had the hard work ethic instilled from an early age and he lost no opportunity in passing it down to me and Trish. Actually, Trish was a few years older and got the full effect. I suppose we could have sat back and

become pampered princesses but, in truth, this was never an option for either of us. He would have disowned us and insisted that we did something. 'Go off and do something that no-one else can do,' he said. 'I don't mind which profession you choose, but that's what I want.' We both ended up doing the same - Business Studies. I was accepted at Harvard for my MBA. Trish was always streets ahead of me, and qualified at the London School of Economics, but Dad was pleased in his own way with each of us. Dad gave us the steel and Mum gave us the love. Dad was embarrassed by any display of emotion and physical contact yet Mum gave us lashings of both. It's what I really miss now."
Suddenly, the black cloud returned obscuring the fleeting sunny view. He knew that it was time to steer the subject away from the dangerous undercurrents threatening his tiny boat of hope.
"Tell me about the business?"

"Dad was more business-orientated, but fascinated by the emerging new technologies - mainly computers. The coal was in decline and the cotton had long gone. He set up a firm supplying electronic components, just as electronics started to boom. It really began as nothing more than a hobby. He was interested in new technology and was amazed at the pace of change, something he hadn't experienced either in cotton or in coal. He struck on the idea of importing American components and devices, and selling them into a home market where such things were non existent, in short supply, or very expensive or all three. He stumbled across a supplier of tape streamers and started to ship as many as he could. That's like a glorified cassette tape that's used to back up a computer," she quickly interjected. "By this time Trish had finished University and helped Dad with the marketing and business side. Far Eastern component manufacturers were becoming more prevalent and choice was increasing as costs decreased. The company's turnover grew and grew. Dad's real love remained in manufacturing and especially exporting. He would always bemoan the decline of British industry, and constantly looked for ways to make a contribution no matter how small. Two new people joined - both engineers. Tony Newton fresh from

Cambridge and Alastair Jones from UMIST. They had ideas and Dad had the money. It was a very productive partnership."

She seemed positively animated as she discussed, at length, their two major technological breakthroughs. A solid state hard disc known as an SSD or solid state drive, and a games chip that would allow very powerful 3D graphics cards, used in fast computers designed for gaming. Melanie explained that each of these were leading edge products that were tipped to become increasingly relevant in the near future, as people demanded higher performance from their humble PC. Most of it was over Smith's head but he did his best to follow as she became more and more positive. His aim to get her talking of things that interested her, and also to find out more about her and what motivated her, was being achieved. 'This is the real Melanie Jardine, I am seeing' he thought to himself as she continued at length. He questioned her about her own career. She went on.

"Trish and Dad had the business running beautifully. I bought a flat, in London, with a bit of help from Dad, and got a job in one of the Merchant Banks. And before you ask, not making the tea. I drove up at weekends and holidays to see Mum and Dad and Trish. I left the bank and bought a flat in the centre of Manchester. Trish was always Dad's favourite but he loved me in his own way, and certainly my Mum and I were very close." The positive, upbeat mood again dipped, like a boat being swallowed by a wave on a stormy sea, into a tearful flurry that seemed to have no end.

Smith was more prepared this time and acted straight away. Once again he moved the conversation on just at the critical moment.
"Tell me about friends. Is there no-one close Melanie?"
"Well, Trish was always popular with the boys at University but I was a bit too choosy. Men either couldn't handle it or saw me as a meal ticket. The men I met were of two types. Those who couldn't cope with the thought of me earning more than they did, and those who felt that having me around was their signal to sit back and relax. I met a few high fliers, but they were mostly too busy on ego

trips to notice me and couldn't stop looking at themselves in the mirror. I had one or two close female friends but when the accident happened and things went from bad to worse, they deserted me like some leper whose right arm has just fallen off. Stella, my personal assistant, is a good friend and very loyal, she's never failed to come and see me each week despite not getting a lot back from me."

He was delighted to see a slight pause for reflection, almost as if she were making a mental note to redress the imbalance, and that in turn meant she could see a future.
"I haven't been into the factory for months. It holds too many memories of Dad and Trish and I feel panicky just thinking about it. Whenever I go near the place I keep getting flashbacks. This is why Stella visits me at home, but even that's an ordeal and we end up gossiping. The bulk of the equity fell to me, of course. It was never really my 'baby', which makes it even harder to get in there and run it in the way it deserves. It could be a fascinating, absorbing interest as we really have some great ideas for new products, but I just can't raise any enthusiasm. It really needs someone at the helm to steer it in the right direction if we're to make the most of our breakthroughs."

"It all sounds pretty interesting, even to a techno-phobe like me. I'd love to see it."
She took the bait.
"Sounds like a dare! Tell you what, how about a guided tour next week? It'll be my first visit there in six months."
"OK, why not; I always did want to see how the other half live."

The consultation ended and Smith felt both relieved and tired. Things were going well he thought, and the depression had at least been checked. A week was nowhere near enough time, but at last she was starting to open up a bit and confront some of the problems, with insight usually denied to those in a depressive state. She had promised to stick with him for at least four weeks, and he was going to make sure that no opportunity was missed. He had offered a specialist, of course, just as he would with any case contemplating suicide. She had refused, just as he expected. Melanie's mother had seen a succession of them, and none had been able to avert the final outcome. He carefully noted all this in the patient records and reflected that no doctor, regardless of training and ability, could extricate any patient bent on self-destruction. If that was what she were determined to do, then that would be the outcome. Smith's assessment of his patient was of course limited to a strictly professional perspective that had been imbued in him since his days as a medical student, and he continued along this line of thought as he departed with his visits for his half day.

Mrs Farnell's powers were far more diverse in this respect, and as he wrestled again with the time-consuming task of starting the Maestro, she mentioned to Dr Michaels that the attractive Miss Jardine was not the only person with a new-found spring in her step. Dr Michaels peered as usual over the wire-rimmed spectacles. Was that a look of genuine and previously unknown surprise that flickered across the usually impassive and unemotional expression?
“Smith is working hard on this one. I think he really has the bit between his teeth. I just hope that he doesn't get too close. It can be a bad thing getting too involved, believe me, Mrs F.”

Despite knowing him for many years Mrs Farnell found new facets of his character to perplex each day. He handed the practice manager a blood test report for Ruby, the old lady, for whom Smith had organised urgent bloods. “Have you seen this Mrs Farnell? Smith was right on the money with this one. He diagnosed temporal arteritis, just by peering from the top of the stairs the other day, and this blood test is lighting up like a Christmas tree. Good job he caught her, she would have gone blind if he hadn't intervened.”
She studied the blood test. Though not a doctor she had enough experience of looking at patient records to know a grossly abnormal result when she saw one. She smiled with delight and as

she did so she caught Dr Michaels smiling back. What a clever man he was. Michaels thoughts echoed her own. What a clever woman she was, and how could he possibly cope without her.

CHAPTER IV

"INSTINCT"

Melanie was a little early for their appointment the following week. She sat patiently in the waiting room. Mrs Farnell gave her a knowing smile that only served to puzzle, almost as if she could see something that Melanie had yet to discover.
"There are quite a few waiting for him, Miss Jardine."
"He told me that he only has three patients"
"No, dear, we try to keep him busier than that," confirmed the practice manager.
"Good job, I think he loves each minute."
Mrs Farnell smiled again by way of reply.

Eventually he appeared and grabbed her hand with his warm handshake that was too enthusiastic to be business-like. Nevertheless, her father would have approved. The firm and decisive shake, the way he looked directly at people with no hint of subterfuge: yes, she knew that her father would very much approve. 'Not bad for a village GP,' she thought. As she followed him into the consulting room he paused, suddenly aware of the remarkable transformation in her physical appearance: the pale blue suit in wool and cashmere, covering the diaphanous silk shirt that revealed a shimmering necklace around the slightly tanned neck; the skirt, just above the knee, and the long legs, enhanced by the beautiful shoes that now seemed to walk with precision and a purpose as she followed him. More importantly, she now walked erect with her eyes forward, not looking at the floor, and the drained, tired appearance had given way to one that was full of vitality, that he had not seen before. He couldn't help but pause as his brain insisted on taking in more of the vision before him. Mrs Farnell smiled as she waited to pop into Dr Michaels' surgery. She had seen this transition long before either of them.

He nodded to the stunning suit purposefully. "Your interview suit,

Melanie?"
"Actually, my factory uniform," she countered as the smile rose on her face like the spring breaking a harsh winter.
"Have you got a job there for me?" he ventured approvingly.
"I'm sure we can always find a job for you, as long as you won't be disappearing every five minutes to save the world."
"How could I, with an offer like that? Besides how can I, now that I've lost my disguise," he rubbed his chin, still feeling strangely naked.
She laughed. "There are some older men who would look very distinguished with a beard just like yours: unfortunately, you aren't one of them, so I guess you're better off without it."
He feigned hurt. "Perhaps I should grow it back for winter?"
"No I'll buy you a nice woolly scarf," she suggested quickly, not being able to contemplate the return of his beard. "You'll be a snug as a bug in clover, with a nice scarf; I might even knit it myself."
"Right I'm ready to go. Shall we?" He raised his arm toward the exit.

She led him out to the car park. Her car was bathed in warm sunshine giving off a palpable heat and a shimmering reflection as they approached. She slipped into the driver's seat, beside him. Out of the corner of her eye she caught the ever so slight stare at her long silky legs, and glanced away quickly as he blushed. Cleverly she nodded to the CD in the tray, as if this had really been his intended sight line.
"Oh, please choose any that you fancy." His composure regained, he picked one or two up, "Let's see now. *Adele*, *Take That*. All a bit too trendy for me these, have you no decent stuff here?" he interjected mischievously.
"I keep an iron bar in my handbag for badly behaved passengers at just such moments," she advised him with mock caution.
The engine purred into life with a visible, though temporary, tremor of the long bonnet. He found an artist with whom he was vaguely familiar, and slotted in into the aperture. As the song came up he started he started singing along.

"What's that terrible noise?" she looked about the car, "I think I must have run over a cat and it's being dragged along under the car."
"My patients love me singing to them," he offered, whilst doing his best not to let her interrupt.
"Miss-teenage-present-each-week perhaps, but if I were you, I would stick to the doctoring," as she laughed again.

He looked at her briefly. Her confidence was returning much more quickly than he had hoped, and she seemed keen to have a joke with him at every available opportunity. His strategy which relied on pure instinct, rather than anything he had learned in medical school, seemed to be working, and he knew that he would run with that instinct until she was strong enough to be considered cured. She stopped the car and began searching under a pile of CDs. Suddenly she found the battered old case of the one she had been looking for.
"OK Doctor, the 'dare' is on. Shall we sing it together?"
The familiar tones of 'Supertramp' came up and one of their most famous tracks, now of many years ago, 'Crazy' came through the speakers, as she encouraged him to sing along with her.

Here's a little song to make you feel good
Put a little light in your day
These are crazy times and it's all been getting kind of serious. Oh Yes
Here's a little song to make you feel right
Send the blues away
It's a crazy game, tell me who's to blame, I'm kinda curious.

He tapped the dashboard, laughing as they sang together. It seemed that he was not the only one prepared to go with instinct. The sunshine illuminated the couple with a warmth that enhanced and reflected their mood. Shafts of sunlight piercing between the trees and their leaves created a softer, dappled effect on the car and its occupants. The Jaguar whisked along with a smooth pulsation that created effortless forward motion. He had never been in such an expensive car, he had never been in an open top car, and had never sung along to 'Supertramp' before today. Though she had done all those things before, she could not recollect a time when it had been so much fun. She glanced at him once again, as she sang. The young doctor, full of a sense of duty, of concern for his patient and determination to do his very best for her, had suddenly been given an interlude that warmed his heart, she was certain, as much as it warmed hers.

The factory was not as he had imagined. It belonged more in a Californian science park than a traditional British industrial estate. The tinted perspex louvres that formed the windows of the building were clicking sporadically as they absorbed the sunshine. The entrance door could be clearly seen as it jutted out from the sides of the building like some monstrous beak still covered with the perspex. Brick courses made up the lower halves of each of the three storeys providing support to the glazing, the whole thing looking like a giant layer cake. On the middle course of dark brick "Jardine Electronics- Jectronics" stood out in gold characters, pinned to the brick. He sensed the tension as she parked in her Dad's old spot and did his best to divert her attention with commendable but futile skill.

Suzy, on reception greeted Melanie with genuine affection. "Lovely to see you again, Miss Jardine," as she rose to her feet behind the laminate and polished metal desk. "Suzy, this is Dr Smith," Melanie began.

He greeted her, a slight nod and the usual enthusiastic handshake. "Please call me James, Suzy, I'm Miss Jardine's personal trainer."

"Stella is on her way down to meet you Miss Jardine."

Melanie pressed Smith's arm gently. "Stop it, or I won't let you sing along again, you'll get us both certified in a minute." She glanced carefully at the young doctor; he seemed strangely carefree, almost like a little boy on the way to the sweetshop, with his pocket money.

"What would you have me do? I thought introducing myself as your GP wasn't quite right. I thought a visiting personal trainer would go down nicely."

"You'll go down the stairwell in a minute: you're just giddy because we've let you out of that surgery for an afternoon."
He laughed. Perhaps her assessment was not far from the truth. Stella's arrival did not help Melanie to keep a serious tone to their visit.
"So pleased to meet you," she said, with urbanity. "I've heard *so* much about you." The deliberate emphasis on "so" left Melanie cringing, as Stella's handshake lingered deliberately and for just a little too long, as she stared expectantly into those chestnut eyes.
"Collect your cards on Friday, Miss Wilson," she whispered *sotto voce* in mock formality through her clenched teeth. Smith chuckled along at the jovial interplay between the two.

As Brian Newman came down, the mood was irrevocably shattered. Smith felt the women grow tense. Newman did his best to disguise his loathing for both women but failed under its intensity.
"Brian, please meet Dr Smith."
"James, please," Smith offered, with almost a tone of relief at being given the opportunity to break up the charged atmosphere that had built within seconds. Newman's handshake was altogether too firm, as if it were some sort of contest between warring warriors. Smith did his best not to wince under its crushing and painful grip.
"Brian is our Finance Director and runs the place on a day to day basis."
Melanie had been fair in her introduction but it obviously wasn't quite enough for Newman. The antipathy returned as he switched gaze back from Smith.
"Actually, I've been running the place, during Melanie's um, absence," he offered with more aggression than clarity.
"May we go into the test lab?" Melanie couched the instruction thinly in the guise of a question.
"Yes of course," Newman acquiesced.

Through more double doors. Stella produced her swipe card to gain access. They crossed to the vast stainless steel bench,

illuminated by an array of halogen down-lighters, which seemed to provide as much light and radiation as a sunny day. Melanie attached an antistatic wrist strap right next to the beautiful Omega wristwatch, bought on her twentyfirst by Trish. She picked up the chip with one hundred and forty-four tiny pins sticking out, rather like a fine-toothed golden comb.
"This chip will sit at the heart of a 3D graphics card. Modern games are becoming more and more sophisticated. They're also appearing in 3D in increasing frequency, which puts even more strain on the graphics card, the thing that puts the image onto the computer screen. Our graphics chip will work at much faster rates with greater detail than anything that has gone before."

Tony Newton joined them and offered much more detail involving frame rates, refresh times and benchmarks against popular modern games. Smith couldn't relate to much of what he said, but of far more interest was the sense of pride and expectation of the people who stood next to him. Melanie spoke. "We're hoping we can offer a really fast and capable games chip on a games card, at a really competitive price."
Smith nodded to mirror their enthusiasm but, in truth, he was more amazed by the transformation in his patient, and he correctly adjudged that this was of far greater importance than anything he would see that afternoon.

"Whilst we have competitors, mainly in Japan and the States they haven't managed to mass produce these chips with the same quality and at such a competitive price," Melanie said. Newman shifted uneasily. "Don't worry Brian, Dr Smith is sworn to secrecy, medical confidentiality it's called," Stella giggled behind him. Melanie continued, "our production process involves several methods which are either closely guarded secrets or protected by patents. We hope to remain ahead of our competitors for at least twelve months, and in that time we hope to ship a vast number of these." She placed the black chip back on the stainless steel surface and took off the antistatic wrist band. Smith came to get a closer

look, his hands held behind him in case he touched something inadvertently. “Are these actually manufactured here?”
“We aim to do as much of the manufacturing locally. The large grey building behind these offices is our production facility. This is simply a test laboratory. The chips need expensive and sophisticated production facilities. The air in there is even purer than an operating theatre, and we also need access to high quality components and other materials,” she said with triumph. “One grain of dust in the wrong place and the whole thing will be useless.” Smith was suitably impressed and stood staring at the memory chip for some time as it glistened in the brilliant overhead lighting.

They moved on to the second laboratory upstairs where Smith met Alastair Jones. Here, he was given an extensive discourse on the new SSD or solid state drive. Smith felt he was back at medical school but had strayed into the wrong lecture. He did his best to sound interested and event tried a question or two, but it was an uphill struggle. He was much more at home looking at the interaction between the two young women and, of course, Newman who would have seemed perfectly at home playing the villain in some stage show, but with much more menace given off at each turn. They spent the afternoon on the impromptu tour. Newman became more and more irritated. What was also patently clear was his dislike, verging on hatred of Melanie.

As the tour finished and they turned to go, Newman seized his moment.
“Melanie we have to talk, about the business, in private.”
“OK Brian, but not now if that’s OK, I have to get Dr Smith back before his adoring patients start to miss him. How about Friday?”
“Fine,” he accepted with ill grace.
“Nine a.m. sharp?” she offered.
“Fine.”

They got back into the Jaguar. Somehow, Newman had shattered the carefree mood that Smith had seen was just starting to establish itself. As Melanie waved to Stella, who had walked out to the car with them, he thought quickly. Once again, the fragile state of her recovery was self-evident. For many minutes during their tour she was that bright, confident young woman he had glimpsed between the bouts of pain, the day he met her. Melanie became quiet again as the mood that had burned brightly whist on the tour had once again been eclipsed by the all-pervading despair. The quiet interlude as they sat in the car gave rise to too many painful memories, and these now weighed heavily upon her, threatening to stall her fragile recovery. The GP reasoned that Newman's attitude toward her had also triggered negative thoughts. Smith was determined to keep up the momentum.

"Can I buy you a cup of tea?" he offered.

"Why, Doctor Smith that's very kind of you. Shall we take a spin down by the river?"

"Let's go. Time to heat the cylinders," he suggested with his infectious enthusiasm.

"Pardon me?"

"The cylinders, Melanie, you know those under the bonnet."

"Oh, I never look under there. Why do you think I need two cars?"

She turned down the road to the river, which led to the café where they occupied the last table on the sun terrace, under the gently flapping sun-umbrella.

"Whoosh, Melanie, I am impressed. That's quite a factory you have there."

"I thought you would be," her face beaming as, once again, he steered the conversation into more buoyant territory.

"How many people do you employ?"

"Much of the production is done by machines these days, which makes us quite capital intensive. We should rise to about five hundred as the production lines start with a vengeance. We're lucky to have skilled workers who came from the car component factory which closed a few years ago."

"Newman isn't your biggest fan, is he," Smith suggested.

"No, he hates me," was her stark reply, and she continued, "he hates me for not being behind a kitchen sink, for daring to have a brain and, of course, for refusing to go out with him."
"Ah," Smith nodded enthusiastically, "seems clear. Have you two got anything going for you?"
"He needs me, believe it or not. Six months' absence, but I am responsible for securing the finance for the development programme that has kept us so far ahead. Don't get me wrong, we've been very lucky, but we have made the most of our breaks and we are in very dominant position. The world beats a path to our back garden, as they say." She continued, "however, the thing that floats it all up is money – as usual. We need development monies and also to support our cash flow whilst the products come on line. I negotiated the venture capital, basically rich people, you know those?" He smiled. "They put a load of money in, and they may not see it again, in return for, possibly, seeing it again, with a load of interest and of course really generous tax breaks."

"Yes, think I see." He looked at her carefully and couldn't help but notice how she impressed on all levels. Not only was she a warm caring person, one who was very easy to look at, but also an accomplished businesswoman who relied purely on her business skills and speed of thought, rather than on those looks or simply her connections.
"You were very impressive in there. You handle yourself very well. It was almost like another person. You are a woman of many talents." He felt impelled to voice.
"You see, when this mask comes off it's just an ordinary person underneath." She deliberately brushed her forehead upwards as if she were peeling something off, now gazing at him intently.
"You can see why Dad and Trish were so committed to the place."
He nodded, deep in thought. "Newman seemed desperate to catch you. What does he want to talk about? Sorry, I hope I'm not being impertinent or nosy am I?"

She laughed. This was typical of the man, his manners seemed to come before everything. Most people would simply ask what they wanted to know, but at all times he retained a politeness that was evident in every word he uttered, and extended to each person that he had occasion to meet. She resisted the urge to tell him that he was being nosy and that she didn't mind one bit. She had, long since, decided that she found his inquisitiveness compelling and it was the male equivalent of a good gossip with Stella.

"Stella says he's up to something. I'm not sure what. I'll get Stella to brief me on Thursday. I'll keep you posted." The serious edge returned all too quickly. "So you see, you are just going to have to get me better." Her eyes were suddenly cast down to the shining metal table-top. The simple words said so much. It seemed that at last she cared whether she lived or died, and she had obviously chosen to live and this was a vital step from which all else could follow.

"Never failed yet, is what I said," he offered incautiously.

"And just how many successes have you had?"

"Let's see now," he delayed deliberately as if in deep thought. "So many cases to count, but as a rough estimate you'll be the first, not including my rabbit who became a bit low for a while, when I was fourteen." His eyes were levelled in her direction, for close inspection, so that she could decide for herself the truth or otherwise in his words.

She laughed. "Sure know how to fill your patients with confidence, don't you. Perhaps I should just take a dive off this terrace now without further ado," she suggested, as she looked down the steep drop to the river below.

"You're not going to waste that nice cake are you, Melanie? It's just that I'll finish it, if you weren't planning on taking it down with you."

She perched a piece on her fork, tantalisingly, just before it entered the elegant mouth.

His jovial mood hid much, but she remained convinced that this was his way of dragging her out of herself, all the while defusing a dangerous situation. Sometimes, just for a fleeting moment, she could catch a glimpse of something that lay below, just below the surface of his smooth jovial persona. She wasn't sure whether it was concern for her, or an inner sadness of his own. In any event, she knew then, that she would remain, at least, at the very least, until she had clarified it.

They ate in silence, each turning to thoughts that their social intercourse had created, and which now demanded immediate attention; each glancing up at the other, as the information was duly processed. She slipped her jacket off and the warm sunshine flooded onto the smooth, supple skin that was rapidly returning to its more healthy, natural shade with the pale olive hue. He couldn't help but notice, too, the pleasing aroma that she seemed to give off with each movement, and he had to check himself from leaning toward her in order to enhance the experience still more. His initial thought that such an attractive person seemed at complete variance with the more confident businesswoman that he had seen hints of, was to be corrected in the days ahead.

"Thanks for coming," she volunteered, at last, breaking the silence. "I wouldn't have missed it for the world," he said, with carefully directed sincerity. "I've had a really nice afternoon. Beats seeing patients any day of the week." There was that intricate defence again that he liked to hide behind, and she wondered if it, in fact, contained a little lie, and he would have preferred to see his patients. The more she saw of him, the more her understanding of the man, the doctor and his methods advanced, one tiny step at a time.

He knew, only, that he had to observe her at close quarters; he was quickly compiling events that brought her out of herself, distracted her from those desolate thoughts and re-awoke that charismatic businesswoman, as well as the charming female that surely no-one would have any problems in spending time with; not even her doctor.

She paused to give some thought to the words he spoke, and understood at that moment his careful construct was aimed solely at restoring her confidence.
"Come now. That, doctor, I don't believe. You're like a six year old on Christmas morning in the surgery. You love it, anyone can tell that; even 'depressed, would rather look at the floor,' me."

She concluded that Smith's character was much more complex than a first glimpse would suggest. The bright, breezy manner was used as camouflage, and only occasionally could even the most sensitive of observers discern any information at all about the real person deep below. The chestnut eyes remained his weak spot, they would always tend to covey a little more of the inner person than he would ideally wish. His enigmatic smile and those intense brown eyes levelled, once again for her inspection, but this time he had to avert his gaze, as he detected that her perceptive powers were rising like the brilliant disc of the moon that would appear in a cloudless sky that night, and with no less wonderment.

He paid the waitress and they found the Jag. for the return journey, to pick up his Maestro.
"Lovely car this, Melanie."
"Yes, it's my pride and joy. I am sorry about the 4x4 the other day. I wasn't trying to be a show off."
"No, not at all, don't be silly. I'm pleased to see it's not just me keeping our beleaguered car industry going. Even if my support was bought more than twenty years ago."
She laughed. "Well at least it was support, and those who bought it before you didn't buy a foreign car. I take it that you're someone who doesn't like to spend his hard earned pennies on motor cars? I know you doctors are always complaining about your wages and so on, but you can't take it with you. Besides my morning paper tells me that all you GPs are on at least two hundred and fifty thousand."

At this moment he wanted to point out the Matalan suit; the shirt that came with a free tie, all for five pounds, and ask her if she really thought that to be true. He decided to keep his own counsel as the car remained silent. He certainly could never reveal his true financial situation even in jest to this, no doubt, incredibly affluent young woman who would never have to weigh the costs of humble items, as he did each day.

She realised she had strayed onto sensitive ground as he looked through the window. It was obviously not something he cared to converse about. To hide the awkward silence she inserted another CD, and Meatloaf's powerful tones flowed from the speakers. As they got back to the surgery she decided to go for the apology rather than leave it.

"I am sorry if I was prying," she offered, the hazel eyes wide and focussed just on him as a sincere apology was conveyed.

"No Melanie, don't give it another thought, please, it's nothing you said." The smile broke through with feeling. "I'm sure I can tell you about all those women I have secreted around the village and this is why I have no money – whoops!" he said, as his hand came up to his mouth as if he had suddenly unwittingly revealed a dark secret.

She laughed. "Well, now you've got rid of that horrible beard, I might just believe that."

"Next week?" he offered disarmingly.

"If you can put up with more of me?"

"All in a day's work ma'am," as he touched, an imaginary peaked cap.

He walked briskly back to the Maestro with a cheery backward wave and a flash of the white, even smile, now liberated by the loss of the bushy beard.

"Would you like me to stay and make sure it starts," she joked.

"No, you could be there all night," he replied, with honesty.

CHAPTER V

"ULTIMATUM"

Stella drove up into the circular courtyard, in front of the grand house and saw that Melanie had come outside in order to greet her with a warm hug.
"'D' is for dishy," she opened.
"Hands off, I saw him first."
"Come on now, all's fair."
"How old do you think he is?" came from Melanie.
"Can't be a day over thirty, I reckon; probably less. He'd get struck off if you made a pass at him," suggested Stella, with feigned concern.
"Stella, he is my doctor," she said with purpose, as if a reminder to both herself and her friend. "Forget it, anyway Stel," she said disappointedly, "he's married to his work, I tell you. What is Newman up to?" she asked as she tried to change the subject quickly.
"Can't really say, but I tell you Melanie, he's up to no good. There have been lots of people coming to see him of late, and he talks as if it's his company, all the time. We really need you back Melanie. I know that the company isn't your favourite place, and I can see why, but I won't be able to hold him off without your help."
"I know Stella, I'm just going to have to get my head round it," said Melanie with a grave tone in her voice.

Though they were such few words, the implication was of far greater moment. Once again, without realising it, she had acknowledged that there was going to be a future after all. Mrs Perkins brought in the tea tray.
"I shall meet with him on Friday and hear him out. He makes my flesh crawl, just as he does yours, but the sooner I find out what he's up to the better," Melanie confirmed.
"So, I'll see you at work on Friday, Melanie. Good luck. I tell you he's planning something. Please be careful."

Brian Newman was uncharacteristically prompt for their meeting. 'It must be something important,' Melanie thought to herself. Newman was a little older than Melanie, about forty, she seemed to recall. His skin and teeth and eyes had not really aged well, mainly because of his habit of heavy smoking, and Melanie had also detected, not for the first time, a smell of alcohol on his breath. The dark eyes seemed to bore into her as if trying to transfix her to the chair, as she sat facing him.
"Melanie, I can understand the pressure you've been under of late, and that the company never really was your first love. We need to move on and make sure our new products are launched successfully, as well as continue to develop new ones."
"I don't have a problem with that Brian."
"We want you to sell your shares."
"Who are 'We'?" She asked.
"All of us," came the icy reply. "I'm afraid it's time for you to let go."
"And if I refuse?"
He laughed as if he had been hoping to hear that, and could already envisage the humiliation that he was hoping to visit on her.
"Then we will vote you out," he said slowly, as if savouring the words he had waited for so long to say.
"I still retain forty percent, Brian."
"I know, but it won't make any difference - you'll see." His eyebrows lifted with gratuitous concern, entirely feigned. "Why not make it easy for yourself Melanie, you don't need this, any of it."
Melanie could tell that he was enjoying himself. He took a strange pleasure in watching people suffer, and was quite happy to exploit their point or time of weakness.

As was typical of human nature, the thought of something slipping from one's grasp, only enhanced the desire to retain it as it became still more precious. Grim determination and a resolve to resist, began to stir deep inside. She was especially keen to deny this

smug, cruel and unfeeling man any advantage whatsoever from the situation.
"What have you in mind Brian?" she said calmly.
Somewhat taken aback by the sudden conciliatory tone, Brian was put off guard. Nevertheless, this is precisely what he wanted to hear. He knew that if he pushed her enough, especially in her weakened form, she would crack.
"We want to buy your shares out at par, and you can walk away."
"They're worth much more than that," Melanie said, knowing that their current value was much higher. She knew, as did he, that the par value was the original value put on the shares long before the company and the share value had increased. She would receive only a fraction of their true worth.
"Who will be doing the buying anyway, Brian?" She knew that he alone would not have the financial wherewithal to fund such a massive purchase.
"I've been talking to Warner Deville."
"Our greatest competitor. I should have known."
"They want to buy in by taking your forty percent."

It all seemed to be falling into place now. At least she now knew some of those with whom he had been conducting secret meetings.
"In what way will that benefit you Brian?" she just had to ask.
"They will retain me as Managing Director and allow me to run the company unencumbered," he offered with a greedy glint in the black eyes.
"Funny, I didn't think that naiveté was your strong suit. OK, Brian, as you are so confident. How about an extraordinary meeting? Let's hear what all the shareholders have to say. You have your say, I'll have mine, and everyone can vote."
"I only want the best for the company, Melanie."
At this point hearing those words from him made her feel nauseous.
"You think selling out to Warner's is the best? They'll transfer the whole line to the States within a month."
"That's not what they say."

She resisted the urge to laugh in his face. Either Newman had lost a few brain cells or, more likely, there was a hidden agenda. She wondered whether Newman had been promised other, more tangible inducements.

“It will take a week or two to get everyone together. I'll arrange it,” he said with more than a hint of menace.

“That's fine. See you at the meeting Brian,” she said with finality.

He left; his hatred of her, as always not far from the surface, had been joined by a hint of disappointment. Newman had been hoping to capitalise on her delicate state, and bounce her into accepting his offer, and simply walk away. His leering smile soon re-established itself as he realised that he would, as he had intended, embarrass and humiliate her in front of all her colleagues and the few friends she had left, at the meeting he was to arrange. How he would make her wish she had gratefully accepted his offer. She had squandered her chance of an exit, an exit with some dignity: the consequences for her having thrown his offer back in his face were no longer any concern to him, and she surely deserved all that was to come her way.

Stella appeared moments later. “I saw him going down the stairwell. How did it go?”

“Not bad. He wants to get rid of me.”

“How can he? Your family built this company.”

“You mean that Dad and Trish did, Stella. Maybe he is correct, and I should hand over with good grace. It’s just that he wants to sell out to Warner's, and as soon as they have our patents they'll close us down and move the line to California. We're calling a meeting Stella; you’ll get a chance to vote.”

“I'll stick with you, Melanie.”

“Hear the arguments first, then do what you think is right.” She linked Stella’s arm and continued, “but I’ll kill you if you don’t,” she joked. “I haven't been in here nearly as much as I should: the company has been idling along and people like Newman have grown restless. There will be more who think as he does, and maybe enough to force it through.”

"Look Melanie, I don't care what that creep says, I'll be sticking with you, come hell or high water," Stella confirmed.
"Thanks for that Stella, your support means a lot to me. I'll try not to let you down."
"I have no worries on that score. I'd rather fail with you, than succeed without you, I guess."
"I'll do my best not to let you down. Stella, can you spare me any of your time tomorrow. Had you any plans for the weekend?"
"Not really, only the weekly shop to get the cat food. I can do that tonight, if I could get away a bit early."
"Thanks Stella. I'll see you here tomorrow as early as you like. Up with the Lark. I need to start getting to grips with a few things."
Stella paused as she considered Melanie's words: "that's what I like to see. Welcome back, Melanie," she said and looked triumphant as if a great battle had already been won. Melanie was more uncertain.
"We're not there yet, Stella, there's a long way to go," she said hesitantly.

Melanie decided to leave and get home. She wanted to take an in-detail look at the state of the company, and wanted to do it unhindered, at weekend. She managed to catch Dr Smith before he left on his visits.
"Forgive me, Dr Smith, is there any chance of seeing you today? I'd like a bit of advice."
"No problem Melanie, suppose I pop round and see you on my way home this evening, about 6:30?"

He arrived a little after 6:45. "Sorry if I'm a bit late. Another hard day saving lives."
"Dr Smith it's good of you to come. I thought we'd eat as we talk, if that's OK with you?"
They sat in the kitchen, Melanie opened a window, as Mrs Perkins fussed with the plates and made sure that Melanie had enough food to keep an Army Quartermaster happy. The large, square, kitchen was an explosion of white with matching cabinets, recessed handles and an expanse of work-surface made of Corian, which

continued as it dipped seamlessly into the twin sinks. Glass shelves supported by chromed, stainless-steel pillars continued the high-tech clinical feel, and the whole array was illuminated by powerful halogen lighting and LED under-lighting.
“I'm all ears Melanie,” he said as she returned from the window. He glanced at the cotton skirt and the baggy vest top that still bore witness to the fact that her weight had not been fully restored.
“How’s the weight doing Melanie?”
“There’s one thing about a bit of depression, the weight just drops off you. I don’t think I'll ever have a weight problem again.”
“I’m certain that you'll soon sort that, with just a bit of help from Mrs Perkins,” as he looked at the embarrassing amount of food that had been placed on the table.
“I have a bit of a dilemma Dr Smith. If we're being a bit less formal, do you mind if I call you James, or Jim, or ‘oohjamaflip’ or something?” she ventured after a slight delay.
“Be my guest," he offered, without being more specific as to which of the options he preferred.

“As you know the company has never been my first love. The charming Mr Newman is seeking to replace me as director, and use finance from our closest competitors in order to do so.”
“Is that not to your advantage?”
“That would leave him in charge,” as a scandalised look crossed her face.
“Would that matter, if you were out of it?”
“What about Stella and all my friends?” she countered, “I feel as if I'm between a rock and the deep blue sea.”
He nodded uncertainly and said, “they would cope I'm sure. It would certainly take a lot off your shoulders, Melanie.”

By deliberately playing Devil’s advocate he could gauge her sense of passion, or otherwise, for the company, and also probably help her to clarify some of her own feelings.
“Do you think that’s what I need?” Her eyes opened as if she needed reassurance.
“How do you feel?”

"I feel a bit better, though I'm still not sleeping, but at least I don't feel like taking all those tablets, you gave me, in one gulp."
"Well, at least we're making some progress," he suggested. "I take it that you don't need to work?"
"I'm 'financially secure', as they say, that's about the only thing I am secure in."
"You could do worse things than give it all up," he suggested, by way of a conclusion.
"My dad would turn in his grave."
"Forgive me, but I'm interested in what *you* want."
"I don't know," she said with desperation. "Suppose I were to depart and not fight for what I believe in, just because it's a bit easier for me at the moment. I'm sure in future years I would hate myself for running out."
That was exactly what he wanted to hear. He knew that only she could decide to fight, or otherwise, for her future.
"I can't tell you what to do, Melanie. If Newman were to take over, it would take a lot of pressure off you."
"Come now. He'd sell the whole thing out to the Americans, and the entire production would shift, along with hundreds of jobs, to the States within weeks," she reflected, as uncertainty was replaced by outrage.
"That wouldn't be your concern, if you were out of it."
"We employ lots of people from the village; have they no say in all this?" was more rhetorical.
"Not unless they're shareholders."
"You know what I mean. What would you do, in my position?"
Once again, she looked at him steadily.

There was something of a pause whilst he deliberated as to the wisdom of a biased view by way of reply. In the final moment before he spoke, he realised that whatever he did, she would gauge his true views, so he might as well do her the courtesy of a frank reply.
"I'd fight."
"Pardon. You'd what?"
"I'd fight him all the way."

"I thought you weren't going to tell me what I should do."
"I'm not. I'm telling you what I would do. Isn't that what you asked?"

Mrs Perkins chuckled to herself, putting her hat and coat on, despite the summer's heat. "I shall be off now Miss," she said in an unusually loud voice.
"Thanks Mrs P. I'll see you tomorrow. Would you like a lift?"
"No Miss, you stay and talk with the doctor. I'll be home in two shakes, on my bicycle."
"Melanie if you want the safe option, then sell out and ride off into the sunset."
"Come now, I'd get bored."
"Perhaps," he said whilst doing his best to hide the fact that he agreed with her. "If you do put up a struggle, I'm not sure how you would hold up." The professional within him just had to caution at this point.
"Remember that you're coming through a serious depression, and it's going to take more time. Are you ready for internecine warfare?"
"If I am going to fight, then I'd better be, I suppose. Besides, I don't throw the bucket in, just like that. Will you help me?"
"Try and stop me," he offered gamely.
She smiled and looked directly at him. "You knew I was going to come to that decision didn't you?"
She sensed his slight discomfort as he said, "how do you know that I knew that?"
Her eyes narrowed as she gazed at him, with still more scrutiny. "You just knew, and I do know that!"

His slight discomfort was transmuted into a smile that beamed back at her, conveying more than any words could. He knew that a patient's insight into their own condition was often the first casualty, in a depressive illness. His smile was an acknowledgement that her insight, her instincts and her sensibility were being strengthened on a daily basis, and his smile also contained more than a hint of pride as he bore witness to such

changes that had occurred much more quickly than he had ever dared to hope.
“I want to thank you for all you're doing. Do all your patients get this sort of treatment?”
“Yes, I look after you both equally well.”
“I've seen your surgery. Packed out,” she said, triumphantly.
“No, they're the ones who think they're seeing Dr Michaels. You should see the look on their faces when they realise it’s me. They spend the first ten minutes telling me exactly what Dr Michaels would do if he were seeing them.”

He thought carefully for a few moments, then became serious once again.
“You know, Melanie, that we all need to strive and to work for something. Everyone has to feel needed and indispensable, at least just a little. I've known patients who retire to do nothing and are often dead within six months. They think ‘I'm going to retire and have a good rest.’ Only then do they realise that they're bored and have no sense of purpose. Those who are busier than ever before, do very well. You always hint that you stood in your father’s and Trish's shadow, but I don’t believe you. I saw you at close quarters as we went round the factory, and to say that you were impressive would be an understatement. Don't take this on if you really have no love for the company but, on the other hand, it would probably be a mistake just to let everything go. Newman has his own agenda and I think that much of it is personal. In any event, I believe you had already made your decision, you just wanted to pass it by me.”
He looked at her carefully as he studied her face, now deep in thought.

The amber flecks seemed to dance as the eyes glowed with vitality that he was witnessing more and more, especially when she talked of things she valued.
“I trust your judgement, and besides, there was no-one else to turn to.” She looked away quickly as if the eyes were about to betray more than was wise.

"Things are on the turn for you now, surely you can see that, just as I can see the good people you do have, whom you can count on. You're coming out of yourself more and more. Lots of exciting avenues will open for you as you recover more."
The kind words, as always, attempting to cushion her discomfort and offer hope for brighter things in her future.
"Thanks for that, It's kind of you. Are you always this optimistic?"
"Optimism is useful in my job. It's no good spreading doom and gloom unless it's unavoidable."
He looked quickly at his watch. "I'd better go; I'm on call tonight.
"Thanks again for calling. I do appreciate your coming."
"Are we still on for next Tuesday? Week three," he noted.
"Same time, same place," she stated.
"I'll see you then. Goodnight Melanie."
"Goodnight Doctor oohjamaflip," she returned, as she realised that he hadn't answered her question.

She filled the dishwasher and watched some television, although her thoughts were far away. Give him a run for his money, why not? Newman had deliberately picked her weakest moment to attempt to separate her from the company. She could only hope that she was now strong enough to make sure that she denied him the expectation of a straightforward victory. She took a leisurely bath and read for half an hour before bed; her mind was still racing, but she succumbed to a few hours sleep before her usual waking time with the dawn chorus. She had wondered what tortured images she would see in her dreams that night, and was pleasantly surprised when, for a change, she could recall none the following morning.

Smith's boast that he could sleep on a clothesline and that he slept the sleep of the innocent rang vexatiously through his head, as he turned restlessly in his long fight for rest. Melanie was treading a knife-edge, and he remained conscious of the fact that he might have just talked her into a death sentence until, at last, the small hours brought but short relief.

The following day Melanie arrived a little early for her meeting with Stella. Melanie found that the passwords to confidential files had been changed. It became apparent that Newman was playing a no-holds barred game. Fine by her, it would lend spice to the occasion. Hours passed as they went through all the manual ledgers, page by page, eventually piecing together most of what she was looking for. "Newman must be lying," she told Stella. "The company is in a far stronger position than he says, so why does he need the Americans? Let's go home, get something to eat, and see if we can make sense of it all," Melanie suggested.

They reassembled in the oak-panelled library. The double-height room contained hundreds of books and tomes that had lain undisturbed for many months. A ceiling- height stone-mullioned window extended across the southwest wall, and the facing wall had a wooden spiral staircase that stretched up to the large gallery rail with still more shelves of books. Hundreds of small leaded lights had been glazed within the large window expanse, to provide light that offset the darkness of the mature oak panels.

"Let's look at what we have," Melanie began. "Our two main products, the 3D Graphics chip and the SSD, should be ready on time. Costs have been contained to a minimum, yet the production line should be capable of ten thousand drives and twenty thousand graphics chips each week on start-up, and rising to at least twice this for the drives. If penetration is only half what we project, the company will make a handsome profit. Stella, we're sitting on a goldmine, so why does Newman want to sell out to the Americans?"
"I'm not sure if I can smell a rat or a red herring, Melanie: he's playing a very deceitful game," said Stella after checking her boss's predictions.
"Perhaps I should expect little else. I wonder what the other shareholders know of all this, and what they've been promised. I think I'll talk to a few people in London and see what I can come up with. In any event our Mr Newman is going to have a fight on his hands," confirmed Melanie.

The two women continued to work in the library; only the lengthening shadows within the bright room bore witness to the sun's transit across the perfect sky as the day progressed. More important than any of the conclusions that came into being that afternoon, was the fact that Melanie could sense that her brain had been set free and was able to think, to assess and to evaluate all the information before it. Living and breathing and thinking had become worthwhile once again, and Melanie could hardly believe that a tiny box of tablets could effect such a change. Stella, for her part, had seen first-hand the resurgence in her boss and her friend, and knew only that she would follow her to hell and beyond, if Melanie had declared that was where they needed to travel.
"Stella it's really late. Can I offer you a bed for the night? I'll go and get you a robe and a few bits and pieces."
"I'd better phone a friend to go in and walk the cat." After the phone call Stella trod her weary way upstairs to bed. Melanie sat in the darkness attempting to piece together Newman's strategy.

Melanie was up early as usual. Stella rose eventually, and Melanie sat her in front of toast and cereal doing her best with her impression of Mrs Perkins, who never failed to make any guest less than welcome, and who was enjoying a well deserved day off that Sunday. "I never knew these things made toast," Stella said, nodding in the direction of the Aga. Having had a quick lesson in toasting on an Aga, Stella showered and dressed and left to go home.
"I'll see you tomorrow Stella, thanks for all your help."
Stella was delighted. "You really do mean business don't you?"
"Just stick around: you ain't seen nothing yet," Melanie declared, as the self- doubt and fear that had run her life for the last twelve months was now displaced by her growing confidence.

True to her word Melanie appeared bright and early Monday morning. She walked in to Newman's office.
"Brian, I see someone has changed the high level password on the computer records. It wouldn't be you would it?"

Newman blazed back, seething, but not quite able to maintain eye contact as she studied him intently. He wondered whether her steely gaze would uncover the lies that he planned to offer her by way of response. As he deliberated, she continued.
“Only, if I can’t get into the system I'll have to bring the whole network down until such time as I can get the information I need.”
“You wouldn't dare,” he said with defiance.
“You come and watch me Brian. ‘Down’ is the command I type, if I remember correctly,” as she approached the fileserver with purpose rather than menace.
“OK: I will restore the old passwords," said Newman as he looked at her with contempt, thinking how he was going to enjoy delivering her just deserts to this air-headed bitch.
“Thank you Brian,” she offered with a calmness bordering on serenity. “I do hope that we can have a fair fight, don't you?”

Her presence in the office was simply a token of her intention to retain control of the company. She no longer trusted Newman, and was not sure how many others he'd approached, and with what promises they had been bought or otherwise seduced. She altered the supervisor password on the server so that Newman could not access or delete any vital information.

Tuesday lunch-time approached and Melanie rose to leave.
"I have an appointment with the ‘DD’," as Stella had long since started referring to Dr Smith. She wasn't sure if he would be very receptive to being known as the dishy doctor, but she would do her best not to let it slip and, at the same time, keep Stella well away. She arrived in good time as usual; the slim, toned figure more or less back to its usual dimensions. The pale blue silk dress made her look tall, slim and elegant, especially when matched with the typical gorgeous shoes that women would kill for.

Sensing her presence, Mrs Farnell looked up from her book. There followed a moment’s pause as Melanie looked back, noting the high cheek bones in her fine face, with its clear porcelain skin, more than giving a hint as to the very attractive woman that age had only reluctantly and carefully changed. Even the harsh light from the spotlights above the reception desk illuminating the older woman was unable to diminish her appearance that shone like a warm summer's afternoon with the sun now slightly in the descendant. "Dr Smith will be right with you dear," she ventured warmly.

Smith had been seeing Molly Fay, who having just been let out of hospital, had come in to thank him and to show him her new pacemaker. She indicated the square object lying just below the left collar bone and making the skin stand a little proud.
"The hospital were full of praise for you. They say if I had gone up in that plane I would have been in dire straits with my heart beating so slowly. I'm really grateful to you especially after the…," as she thought better of revealing that she had inadvertently heard the tirade that the ambulance man had heaped upon him after he had gone inside, "especially after me turning up on spec. like that."
"Not at all Molly," he said as he motioned to take her blood pressure, which like her heart rate was now excellent. "Many thanks for coming in Molly."
He showed her to the door, and Mrs Farnell caught the next words.
"You saved my life doctor, how can I ever repay you? I wanted to drive to the hospital and they said I could have collapsed at any time, and it was a good job you acted as you did."
"Think nothing of it, I'm pleased you got here when you did, and there will now be many more holidays to come," he offered breezily.
Mrs Farnell smiled to herself. She couldn't wait for Dr Michaels' next patient to come out so that she could slip in and inform him of the latest news.

As Melanie entered, the young GP greeted her, as always, with his boundless enthusiasm and friendly manner. He tried not to stare as he detected that her recovery had liberated other positive facets, like the keen attentive expression and the bright, agile mind.
"How goes it?" he ventured.

"Well," she said. She told him of her opening skirmishes with the puerile Newman and the passwords. "Of course I didn't tell Newman that we had extracted all the information we needed; I just wanted to see how much of a stand he would make at this stage. He's playing a duplicitous game, and I'm not quite sure what he's up to. We've called an extraordinary meeting but it'll take a couple of weeks before we can get everyone together, with summer holidays and annual leave."

"Are you confident Melanie?"

"I'm not sure; he's very crafty, and he seems to be in constant contact with Warners. They pack a very big punch, but I do have some allies."

She was aware that Newman wasn't going to give in without a fight, he was too close now to his goal to let it slip from his grasp. Undue confidence on her part would surely be premature and her long illness had taught her that she could not allow herself that luxury.

"How are you holding up Melanie?"

"I'm better by the day. I just don't sleep. I don't suppose you could let me have a few knockout drops could you?"

"Those are heap bad medicine," he pronounced, rather like a First Nation Chief doubting the wisdom of a particular strategy. "Sleeping tablets will put hours on the sleep clock, but don't give the quality that's needed. They're addictive and tend to have what we call a hangover effect the following day."

"I sense you're not too keen on these doc. Any suggestions?"

"You've tried the hot bath, the hot cocoa, a good book and the rub down with an oily rag?"

"Yes, well some of those anyway," she replied, being temporarily unable to dispel from her mind the image of being rubbed down with an oily rag as a means of promoting sleep.

"How long has your sleep been disturbed?"

"I've been awake with the dawn for fourteen months now, two weeks before Dad and Trish....," the words trailed off before completion, as if the very mention would bring pain which was difficult to bear.

"How come two weeks before?" he asked somewhat puzzled.

Her eyes widened as she faced another beast in her memory. With an amalgam of tension and fear she told him of her visit to the gypsy, 'just for a bit of fun', and of the damning prophecy that had come about as a result. He gazed intently, and gently stroked his chin as he always did when deep in thought, reflexly reaching for something that was no longer there. She unleashed the terrifying tale without interruption, feeling sudden relief at having told someone, at last, the thoughts that haunted her.

He paused for some time, choosing his words with accustomed skill, almost as if talking someone perched on a high ledge. One mistake or hasty word and off they would go. "Medicine is a strange blend of science, skill, hope and belief. I've seen people die from sheer worry, and others recover from what were considered to be terminal illnesses. Whether it be the physical or the metaphysical, one thing remains supreme."
"Go on, I'm fascinated."
"The power of the human brain. You showed me some of the wonders in your factory. Do you ever stop to think about the sheer capability of the human brain? Certainly the most complex thing seen in nature and, I don't know if I dare offer, Creation. You see wonders performed by hypnotists and acupuncturists and Chinese herb medicine as well as homeopaths. Whilst I don't decry any of those, I believe firmly that it is the brain that catalyses all those events and brings about the healing or whatever."
She looked intently at him as he continued.
"The gypsy told you only one possible outcome - a future that may lie in wait for you. Men can change history; think themselves well, or change continents. I do not accept that you're a passive player in all this, without any possible chance of affecting its outcome. Perhaps by seeing the future, we have the opportunity to change it?"

His words achieved their aim. Not for the first time; he had he had checked abject despair and turned it with understanding, empathy and skill into something much more positive, and in so doing had created a *modus operandi* that would strengthen and restore her, as might a flickering flame in the wilderness. He would seize every opportunity to turn that glimmer into a glow and then on to a blinding flash that would banish the depression forever. She believed his words, and hope waxed somewhere in the dark despair, like a tiny seed that would grow.

Melanie remained impassive for a few minutes and he sat back, drained, almost as might a faith healer who had just completed his latest miracle.
“I'll never be able to thank you enough for all this,” she concluded after the pause.
“As I said, Melanie, my job is to get you well. I don’t give up without a fight. A bit like you and that factory of yours. We are not dissimilar you and I.”
She nodded approvingly with the words. She slowly regained her composure and got up to go.
"I'd better go, you will have your visits and your half day."
As she stood, she extended an elegant hand and a firm handshake, and paused for a moment as she reflected on this unassuming and almost humble man who could bring to bear such consummate expertise and such skill.

Just as she turned to go, a flashback came as she remembered something else that the gypsy had said, something that she had either discounted or repressed all those months ago. She repeated the words. “*Those who try to help you shall be the first to die*.” Her recollection of words from which her subconscious had sought to protect her, were now out, once again, in the open, and she remembered how few of her former friends had returned once she had voiced them. She had to warn him.
“Dr Smith, you are in danger. The gypsy told me those who help me will be the first to die. James you are going to die,” she repeated as the recollection stayed within her mind.

The tension was too much for her fragile state. She fled from the room and out to her car. He ran after her as the doors flew open. Patients looked with amazement and raised eyebrows as he called to her. Mrs Farnell nearly collided with him as she rushed from behind her desk to see what emergency was unfolding. He caught up with Melanie as the driver's door closed. He opened the door with a tug.
"Melanie listen to me, I don't die that easily and I don't accept the unalterable vision. I am in this with you now, and I don't intend to run away or to fold under a gypsy's curse."

Even without turning Smith knew that a significant weight of stares would be coming from the waiting room with its large window. He could only hope that Dr Michaels' was not amongst them, as both doctors knew that such events were very unusual in the normally restrained proceedings of Lorne Street surgery. Whatever would Dr Michaels say about this? Mrs Farnell waited for the opportunity to slip in between patient to apprise him of the disturbance.

"Smith has his hands full with this one, eh, Mrs F." Dr Michaels repositioned his glasses. 'Time for a cup of tea,' he thought to himself, 'with just a drop of something a little stronger.' "The boy did well with the Fay woman, eh Mrs F. Have you seen this letter from Casualty. I was rather hoping the Ambulance would make a complaint. I can't wait to tell them."
She nodded affirmatively, as always, carried along by his infectious mood.
"Well, do the boy good. I suppose these young'uns need to get their hearts pumping every so often."
Looking at him as he sipped his tea while the hot drink slowly misted the half-moons, she wondered coyly whether his blood had ever been moved with such force. He seemed to sense her musings and gently chuckled into his tea. "Please send in the next patient Mrs Farnell, someone has to keep this ship afloat."

Melanie sobbed, her mind once again firmly under the spell of perfect despair. He grabbed her hand tightly, the skin whitening under his grasp.

“We see this through to the bitter end, and I am not a man who likes to lose. It’s just not something I intend to get used to,” he offered with defiance.

“I shouldn't have involved you. I wouldn't forgive myself if you came to any harm,” she sobbed.

“You didn’t involve me, I believe I was the one who visited you, if I recall. Well, I'm not planning on going anywhere, and besides it’s probably too late now anyway, so looks like you are stuck with me.”

It was almost a challenge to fate itself. His words, clear, firm and unwavering, hit home as she calmed under their impact. His whole demeanour, as well as his words admitted no possibility of being wrong. It was almost like talking with a member of the clergy about whether God existed or not. She accepted those words, with a smile slowly breaking under the last sob. Once again his unwavering belief, his commitment, to the right thing and to his patient, were unalterable. She could see this in those deep chestnut pools that looked so intently, without blinking, at her.

“OK, Dr Smith - the floor is all yours; let’s go for it.”

“That’s more like it Melanie. Now you get out of here before I get struck off.”

“You should be so lucky,” she managed with a more teasing smile.

That night Smith realised that the unwelcome visitor of sleeplessness was about to descend and, like many unwelcome guests, was to remain for some time. No matter, he was not about to quit now. The only way was forward. Doing nothing was no longer an option. He had made a promise: a promise to get her better, a promise to stick with her, a promise not to cut out at the first available opportunity, and he knew he would make good on those promises.

The moon rose in a perfect July night sky as if to bear silent witness to the challenge thrown to the unseen and unknown fates.

As he turned restlessly in a futile attempt to seek somnolence, he knew that sleep was to be the first casualty in a long struggle. His strategy was to be a simple one. His training, his belief in the skills he had been taught, combined with his need to assist his patient, would be used to create stability in the turmoil. The work he loved and the skills he applied, would form a barrier against the imagined evil that confronted them. Just before sleep came to him, in the early hours, he knew only that he would do whatever it took to save her.

Melanie too was facing her own battles. His words of defiance had strengthened her resolve and she believed implicitly in his ability to guide them both calmly from darkness into light. His strategy of assuring her that it was too late now, and that he had no intention of leaving, caused a calm that flowed through her. Her thoughts turned to the meeting at work that had been arranged for two weeks time. Newman had deliberately chosen a week when Stella had booked her annual leave. Both knew that Stella controlled five percent of the voting shares, and that her loyalty to Melanie was unswerving. This underhand move had not been entirely unexpected on Melanie's part. It was a battle to the death and she was either going to win handsomely or face oblivion. Slowly and with great care she had built up her business- plan with which she hoped the company would move forward. Newman too had been busy, and confidently talked of his plans, as if those with voting rights had already backed him without reservation. The meeting would give her a chance to show her resolve and, hopefully, her ability to transform the company into a world- class player. In any case it was on the verge either of a breakthrough or being swallowed up by a larger competitor, and she would do her utmost to bring about the former. Newman would have the fight of his life on his hands. And his smug confidence together with his misogynous tendency might just give her the chance to deliver the lethal blow to his misdirected plans.

CHAPTER VI

"INCAUTIOUS EXCESS"

The following day Melanie arrived at work early. She was attempting to write the speech of her life when her mobile phone rang.
"Hello, Melanie?"
"I thought I told you never to phone me at work," as she pretended not to recognise Smith's calm voice.
"That's a bit rich, having shown me up in front of all my patients yesterday. I wondered if you would care for a rematch. I was going on some visits and I wondered if you'd like to come with me?"
"Why not. I'd be delighted." Her speech had only got as far as 'Dear Colleagues', so a bit of a break could do no harm.
"I'll pick you up in fifteen minutes," he suggested.

The battered Maestro made its usual noisy entrance into the car-park, as she waited in reception before running out to meet him. "I thought I'd better wait for you, so you wouldn't have to turn off the engine."
He reached over to open the passenger door which slowly creaked as rusty metal moved on more rust.
"This will do nothing for my image," she informed him mischievously. "That door sounds like the creaking door as Vincent Price does the voiceover on 'Thriller. 'darkness falls across the land'," she started, as suddenly she looked at the driver's console. "Not the talking car! I remember these, my Grandad used to tell me about them."
She pressed a button on the trip computer to bring the synthesised voice to life. "Average Speed", "Average Fuel Consumption" and a variety of others generated by the female voice as she attempted different actions.
"Well, you must have a good memory if you remember all that Grandad told you about the MG Maestro," he said. "You sure know how to hurt a guy's feelings."

"No, actually I quite like these old biscuit tins. A former boyfriend had one when I was in my teens. That must have been nearly ten years ago," she exclaimed with triumph. "Mind you, it was an old car then!"
"Go on, continue to mock."

"How are you today, doctor? It must give you a real lift driving in this to work every day."
She couldn't quite hide from him her mixture of fascination and horror, that someone could still own a car that had belonged in the crusher some ten years before.
"You could always walk, you know. How are you anyway?" as he hoped to move the consultation on, despite her deep-rooted fascination.
"Fine thanks. I've been thinking about what you said. If you were to drop me now, you might get away unscathed."
"Now Melanie, we settled this yesterday, I believe. I told you, we're in this to the end. I never desert a patient in mid-treatment, even those cursed by Mancunian gypsies. I have a special clause written into my Defence Union subscription, 'licensed to treat those cursed by gypsies and other fortune-tellers'."
She smiled with an inner contentedness that had been missing for many months. She looked through the passenger window away from him, hoping that his powers of observation had not detected the tear that had suddenly formed in the corner of her eye. She anticipated that would be his response but, as she saw herself as the ill-fated one, she sensed that she owed him a chance to exit now.
"If you are sure," she deliberately held on to the 'sure'.
"Never in all my life," he offered with sincerity.
"OK, on your head be it. Have we any in-car entertainment?"
She almost didn't dare ask. She found a dusty tape. "Ah 'Tears for Fears' my favourite," she teased. "This cassette tape belongs in a museum too, you know," she said, as she realised that the car and its contents were encapsulated within a rift in time that was almost twenty years old: and how at variance this was with its youthful and energetic owner.

"These new fangled things like CDs don't play music like an old TDK cassette tape," he confirmed.
"This album must be older than the car," she said as she brushed off the dirt and the dust from the tape. She ejected a tape, in a similar state of dusty decay and peered at its title. 'Medical Management of Piles' she read, just before tossing it disrespectfully into the back, over her shoulder, as she observed, "Doctor, you are not getting out nearly enough."

The tape player crackled into life and she discovered, with some surprise, that the music wasn't as bad as she feared.
"Wow, what a car," she said facetiously.
"You will be walking in a minute, I swear."
"Where are we off to?"
"I was driving out to Seabridge to do some visits."
"Seabridge?" she enquired. "That's a bit off your patch isn't it?"
"A few patients asked us if they could join the list and as Dr Michaels says, we'll have to take on few more patients if he is going to be able to keep me as a full time partner. It seemed the logical thing to do."

Seabridge town, though not far from the genteel and affluent village of Little Dunham could not have been more different, with the remnants of decaying industry and dilapidated housing stock as a constant reminder of more active and affluent times. He drove to the first visit. It reminded Melanie of a scene out of war torn Beirut that she had seen on the telly.
"Glad we brought your car after all," she acknowledged truthfully.

The houses lining the streets had been built well enough, thirty years ago, but had long since finished their terminal decline into uncared-for decay. Old bangers, even older than Smith's, littered the road. Front gardens had been flattened to make way for off-road parking for many of the wrecks that presumably had no right to be on any public highway. Small, poorly dressed children with chocolate and food still lingering around their mouths; their clothes, either the wrong size or filthy with prolonged wear, played

amongst the litter and the detritus, followed round by a variety of cats and mongrels in a state of excitement that seemed to add to the chaos. Melanie reflected what lovely children they were. Eyes shone from beneath hastily cut fringes in varying shades. Peach-like skin was smothered with ingrained dirt.
"Dr Smith, you do show a girl a good time! I, I am speechless Doctor, you have exceeded your finest efforts."
"Number thirty two," he announced, ignoring her jibe.
Two little boys came up to them and asked if he was a doctor and if she was a nurse and which house he was going to. Smith answered the former but ignored the latter. Every patient had a right to privacy regardless of their status. Melanie followed him quickly, anxious not to be left behind. They were shown into a small, dimly lit lounge. Despite the full sun outside, the window made little concession to the rays attempting to pass through the caked-on smoke of a thousand cigarettes. Melanie looked down, wondering what was sticking to her feet and whether she had walked in something. She was surprised to find that it was only what was left of the carpet. It had long since been replaced by a black sticky mixture of dirt, food, smoke and other things she shuddered to even consider.
"I'm Dr Smith," he announced, "and this is Melanie, who is taking a look at my practice; do you mind if she comes in?"

Here it was, the Smith charm. Everyone was smiled at, everyone was shown respect, everyone was engaged by eye contact, everyone was greeted with politeness, nobody was treated any the less for being of modest means. The young mother motioned to a baby lying on the settee. "It's Matthew, doctor, he's been throwing up for days and he keeps getting diarrhoea."
Smith looked at Matthew. The young fellow was chirpy enough but covered in vomit and diarrhoea.
"Have you no nappies?" he guessed.
"I couldn't afford no more, doctor. I had to tear up an old bed sheet." The sheet had long since been exhausted with the frequent diarrhoea.
"How old is he?"

"He'll be ten months next week doctor."
"Is there anyone else in the house?"
"No, just me and 'im. My boyfriend moved out last month."
A half finished bottle lay next to the baby.
"What's in here?" Smith asked expectantly.
"It's tea, doctor. He likes tea normally, but he's hardly touched it."

Smith applied himself to the examination of his young patient with painstaking care. A few minutes later he stood upright to engage the baby's mother.
"Mathew has a virus in his tummy. Now, the virus won't harm him, but dehydration just might. It's important to get fluids, drinks," he explained when he thought that mum was looking a bit puzzled, "down him. I'd like you to try these sachets, little packets, that you dissolve in water to make up drinks. If he'll take them, these are ideal. It's important that he doesn't have any milk, as that won't feed him, at the moment, it'll just make his diarrhoea worse."
Eventually mum signalled that she understood the instructions, and Smith and Melanie left to retrieve the car from the shattered streets.

"There isn't a lot of sunshine down here, Melanie, but these are real people who still need and deserve as much help as someone like me can give."
"Do you think that these people suffer that bit more because of their circumstances?"
"Suffering is a relative, not an absolute, term. I do think they suffer, either because of what they do, or do not do to their bodies; because of the people they associate or are in contact with; because of mistakes made by their parents; because of poor social conditions or because of a limited grasp of some of the essentials of life and of longevity."
She listened intently as he talked of his work and of his patients, patients that he was here to serve as best he could. At last she had been allowed just a tiny glimpse of the real James Smith, and some of the things that moved him.

"It's a bit of a battle, I'm afraid, and one that we're slowly losing. Beautiful, healthy children are born into environments that will destroy their health, and sabotage any chance that their intelligence, under ordinary circumstances, would give them some sort of success in life. A lot of GPs write these people off. The estate is a no-go area at night with older youths gathering in the streets, with fighting, petty crime, drugs and of course the joyriders."

He stopped the car outside a heavily-fortified corner shop, and ran inside. He came out with a packet of nappies and tossed it into her lap.
"Now I know where your money goes. I take it we're going back with these?"
"Would you like to leave the little fellow in that condition?"
"Surely the state provides?"
"Yes, of course it does. Do you want to come back and tell her that they should spend their cig. money on clothing their kids, or maybe send the satellite TV back, or the plasma telly? We can't change the world, Melanie, but, we can do our bit, here and there, to spread a little sunshine as we go. Many do a really good job of bringing up their kids on a limited budget, but you won't find many of them on this estate."

He stopped outside Matthew's house while Melanie ran in with the nappies. "Please tell her that it was a sample we found in the boot, Melanie," he called after her.
Melanie was quiet, deep in thought as she got back to the car.
"Did you see what a handsome chap he was? What a life. Does he have any chance at all?"
"Not really, Melanie. You could see that his Mum is still a child herself. She can only care for him as well as she cares for herself."
"Why do they still smoke if they know it's so bad for them and their children?"
"It's not quite that easy. The cigs are extremely addictive, and I suppose we could say that they have little else in their gloomy lives."

Melanie became silent again as they moved on to the next call. They drove past the shattered playground where all the rides had been vandalised, and the concrete surface was littered with glass and dog excrement. Melanie noticed the untidy gardens and run down houses, many of which were boarded up.

“Why do they board houses up when so many are looking for homes?”

“As people move away, or whatever, the homes they leave are in such a bad state of repair that it takes teams of workers weeks, just to get them habitable again. If the houses are left open they'll be vandalised, stripped bare or used as all-night drug dens, or all three. Many of these people are forgotten.

“I'm sure I could pull myself out of the gutter,” she concluded.

“I'm sure you could: but your father has given you pride, your mother love, they both gave you an education and something to strive for, as well as a sense of belonging to the community as a whole. These people are used only to Dad coming home drunk every night and beating their mother up, and a world that wants them to go away.”

“Well you have opened my eyes, James. I feel really sorry for them; the children deserve so much better.”

“It’s getting worse Melanie, not better. I think the Americans call it the ‘underclass’ but I prefer the phrase ‘long-term poor’. In any event whatever we mean by it, this is it – all around us.”

They drove on past the decaying Elderly Folks Club with its rotting wooden frames and it bedaubed exterior. He pulled up at Mr and Mrs Davis' on the edge of the estate. Here was a contrast, with a neatly-tended garden and a well-cared-for domicile. Mrs Davis was suffering from a flare up of her arthritis. Dr Smith took time to examine her and explain why her joints had become so painful. He discussed the pros and cons of the various treatments available, and agreed a treatment plan with her. They turned to go.

“I would like to thank you and your young colleague,” Mr Davis said as they went through the door, “we don't see a lot of doctors round these parts, and those we do see don’t give us the time of day; because we're old and we live on this estate, they don't want to know." He shook Smith's hand warmly and also Melanie's. "Thanks for coming again doctor and for what you've done for the missus."

"I am truly impressed," she began. "I can see that you have a real calling."
"Not really Melanie. I like people, and it's a pleasure to do what I can. Money isn't what drives me, I simply want to help as many as I can, and do my best with them all, regardless of who or what they are."
"I'm proud of you," she continued, "I feel ashamed. Here am I, with the gold spoon in my mouth and floods of tears in my eyes, and these people are at the sharp end. These are the ones who have a right to be unhappy or depressed or suicidal, not me."
"Please remember Melanie, that it's all relative. That elderly couple would not change places with you. They have each other, and they're happy with their little lot. It's an outdated concept these days – contentment, but there are still a few who've found that the secret of happiness is to want what you already have, rather than lusting after what you can't have or what someone else has."
"Does that mean you don't believe people should try to better themselves?"
"No, not at all: if they don't lose their perspective, and as long as they don't equate material acquisition with life-long happiness, because it just ain't, as I'm sure you could tell any one of them."
Before she could reply the phone rang. It was Mrs Farnell.
"Dr Smith sorry to disturb you but another call has come in, down the road from where you are; it's a little boy of eight, with breathing problems."
"Never trust phone messages," he began, as the engine roared with new-found life, "it may mean he has a cold, or it may mean he is on his last legs."

Unfortunately it was the latter. Daniel was an asthmatic, whose inhaler had run out a few days before. Mum had not had chance to

get a new one. He was unable to speak, and in obvious distress. Smith placed the Oximeter on his finger to measure the oxygen in his blood.
"Whoosh," she heard him say to himself, "oxygen is a bit down. Melanie would you get my nebuliser from the boot and my red toolbox. The nebuliser is the large white plastic case."
Smith listened to Daniel's chest to make sure that both lungs were still inflated. As soon as Melanie returned he set the nebuliser up, with well-practised ease. He opened the red box, squirted the contents of a small plastic bubble into it with a tiny bit of adrenaline.
"Melanie 999, please," he said, as he threw her the phone.

While Melanie made the call, Smith went to get the Oxygen cylinder from his boot. When the nebuliser had finished, he set up the oxygen and mask to ease the child's breathing. Gradually his condition stabilised. A couple of minutes later the Ambulance had arrived and whisked him off to hospital. Dr Smith phoned ahead.
"Young lad on his way in status asthmaticus, he's getting tired and may well need ventilating. He'll be with you soon."
They both sat in the car letting their nerves calm on the over-warm summer's day.
"Will he be all right?" Melanie asked.
"It'll be touch and go. I'll phone them later to find out and I'll let you know."
"How could his mother have let his inhalers run out?"
"Mum needs to know that that isn't a wise move, but you never really know what's going on in their life. Dad may have run off with someone at work, the dog may have just died and so on."
"Do you think of everything?"
"Well, I do my best to understand human nature. It's the only way to get to grips with some of the problems we face. As I said, increasingly, people bring us social rather than medical problems."

Once again after a struggle with the car they drove off.
"Thanks for bringing me along, but can I ask you why?"
She already anticipated his reply.

“Life is a funny thing. One person may be in paradise but be in a personal hell. Another person, who may be in what onlookers would view as a terrible state, may be quite content. Depression tends to make you look at everything from the blackest view. It's a bit like wading through porridge with no clue as to where you are and how close to the edge of the dish you are. As I told you, the half-full glass becomes the half-empty.”

“Am I a spoilt little rich girl, who should pull herself together?”

“You know better than that, Melanie,” he suggested with gentle reproach, “I thought you might like to know what goes on down here in this ‘forgotten’ estate with its forgotten people.”

“I know these aren't quite the words, but I am glad you brought me.

"I feel really sorry for some of these people; they don't have a lot to look forward to and their chances in life already seem to be non-existent,” came from him.

“It’s the little children I feel sorry for. What lovely children and what a waste of their potential,” Melanie said, still deep in thought. “Can anything be done at all?” she asked.

“Not a lot Melanie; we're just two people and we can't change the world. We can do just a little bit where and when we can, like buying nappies.”

Melanie nodded in agreement, but had one or two ideas of her own. Smith dropped her off in the car park and drove off to start his evening surgery.

The following morning she installed herself behind her desk so that she could make one or two phone calls. Newman was in early too. He barged into her office, as if not expecting to see her.

“Sorry, to interrupt you,” he said in his usual insincere tone, “mind if we just do a bit of measuring up?” Two workmen followed him and started measuring for new office furniture. At first Melanie was annoyed then bemused. She waited for the men to finish and as Newman turned to go, she quietly said, “Brian, just remember that you, too, are an employee here. You may seek to change your status, but only a full meeting of the shareholders can do that.

Until such time as they do, I would be grateful if you would keep out of my office."

He left with an icy stare. At the door he hesitated, the snarl forming on his face, and then checked himself before continuing on through the door. He was doing his best to get her rattled, but Melanie had a much more positive train of thought than the malevolence which, it seemed, was all he knew. Perhaps things would have been better if she had accepted his offer of a date all those years ago, when she was working there as a student in her summer holidays. Trish had always liked him, but Melanie felt her skin crawl at the smoky breath and the greased hair slicked back over his head. Despite her brilliance as a business woman, Trish had never been a good judge of character. Melanie could see through the shallow, cocky exterior, deep into those dark eyes and to the person below. She looked up the Finance Director's cruel and unfeeling face and realised that such experiences now lay firmly behind her: and she knew only that whatever it took and whatever it cost, she would want to make no accommodation with him whatsoever; even if this meant her departure.

Her mind cleared quickly and she set about the task in hand. She brought up an online directory on her laptop and positioned herself next to the telephone handset. She agreed with Smith, you could make a small difference to the plight of the people she had met yesterday, a little bit at a time. She phoned Seabridge Borough Council and spoke to the senior Treasurer. "It's Miss Archibald here from the National Lottery finance allocation board. We hear that the playground in Weaver road is in need of urgent repair or replacement? Would forty thousand pounds be enough to replace it with an adventure playground for use by all local residents?" The Treasurer whooped with delight and barely heard her say that a banker's draft would be transferred electronically that very day, provided work could begin at once. The anonymous benefactor also arranged for the complete refurbishment of Foden Lodge, the elderly persons' club and bowling green, which was in a similar dilapidated state. A few days later a mini bus appeared outside the secondary school, complete with sign-writing down its side

'Seabridge Comprehensive'. The headmaster had been phoned some days before and informed that his school had come top in a charity prize draw for school equipment, and asked what were they most in need of.

An envious motor mechanic steered the beautiful brand-new Mini Cooper Special into the surgery car park. He, himself had always secretly desired a car identical to the one he was driving. The Mini was of a deep, cherry red and looked resplendent in the beautiful August sunshine. He found a small speck of dust to polish off with his overall sleeve and then walked inside, jingling the keys with proud, boyish delight. He walked into the surgery and asked for a Dr. James Smith. The protective receptionist as ever wanted to know who was asking for him and why. The mechanic said excitedly that he had his new car in the car park, and wondered if the doctor would like him to demonstrate the car and its controls. Smith was upstairs in the office with Dr Michaels, who was contemplating another chocolate biscuit with a certain guilt about the example he was setting to his patients. Mrs Farnell ran upstairs with just a hint of prescience as to what was about to happen.
"Your new car is here Dr Smith."
"What new car Mrs F.? I haven't ordered a new car."
"Must be paying you too much, my boy," came the considered response from Dr Michaels, who was now well into his second biscuit and who, too, had a sense of the drama which was about to unfold. He chewed a little more vigorously as he sensed the excitement in the air. Smith ran downstairs to see the mechanic holding the keys up in front of him. "She's a beaut. Doctor. What a good choice," confirmed the mechanic.

The new Mini looked truly magnificent, especially next to the battered 'biscuit tin', as Melanie had christened it. Smith, too, had inwardly desired such a car ever since they had been launched, now some years ago.
"That's not mine," Smith began incautiously.

"Well, I, believe it is, at least your name is on the registration documents and I was told to deliver it to you. You are Dr James Smith of Lorne Street surgery?"
"Yes that's me, but that is not my car."
"It says here it is sir," the mechanic said, in a stupid, but matter-of-fact way holding the documents for his inspection. "One moment, Doctor, I'll just phone the garage."
The mechanic spoke to the sales director and handed the young doctor the phone as he, also, gained insight into the events now before him.
"Ah Dr Smith, sorry I couldn't come in person, but as you can imagine with it being the new plate we are very busy. Might I say what a wise choice and how pleased we were to be able to get one for you at such short notice," enthused the sales director as he continued to eulogize about the doctor's choice, so much that Smith eventually had to shout to interrupt him.
"This is not my car," insisted Smith, somewhat forlornly.
"Did you not send us a banker's draft yesterday for the full amount, Sir?"
"That was not me."
The sales manager was very puzzled by this time. "Well, who was it sir?"
"It wasn't me," offered Smith realising that his didactic stance was already redundant.
"The lady who telephoned, said that she was your secretary and was ordering it on your behalf. The draft appeared the same day. We had to move heaven and earth to get one for you at such short notice. I'm told your old car just won't start, is that correct? You'll find that this one will never let you down, sir. What a good choice you've made."

Smith realised that he was getting nowhere. To make matters worse, it was obvious that they had been given enough facts to lend authenticity to their argument whilst destroying his. The salesman thought he knew from reading his paper that these GPs were paid far too much money, and considered that perhaps he was simply trying to appear more frugal in the eyes of his colleagues and staff, and didn't wish to be embarrassed. Perhaps he hadn't even informed his wife of the car's arrival. The mechanic looked at the young doctor carefully, as a new thought came to him that the doctor had been working too hard and was probably so stressed that he'd forgotten. No, he discounted this instantly, everybody knew that doctors, these days, worked so few hours. Smith realised that he was against a carefully disguised trail, but was in no doubt as to where it had come from. He asked the sales manager to leave the car with him, while he checked things out. The sales manager, increasingly puzzled, agreed with some relief. The mechanic was picked up by a workmate who had been patiently waiting for him throughout the exchange, and the Mini remained poised on the car park.

Dr Michaels was finishing his seventh biscuit. The common room window was open and he remained glued to the unfolding story he could hear below as he continued to listen with no hint of shame. He might have told himself at one time that it was rude to eavesdrop, but these days, he realised such sentiments belonged more to a person with more days left on earth than he had.

"That young man has his hands full, Mrs F. It's a good job he's young."

"He needs a good wife," concluded Mrs Farnell. Her mind, as always thinking furiously about all that was, and was not apparent. They moved quickly away from the window as Smith returned from the car park with a handbook, cleaning kit and bits of literature that the mechanic had hastily handed him.

He grabbed his notes from the downstairs office, his usual calm manner having been shattered irrevocably, and disappeared on his visits muttering to himself. The Maestro eventually started with what seemed like an even longer delay than usual, and he disappeared in the familiar cloud of dust and smoke. The engine seemed to be firing in a more uneven way than usual, as if it had recognised that it had been put on notice of an imminent visit to the crusher. His agitated state continued even as he pulled into the car park. He jumped from the Maestro and went through the glass and chrome doors to reception. "Suzy, could Miss Jardine spare me a minute?" – only by employing exceptional effort, did he manage to restore some semblance of outer calm.

"She'll be right with you Dr Smith," she confirmed, as she replaced the handset.
Melanie appeared in the foyer. Her smile had banished most of his agitated thoughts, and for a moment he hesitated, as he bore witness to the glorious sight in front of him; not wanting his words to damage what he could see. He would tell himself later that this was the first time that he had recognised that her depression was lifting. He knew in that instant that she was now firmly on the road to recovery, and also with a hint of a smile that could brighten the darkest day – almost. His eyes as usual reported all that they saw faithfully with their customary unswerving sensitivity, but it was only weeks later that he would gauge everything that he had experienced that day, and he would look back at this time with more than a little wistfulness. Melanie at once registered the pause, as his thoughts and intended words were hastily being re-aligned. She sensed his agitation, which concerned her, but it was accompanied by just a hint, an impression, of something far more uplifting which couldn't be totally extinguished by the words she was about to hear. He had rehearsed what he was going to say on his way over, but her presence seemed to nullify his thoughts.

"Melanie can we go to your office? You are looking well," he ventured as she led him away.
"Why thank you Dr Smith." The smile returned with full force, as she gazed at him. It was he who looked away, as if he was not quite able to meet the full intensity of the look that she had applied in his direction. She couldn't fail to see, nevertheless, that he was deeply troubled.
"Melanie, you know that I'm flattered and I'm overwhelmed. You know that I cannot accept such a wonderful present, don't you. It was really kind of you and...." his words began to break up as a nervous agitation took control. "What would people think of me if I were to even contemplate accepting such a gift?"

She thought briefly about denying everything. She had covered her tracks very well and it was impossible to trace back. Seeing his discomfort, however, she knew that she would have to confess. Ultimately she realised too, and also should have known, that his sense of duty, of propriety and regard for his public image were just too unshakable.
"Forgive me, James. I wasn't thinking. I just wanted to thank you. Thank you for all that you have done. To show you how much you've done for me. How much you've helped me." Sentences were short and choppy as if the emotion that was now in force could not be held in check by anything longer. As his distress eased, hers increased in equal measure. Slowly her words too broke under pressure of that emotion as she elected for a simple, "I'm sorry."

He held her hand gently in his but she could feel him tremble, or was it she?
"What a beautiful car! I've never been more flattered, nobody has ever given me anything like this!" The truth, he couldn't voice, let alone admit to himself was that he had never been given anything, by anyone apart from the occasional hurried birthday present from his mother. "I want to get you better, Melanie, this is my job and that is my reward." Her acutely attuned instinct was hardly needed for her to know that each word he uttered contained the undiluted truth.
"I know all that, it's just that I really thought it would be a token of my gratitude."
"A token!" his words failed him at this point as he struggled to say more. "Melanie it has to go back! You know that don't you?"
"Please forgive me, it won't happen again."

There it was before them, words that by others might be spoken freely and without restraint were modified or even blocked completely, by professional ethics and conduct that dictated his actions and therefore hers. She had no doubt as to the feeling he had for his work. May be that was all there was. They parted, each looking dejected. "See you on Tuesday," he offered as the last parting chance to rescue the conversation from the icy waste that seemed to surround them. She nodded in agreement, but it was almost as if a veil had descended between them. Despite the fact that it was invisible and impalpable, she had no doubt as to its presence.

Mrs Perkins carefully removed the heavy steaming kettle from the Aga plate and deposited the boiling contents into two mugs. She placed one in front of Melanie and sat facing with the other. "I've seen a big improvement in you of late, my dear, and you're almost back to your old self. I know that you wanted to thank that nice Dr Smith." After some delay, while she searched for the right words, she continued, "you know that he is just a little shy, and maybe such an, an, osten...., generous," she corrected before finishing the wrong word, "present made him very nervous. Also you know how people talk in village. They would have a field-day if it ever got out."

Melanie acknowledged all that was said with her usual good grace. "I just wanted to show him my gratitude," she said a little sorrowfully. "That old banger of his is on its last legs anyway," as if searching for a more consummate logic to defend her actions. She sniffed at a hankie, as Mrs Perkins looked on with her worried mother-hen look.

"He knows my dear, what you tried to do. These men get a bit frightened, you know, with their stiff logic and misplaced pride 'n' all. You have to try to see it from his point of view."

Mrs Perkins saved the day, once again and, though still miserable, Melanie could at least see merit in the homespun rationale delivered with care and genuine affection.

"I don't know where I'd be without you Mrs P. you're so kind to me." The tears flowed once again as the hankie struggled to stem the surge.

"You and Mrs Lydia have always been so good to me and I'll never forget it. You know that I could never do enough to repay you for all the kindness shown me over the years."

Melanie finished her coffee and went through to the high-vaulted conservatory to catch the sun as it declined in the late afternoon over the rock garden to the west. She switched on the television but her thoughts were elsewhere. How she missed her Mum and Trish. Mrs Perkins popped in to say that she was leaving, and Melanie thanked her as she folded her pinny and shrugged off her thanks with a waft of the hand. Melanie sat all alone in the big house as the first star of the evening blinked into the perfect sky.

Melanie arrived early as usual for her next appointment with Dr Smith. Mrs Farnell, seized the opportunity to pop into Dr Michaels' surgery. He threw his new electronic stethoscope onto his desk with disgust. Mrs Farnell knew that he had just purchased it at great cost. "Look at these notes Mrs F.," he began. She saw some squiggles in the notes that didn't mean an awful lot, "Smith saw Eunice Jenkins last week. Look here," he pointed to the notes again and read Smith's notation, 'rough, rumbling low-pitched diastolic murmur at the apex, loud, long pansystolic murmur. Diagnosis mixed mitral valve disease. Refer for Echo.' Eunice came in today to ask me if she needed to go. I can't hear a damned thing, even with this new fangled thing," he prodded the new stethoscope again with disgust. "Smith only has that old second-hand stethoscope that is on its last legs, and he's picked all this up. I told Eunice to get herself over to the hospital. That boy is jolly good Mrs. F. we were lucky to get him. My old ears just can't keep up with him." Mrs Farnell smiled at the more elderly GP. He had obviously forgotten that bright young GP, not unlike Smith, who had interviewed her more than thirty years ago. How bright, keen and handsome he was, perhaps even more so than the young Dr Smith. One day soon, she was going to have to remind him of those times. For now, she placed his tea on his desk and left with a little smile as she knew at a time like this he would want to add something a little stronger to the brew, as soon as she had gone.

When he and Melanie met for her consultation Smith was warm and friendly, as always, his gentle and caring smile shone out from the brown eyes of polished teak. They sat facing, as usual, in his

consulting room. He was polite, as always, yet a subtle distance had crept in between them; the same undercurrent that she noticed last week after the fiasco with the car. Once again she sought to close the gap.
"I am so sorry about the car. I know now how embarrassed you must have felt," she offered.
He passed a copy of the 'Seabridge Advertiser' over to her. "Have you read about the mysterious benefactor of the Seabridge estate?" he enquired.
She knew that he knew, and felt that she should defend her behaviour. "I just wanted to do something - a little to help some of those people. Did I do wrong?" she said nervously as his palpable discomfort was mirrored within her.
"No, I think it was a lovely act. Not many people would have done what you did," he deliberated.
"Money is no use, just stuck in a bank," she continued defensively, "It won't bring people back to life and it won't make an ill person well, but it can spread a little sunshine where there was none before."
"Have your magnanimous deeds ended for the moment?" he asked, a little irritatedly.
"I have one or two little projects on the boil at the moment. I'll set them in motion as soon as the time is right. I would rather spend my money on helping some of those in need," she repeated, but with more uncertainty.

He changed the subject quickly, almost as of he had been struggling all along to get his real thoughts into the open.
"Melanie, you seem so much better now. I wonder if we should leave things for a bit, and perhaps I can review you in a month, or two?"
Her reaction was as swift as it was unexpected.
"You running out on me too, now, Doctor? I'm sorry to be such a burden."
"That's not what I'm saying," he began, but she was already in flight toward the door.

Once again, she made for the car park with indecent haste, which only served to clash with her normally cool exterior. He started to run after her but he knew he could not contemplate what he would do or say if he were to catch her. Eyes once again were raised with incredulity by staff and patients in the waiting room. He stopped in reception. A few seconds later he could hear the Jaguar roar into life as the engine caught first breath without any hesitation. Mrs Farnell gazed from behind her reception doing her best to look as if nothing had happened at all. No doubt Dr Michaels would have heard the commotion and the muttering from patients, and would expect a full report after surgery.

The persistent insomnia he had faced ever since Melanie had told him about the gypsy, was as nought compared to the unrestrained turmoil that was unleashed through many of his days, and nearly all of his nights, as he attempted, and failed, to calm his raging thoughts and unsettled mind. How he got through his surgeries was a source of amazement to himself and also to the watchful Mrs Farnell who reported all to Dr Michaels as she popped in, as always, between patients.

“I don't know what’s going on Dr Michaels, but he's been looking dreadful since Miss Jardine ran out in a hurry the other day.” Mrs Farnell lied deliberately, in order to persuade her employer to part with some of his feeling on the matter. She knew exactly what was going on and she suspected that he did too. Michaels was his usual efficient self, never using more words than were needed to convey his point. “I expect he's got it all under control,” suggested her boss in a disinterested way. Mrs Farnell doubted that very much but nodded as if acknowledging the point he was making. Perhaps she was being too protective or even too inquisitive and should leave Smith to his own devices. Dr Michaels had the best idea. She would follow his example in future. He was no fool and she knew that he would simply leave Dr Smith to sort himself out.

Emotion was a very rare visitor to Dr Michaels’ face but she could have sworn that a worried look flashed across his visage as he stopped Smith, at the end of the surgery, to ask him if he was all right. She had never seen the like, in nearly forty years of working with him.

Chapter VII

"Forgiveness"

The next day, as Melanie once again sat impassively in front of the television that was on but registered nothing at all on her consciousness, the doorbell rang. It was late and she was not expecting any callers. She opened the door with a mixture of nervousness and puzzlement. Smith stood on the steps looking wretched.

"Hello madam, may I interest you in an apology?" as he held open an imaginary suitcase for her inspection.

She paused just for a moment, she looked carefully at him as he stood there, her face impassive and giving no clue as to what would happen next. The pause was expedient and served two purposes. Firstly, it stopped her from mining, too soon, the rich seam of forgiveness that ran within her, at times just a little too close to the surface. Secondly, and more importantly, she needed to convey that she had been hurt by what had passed between them, and whilst recognising that it was in no way intentional on his part, she needed him to acknowledge that it had been so.

Without a word she led him into the drawing room and motioned to him to sit down. He attempted to speak but she held up her hand, as if such a step would be unwise. She perched on the edge of a chair some little distance away.

"I was wrong to give you the Mini as a present. I believe I have apologised, unreservedly. I was starting to feel better, and I wanted to show you my appreciation. I am sure that patients buy, even you, the odd bottle or tie or the like, from time to time. Have you any idea what I've been through, and have you any idea of what you have done for me? You knew that first day I was going to swallow those tablets, and it's mainly through your efforts, and acute appendicitis," she added quickly, "that I didn't. It may have seemed like a lavish gift to you, and I'm sorry it appears so, but I wanted to convey some idea of how much I had been helped. It was a bit of an impulse but it seemed at the time like a good idea. For that I apologise." She held her hands up. "I am guilty, but tell me, Doctor, is there some other crime of which I have been guilty, because if so I would be grateful for some hint." She spoke quickly almost as if to outrun the tears that then flowed.

He looked even more wretched at the sight of this young woman driven to tears by his misconceived actions, but used the silence to respond.
"Melanie, I'm the one who should be apologising and asking for forgiveness. I was confused and frightened. I've never seen such a beautiful thing," he paused as he looked at her and considered what he had said was not quite true, "I've never owned anything remotely like it. How could I possibly accept such a wonderful gift? All for just doing my job; I'm not worthy of such a thing."

The tears stopped quickly as she received words that she was never expecting to hear. Surely he must know that he was worthy of the moon and stars. He continued, "I knew that I had to pull out all the stops if I was going to get you better. I was aware of how far down you were, and that I was dealing with potential suicide. I had to see you more often and get closer than is usual in a doctor-patient relationship." He hesitated, then continued. "I was worried in case I was losing sight of my rôle and whether others would misconstrue things."

The tears had been replaced, as a look of mixed amazement and relief crossed her face. All had not been said.
"So that's it! I don't remember you behaving in anything other than a proper manner at all times. I don't remember you putting your hand on my knee, or making improper suggestions, or any of the thousands of other things that the Sunday newspapers tell us you GPs are supposed to get up to all the time, in between spending afternoons on the golf-course. Excuse me, but if you do feel that you are guilty of any of those things, we can phone the BMA,"
"General Medical Council," he corrected.
"The General Medical Council, and have you struck off at once!"

They laughed in unison as the image flashed through both minds simultaneously.
"You're my doctor, and I'm grateful for all that you've done. Is it really too much to ask to be called a friend also. I am sure the GMS wouldn't be too worried by that, would they?"
"GMC," he corrected.

He smiled again. There was so much more he wanted to offer at this point but rather than risk incautious words he sought refuge in changing the subject quickly. "I was wondering if Newman stood any chance at all," he ventured.
"He's up to no good, but I'll sort him. Now, stop changing the subject. Have I still got a doctor or not?"
He had to check the impulse to tell her that he would be her doctor until the Earth had stopped spinning upon its axis, and decided, more cautiously, that an alternative form of acknowledgement was needed. He held out his hand and grasped hers in his usual firm manner. "Didn't I tell you that we were in this right to the end, whatever happened. I'm sorry if I gave you any other impression."
There followed a slight but palpable delay as she assimilated the new information. The smile and the cool hazel eyes were fired with the warm glow of amber accompanied by forgiveness as it crossed her face, bringing relief to them both.
"You look worse than I did with appendicitis. I was just going to have a snack. Can I tempt you into joining me?"

He accepted eagerly. He looked as though he hadn't eaten in a week, or slept.
"When is your meeting?"
"Next Wednesday."
"Nervous ?" he enquired.
"Newman is doing his best to spook me. He was actually having my office measured for furniture the other day."
"How strong a hand does he have?"
"He's playing for very high stakes, and Warners would love to gather us under their belt. They knew that I wouldn't sell in a million years, but I wonder just what they've promised him if he

can pull it off. That, I would love to know," her eyes suddenly becoming even larger and darker.
"Will it depend simply on votes?"
"Yes, and also how many shares each person has. I have forty percent of shares, Stella five. I think Stella is pretty solid, but Newman has managed to call the meeting when she is away. Newman has ten percent and each of the two engineers ten percent, and several others hold the balance. Technically if everyone voted with Newman they could outvote me and carry through their resolution. I know that I've not been in there much of late, but I can't believe that they've all turned against me. That can only mean that, not only has Newman been bought, but perhaps others too. Things are on a bit of a knife-edge and I honestly think it will be sudden death for one of us. I don't like losing to a creep like him, but on the other hand if the majority have decided that it's time for me to go, I would rather do that than try to hang on. My Dad would have wanted me to fight, just as you did, but always taught me when it was time to cut my losses and turn the other cheek as they say," she offered with one of her typical mixed idioms. "Do you think you *will* be able to get to the meeting? It would be an enormous boost to me if you were there."

"If it's good for my patient how could I possibly refuse. I'll do my best to sweet-talk Michaels. Actually after all the ferment that surgery has seen in the past few weeks I think he may not renew my contract at the end of the mutual, trial period."
"Is there a chance he won't?" she asked, with sudden concern.
"He plays his cards close to his chest and, believe it or not, my fate probably rests more with Mrs Farnell than anyone else.
"Is she really the *Eminence Grise* then, the seat of all power? She's always very nice with me on the odd occasion I've attended, but I have no doubt she has her finger on the pulse, as you medical people say."
"Yes, you could put it that way. I do my best to keep on the right side of her."
"Don't come if it will cost you your job."

"Well I might as well be hung for a sheep as a lemon," introducing one of his own, with less skill. "I'll be there, even if I never work again," he said with grim determination, "we see this through to the very end, remember?"
"I'm putting the finishing touches to my speech."
"How much have you written?"
"About two words."
"You really do fancy strawberry picking in Lincolnshire, don't you as your next career move?"
"Don't worry, I will finish it; it's just that Newman and you," with some emphasis, "have been distracting me. Which reminds me."

She collected a tiny plastic tape from the mantle of the magnificent fireplace and handed it to him.
"What's this, have you been dusting off the policies?"
"Not quite, but I will tell you that it is very valuable. Please keep it in a safe place. If anything goes wrong at all, please give it to Stella: she will know what to do."
"Do you think things could turn that ugly?"
"It's do or die time for Newman; he knows that if he fails now, he will be taking the long walk. Actually a bit of strawberry picking would do him good. He has a black heart and there's no telling what he might do."

He placed the four millimetre tape in his pocket without really knowing what it was. "I will guard this with my life, my lady," he offered, "and keep it safe from all evil.
Tell me about your public works programme?" he asked.
At first she didn't know what he meant, then it dawned quickly.
"I drove past there the other day. I was doing some more house calls," he clarified.
"The new playground is coming on a treat. It's going to look super," she enthused. "Though, they will only vandalise it at night," he concluded, sadly.
"I thought of that one. The same mysterious benefactor has hired a security firm to patrol at night, and a sum of money will be made available for regular maintenance."

"You are a kind person Melanie, your selfless act will bring a lot of sunshine into their lives."
"I've also donated to a youth club that was desperately short of funds and a nursery that was about to close due to vandalism and shortage of equipment. No-one knows where the money has come from and I covered my tracks very well. The local news has been sniffing, but I don't think they'll pin it on me. Maybe some millionaire recluse, rather than some spoilt little girl who tries to cut out when the going gets tough."
"I don't see that person anywhere in sight."
"Thanks – it's all due to you."
"You do yourself down, madam."

"For the first time in ages I can see the sun rise in the morning and hear the birds in the trees. Life is worth living again. It's as though the sun has come out and cleared away the fog that was occluding everything from sight. Whatever happens, I don't want to go down there again. Do you think a little box of tablets can do all that?"
He did think that but, of course, he was wrong, he had missed the real reason.
"You won't go down there again," he said.
"Do you really think that the gypsy's vision can come true?" she asked.
"The trouble with prescient vision is that it presents only one possible option. I believe it's up to us to attempt to create a more favourable one. As I told you, I don't give up easily and there is still a lot more for me to do."
"Try telling that to Mrs Farnell," she offered and then, after a long silence, "I believe you."

They sat in the kitchen and continued to talk. The clock in the great hall struck midnight and still they talked: the relief on their faces mutually apparent. Peace came in equal measure with forgiveness, and the price that these demanded was one that both were happy to pay. A compromise had been struck which was as expedient as it was comfortable. Neither dared look further than this, for fear of disturbing the delicate but essential bond that lay between them. He with his duty to a patient, and she with the need for support in order to recover. Purely at a subconscious level each had realised that exposing their relationship to more scrutiny would shatter it, and neither was prepared to do so.

All too soon, he rose to go and began the time-consuming wrestle with the car that would eventually start in the balmy summer's night. As he left, she handed him a small packet. He withdrew a silk tie.

"I thought I'd buy you the usual type of present that a patient would buy for her doctor."

He smiled and thanked her and withdrew a CD from his car. "What's this, doctor, a present?"

"A bit of a peace offering."

"What would the GMSC say?"

"GMC," he corrected, once again.

"Well, as long as it doesn't contain anything too suggestive, I suppose it would be OK."

"Kayser Chiefs – *Future is Medieval* - suggestive enough?"

"Thanks very much. I'll play it on my way to work tomorrow. An up-to-date CD – well I never! I think this one may still be in the charts, rather than thirty years ago this week !"

"You see, a surprise each day."

She paused as she considered his words. Surprise or otherwise, he had certainly brought new experiences to a mind that had misguidedly sought only to be free from such things.

Though it was already well into the small hours, a little sleep came to each of them.

Dr Smith certainly looked much better: a fact that was not lost on the ever observant Mrs Farnell, nor was the smart silk tie, with its beautiful, striking pattern, woven with expertise and care into the silk threads, no doubt at great expense; and was a world away from the cheaper and boring one of printed polyester that he normally sported around his neck.

As Melanie drove Stella to the airport she too had noticed a lightening of step and purpose.
“Everything all right?" she eventually asked, as the curiosity overwhelmed her.
“Fine thanks,” teased Melanie.
“You saw him last night, didn't you? You'll get him struck off, you know,” she said provocatively.
“Oh I think not, Stella. I only gave him a tie, and he gave me this CD, like a peace offering.”
“Only gave him a tie! A tie! Have I taught you nothing gal? I would have given him much more than a tie.”
She detected the wisp of an enigmatic smile forming on her friend’s face. She read just a little too much into that. “That’s it: he's bound to get struck off. I'll report him when I get back.”

The car purred sedately into the terminal building. Heads turned as they both got out, and a passing van driver nearly shot into the back of the vehicle in front, as his head swivelled a little too far and a little too long. Stella laughed, sensing that she and her friend were the focus of attention from those in the drop-off area.
“See you as planned,” she said.
Suddenly a taxi pulled up just in front of the Jag. Melanie saw the shock of blond hair before even the large muscle-bound figure. The young man charged out of the taxi and lifted Stella right off her feet with an enthusiastic hug, whilst still managing to carry his large holdall. Melanie smiled without undue surprise. She had seen Stella with a succession of boyfriends, and no doubt, this was the latest in the ever- lengthening line.
“Melanie, this is Tony.”
Tony managed to put Stella down after what seemed like a breath-defying age, dropped his holdall as a massive hand took Melanie's with controlled tenderness. A row of brilliant white teeth, framed by the large jaw, appeared across the suntanned open face followed by a quick, “Hi.”
“Pleased to meet you Tony,” as she revealed her own perfect but less substantial array of white teeth.
Melanie moved up to Stella to give her a farewell hug.

"Enjoy yourselves," and more quietly in Stella's right ear, "Cor! Practise safe sex won't you," followed by a, "not if I can help it," from Stella.

Melanie laughed; the young couple disappeared through the automatic doors and into the terminal building. Melanie walked back to the car, swung open a weighty door and slipped back into the soft leather seat. More admiring glances were directed as she selected drive from the control and the engine connected once again with the massive tyres. A purr, then a roar and she was gone, followed in her wake by still more glances and the odd open-mouthed 'wow' from young males.

She returned to the factory and to her preparations. As she sat at her desk her mobile announced an incoming call. She recognised that it was Smith.
"I was driving out to see my Mum and I wondered if you'd like to come too?"
"Gee hon. ain't this a bit sudden n'all. I am flattered," she said, "I bet, you don't take just anyone to see your mummy. Yes, I'd love to."
"OK: I'm on my way; see you in ten."

He waited in the car park, for her to come down from her office.
"This is exciting, Dr Smith, I am curious."
"Sorry to disappoint, but there are wall-to-wall surgeries for the rest of the week. Dr Michaels is off till Monday and I needed to pass something by you now," he said, as soon as she had braved the creaking passenger door once again.
"Is there any chance at all that your Dad's accident was not an accident? I just wondered."
"You mean murder? Who would stand to gain from such a thing? You mean Newman?" she said at last. "I know that he's a low down rotten skunk if that's not an insult to skunks," she added on reflection, "but I don't think he would sink to murder."
"He wants Jectronics badly, Melanie; I wondered how far he would go to get it?"

"I just couldn't believe it at the time, Dad, was really fit, he'd never been ill. He used to have a private medical every year and it had never shown anything. The Police were adamant that it could only have been a heart attack. What else could cause him to crash in that way? The car was in perfect mechanical order. If Dad had been taken ill, surely Trish could have grabbed the wheel? Bentley themselves went over it and checked every nut and bolt. They did find some tiny shards of glass in the footwell and a small battery. Apparently Newman had asked them to test his new Satnav. and it had a long dangly wire, because he had modified it, but the engineer's report stated that there is no way that it could have caused the car to veer off course so violently. Surely a tiny box like that stuck on the window couldn't crash a modern Bentley with every conceivable safety feature, even if these Satnavs do send delivery trucks down tiny country lanes! The Police say that there is no other explanation: sudden violent heart attack or collapse is the only thing that fits. Post mortem was inconclusive, too much damage," her words trailed off as her thoughts wandered into more painful territory.
"Sorry Melanie, it was just a thought," he began, "you have to look at all the possible explanations when faced with something like this, and I just wanted to be clear in my own mind."
"Surely, not even Newman could stoop so low. He is a conniving, two-faced rat, but would he be capable of such a thing and how could he bring it about?"

They reached Mrs Smith's house in silence; each once again plunged into deep thought as new information was presented. He had obviously been thinking about things furiously, Melanie acknowledged to herself.
"Are you coming in Melanie?"
She jumped quickly out of the car and walked with him up the overgrown path of the modest semi, situated on a quiet street of the adjacent village to Little Dunham. He opened the door with a key.
"Mum it's only me," he called.

He led Melanie into the lounge that had been converted into a bedroom-cum-sitting-room. Melanie saw the frail tiny woman huddled in the chair, her body obviously wrecked by a painful arthritis.
“Mum, this is Miss Jardine, she's a friend of mine.” Melanie did not look at him, but instead offered her slim, elegant hand to make gentle contact with the twisted claw that had itself once been a hand.
“Pleased to meet you Mrs Smith,” she said as she looked carefully at this frail elderly lady who remained keen and alert.
“My, I'm very pleased to meet you, dear.” Age and infirmity had long since destroyed any pretence. She was frank and direct, but she knew that people would forgive her this and more, given her condition.
“Isn’t she lovely, James,” as if she were trying to convince him of something he already well knew. Melanie and Smith blushed in synchrony. He pretended to speak quietly behind a raised hand. “Gets a bit confused, my Mum, and that white stick doesn't help," as he nodded mischievously in the general direction of her walking frame.
“My body may be wrecked, but my head is in fine fettle,” she corrected. “You're lucky to have someone so pretty as a friend, you old curmudgeon, more than you deserve,” she joked, as she looked admiringly at her son, of whom she was obviously very proud.

Time had evidently not altered her ability to bring him back into line, nor had it corrupted the fact that she continued to view him in many ways as her young son. From anyone else, the tone would have been immensely embarrassing, but her crippled frame and what was left of her world, firmly revolved around him.
“It’s some time since James’ father died, and I don't know what I would have done without him. My health was failing quickly and I didn't want to go in a nursing home. I can only stay here with lots of people coming in every day to help me.”
Melanie nodded sunnily as another mystery about the retiring Smith was solved. ‘So that’s where all the money goes, I bet he

contributes to the support,' she thought quickly, as other pieces of the puzzle that was 'Smith', fell into place.

Smith quickly disappeared to make some tea. Taking advantage of his absence, his mother angled her head towards Melanie and lowered her voice, ever so slightly. Melanie thought that whilst the body was wrecked, the perceptive mind was still capable of gaining insight into any given presenting situation, as she detected a gentle subterfuge.
"Tell me, Melanie, are you working with James?"
"No, actually I'm a patient of his."
Melanie's embarrassment was immediately dissipated by a knowing calm on the elderly lady's face, and she continued nervously. "I've been quite ill, I guess, but he pulled me through. I'm feeling so much better now, thanks to your son's efforts"
"Well he always does his best for everyone, but I 'm sure it was no effort to help someone as beautiful as you."
Melanie's embarrassment returned in force as she continued. "I'm so pleased that you're better. I just can't imagine a young person like you becoming ill."

Melanie was about to offer more explanation than her discomfort suddenly told her was needed, when Mrs Smith nodded knowingly as if clarification was unnecessary.
"You know Melanie, he's not really got a lot in his life. He has his work, and he comes to see me every day, but it's not really enough. He needs to come out of himself a bit more."
Melanie's reply was foreshortened by Smith returning with a tray with tea and biscuits. He helped his mother carefully with the steaming tea, as she seamlessly changed the conversation in an instant.
"Yes, it is a nice little house, Melanie. I moved here when James went to medical school a few years after his father died. I needed something smaller, and my rheumatism was just beginning to become a nuisance. Look at it now," holding up a twisted hand whilst nearly spilling her tea, "cruel this rheumatism. You'd have thought they'd have found a cure for it by now, never mind all

those Gold injections and tablets and blood tests and so on. These doctors," she looked with feigned accusation in her son's direction. "Well, Melanie, what do you do then?"
"I have a small company that makes bits for computers."
"Small!" Smith repeated – "it's as big as a football pitch and two stories high."
"Bits for computers, is it what they call one of those sunrise companies?" The elderly lady asked.
"Yes, you could say that. Certainly it's pretty modern technology," Melanie confirmed, impressed by her knowledge.
"So are you a scientist or an engineer, Melanie?"
"Neither; more of a businesswoman. I'm supposed to keep the place running and obtain the funds whilst the engineers and scientists get on with it."
"It sounds quite exciting. I bet you're very good at your job."
"I do my best, despite the fact that one of the directors is trying to get rid of me."
"Oh, I don't think he'll do that," as a slight smile crossed Mrs Smith's wrinkled and deathly pale face.
"Better be getting back now, Mum," Smith suggested.
Smith could see that she was getting tired. The weakened heart and lungs were incapable of powering such a failing and painful body for too long without rest. The twisted claw touched Melanie's once again. She glanced appreciatively at the lovely elegant fingers - having already noted that they were without adornment of any kind.
"Lovely to meet you my dear, please call again any time. Even if you're just passing, I'm always here."
"I'd like that very much," she offered with sincerity.

A quick kiss on the forehead and a, "see you later" and they were back outside. Smith fumbled unsuccessfully for the car keys. "Melanie won't be a minute I've left the keys inside." As he re-entered the house his Mum quizzed him eagerly.
"What a lovely girl. James, she tells me that she is a patient. You've never brought anyone here before. Why now?"

"We're in the middle of a bit of a crisis just at the moment, and I need Melanie to keep her feet firmly on the ground if I'm going to pull her though." The partial explanation only triggered the need for more questions which he could see queuing on her face.
"I'll tell you more tomorrow, Mum," he offered, by way of consolation.
"James you could do worse than have someone like that in your life."
"Patient, I said Mum, no more no less," he said firmly as once again the door closed.
Mrs Smith chuckled to herself. There was no doubt that her son firmly believed that.

Melanie was leaning against the bonnet of the ageing Maestro as he returned with the keys. "This is not doing anything for my image, you know; being seen waiting to get into a twenty year old Maestro. You should see the admiring looks I get when I'm in my car."
"I bet you do," he said with conviction.
"The only problem is it either turns men into sex maniacs who start whistling at you as soon as you get in, or maniacs determined to force you off the road."
"The car is the greatest of phallic symbols. It's like a badge that men wear on their chests telling everyone about their testosterone levels. You women come along in bigger cars and they feel threatened and envious. I suppose many of them can't accept that you drive a car like that, for the sheer driving enjoyment, rather than to show off or to impress them."
"Just about sums it up," she said with a smile, "not bad that, Dr Smith. Is human nature a bit of a hobby of yours or are you just nosey?"
"No, it's definitely a hobby. People-watching, I think they call it. Of course, I am nosey as well," he offered with a slight tap of the side of his nose. "Some people play Golf, some collect stamps - I'm just inquisitive."
"Well at least you're honest. She doesn't look too well your mum."

“No, in fact, she's dying slowly. It’s not a very nice thing to see. She's always been pretty active, but the past six months she has been more or less chair-bound. She needs fleets of people to go in through the day and help her. I go round when I can, but of course it's a bit difficult. Work tends to get in the way. Her mind is still active, as you saw, but the body is just a twisted shell. I think that if she had her choice she would rather be out of it, but I don't think she would hold with euthanasia or anything like that. She's fairly religious and she'd definitely be at odds with that.”
“What do you think about doctors being involved in euthanasia?” Melanie asked.
“Bit of a tricky one that. I'm sure it goes on quietly, but although we pay less lip service to the Hippocratic oath these days than we ever did before, most don't cross the line. Who could decide who lives and who dies? And where do you draw the line? The thought of us playing God is abhorrent to most patients as well as most doctors, I believe.”

She quietly digested his words. A surprise every day, he'd said, and he hadn’t lied. Though she did not see it at this point, here lay the secret of her recovery. He had changed the axis upon which her life rested. He brought new experiences, new thoughts and new challenges for her each time they met, and the success of this strategy was now firmly in evidence.

“I'd better get you back to work before old Newman sells off your desk. Do you mind if I just pop home and get my bag for surgery?” he asked.
“Thanks for taking me along today, I feel almost privileged.”
“Melanie, I feel really bad about nearly deserting you in surgery the other day. I suppose I just wanted to apologise, to atone for my sins. My job now is to make sure that you continue to improve and remain on that tack. I know that you have a lot of things facing you just at the moment, and perhaps when you get through that, you won’t need my services any more. Either way, we see it through to the end.”

Melanie realised that insight, that had been absent during her long illness, was now rising like a column of mercury in a thermometer placed in boiling water. Such insight revealed clearly, much of the strategy and the tactics that were being called into play by the young doctor. Now, she could clearly see the effort he applied in all that he said and everything he did, from the subtle nuances and the delicate gestures to the more obvious manoeuvres that no-one could miss: each action, great or small, was geared to supporting and restoring her. By contemplating his strategy, in this way, she realised that she could now see more deeply into the man himself: and she knew too, that he would not, under ideal circumstances, have wanted to reveal such information to her, his patient. The depth of despair in which she had been trapped and the urgent nature of providing help for her, had simply subjugated any other consideration. She recognised ultimately that it represented a pure selfless act of which few in modern times were capable. Mrs Smith had seen all that was slowly dawning on the young woman at their first meeting, and her perceptive but failing grey eyes had seen even a little more that Melanie was yet to discover.

Jectronics appeared a short time later. “I'd better get going now. I’ve got to keep on the right side of Mrs Farnell if she's going to put a good word in with Michaels.”

“He'd be mad to let you go - wouldn’t he?”

“Well, I suppose it’s how you look at it. I seem to have got on with everyone and it's a really nice place to work. Even the Seabridge estate has its attractions especially since they started doing it up,” he suggested with a cheeky grin. “The six month mutual assessment period is a good opportunity to either leave or get rid of someone, and usually after your assessment period your partnership share starts to increase.”

“Does that mean you'll be able to change this car?” she asked excitedly. Before he could look too hurt she interposed, “actually I'm quite getting used to it. Not bad for a biscuit tin.”

“Well I suppose that's as far as you're going to get towards a compliment,” he noted.

She disappeared into the factory and up to her room. She had made all her preparations, except for the speech which seemed as elusive as ever. She had got her facts and figures together, and her charts and diagrams, but not the 'hearts and minds' speech with which she was hoping to carry the day. If only she could get some sleep, it might appear to her like many of her flashes of inspiration in the small hours of the morning. Not since visiting the gypsy had she had any such creative visions. It was almost as if the omen that lay in wait had sucked in part of her very being, where it would be held hostage until the terrifying prophecy had been delivered, whereupon, she presumed, it might be restored to her - if she were still alive to receive it.

She saw Tony Newton in the main lab: his white coat as pristine as ever, but strangely at odds with the untidy beard and moustache that seemed to have a messy stranglehold over all of his face apart from the bit where the glasses were perched. She sensed a slight stiffening as she approached. She decided to keep things strictly business-like. "How is the conformance testing coming along, Tony?"

"It's gone really well, Melanie. The chips are holding up better than we feared and though at one time we thought that the core temperature tests were way off-line and would lead to chip degradation unless we specified extra cooling - we now know that in fact they are very temperature-stable. Looks as though we have a winner, Melanie. Testing will be complete at the end of this week. We can then transfer the final schematics to the production plant and start a limited run off by the end of the week. That will then give us a chance to test the whole 3D video card."

The engineer studied her carefully as she described in more detail how she was planning to augment production as soon as he could give her the go-ahead. It was almost as if they had been strangers up to that very point. He had worshipped her father, as a man who worked harder than anyone, could always be found in the thick of things in a crisis; and was the first to congratulate when breakthroughs were made. He was also someone who made it happen. If more equipment was needed or certain materials, they were provided without question and as soon as human effort would allow. Trish too was very much in the same mould but he had not realised how alike the two sisters were, until that very moment.

Melanie could sense his thoughtful expression and was pleased with the courtesy with which her questions were answered and her own proposals received. She sensed that he was about to say something of great moment, but both were interrupted by Newman, who suddenly approached. Melanie made her excuses quickly and moved up to the laboratory where the final prototype of the Lightdrive was being assembled. She found Alastair Jones in a similar ebullient mood. He was much younger than Newton and imbued with a certain genius. He too sported a beard, but much less dense than that of his colleague though the head-hair had receded quickly in the time she had known him, to reveal the featureless and shiny pate.
"Look at this, Melanie; you will love this."
The monitor flicked on and a feature-length pop video appeared on screen. "The drives are behaving beautifully and formatted capacity is just above two Terrabytes." Melanie knew that such capacities were rare even with old traditional drives that spun at great speeds, but were unheard of for solid state drives.

"The new discs are little harder to mass produce than we had hoped, but I'm working on this. We may need to downgrade our production estimates."
"Is there any way we can redress this?" Melanie's skills of listening and comprehending were resurgent, and increasingly this was demonstrated by her ability to ask the most pertinent question.
"Only by a certain amount of preassembly. The Silicon/Gallium wafers could be pre-layered for us on the lamina of the disc, but I'm not sure if the supplier of the Gallium is up to this."
"Will we reveal anything of our production process, if we ask them if they can do it?"

"No: the really clever bit comes after this, and the preassembly I had in mind is just time-consuming rather than anything hush-hush."
"I'll speak to them and get them to quote us for pre-layering. If they were able to deliver on this, how much faster would the line run?"
"At least a factor of forty percent."
"This would allow us to exceed our initial projections for the run-offs?" she asked.
"Comfortably," he confirmed. Alastair could hardly contain his enthusiasm at this point, and Melanie found the youthful optimism infectious.
"I'd like you to press on with testing the final prototype," she suggested. "Have all the schematics been transferred to the file server for downloading to the production lab?"
"Yes, a couple of weeks back," he confirmed again.
"Fine. I'll get on with chasing up the Gallium supplier and get some revised production figures together. I'll get back to you when I've got some firm proposals from them."
"Melanie, thanks for your interest," he offered with a mixture of guilt and gratitude.

Newman has definitely been getting to these two, she thought. She was only doing what any interested and committed manager could be expected to do, yet both men seemed really surprised as if they had expected nothing from her. She wondered what other surprises he had in store.

She sent out for a quick sandwich and kept out of Newman's way. She also spoke to Lawrence Ward, the MD of Silicon Etchings, the firm that produced the Gallium Arsenide for the new Lightdrive discs.
"Thanks for speaking to me, Mr Ward. We have been purchasing small quantities of Gallium from you for a new project we're working on."
"I knew your father well, Melanie. I'd like to say how sorry we all were to learn of his death." A silence followed, as he searched for

words to express his feelings about the rest of the Jardine's tragedy.

She intervened to spare him too much discomfort. “It's kind of you to say that Mr Ward: really there were two things I wanted to mention to you. Firstly, our new product will be brought to market soon, and we'll require large quantities of the Gallium, especially of the quality we have received from you. Would there be any problem with that?”

“I don’t foresee one, Melanie. Obviously we specialise in providing raw material for firms such as yours. As you will know, it’s a difficult process extracting the material to the required standard and then to etch it to such fine tolerances, but we would be delighted to look at your requirements in more detail. Just how much Gallium were you looking for Melanie?”

“How much can you supply us with?” she asked unequivocally.

“This is my kind of talk Melanie - it must be a pretty big project you're working on. We have a sample of the optical drive you launched two years ago. It's really setting the pace these days. Has it anything to do with that?”

Melanie decided to carefully steer the conversation away. He smiled as he sensed the polite deflection.

“Well, we can discuss that in more detail, as secondly, I wanted to talk to you about the possibility of pre-configuring the Gallium into laminas that we need for the production process. I was wondering if I could arrange a meeting with you to demonstrate our exact requirements?”

“That’s fine Melanie. I should be free for the rest of the week.

“How does Friday sound to you?”

“Perhaps we could meet up late morning?” he suggested.

“Fine, Mr Ward I'll see you then.”

A delighted Lawrence Ward put the phone down and went off to talk to his colleagues about a sudden uplift in their business. He asked his secretary to cancel everything from 11:00 am on Friday, and arrange a meeting for the day before so that he could inform his production team.

Melanie smiled as she replaced her receiver and wondered if he was going to be prepared for some pretty tight delivery schedules and pricing. She went over to the 'lightdrive' laboratory to inform Collins.

"That's good going Melanie, didn't expect you to get on with it so soon."

"No time like the present as they say, and we don't want to be hanging about or just rely on our 3D graphics chip when we may be able to get both ready this autumn."

He too found himself rapidly re-evaluating the head of the company. He had been very impressed with her grasp of the technical aspects of the production, as well as her formidable knowledge of setting up the production lines. He could only think that perhaps Newman was wrong in his assessment of her. Pity it was too late to change things.

Melanie was pleased with her day's work, and at last found herself actually enjoying what she was doing. Her interest was becoming awakened again, and the people she talked to around the factory reinforced this. Up to that point she had viewed, with some equanimity the possibility of being forced out, but the more she prepared for the meeting and the impending production commencement, the more she wanted to remain a part of the whole thing. For the first time she appreciated the intensity of emotion that the business had generated in her father and Trish. She had also witnessed first hand the passion that his patients could generate from within the normally passive Smith. The pieces were slowly falling into place. At first she had remained in contention simply to spite Newman, but now a different game was in progress.

She found her laptop in her office and walked slowly down the stairs and out to her car. It was a beautiful day and she looked forward to the drive that awaited her. She could not have seen Newman as he stared from the upstairs window.

Chapter VIII

"Dead Girl's Curve"

The Jag. cruised out of the car park. It made effortless progress down the long, narrow road that led to the village. Strong sunshine filtered by the trees created a stroboscopic effect as her journey continued. She prodded the CD player until she had selected her favourite sequence of tracks, whilst at the same time managing to find her sunglasses, which she slipped over her pert nose. The car made little complaint as it sensed that, for a split second, neither hand was in contact with the steering wheel. She glanced in the rear-view mirror just to make sure that her distractions had not inconvenienced a driver behind, as the car must have swerved just a little, at least once.

She noted the white Mazda Rx8 coupé. She had seen these in action and knew them to be very fast. She also knew that they had an unusual engine, creating a fast, light, free-revving power unit that could embarrass many a performance car. The Mazda was closing on her very quickly. She decided to slow down and move just a little to the side so that the press-on driver could easily overtake. 'Another male demonstrating his testosterone levels,' she thought. Rather than speed past her, however, the car slowed and seemed to be heading straight for her, as if poised with menace.

She could now clearly see the two young men in the front seats laughing, with a casual disdain for their lives and hers. The coupé slammed into her back bumper, just as she had braced herself for the impact. Her car was shunted forward as the Mazda hit her with explosive force, a loud bang reverberated through the frame of the car as it absorbed the violent collision.

Unadulterated panic replaced rational thought. Smith had asked her on more than one occasion just how could she drive in the heels that she nearly always wore. Today, she had a feeling she was about to find out. She knew, certainly that she would be allowed no time to slip them from her feet. She dialled sport mode from the cylindrical, central control dial, her car now growling as it detected that a pursuit was afoot. The speed whipped up quickly. The Jag. moved away with effortless ease, which seemed completely at variance with the sheer terror that now held her within its grasp. Her pursuers relished the chase and thirsted for the torment and suffering they planned to visit upon her. Once again, that turbine-like engine was revved without mercy to close with her.

She wondered, in a split-second and solitary moment of calm, whether some poor person was missing the car, and exactly how the two young men had managed to obtain it. The Mazda charged forward as the young driver dropped down a couple of gears to harness more power from that rotary engine, as it revved easily into areas that ordinary cars simply could not match. This time the Rx8 slammed into her car's rear quarter, as they dealt her a glancing blow. The Jaguar's rear track was jolted sideways by the collision, as another loud report came from the impact like the sound of a shell leaving a gun. She occupied the middle of the road to prevent them from pulling alongside her. They accelerated again, as another violent blow impacted on the rear bumper. She silenced the CD player and dabbed the touch screen to contact the Police. The men in the Mazda seemed to sense her efforts, as an even more violent thud came from the rear bumper which now splintered with the repeated trauma, and fragments started to fall away, as once again she tried to escape by raising the speed still further. She reported her position to the Police, the control room promising to send a patrol car as soon as one could be contacted. As she glanced at the speedometer, now into three figures, she could only hope that it would be a fast one.

Her knuckles whitened on the leather rim as her grip fought off the sweat exuding from her palms. She was aware of her heart nearly exploding in her chest with every beat. She desperately wanted to get away, but her pursuers, gaining from her momentary distraction while she had talked to the Police, closed within seconds. She pressed the accelerator, in desperation, as the magnificent car once again responded with even higher levels of speed.

The fork in the road was approaching rapidly, and a difficult dilemma presented. The straighter road ran into the village town centre. The lollipop ladies would be gently seeing their charges across the normally quiet roads, as Mums and Dads did a bit of late shopping on their way home from school. To choose the straighter road would perhaps allow her to stop and shout for help, but would surely put innocent people at risk, especially as the two young thugs pursuing her had acted without any hint of restraint, and without regard to anyone's safety including their own. To opt for the winding road that ultimately would lead to the dual carriageway and on to the M6, would risk a confrontation in the close bends that came first, and place Melanie at greater risk if she should slow even in a moment's distraction. She made as if to take the right fork but swerved at the last minute in an attempt to throw them off the scent of violent pursuit.

The car flew left into the winding lane that would eventually lead to the motorway and certain escape - if she could negotiate the next few miles successfully. Unfortunately her two pursuers had anticipated this manoeuvre. They appeared within a second, the white car filling the rear-view mirror, and then slammed into her again as if to underline their persistence and malign intent. Panic was enveloping her completely at this point, accompanied by fear as it rose to take charge unequivocally. She knew that her only course now was to stop, and both fear and panic agreed with this strategy. To make matters worse, self-mocking doubt conflated with those emotions which were about to dictate her next move. Surely she had made the wrong decision, she could have stopped in the village and screamed for help, rather than try to outwit her unfeeling pursuers in deserted winding roads where the next mistake could be only a microsecond away. With further thought, she realised that mercy was the last thing that her pursuers were intent on demonstrating that day. She could now see the road ahead as it closely and sharply wound around the granite bluffs, with a steep, precipitous drop as they fell away from the road. The young thug slammed the Rx8 into her again, the rear bumper now so compromised that it parted in large fragments from the car: the Mazda swerved, nimbly around the debris. She could see them laughing with delight. She wondered if the unrestrained menace that she could see clearly in their eyes was drug-fuelled, or if they had been simply paid, as one might pay someone to do a routine job of work.

They made to start another run and she pressed the accelerator again, as she demanded more speed, faster than she had ever driven before, and the engine now roaring its response like some feline beast as befitted its name; but perhaps mercifully oblivious to the destruction that lay in wait in the winding road ahead. The sharp bend was now almost upon her. The men behind her sensed that this was their moment and moved the Rx8 out, as if they were poised to overtake her. The road was now simply too wide for her to occupy all of it, especially with the blind bend in prospect. They started the manoeuvre that only someone with absolutely no regard for their own safety could contemplate. Unabridged fear gripped her with the same intensity with which she clung to the steering wheel, now not daring to loosen that hold as she knew her life depended upon her next movement from it. The Rx8 was poised like an executioner, and the final stage was the impossibly tight bend that lay in wait for each of them.

She knew only that she had to keep going. The young driver changed up into 6th gear as the revs dropped. He knew that a simple flick down into 4th gear would cause a surge of power as the revs screamed again, and would carry the Mazda past the Jaguar, now being forced onto the outside track. It was then a simple matter to close her out of that curve completely. He waited for her to crack, as he knew she must. They laughed to each other as they recognised that the moment was about to be delivered to them. The 'posh bitch' they had been sent to terminate in this way had done well, but not nearly well enough, and they sensed that she was now at the limit of her nerve and her skills, such as they were, as a driver, that would see her depart from the road at the place they had assigned for her. She was now theirs, and would surely be begging for mercy that cold hearts and a vast payment were not inclined to allow. Time for her to die; here almost, was her exit down the rocky bluff, falling away steeply to the left. The sheer drop had claimed victims before, but none deliberately, and none so violently at the hand of others, who relished the destruction they feverishly planned to impose upon a terrified young woman. His hand was poised above the short gear lever as he readied to flick it into 4th in order to unleash even higher revs and yet more power from that beautiful engine, still hardly making a sound, as it spun with its turbine-like precision.

Melanie knew the section of road very well. She had traversed it by night and by day, in wind and in rain, but always at slower speeds than those to which this most disturbing of cruel nightmares could have exposed her. Surely the speed must be too high. Surely the car was now going so fast that it would be incapable of carrying that sharp bend and take the only available route – straight on. The laws of Physics demanded that a straight line was now the only course open to her at this speed. The narrow trajectory that would plot safe passage around the curve, was precisely the one they would occupy in order to deny it to her. They moved the Mazda out still further and began to accelerate as the revs. climbed to the maximum, to gain the position that would ensure their safety as hers was denied. It was, however, panic that would claim her. Panic that would dictate that the entry speed into the bend was simply too high. She knew only in those microseconds of time that she had to brake, to reduce that entry speed. Panic insisted that this was correct. They laughed with unbridled delight as they saw the brake lights flick on; lights that signalled her last fatal move, that would mark her demise and not her surrender. The stupid 'toff bitch' had shot her last bolt: they would not have to wait long now. They drew alongside as they floored the accelerator. Revs. climbed, incautiously, in the first hint of an unguarded moment. The driver placed his had on the gear lever to change down into 4th. The ten thousand pound bonus was theirs with a simple flick of the front end, sending her sharp left and them round the corner and on to glory.

The last scintilla of her life, however, saw panic pushed to one side as a reserve of courage that she had never tapped before, presented itself with a death-defying assertion. Panic's counsel would assure her destruction, not her safety. She had to enter that bend ahead of them, not at their side, in order to plot the track that might, just, allow passage; if only the tyres could hold the weight of the car, and her, in that curve of certain death. Her final thought was that she needed more speed, not less, to come first into the bend not second, as death lay hungrily in wait for one of them that day.

In those fragments of time that only high-speed cameras could have captured; images could, perhaps be replayed and pored over and discussed later at length. During those real-time moments, however, where the balance of life and death lurched uncertainly from the cocksure to the terrified; only the most acute of human brains, the sharpest eyes and quickest of reflexes could still function in order to assimilate enough information to be able to effect an escape. In that instant, her pursuers learned that they had underestimated her and her desire to live, a mistake that would cost them *their* lives.

She floored the accelerator violently: the car responded without hesitation just as the young driver rammed the gear lever into 4th and prepared to flick the Jag's front end, with his. The Jaguar shot forward: as the clutch came up to synchronise 4th gear the Mazda's revs. climbed again. Ultimately courage saved her, with invaluable assistance from a peculiarity of the Mazda's rotary engine, inbuilt to ensure its safety at all times. As the clutch was released, the revs from the Mazda's engine moved to go past the 9,000 absolute limit. Just at this point the rev limiter cut in, with a loud 'beep', to protect the engine from revving too fast, a particular danger of a rotary engine; an infinitesimal, but crucial delay as the gear-lever crossed into fourth dictated that the power output must momentarily diminish and not rise, as the thugs' overblown strategy now demanded, causing the Mazda to slow imperceptibly precisely where they needed speed to match hers. As he flicked the front end violently, the Jaguar was already moving ahead. Even the slightest move to the left at this speed was enough to assure death to any that had been so foolish. Just in that instant the revs were allowed to remain at the 9000 rpm red line, and maximum power surged back, causing them to head straight for the barrier as they now occupied unequivocally the track that they had planned for her. Fast, young reflexes were simply impotent in the nuances of time that remained, a scintilla of time that could neither sanction nor allow any change of course, and the Mazda transected, cleanly but fatally, the safety barrier, as the sharp nose moved straight through it almost perpendicularly.

She was aware only of a white blur passing behind her. She eased off the accelerator but the speed was now very high, possibly too high to save her. She gripped the wheel, as one might a safety buoy in a stormy sea. She continued to grip with all her might, as she desperately tried to coax two metric tonnes of car into a curve and not a straight line. The tyres, the steering geometry, the traction control and the differentials all combined to assist her at this point, counterbalancing the unyielding laws of Physics with man-made forces that theory, backed up with endless calculations, arrived at in a laboratory, dictated would also apply in real conditions. She was about to test those calculations with her life. The rear end slammed against the barrier as the car drifted sideways into the curve, but the impact was oblique, involving much of the flank of the car. This was the sort of impact that the barrier had been designed to take, and it held with only an explosive sound, by way of protest, as the car bounced back and was returned to the road. Smoke and dust billowed from the rear end as the tyres sought only to embrace that tarmac and safety. The magnificent car held the curve, as the panorama before her flashed from certain death to a straight road that assured life.

She braked; more smoke billowed off all the tyres as rubber was burnt against tarmac, wide slicks of rubber were deposited in tracks on the road as the car stopped. She opened the door and swung her legs from the front seat, cradling her head in her hands, as she wept with the release of forces within her that she had not experienced before. She remained like this for moments whilst she attempted to steady her raging thoughts that queued remorselessly for attention from her now-overawed, brain. The adrenaline surge that had fuelled her conveyance from death to life, now made its presence felt in her legs which crumpled uncertainly as she attempted to stand. Her body started shaking all over and light-headedness dictated that she sit down again. She sat on the crash barrier from where she could see the jagged gap in the metal and from there down the unforgiving rocky slope that was to have been the route they had planned for her. The Rx8 lay as a twisted shell of metal, now being licked by all-consuming flames. Other than the flames, which were going about their grim work with relish, there was no sign of movement or of life. The scene seemed oddly peaceful, as if nature had stepped in immediately to counterbalance the violence that had erupted a few moments before.

After some time she managed to stand, and continued to gaze at the horrible scene. Still no hint of movement existed, save for the tongues of flame which licked like hungry lips devouring flesh and unspent fuel. Emotions of courage and determination that had powered reflexes, instincts and actions that had conveyed her from certain death to life, seemed in that moment to generate free flowing tears as their only by-product.

Moments later a Police car came rushing to the scene, followed by another from the opposite direction. An Ambulance could be seen travelling round the twisting road in the distance. The Police driver rushed to her side and knelt by Melanie who had had to sit down once again. A blanket was offered to cover her shoulders which were still shaking uncontrollably despite the warm afternoon.

"Are you all right? Are you hurt? Can I get you anything? Is there anyone we can contact Ma'am," the policewoman asked solicitously, as her mind, too, digested the horrific scene on the beautiful hillside. Melanie shook her head, still not quite able to formulate words. There wasn't a soul in the world who would come for her.
"The ambulance will take you to casualty for a check over."
"No, honestly, I'm fine: could you take me home, perhaps?"
The Police Officer paused for a moment as she doubted the veracity of Melanie's statement, but nevertheless she nodded her acquiescence.
"Just give me a moment to organise my colleagues and I'll drive you home."
Melanie nodded but did manage a "Thank you", despite the shock which continued to engulf her, making her look ghost-like in the afternoon sun.

A car-transporter and Fire Brigade were summoned and the Police started to mark off the damaged section of barrier and take measurements and digital images from the road.

Melanie strapped herself into the rear passenger seat uncertainly. The Police driver set off slowly but with no hesitation. Whilst in the car Melanie was able to provide what few details she could to the other Policeman in the front seat.

"The car was reported stolen yesterday, two masked men appeared as the owner was coming out of a branch of Halfords, demanding the keys. The same car was later recorded at a petrol station as a "drive off" when two men, whose faces were covered by scarves, filled up without paying," the police officer informed her. Melanie did her best to supply them with as much information as she could, though ultimately they realised that she knew very little more than they did, and she spent much of the journey too numb to speak.

Mrs Perkins came rushing out of the great house. "Oh my dear what has happened to you? Are you all right?"

The police officer gave what few details she had. "Your car will be returned in a day or two, you may wish to notify your insurers so that it goes directly to the repairers as soon as we have released it. Are you up to a statement ?"
Mrs Perkins was about to intervene when Melanie spoke with a slight return of her composure.
“Yes, of course.”
Melanie told her terrifying tale as both women listened.
“This is very unusual in these parts. Have you any idea why they picked you? Has anyone a grudge against you?” asked the Policewoman.
Melanie hesitated, then said that she couldn't think of anyone in particular.

The Policewoman finished the hastily prepared cup of tea that Mrs Perkins had summoned in record time. Melanie's still stood untouched on the table.
“We do have a counsellor for violent crimes of this type. I could contact her for you?”
Melanie declined with thanks.
“Perhaps we could contact your doctor?”
Melanie hesitated but Mrs Perkins replied in an instant. “Good idea officer. Dr Smith is his name, at Lorne Street surgery.”
The officer disappeared to use her radio and a few minutes later returned.
“Dr Smith is not in surgery at the moment but they will get a message to him.”
The officer turned to go with a thanks to Mrs Perkins and a supportive grasp of Melanie's hands. “Please don’t hesitate to get in touch if we can be of assistance. I'm Sergeant Rogers.” Melanie was handed a copy of her statement and the details of the police officer. Rogers found her car in the courtyard and turned to Mrs Perkins who had followed the Policewoman. “Please keep an eye on her tonight. The after-effects of shock can be very unpredictable. It might be worth giving Dr Smith another ring.”
Mrs Perkins indicated that she would, but she knew, somehow, that he would be along just as soon as events would allow.

After surgery Smith had pointed his car in the direction of his mother's. She had been bursting with questions, just as he had anticipated. He sat down patiently next to her, after making her a hot drink, so that the inquisition he knew to be forming, could begin. As he made the tea, his mother was firing questions from the other room. He could barely hear over the hissing of the kettle. Eventually he sat facing her, so that she could slake her thirst for information.

"What a lovely girl. She's so pretty, kind and gentle. Are you sure that she is only a patient?"

"I told you Mum, no more and no less."

"I don't remember you bringing a patient here before, James."

"Well Mum, Melanie has been through considerable traumas of late and I think that at one time her health was badly affected. In a way we've been dragged in by her illness into something that we must see through together."

"So why is her illness linked with you?"

"Firstly because I'm her doctor. Her mother killed herself last year in a deep depression and no-one seemed able to help her. I didn't want Melanie to go the same way."

"What makes you think that you can stop her?"

"Nothing, but I am pulling out all the stops."

"I can see that," as she softened a little, and adopted a less intense tone. "And secondly?" she prompted.

"Ah yes, well." Then he told her about the unfulfilled prophecy that had been delivered by the gypsy.

"Do you believe that is what will happen?"

"I'm not sure what to believe, but I hope that each of us maps his or her own future, and I'm not sure that what the gypsy says she can see, is incontrovertible. As the gypsy sought to include me or at least any who may try to help, I thought that I may as well see it through to the end."

"Well, in any event, she is a lovely girl and…"

"Patient, Mum, patient," he interrupted.

His Mum smiled and permitted herself a momentary self-satisfied impulse as she reflected that she was not the one he was reminding.
She coughed and suddenly looked tired.
"You aren't too well at the moment are you?"
"No worse than usual."
Until that point because of the interest of the conversation he had failed to notice that his mother was even more breathless than usual and was definitely coughing more.
"I'll get Dr Stephens to visit tomorrow shall I?"
"Waste of time. You know I'm done for."
"Now, Mum, don't say that. I'll ask him to pop in after his surgery."

Just then his mobile phone rang. It was the surgery telling him that Miss Jardine had been involved in an accident. Mrs Smith smiled.
"Well, what are you waiting for. Go and save your patient!"
Smith kissed her, and told her that he would call the next day, as he knew she hadn't quite had her fill of questions, and rushed out to begin the laborious business of starting the Maestro.

Once again a smile passed her lips as she considered the information that had been imparted. She knew that he believed it to be the truth, and certainly the logic was there, but there was much more that had not been said. She could see also that they had not begun to recognise, still less to quantify the powers as seen by the gypsy that were being ranged against them. She could only hope that even in this state they would be still strong enough to counter the forces that she now guessed, as she closed her weary eyes, would demand that she be the first domino to fall in the game of rampant destruction about to be released.

Mrs Perkins met him at the imposing entrance hall.
"Thank you for coming Doctor. She's in a terrible state, just when she had started to look a bit better."
She gave him as many facts as she knew, and led him through to the conservatory, where a very quiet and dejected patient sat

almost motionless. He sat beside her and asked her how she was. Her body was trembling with shock and fear as she relived the brutal intensity of the accident.
"I know now that they were really after me. Why would he do that James?"
"Who?"
"Newman."
They almost said the words together.
"If he wants Jectronics that badly, he can have it."
"Don't you see Melanie, he's frightened. Since you started going back in, he realises just what you are capable of. You've got him on the run now. Don't quit now."
"I'm not sure I can continue. I'm not sure I want to."
"You must, Melanie. I won't let you go back down there again." The determination in the calm voice was augmented by a firm grip of her right hand as he sat next to her. He knew that her recovery still lay in the balance, and giving up on her work would cause a slide in all areas of her life. "Tell me about it?"

He sat, as she re-lived every painful detail of the afternoon's events. She cried with free-flowing tears as the detail was carefully brought back to the surface of her consciousness and slowly, but painfully, acknowledged, countered and expunged by his gentle yet painstaking skills. Mrs Perkins returned with a tray of tea and sandwiches, and quietly withdrew so as not to disturb the steady momentum of the recovery that gathered pace as the light faded over the west lawn and the plains of Cheshire beyond.

"Are you certain that Newman was behind this?" Smith asked a little later.
"It was deliberately contrived. The men in the car knew who I was and where I would be. I am certain of that. The Police told me that no-one survived, there were two charred bodies in the wreck. We may never know for certain, but they were on me so quickly after I left the factory. Newman is playing a vicious game and you're right: he must not win."

"So how do you view things now?" he asked, as always, open questions allowing her to answer whatever was uppermost in her mind.
"I am beginning to see the attraction that it held for Dad and Trish. There are so many good people there who deserve better than the attention they have had from me for the past twelve months."
"I think that perhaps you're blaming yourself a little too much," he offered.
"I'm sure everyone was sympathetic at first, just like many of my friends, but *they* all left one by one."
"People's ability to grieve is saturated quite quickly, and after that they must act to protect themselves."
"There are very few who can stick with it. Mrs Perkins and you are the only two I can think of," she offered as the realisation came to her.

In a way Newman's appeal is almost that of a gifted revolutionary who's about to sweep away the ideologies of the past and replace them with a more sound egalitarianism, where all can share in the success of the company, rather than worry about whether I'm ever going to recover again. The thing that they can't see is just what sort of man they're dealing with, and that they're about to jump from the frying pan into the fire. I should be grateful to him: his antics with the Mazda should have warned me as to which depths he is capable of sounding. I know now just what he is capable of, and if he thinks I am just going to fold and walk away, he'll have another thought coming. If he wants the company, he's going to have to come up with much more. He has evidently been speaking to everyone who has equity in the company and, no doubt, has done his utmost to ensure that they vote with him."

Slowly and with great care, he drew from his patient all the positive aspects of her current situation, and quietly suppressed the negative ones. She had grown steadily in stature and confidence in the time that he had known her. His role, now, was to encourage her to see just how far she had come, to recognise and to promote the skills he believed she held in abundance, and in turn to use those skills to withstand any reverses that she might yet encounter and most crucially to be able to do this without his presence. This he did slowly, patiently and with self-surpassing skill.

"Do you think that you can beat him?" he asked, after some moments had passed.
"They say that good will always triumph over evil, but sadly we both know that that's often not the case. I have to beat him because the alternative is unthinkable. Dad and Trish would turn in their graves."
"Surely if you hold forty percent of shares, you are capable of blocking just about any move to unseat you."
"On paper, yes of course. Things aren't quite that easy. The Captain of the ship tells you to sail to the edge of the world. Not only that, but he is so new to the crew that he has neither had chance to display his qualities, or absence of them, nor had the opportunity to build trust in his men. Technically his authority is insuperable, but does that mean that the crew will blindly follow to their possible destruction? Come now, Doctor, you have ten minutes to make your mind up."
She laughed for the first time that evening, as, once again, the hazel eyes, now at their deepest meditative yet discerning phase, were levelled unequivocally in his direction. He raised his hand as if swearing an oath of allegiance.
"I follow my captain to the death. I see your point. Surely you haven't got enough time to convince all the shareholders that they should back you. Presumably Newman has been working on them for months. What chance have you?"
"The meeting itself represents my one and only chance. It will be a sudden death play off between Newman and me."
"If I were a shareholder, you would have my vote."
"You'd better." She looked at him with slightly narrowing eyes as if scrutinising him carefully.

A beautiful starlit night appeared to augment the warm August evening. As they continued to talk they seemed oblivious to the oncoming darkness, neither seemed to want to cross to the light switch. It was as if the darkness protected one from the searching gaze of the other, almost as if, under such cover, immunity would be granted for any statement or question.

As Mrs Perkins returned at the start of another brilliant day she found the two, still fast asleep. Miss, stretched out on the sofa and he, recumbent in the large arm chair. The housekeeper quietly withdrew and began preparing breakfast for two. Melanie was the first to awake. She knelt beside him and gazed at the peaceful expression, almost like that of a priest who had saved one last sinner from certain doom. They had talked on and on into the night, until sleep had intervened for each of them. She looked at the lustrous dark-brown hair, hastily cut, but which seemed to complement those shining brown eyes, still asleep, but as always capable of demonstrating unbounded interest in everything and everyone and especially in those, like her, his patient: eyes that she had noted at first glimpse all those weeks ago. She gently touched a slim hand with its strong fingers as it lay motionless on the arm of the chair; as might a little girl to see if the wizard was real. Suddenly he stirred. She quickly rose to her feet, as he slowly sat up, not wanting him to see the closeness with which she had approached moments before.

His aching muscles, dry mouth and sore eyes were now protesting vigorously as they recalled the posture that eventually an exhausted brain had sanctioned for rest some hours ago. He looked upon Melanie as she sat facing him, smiling intently as his discomfort slowly eased.
"Good morning Doctor Smith. I wonder if this would make the Sunday tabloids?"
"Not quite Melanie, I think we'd have to do a bit more than this, but you never know, they might just be scraping round for a suitable story this Sunday. I always wondered what would be worse - fame or infamy."
Careful design rather than careful timing brought Mrs Perkins to the large double doors.

"Good morning Miss, I see Doctor Smith has joined you for breakfast. What can I offer you? Would you like to stay and eat in the conservatory, Miss?"

The conservatory with its splendid vault of white metal and plate glass was refreshingly cool. Ornate aluminium brackets supported long slender spars which in turn encompassed that large expanse of glazing. The early sun gave a hint of the heat that it would provide, only later that day, but even so Mrs Perkins had already switched on the slow fans and opened the roof lights in anticipation of another scorching day.
"The cleaners will be here in about fifteen minutes, Miss," she offered.
"I'll just pop in the shower before they get here," Melanie said as she rubbed her chaotic hair.
"I'd better skip breakfast thanks Mrs P, I'll go home and get ready for surgery."
"You're welcome to use one of the guest bathrooms, and I'm sure we can find you a new shirt somewhere from within this vast house," suggested Melanie.

Mrs Perkins showed Smith to a bathroom, and found him a new white shirt to replace the one that his sleeping torso had creased irrevocably. She set the trouser press and whisked away his jacket for a quick press. They both returned to the conservatory looking refreshed and invigorated. Their minds had obviously gained far more from the convivial atmosphere so generated than any discomfort that their bodies had endured from poor posture.

Smith gazed, like a man finding an oasis in the desert, at the scalding coffee, chilled juices, hot croissants and other delights that Mrs Perkins carried in seconds later. He despatched a croissant and jam with embarrassing speed and found himself apologising at Melanie's more sedate eating habits.
"Please don't apologise. We like people who enjoy their food don't we Mrs P?"

"What's your schedule for today then, Melanie?" he asked brightly as some of the aching started to fade.

"I am driving," she hesitated for a moment, then again as if to reinforce her intention, "I am driving over to see Mr Ward MD at Silicon Etchings. I need to shore up supplies for our new Lightdrive. And you?"

"I have surgeries for much of the day. As you know Dr Michaels will be back soon and he was planning to have a meeting when he returns from holiday. I also must get my Mum's GP to see her today, as I don't think she is too well. She refuses, as always, but she seemed more short of breath than usual."

"I do hope she will be all right, James."

"Well, she always seems to bounce back, but against that she seems to get weaker with each bounce."

"Will you let me know later?"

"Yes of course."

He thanked Mrs Perkins for the breakfast and the restoration of his suit from almost certain ruin.

He looked at Melanie with the concerned look that she somehow could not meet. "Do you feel confident enough to drive?"

"Yes I must; the meeting is important and I'm going to have to get behind the wheel sooner or later."

"Phone me if you have problems." He looked somewhat forlornly at his portable phone whose battery had faded below a usable level some time in the night.

"I can always get you at the surgery," she interjected, as she looked at the old phone with evidently, an even older battery. She looked at him carefully, amazed at this unassuming man's ability to somehow restore her, and give her the determination to stay the course.

"Fine, I'll perhaps speak to you later."

He waited while Melanie got into Range Rover and started the engine with the flick of the key. His own engine start would take considerably longer than that, but as he sat there he reflected on the progress that had been made steadily through the night, and uppermost were thoughts of her restitution from the distressed gloom of the previous evening.

CHAPTER IX

"SUBTERFUGE"

Melanie coaxed the 4x4 along, uneasily at first. It seemed far less happy with the short dab of the accelerator followed by a quick switch to the brake. She clung nervously to her rear view mirror as she re-lived the events of the day before. Smith's calm voice came into her mind, with its usual steadying influence, and slowly she released the car as her confidence returned.

Just over an hour later she managed to find 'Silicon Etchings' and was shown in to Lawrence Ward's office. A portly but well dressed Lawrence Ward rose, quite quickly, to his feet, considering his size.

"I am pleased to meet you, Melanie. As I said, I knew your father and Trish very well. I was so sorry to hear of their tragic deaths."

"Thank you. It's kind of you to say that. It's taken quite a while to even begin to pick up the pieces, but I am getting there slowly."

He motioned to a seat with a large and puffy hand and she sat facing him across the oversize desk. She withdrew some figures from her briefcase.

"These are the projected quantities we will require in the first year, if market penetration is half of what we expect."

"Melanie, I'm not sure that we could supply you with these quantities. Since I spoke with you yesterday, we've had a large order come in from overseas, and I'm afraid it will tie up most of our production for at least the next twelve months."

Ward seemed to hesitate before each word. It was always said that bad figures took accountants longer to add up: obviously Ward was of the view that bad news should be delivered more slowly. Each word that he uttered surprised her more, his attitude today at complete variance with when she had spoken on the telephone a short time ago. His words came as a great disappointment.

"I was rather hoping that we could source most of our raw material

from you. How much do you think you will be able to let us have?"
"Not really much more than you have at present, Melanie. I am sorry."
"The amounts you have supplied us with thus far, will not support a full production run, and we would have to delay release of our product."

The massive black suit he was wearing, made the room darken as he shrugged his shoulders, causing the abundant span of material to spread in front of the window.
"As I said, I am sorry, Melanie that you have come all this way for nothing."
She rose to go and once again his massive bulk appeared to completely eclipse the sunshine coming through the very large window behind him. Dejectedly, Melanie shook his hand. A weak, slimy, almost cold handshake, she thought to herself. 'Dad would not have liked this man at all.' She gently closed his office door behind her as the secretary came up to show her back to the car park.

The door to the adjoining office opened and out stepped a beaming Newman.
"Excellent Lawrence. That should put a spoke in her wheels for a bit."
"Are you sure this is right," the ponderous Ward said as he began to perspire with the exertion of getting out of his chair twice within five minutes, and also feeling very uncomfortable under the weight of the self-satisfied smirk on Newman's face. Betrayal did not sit easily.
"I tell you, she'll be out of her office within days and I'll be in charge."
"We cannot afford to lose an order like this. I've already told my partners that this is on the cards, and they won't be very pleased if we lose it for any reason," said Ward even his voice now becoming shaky with his exertions and with fear that now stalked him like a hungry panther.

“Trust me Lawrence. When I'm MD of Jectronics we'll be asking you to supply even more.”
“What was this about preassembly of Gallium lattices?”
Newman hesitated so long that even the obtuse Ward noticed it.
“Oh that’s nothing, she doesn't know what she's talking about. I tell you, all she knows is what colour of lipstick goes with her shirt, , and what height of heels she can wear before she falls over, that sort of stuff, women stuff, not running a company sort of stuff, like we know.”
“It seemed to me that she did, when I spoke with her yesterday. In fact, I thought how well-informed she was.”
“Trust me, I tell you Lawrence, she knows absolutely nothing. She's been watching daytime TV for twelve months. I'll remember who my friends are when I'm in control.”
He smiled his usual false and disingenuous smile that seemed almost as meaningless as his reassurance. Ward smiled uncertainly as his back was patted by Newman’s firm hand, causing his flesh to ripple under its impact.
“Well, I just hope that you're right, 'cause if it goes wrong I’ll take you down with me.”

Newman moved quickly, almost as quickly as his mood had changed. He grabbed the large man firmly by the throat, the sweating flesh quivering under his grip of steel.
“Don’t think about threatening me, Lawrence. I eat even bigger men than you for breakfast, you don’t want to be upsetting me. I am not a nice man, especially when I am upset.”
Ward spluttered convulsively as he struggled for breath under Newman’s grip. Newman now smiled as he saw the terror appear on the other man’s face, deriving delight from his distress.
“Now, let’s not fall out Lawrence, she hasn't been in there for months. The place is going to the dogs. Everyone is fed up to the back teeth, and they want someone new and dynamic like me to take the thing forward. I have backing from Warners, who want to buy up as much stock as they can get their hands on. No-one is going to back that posh-totty, airhead. She'll be faced with a *fait accompli*. Leave now or get pushed out. I tell you, she can go back

to her mansion and start growing roses, for all I care. I'll have a company to run and we'll need supplies from people like you."

Newman smacked Ward's cheek by way of confirmation, sat down and put his feet on Ward's desk. He took out a cigar from his shirt pocket and large clouds of smoke began to obscure, ever so slightly, his self-satisfied, conceited grin. After some moments, Ward too, sat down but he felt a little more deflated than anything else.

"Just when is this meeting then?"

"Wednesday, Lawrence, high noon," Newman said as he puffed away unconcernedly. "It will be all over within five minutes, I tell you. I'll phone you from my new office suite on the top floor."

A few more puffs and even Ward was enveloped by stale, reeking smoke from the large cigar. This seemed to please Newman in a perverse way, as he continued to savour the moment and revel in his impending, certain victory over the woman who should never have crossed his path in the first place.

The secretary came in and managed to find her way to Ward's desk as the smoke temporarily cleared in the waft from the open door.

"Would you like coffee, sir ?" she asked.

"That would be splendid," came the reply from Newman who was intensively studying her delicate blouse in unashamed detail, as he undressed her with his cold eyes, which appeared almost black in the dingy room.

"Not for me thanks Cynthia, I'm not thirsty," came from Ward's side of the desk, suddenly sensing a nasty taste in his mouth.

Cynthia quickly retreated as she became aware of the overbearing gaze from her boss's guest.

Out in the car park Melanie sat dejectedly behind the wheel. On the other side of the car park she saw the gates open to the factory yard and a large articulated lorry emerge. Still feeling a little nervous, she decided to wait for the lorry so that she could tuck herself in behind and simply take her time. Reflexly she looked into the factory yard as the gates were slowly closed. There in the corner, she spotted the red BMW with the distinctive private registration plate. She should have known that this was Newman's work all along. The sudden massive order that had materialised within hours of her contacting Ward was a simple ruse to offset her plans. Not only was Newman playing his usual underhand game but he obviously had spies in Jectronics revealing her every move. Her instinct to do most of her preparation from home had been advantageous.

Initially distaste was the main emotion that appeared, when she thought of the obese Ward, but this view softened on contemplation. He too, was a simple and relatively innocent pawn in Newman's dastardly game. She had not yet finished her business with Ward, however, and if business negotiations were to be entrained he was going to have to view her as an equal. In order for him to make this ponderous step, a sharp lesson in simple economics would be required.

She followed the lorry down to the motorway junction and then accelerated carefully past him. Her thoughts turned to Smith. It was his meeting with Michaels today, who would no doubt be refreshed after his holiday, but by all accounts would place a great deal of weight in the testimony, whether it be good or bad, of the all-seeing, all-knowing Mrs Farnell. Michaels would be a fool to let such a fine young doctor go. She just hoped that she had not impaired his chances. She smiled to herself as she tried to visualise the events that had taken place the day the Mini Cooper was delivered to Lorne Street. She could not help laughing as she imagined Smith's momentary discomfort under the calm, imperturbable gaze of Mrs Farnell.

Smith's own first task was to phone his mother's GP to ask him to pop in and see her after surgery. It was always difficult making medical decisions for close relatives. Objectivity was a vital force to aid the diagnostic process and allow an efficient management plan. Fortunately Dr. Stephens understood this and would make the necessary decisions for him. The surgery was quiet that morning. There were still a few regulars who would prefer to wait for Dr Michaels' return, but most were happy with the new GP and had quickly come to like his painstaking history-taking, thorough examination and above all his patience, coupled to a friendly manner that seemed impossible to disrupt.

Dr Michaels appeared at the end of surgery looking relaxed and tanned.
"Good holiday, Dr Michaels?" Smith said, doing his best to imitate the older man's matter-of-fact style.
"Superb, Smith thanks. Must go again soon. Now then, Smith wondered if we could have a chat in the common room?"
At this point the phone rang. Dr Stephens had been to see Mrs Smith and was unhappy with her. He would be admitting her that afternoon to the chest ward with suspected bronchopneumonia.
"Sorry to hear that Smith. Meet me upstairs when you're ready."
Smith tidied his papers and placed his equipment back in his capacious case. He wasn't surprised that Dr Stephens had admitted his Mum, she had been deteriorating of late. He walked briskly upstairs to meet Dr Michaels. As he ascended the stairs he passed Mrs Farnell, on her way down. Was that inscrutable smile one of commiseration or congratulation? He was about to find out.

"Sit down Smith. Have one of these biscuits. Almost worth coming off holiday for. Now then Smith, I'll get straight to the point. I think you've done sterling work here in the last six months. Patients and staff seem to really like you. Our list size has slowly increased since you came. I think we have even taken some back from the Oak Lane practice, despite them being much larger than we are. As you know, we don't have a large list, but I'm sure with a young, dynamic partner things will really get going. I would be delighted if you'd consider joining me as a full-time partner. You've worked your parity to a half share of the income, and if it would interest you, I'd be happy to take you on as an equal partner from October first. What do you say?"
"I'd be delighted Dr Michaels."

"Fine, then all settled. I've never been one for partnership agreements, but if you want one, we can draw one up, I suppose. Anything you want to ask me?"
"No, Dr Michaels, many thanks for giving me a chance. I am very happy here and I'm really grateful and pleased."
Dr Michaels considered for a moment his gracious comment. Many a young doctor would not want to work with a fusty old man like him. "Everything alright with the Jardine woman?" Michaels felt the need to add quickly, "you've done a great job there, she seems so much better," and served only to heighten his embarrassment as he continued, "her mother's death was tragic. For all our modern treatments, antidepressants and specialists, nothing I tried seemed to stop her self destruction."
Dr Michaels was obviously re-living some of his own personal horrors to do with Lydia Jardine, a patient who had died before her time, on his watch. Medicine was a tricky specialty and he knew that a doctor, any doctor, was only as good as his last misdiagnosis.

Fortunately Smith was facing some deep thoughts of his own, at this point, and did not notice the depths of regret on his senior's expression as he formed his reply. "I felt a bit out of my depth at first, as I don't think she was too keen to accept any help at all. I was so worried about her that I wanted to bring in the Psychiatrists but she refused. I managed to persuade her to keep coming back and though it's taken a lot of work, we are getting there."
"There's a bit of gossip floating round, so Mrs Farnell tells me, but I'm sure you have it all under control. People won't leave the poor girl alone, which doesn't help, and then along comes this handsome doctor, eh Smith."
It was Smith's turn to be embarrassed.

"Fine, well, that's it then. Now then Smith, you'd better get off. I'll do the visits. You try and start that car of yours, go and see your mother. Hope she's better soon. May be now that you'll be earning a bit more you can get yourself a decent car." A grin now visited

Dr Michaels' face, albeit fleetingly, as he remembered the recent events in the car park with the Mini Cooper.

Michaels disappeared after picking up yet another biscuit. "To save for later," as he would often say, and went downstairs to obtain the notes for the visits. Smith sat motionless for a few moments. He was delighted to be staying at Lorne street. Michaels was at times a little brusque and had a habit of using few words where more were usually needed, but he had a respect for the wily Yorkshireman and knew that he could trust him both morally and professionally. His rapture about staying on was more than counterbalanced by worry about his mother. He knew that something had been brewing the day before, and he also knew that Stephens would never have got his Mum anywhere near a hospital unless she was too ill to resist. This fact, together with a sense of foreboding, overshadowed the genuine congratulations delivered by the staff when he finally went downstairs and out to the car park.

He drove quickly over to the District General and found the doctors' office on the ward where his Mum had just been admitted. Kim White, the chest consultant was still there having just seen his mother. He approached the desk as she looked up from her work, the greying hair giving way to the reflected image of the desk lamp in her glasses. Her plain looks were more than counterbalanced by the warm, friendly smile that shone from the slightly angular and narrow features. The reflection from the lamp passed, as did the smile, revealing her calm but steady gaze. "Hi there, James, are you well?"
"Fine thanks Kim."
"Long time, no see."
"You know we GPs keep well away from these places, just in case you proper doctors start to show us up."
"As I recall, it was always your diagnoses that were keeping me on my toes," she remembered as a look of delight crossed her face, her grey eyes studying him with the pride that one would bestow upon a skilled protégé.

“I'm sure that wasn't the case.”
The reflex smile was delivered across the desk, once again, and suddenly her face hardened with the changing subject matter.

“I am afraid she isn’t too well Jim. She has a virulent bronchopneumonia and though we have started intravenous antibiotics we haven’t got any sensitivities yet.” Her expression grew darker. “It’s going to be touch-and-go I am afraid. The physio. will be coming up soon, but the problem is that she is so frail.”
“Yes, she has been unwell for many months. Bob Stephens has been excellent with her, but she can be a bit stubborn. I knew she must be ill when she agreed to come in.”
“She's in the side ward if you want to pop in.”
“Thanks Kim, and thanks for seeing her so soon.”
“Not at all, could never do enough for the best junior I ever had.”
Kim could not think why he had gone into General Practice, what a loss of a fine young doctor. Surely he was wasted in that quiet backwater. Memories came flooding back of all the lives he had struggled with, well into the small hours, in this very room, sometimes successfully and sometimes not. He wondered about the drama unfolding now.

His mother was awake; the oxygen spectacles hissing in the background as she fought for every breath. A drip-stand with an intravenous pump, stood beside the bed, its panel of lights blinking as another tiny amount of the antibiotic was infused into a vein.
“Ah James. Have they dragged you here in the middle of your surgery?”
“No Mum, surgery has finished and Dr Michaels said he would polish off the visits.”
“Well I'm sure you're much too busy to waste your time here with me.”
“Not at all. I was stuck at a loose end and I didn't have anyone else to spend the time with, so you were my only option.”

She managed a smile despite her breathlessness and the discomfort from the tubing which continued to hiss. “Now tell me, how is that nice Miss Jardine?”
“She's well, Mum. Not bad at all, for a *patient,”* he reminded her deliberately.
“Well I tell you, she's absolutely lovely that girl, and you could do a lot worse than that.”
“I don’t know what the General Medical Council would say about that.”
“I'm sure they would be very jealous of you if they saw her,”
He laughed at the thought of jealousy being the predominant emotion at a Service Committee Hearing, to decide whether he should be struck off or not. She continued, “anyway, doctors have been known to marry patients.”
“Not if they want to keep their jobs. Mum she is my patient, my charge, my responsibility. I have to get her better, not propose to her.”

Tiredness suddenly engulfed her as the extra exertion of talking demanded payment in full. She coughed that moist, bubbly cough of which he had much previous experience in his patients; unfortunately most of these occasions had gone against the patient and him.
“Mum, you're tired, I'd better go. The physiotherapist will be along soon, so keep your strength up for her. I am told she's an ex-Russian shot-putter!”
He kissed her quickly and left the room. Something told him that he had been through this scenario many times before, but never before as one of the relatives.

He decided to pop back to the surgery and as he entered the office Mrs Farnell handed him a message.
"It’s from Miss Jardine, Doctor. I tried to reach you on your mobile but it was switched off."
“Sorry, Mrs Farnell, the battery was flat.”
“She'll be on this number, if you have the time to phone her.”
He went to his surgery and punched in the number.

"How are you Melanie? Everything go well with Silicon Etchings?"
"Oh, I'll tell you about that later. Mrs Farnell told me about your mother. I am sorry to hear that she is unwell. How is she?"
"She isn't too well, to tell the truth. The next few days will tell us. She's in good hands and is being looked after by an old boss of mine from my hospital stint."
"Is there anything I can do?"
"Not really Melanie, but thanks for asking."
"Do you think she would mind if I popped in, just for a few minutes?"
"She is very tired Melanie, but I'm sure it would be OK, if you don't stay too long."
"Fine. Would it be all right to phone you later, I just wanted to pass something by you?" she said somewhat hesitantly.
"By all means, Melanie. Where will you be later? I'll stop by your house on my way to the hospital tonight?"
"Oh and by the way, Mrs Farnell told me that congratulations are in order, well done. Not that I ever doubted you. Dr Michaels is a very lucky man." She thought, as she put the phone down, that this applied to his patients too.

Melanie finished a quick sandwich in her office. Her presentation was all but complete, but the speech remained as far off as ever. Each time she attempted to write the words down, she would either be distracted, or the words would simply fail in their ability to do the job she demanded of them. The mendacious Newman continued to surprise her, as he sank to lower and lower depths. That he wanted control of the company came as no surprise, but it was the extent and nature of the wickedness that he was happy to display that she found most shocking.

Once again her mood had swung too far from its norm to be constructive, and she decided to take a drive over to the hospital to see Mrs Smith for whom she had developed a genuine liking. The Range Rover made short work of the journey as she drove down to the village to purchase a bunch of flowers. She eventually found the ward: she knocked gently on the open door and threaded her

way between the drip stand and tubes to the far side of the bed. Mrs Smith looked dreadful and extremely tired. On seeing Melanie she brightened visibly.
"Oh, Melanie how lovely to see you."
"I've been given instructions not to stay too long."
"Ignore him. I'll sort him out later. Are you keeping well Melanie?"
"Never better, thanks to the efforts of your son."
"Have you been very ill?"
"If it hadn't been for acute appendicitis and your son dragging me from my moroseness, I think I would have taken my own life."
"That would have been a great tragedy, my dear."
"It's kind of you to say that. I am very grateful to him. I hope that I haven't been too much trouble for him."
"Between you and me, I think he has enjoyed every single second. Since that Annabelle walked out on him, you know .....," she sensed that she was about to say too much and checked herself whilst changing tack quickly, "he told me about the car."
"I was put in the dog house for that, well and truly."
"It was a very, very kind thought and you know, he was really touched by it. I don't think he's used to receiving any gifts, let alone, one so wonderful. He tells me that Michaels has made him a full partner so his partnership share will go up nicely. I'm afraid he spends all his money on me. It's not cheap keeping an old crock of a patient like me, at home. Even with the various allowances. Hopefully he'll be able to afford a better car soon."
"I don't think he would want it any other way."
"Melanie, he's been a marvellous son to me. I couldn't begin to tell you what sacrifices he's made for me."

Melanie could almost palpate the painful emotions that had flooded her mind. It was Melanie's turn to change the conversation abruptly.
"So, will he be coming to see you later?"
"Yes I expect so," her mood lifting a little with the change in subject.

Once again the tiredness and breathlessness caught up with her. The nurse arrived and told Melanie that the Physio. was waiting. Melanie leant over and kissed her on the cheek quickly.
"Melanie, he is very lucky to have a patient like you!"
She managed the mischievous smile that mirrored the one that had appeared on Smith's face increasingly of late.
"Thank you for that, but I think I am the lucky one, Mrs Smith. May I come again?"
"I would be very pleased if you would. Thank you for the flowers, my dear."
As Melanie turned to go, a large, thickset lady waited in the corridor, her uniform bulging more with muscular than fatty bulk. Melanie's eyes widened a little as she passed, thinking that she would not want to arm-wrestle her for the next pint.

Melanie found the car in the car park: the Jaguar was still away at the repairers, but she liked the elevated driving position of the Range Rover, and the feeling of safety which that seemed to engender in return. Melanie's mind was racing even faster than the engine. Annabelle could only be the attractive brunette in Smith's room. She wondered quickly whether the photo had been placed there more as an icon of unfulfilled love, rather than as a deterrent to hot-blooded teenagers who had come to swoon at the new doctor. Her question was to be answered much sooner than she realised.

Melanie sat down to a typically tempting platter that had been filled enthusiastically by Mrs Perkins who had discovered that avoiding the use of serving dishes meant that her boss was more likely to clear the plate than simply leave food untouched. Melanie started to attack the mound before her with new-found gusto. Mrs Perkins grinned with delight as she remembered the months and months of toying with food that Melanie didn't want and was not going to eat, regardless of any amount of encouragement. Things had changed for the better since that nice Dr Smith had arrived on the scene. The self-satisfied smile was doubly reinforced when she

heard the familiar racing engine on the courtyard outside. She removed her pinny reflexly and went straight to the door.
“Doctor Smith. This is a pleasure,” she said with her usual sunny smile, which seemed to be perfectly at home on her pink round face. “I was just making Miss some dinner, could I get you something, Doctor?”
“No, Mrs Perkins, but thank you. I hope that I'm not disturbing Melanie am I?”
“Not at all sir. She's just on her dessert. Perhaps a tea or a coffee?”
“Tea would be great, thanks.”

Melanie was just finishing what had been a rather large slice of lemon drizzle cake, that was generally regarded as Mrs Perkins's masterpiece. She got up from the table, looking a little embarrassed at the thought that he might have witnessed the inelegant speed with which she had been consuming it, and hoped that the warm smile she sent in his direction would distract him whilst she attempted to swallow a mouthful.
“Please don’t let me stop you Melanie,” looking at the plate that had almost been swept clean of even the tiniest remains of cake. He smiled inwardly, savouring the return of her appetite as being a reliable index of her recovery. Mrs Perkins brought in a tray with a teapot, saucers and plates. Smith watched as Melanie’s long fingers grappled with the large tea pot with delicate ease.
“I saw your Mum. She doesn’t seem too well. I hope she will be all right. She seems surrounded by tubes and flashing lights and things and that was just the radio! When I left, this big girl was waiting outside. I am sure she was the Physio.”
“Ah Helga,” Smith said with a wry smile.
Melanie took him seriously at first a look of horror crossed her face as the image of the sturdy Helga breaking bones in the frail old lady, then laughed as she saw the joke.
“Actually, she is very gentle, if it’s who I think it is. I'll pop in and see Mum on my way home. How did your day go Melanie?”
She interrupted quickly as she remembered his mutual assessment period had ended today.

"Oh congratulations by the way. Michaels would have been stupid not to take you on. Mrs Farnell told me, without me having to ask. I don't know how she knew, I was burning to know?" Melanie had perhaps missed the fact that there was not a lot that Mrs Farnell was not aware of. "He would be mad to let you go," she said earnestly, "and besides, I've seen the way Mrs Farnell looks at you."
"Well, Dr Michaels was unusually talkative. I've never seen him like that before. Anyway he told me that things were going well and that my face seemed to fit and that Mrs Farnell had said that I was passable."
"He didn't!"
Melanie hadn't quite learned the art of spotting when he was joking, but her study of him was advancing her knowledge daily.
"No only joking," he replied, the smile bursting on his face at the sight of her indignation. "He did say that the list size was increasing nicely and that we were starting to woo patients back from the Oak Lane surgery, that's the large practice, you may know it? He seemed well pleased and even took all the visits when he learned of my Mum."

She stumbled with the words at first, then decided to simple say what was on her mind.
"Would you let me buy you dinner, or something, to celebrate? Tell you what how about Wednesday evening? THE day," she said with emphasis.
"That would be fine for me. Are you sure? What if you lose, and they decide on nasty Newman?"
"Well, in that case, it will be a commiseration tea and you can buy, in that event."
"Fine, it's a deal," he confirmed instantly.

She told him about the events that day and how by chance she had managed to spy Newman's car within the factory yard where he had hoped it wouldn't be seen.
"How did he know you'd be there?"

“Probably Suzy, on switch. He has most of them in his camp. I don’t know what he's been saying, but they are all backing him as if he's the new MD already. Most of them seem terrified to speak to me.”

“As you said, it's ‘do or die’ on Wednesday. Is Stella still away?”

“Yes, Newman knew that she would vote for me, come what may, and deliberately chose the meeting at a time when she would be in the Gambia, but I have one or two surprises for him. By the way, here is another little box for you.” She handed over yet another four milimetre tape to match the first. "As before nothing too important, just guard it with your life. Tuck it under your pillow, with your stethoscope.”

“I'll put it next to my ‘Superdoc’ outfit,” he said reassuringly. “So what do you do now? Is ‘Silicon Etchings’ essential to you?”

“Not at all, it’s just they were convenient and are nearby; we could have subcontracted some of our assembly to them. I couldn't understand why he changed his mind so quickly, and then when I saw noxious Newman’s car there it fell into place.”

“So what will you do?”

“The Sumitomo factory in Japan is the world’s biggest supplier of the components we need. I’m going to contact them tonight, when their managers are in. I’m hoping to get a price and a supply contract out of them.”

“So will you cut out Ward completely?”

“At first, when I was angry, I thought so, but then I thought that he's probably a pawn in Newman’s dastardly game. There’s no knowing what Newman has offered or threatened him with. It seemed to me that Ward was someone who was swept along by events, rather than someone who shapes them. If his partners found out that he’d been got at by nasty Newman, the strawberry fields in Lincolnshire would be swelled by one more recruit. I may just get back to him when I have some competing prices from Japan, and then put the fear of God in him. He won’t want to lose this contract. I bet nerdy Newman has already told him that my cause is lost, so there is no point in dealing with me.

“Well, mark my words, this is a fight to the death and old necrotic Newman isn't going to win without a fight,” she continued.

“Not bad Melanie – quite like necrotic,” as he picked up on her skills of alliteration.

“Do you think I am doing the right thing?” she said as her confidence evaporated in an instant to uncertainty.
“Melanie, what do you think?”
“My father and Trish would want me to fight for what was mine.”
“What do you want?”
“What they would want.”
“Do you? What do *you* really want?” this time with pleading emphasis on the 'you'.
“I want it. I want to give nauseating Newman a bloody nose for what he tried to do to me. I want this company up where it belongs, and I want those who’ve worked for it to get their just reward. I don’t want some outside firm to come along, strip out the patents, ship them overseas, then close us down and throw a lot of good people onto the dole.”
“There Melanie, in that case, that is the right thing.”
“How do you know?”
He laughed. “Because you told me! Deep inside, this is what you really want. I know you draw reference at all times from your Dad and Trish, but increasingly you will find you have to plough your own bed of roses, as you might say.”
“Thanks.”
“What for?”

The pause said much more than the simple words that followed. She knew she had him to thank for everything, for saving her, for restoring her, for catching her when she wobbled, for making her strong and fit for the trials ahead, and most of all for being something that she knew she could not have been without him.
“For restoring my confidence.”
“It isn't me Melanie, it’s you. You may have taken a severe knock in the past few months, but you are the person who has that inner strength. It emanates from within you and not from me. I'm just helping to reinforce it."

Before he could voice more than was wise, his phone rang and instantly started beeping as its battery signalled distress.
"Smith here. Annabelle ! Long time no see. How are you ? How is Peter? Divorcing? I am sorry to hear that. Yes, It's good of you to ring. I'm afraid she is unwell. Yes she's on Kim's ward. They're doing the best they can. Look Annabelle, I can't talk just now," Smith said, sensing that the surprise that engulfed him, now made his behaviour border on rudeness, "I'll phone you later? OK then, goodbye."
Melanie sensed acute embarrassment rise. She motioned that she would leave the room and allow him to finish his call unencumbered. He touched her arm and waved to stop her from leaving. "Listen Annabelle, I am a bit busy at the moment. I will phone you later."

He replaced the phone in his top pocket. Both were shaken in equal measure but for entirely different reasons. "Please forgive me, Melanie. A bit of a blast from the past. The photo in my room?" he reminded her. Melanie nodded. "She is married, or is divorcing, the brother of the Registrar who's looking after my Mum."
"News travels fast," Melanie commented.
"Apparently she heard about my Mum and thought she would phone to see how she was. Listen, I had better go Melanie, thank you for the tea and cake."

Melanie did her utmost to fashion a look of passive disinterest. She nodded and played her part, so well that he was never aware of the turmoil that it had unleashed below that veneer of outward placidity. As he turned to go, she was unable to define her true emotions, but she could discern that something sizeable had hit her in the pit of her stomach, and had left an emptiness in its wake. He too walked half-stunned and half-intrigued back to his car. For once he had no recollection of just how long it had taken to start that engine, so deep had his thoughts become. He smiled to himself as he now remembered, once again, some of those times he had spent with Annabelle. The more he tried to examine his own emotions, the more diffuse they became. Something had stirred from deep inside, but he too, was unable to say exactly what.

Smith drove straight to the hospital deep in thought. The more he thought, the more difficult it was to crystallise his own line of logic. Eventually he realised that his thoughts had become too detailed and too complex and, when all was said and done, he should simply take things one step at a time. One thing was clear, it would be unwise to mention her name to his mother, especially in view of her weakened state. He would phone Annabelle back, as he had promised, but for reasons which he could not fathom, he failed to summon enthusiasm for doing so.

His mother looked much better despite the usual evening dip most people with chronic chest problems experienced. She sat up in bed reading a magazine. The oxygen spectacles lay on the bed next to her, still quietly hissing. She showed him the beautiful flowers as she said, “I do like that girl.”

“Yes Mum I know.” He was unusually irritated by the mention of Melanie and could not say why. As usual, his observant mother did not fail to notice the inner turmoil but chose to keep her own counsel rather than add to his restless state. She steered the conversation well away and concentrated on more clinical aspects of her stay in hospital and the excellent and ever so gentle physiotherapist who had seen her earlier. His smile crept back.

“She is a big girl, but I am told that she's very gentle and also a very good physio.”

His mother reinforced this view.

“The food isn't so good. It’s a good job I'm not very hungry. Kim was telling me how much she misses having you as a junior doctor on her team. So, how do you feel at being made a full-time partner?”

“Very pleased. Michaels is a good man, and I think that we'll get on very well. There is a lot to do, and quite a few things that we want to bring on board. All in all, the next few years should be quite interesting.”

"I am so pleased for you. You've done so well. I'm very proud of you. All you need now is a wife. I've never heard you talk of anyone since Annabelle walked out on you, and that was four years ago now."

He sensed what was coming next and deflected it quickly. "I notified the home helps that you would be in hospital for a few days. They asked me to let them know a couple of days before you come home."

"I am hoping not to be in here too long. It's very nice and people are very kind. I'm not sure why they put me in a side ward, probably courtesy toward you but I'm sure that I'm undeserving of it."

"No, they usually put the troublemakers in the side ward."

She looked at him over her glasses as he grinned back.

"Listen Mum, I'd better go. You still look pretty tired and a good night's sleep will do you good. I'll visit tomorrow after surgery."

"Melanie said she would pop in tomorrow."

He kissed her quickly and walked toward the door, once again fearful as to what might come next in the conversation.

"I'll see you tomorrow."

CHAPTER X

"GHOST TO REST"

As he walked back to his car, several things were gnawing away at him. He felt tetchy and anxious but could not say exactly why. Things had gone so well, he had no right to feel the way he did. As he walked, his thoughts crystallised a little and he was able to define exactly why he felt uneasy. He had promised to phone Annabelle back, and it was the conflict of uncertainty and excitement that was unsettling his inner psyche. Yes, he was certain, that must be what had unsettled him so. He drove home and made himself some tea. He picked up the phone three times and put it down again before he decided to take the plunge and key the numbers. Annabelle answered quickly, as if she had been expecting him.

“Thanks for phoning back James. I was hoping we could have a little chat. It’s been so long and it would be very nice catching up with things again.”

“I'm not so sure about all this, Annabelle. As you say, it has been a very long time. I am sorry you're divorcing.”

“It’s amicable enough, but I do need someone to talk to. Please say you'll come.”

“Very well. Suppose I meet you at Delphino’s tomorrow 8:30?”

“Fine, I'll book the table. Thanks James. I'll look forward to it.”

Melanie smiled to herself as she filled her tenth cup of coffee. It was always the same. When you had to stay up your body screamed for sleep, and when you tried to get an early night you found yourself pacing the floor. She was now no stranger to a disturbed sleep pattern; she had heard the Psychiatrists discuss it with her mother and Smith with her. Early morning waking was typical of depression, and difficulty getting off to sleep was an anxiety pattern. She must be a hopeless case, as she had suffered both, ever since her visit to the gypsy. Still, Smith had worked wonders together with his little tablets, and though she was not getting any more hours of sleep, she was at least feeling a lot more refreshed in the mornings. Her thoughts turned to the unexpected phone call and the mix of emotions that she had detected on his face. It seemed fairly obvious that Annabelle was intent on featuring in his life once again, and no doubt carrying him off as her next prize. She wondered how Mrs Smith would view this.

Suddenly the fax chattered once again as another series of sheets was issued. She looked at the information they contained as she sipped her coffee. Things were coming on very well, and it seemed as if Sumitomo were happy to deal, provided Melanie could guarantee a minimum volume. She sat in front of the web cam and dialled their number. She knew there was an eight hour time difference but business was business. By the early hours her work was done and she collapsed back in her chair, too exhausted to take herself upstairs and to bed.

Mrs Perkins found her the following morning stretched out on the settee in her study, the sheaf of papers by her side.
"Where would you like breakfast this morning, Miss ?"
Melanie elected to sit in the kitchen with the housekeeper. She usually did this when she wanted to discuss key issues with her. Since her mother had taken her own life, she had very few people to reflect her thoughts, and whilst Stella was ideal for sounding out as regards business ideas, Mrs Perkins was unequalled when it came to things of a more personal nature. As she munched her toast, she told her all about the events of the previous day, and about Mrs Smith's admission to hospital. Mrs Perkins remained her usual attentive self, but knew that Melanie had not yet reached the vital piece of information that she needed to communicate. Suddenly she mentioned the phone call from Annabelle, and the photo she had seen in Smith's office, and the unguarded comments made by Smith's mother. Mrs Perkins was her most delicate and discreet self as she formed her reply to the one vital crumb of information, in all that had gone before.

"Sometimes men aren't the most sensitive of creatures," she deliberately understated. "It often takes them a considerable time to know their own feelings, and then perhaps not until it has hit them right in the face. They can also be just a bit gullible, weak willed n'all, especially when it comes to dealing with us women, who can turn this weakness one way or 'nother to our own definite advantage. If one were interested." Her eyes moved away from Melanie back to her own coffee cup, "then under normal circumstances it'd simply be down to 'may the best woman win', but these are not normal times, and beggin' your pardon Miss, I'd be advisin' caution. I think that'd be for the best. Course that don't mean to say that you should do nothing. In fact I'm sure like, that there is quite a bit that could be done. Let's see now." Her voice seemed to dip just a little as she poured another cup of tea almost as if the words she was about to utter were known only to a secret few, a bit like a dark art, but much more compelling. Melanie smiled a little as she nodded to the hushed words of a more animated Mrs Perkins than she had ever remembered.

Melanie finished her breakfast, kissed the elderly housekeeper with new-found animation, and rushed upstairs to shower and to change. A bemused Mrs Perkins went about her usual routine. She stopped as she cleared away the breakfast table to marvel at the transformation she had witnessed in the young woman. Surely she was cured by now, and surely nothing could touch her now. Without prescient vision of her own Mrs Perkins could have been forgiven for failing to spot the dark forces massing for the final conflict.

Melanie returned a few minutes later to tell Mrs Perkins that she would be gone until early afternoon. She hugged Mrs Perkins and jumped into her car. The usual spring in her step had returned, and Mrs Perkins once again smiled as she watched the car disappear down the long drive. Mrs Perkins could see that some of her advice had already been put in place. The skirt, just a little higher than usual, those endless legs now unashamedly out in force, and the top, a teeny bit lower to enhance the curvaceous breasts and, as always, those beautiful shoes, that women would kill for and men would die for.

Lawrence Ward was quite unaware of the visitor who would be descending on him that day. The first he knew of it, was when his secretary rushed in to apologise for disturbing him. "I have a Miss Jardine outside, Sir. She insists on seeing you without an appointment." Ward sat down a little more heavily than usual. His chair creaked, uncertainly, under the forces so unleashed. He sat silhouetted against the large window and the pine-panelled office with his pictures of his family and great fishing catches he had made, seemed just a little foreboding as he waited for her to enter, like a stunning Nemesis. Melanie was shown in by the secretary, who held a secret admiration for women who could hold their own in what was usually a man's world. The secretary, Cynthia, had no doubt that this impressive young woman was about to reveal her business prowess today unequivocally. There was something in her walk, a sense of purpose perhaps, even a sense of destiny. No matter what it was, it was definitely flowing with this bright young woman. Cynthia could not help but smile a little, despite the effort she maintained in order to keep her face straight, when the thought 'he's toast' refused to depart from her brain.

"Melanie, so nice to see you," he began, as the first move to surrender.

"Please Lawrence, spare me the pleasantries. I'm here to talk business."

Her coolness in the blistering heat only seemed to exacerbate his own discomfort, as the layers of fat insulated him rather more than his body would have liked. His tiny eyes widened in the large, rotund face as he swallowed heavily against that tight collar.

"I have here, some figures from Sumitomo. They are more than happy to supply us with all we need at some very attractive prices."

Wade began to sweat profusely, just at the mention of the Japanese giant. He knew that the firm had outshone his business at every level. He knew that once his partners learned this information, he would be history, just like hundreds of other lay-offs they had been forced to make as a result of losing business in precisely this way. He shivered, despite the sweating, as if someone had just walked over his grave. He knew that he would never find another job, not after this young woman had destroyed him. He was just about to beg, to plead and explain to Melanie how Newman had blackmailed him. That deal, done so long ago, he thought nobody, nobody except Melanie's father knew of his transgression, until Newman had contacted him days ago. Melanie's father had been kind and shown him more mercy than he deserved. He was about to lose everything, as those beautiful eyes locked upon him like an assassin sent from heaven, to put him out of his misery. Blind panic set in, rendering him speechless. He knew that his legs were trembling, thank heavens she could not see them behind the desk.

Melanie, however, did not need to see his legs, she could plainly see the terror course across his ample countenance. Tears were welling in the corner of his eyes, queuing to start, with emotion that was about to flow without restraint. Melanie, knew then that Ward was beaten, all she now had to do was to deliver the *coup de grâce*. In that moment she thought of her father and, so it seemed, she also thought of Smith, as kindness dispelled anger, and mercy outshone the rampant ruin that she realised she could unleash if she so chose.

"It would be a pity, don't you think, Lawrence?" The use of his first name seemed to underline how far he had slipped in her esteem. At their first meeting she had always referred to him as Mr Ward, the more formal title that was usually reserved for those who had worked with her father, "if this nice contract went overseas when we're on each others' doorsteps, and when your firm is more than capable of supplying us with our exact requirements, as well as undertaking much of our subcontracting. Would you like me to pass this by your partners, Lawrence? Perhaps they would be very interested to hear what I have to say."

Ward knew then, that that ever so pretty face concealed a resolve of steel, and that he gazed admiringly also at a businesswoman who had beaten him resoundingly. Shame now replaced panic on his face, as his large legs continued to tremble, like those of a big dog who had heard the term 'visit to the vet'.
“No Miss Jardine, that won’t be necessary. Forgive me Melanie. Would you be prepared to let me look at some of the figures you have?”

She hesitated only for a moment. She realised that use of her full title signified capitulation. The temptation to let him produce his own figures from a position of weakness was rising within her, but her father’s teaching, about allowing a defeated opponent some means of recovery, remained uppermost as she handed him her folder. Only the slight sideways glance hinted at the fact that she really ought to have done otherwise. 'Always, but always, show good grace to your opponents,' came to her in that moment; they were her father’s words, and she remembered them now, as more uplifting emotions eclipsed Ward’s tawdry dealings. His usual ponderous speech had certainly sped up considerably as he digested the figures in commendable time.

“Melanie, we would be pleased to supply you with these quantities and say, as a mark of our sincere apologies for any inconvenience we have caused, we come in at ten percent below these prices, and also offer to do the preassembly at our cost for the first twelve months?” He looked at her expectantly, not daring to breathe.
Melanie was delighted and her countenance softened from one of anger to one of unrestrained happiness. Her face beamed at him as she held out her hand without saying a word. As his sweating palm engaged her cool firm grasp, his relief was manifest. She thought for an instant that a jet of steam was about to issue from beneath that very restrictive collar. She rose to go.
"My father would be proud of you, Mr. Ward.”
“No Melanie, I rather think he would be extremely proud of you, and I think, if I may venture, with just cause.”

His secretary appeared in an instant, she had been listening through the thin door to his office.
"Is a handshake enough, or would you like a contract drawn up?"
"*Your* word is more than enough for me, Mr Ward," she offered without hesitation that implied forgiveness coupled to her mercy. The emphasis also hinted that she knew who his associate was.
"Melanie, good luck in the meeting on Wednesday. I do hope that we will have many years of mutually beneficial business dealings." His head bowed almost imperceptibly whilst he shook her hand again, as he recognised a person who conducted herself in a manner, that from this day forth, he would aspire to. He looked at the picture of his wife, and son, who had just gone to University, as the tear formed once again.
"I hope so too. Many thanks."
"Thank you for saving me today, Melanie, I won't forget the kindness you have extended to me."

The beautiful enigmatic smile, rose like the sun over a lush oasis that promised better times for him, from the previous unforgiving desert. She turned and was gone without further word, the secretary following behind almost as a matter of homage rather than courtesy. Ward sat down feeling heavy with guilt, and downcast with his foolishness.
One thing was certain. Newman was going to have to pull something very special out of the hat if he was going to have even the slightest chance of stopping this impressive young woman. He found himself wishing firmly that he would fail soundly.

She walked slowly to the Range Rover, where she had left it, in the visitor's spot. A refreshing breeze chose that moment to play over the pretty face as she extended her neck and reclined her head backwards to bask in the comfort that it created, more than simply by its physical presence. She noted that the yard gates were firmly closed and wondered just how often a lorry would arrive, to cause them to open. Newman was obviously so confident as to be getting careless. She hoped his confidence would be the first link in the chain to shatter. She looked up at the unwavering sun in the cloudless sky. For that moment she dared to hope that her father and Trish would be proud of her and without intending it to be so, she acknowledged that her mother would be nothing but delighted that Smith had facilitated that transition. Somehow the GP's tireless patience, interest and hard work had liberated things within her that she either had forgotten, or of whose presence she had been unaware.

Mrs Farnell took the notes down to Dr Michaels who was about to start his surgery.

"Just as you predicted Dr Michaels, everyone seems quite excited at the changes in prospect, now that we know Dr Smith will be staying on."

"You know. Mrs Farnell, I feel the same way myself. I think the next twelve months will be very interesting. If he can persuade the PCT to back his plans, I think that we'll even be giving Oak Lane surgery a run for their money in spite of their being much larger than we are."

Mrs Farnell smiled the usual restrained, discreet smile and left him with the box of notes.

"Your first patient is here. Miss Spencer is three quarters of an hour early, as usual."

"Why do I get the eighty year old spinsters. Mrs F. and Smith gets these young attractive heiresses?"

"Now, you wouldn't want me to answer that, would you, Doctor?"

As usual, her professional manner and carefully angled anti-reflective glasses would hide the adoration in her eyes as she looked at him. Thirty years and more, she had waited for those most simple of words from him: it seemed she would wait a while longer. "Besides," she continued "I'm sure that Doctor Smith would gladly swap with you."

He looked at the practice manager carefully: what a clever woman she was. She always, absolutely always, seemed to know and say and do the right thing. In thirty years she had not once let him down.

"You may just have a point there, Mrs F. The boy has done a marvellous job though, she's looking so much better. I thought for

a while that she was going to follow her mother and take her own life. By all accounts Smith seems to have pulled it off. Perhaps it's best if I look after the old fogies and leave him to look after the young ones."
"I think that if you did that, you would disappoint a large proportion of your following. Your *devoted* following, if I may say so."
The slight emphasis on the repeated words did the trick in pulling him out of his reverie.
"Yes, I suppose you are right Mrs F. Thanks for that. Why not send in that nice Miss Spencer?"

She smiled and quietly closed the door. Things had not changed in the past thirty years, he still needed the re-assurance that people were coming to see him. For all the new ideas and changes that had taken place in general practice, if young Smith could do half as well as Dr Michaels, then he would be very fortunate. She went to find Miss Spencer, eagerly tapping the tessellated pattern on the lino with restless impatience.
"Dr Michaels will see you now, Miss Spencer."
"About time too. I had to wait a week for this appointment, you know."
Mrs Farnell thought of reminding her that that was only because Dr Michaels had been on holiday and, as usual, she refused to see anyone else, but dismissed the idea as a futile waste of breath, on the very warm August day. Miss Spencer scurried into the consulting room, nearly forgetting her stick in her rush.

Slowly, but steadily, more and more people filed into the waiting room. Though Smith's popularity was growing steadily Mrs Farnell was always amazed at the numbers whose problems had waited until Dr Michaels' return.

As always, when a surgery was in progress the time seemed to fly. It hardly seemed two minutes, but the surgery clock assured her that her estimate was out by a factor of hours rather than minutes

as Smith, still rushing, charged in from the car park, just in time to catch Dr Michaels as he was finishing his surgery.
“Dr Michaels, I've been to the PCT, they seem pleased with our ideas and seem happy to back us providing the list size continues to grow at its current rate.”
“Excellent, I don't see a problem with that, do you Smith?”
“Not at all, in fact if we continue taking patients off the Seabridge estate I would have thought that we can even increase the rate of growth.”
“Steady on there Smith, we don't want to take on too much now do we?”
“I’d be happy to do more surgeries Dr Michaels,” and when his partner looked concerned, continued, “I'll keep a steady eye on things, I promise.”
Michaels nodded. His word was good enough and Smith already knew that at his time of life he did not want to be pushing his workload up too much, but neither did he want to flog the young doctor, just because he was keen. Smith’s mood was infectious and Michaels had noticed that the whole place was simmering with new-found excitement, not seen since Michaels had been the junior partner, now more years ago that he cared to remember. The young man certainly had a lot of ideas and made a case for their gradual implementation rather than by overnight upheaval, which would have upset the normally conservative reception staff, and him too, of course.
“Now then Smith, I've asked Mrs Farnell to book your evening surgery a little lighter than usual as I expect you will want to get off and see your Mum. How is she?”
“She seems to be holding her own thanks. That was very good of you. Thank you, Dr Michaels”

Smith soon finished the surgery and drove straight to the hospital. He tapped on the door, which was ajar as usual and walked in. Melanie was sitting on her bed and the two women were obviously deep in conversation.
“You seem a lot better, Mum. Good evening Melanie.”

“It's the excellent company, I can assure you James,” as she pointed firmly to Melanie.
“Yes, I can see that. You seem to be having a good gossip.”
“We were just talking about you,” Mrs Smith said, as Melanie smiled; she seemed keen to tease him, just a little, which must surely signify her improving condition.
“Oh yes, perhaps you'd like me to go out?”
“No we've finished, I’ve told Melanie all the juicy bits already.” Smith blushed. “Actually, Melanie was telling me all about the tussle she was having for her own company.”

Melanie stood up, looking just a little embarrassed, sensing that he needed a moment. As she did so, he felt his eyes being drawn into what was just too long to qualify for a passing glance. He could not help noticing the sun-dress as it extenuated her taut figure, the slim arms, with their only adornment being the Omega Ladymaster watch, as always on her left wrist. She brought herself up to her full height and the movement was enough to give off the slight but sensual wisp of her perfume that seemed to tantalise his sense of smell. The momentary contact of their eyes, as his shining brown ones met those of pale hazel with a hint of amber that seemed to be aglow in sun or shade, or even artificial light, was quickly detected by his ever-vigilant mother, and the slight awkwardness between them, patently exposed to her attentive mind. Nothing, was missed by her acute gaze as she looked carefully at the two of them, and noted at once the slightly awkward look they gave each other, as eyes were averted after an interval that had bordered more on longing than not. Though such things seemed plain to her, she realised that the delicate subterfuge that existed between them hid much deeper emotions, and for the time being this denial was the only way their relationship could continue.
“Please don’t let me disturb you, Melanie. I have to get going. I was only popping in to see if you are OK, and I can see that you are.”
“Are you on call tonight James?”
“No, actually I'm going out.”

The direct question left no time for a more delicate stratagem to prevent her from knowing his true plans that evening. Rather than face the next salvo of questioning, he opted for retreat and slowly moved to the door. Sensing the urgency of his need to escape and aware of her chance to quiz Melanie as soon as he had gone, his mother simply said, “Thanks for coming, anyway, and whatever you are doing, enjoy yourself.”

As soon as he had gone she redirected her attention to Melanie.
“I wonder where he is off to in such a hurry? It must be something important, if not exciting.”
Melanie did her best to engage all facial expression in firm neutral, but she was either too late, or a deeper involuntary process had already supervened.
“I don’t suppose you have any idea, have you Melanie?”
Her initial strategy having failed, Melanie attempted to avert her gaze, but this only served to seal her fate.
“Go on Melanie, you can tell me. Just where is he off to in such a hurry.”
The open, grey eyes levelled, this time, directly at her.
“I don’t think he would be too pleased if I told you.”
“You don't mean that horrible woman do you!”
Though the body was weak, Melanie was in no doubt as to the acuity and sensitivity of an acute mind in full flow. Melanie's expression remained impassive.
“I just knew. I knew it! What is she doing back in his life,” was offered more rhetorically. “I tell you Melanie, this is absolute disaster. How could you let him go Melanie!”
The young woman had to pause for a minute as she realised the literal meaning behind her words.
“She ruined his life the last time, and it looks as though she's coming round to repeat the performance. Melanie we must put a stop to this.”
“Mrs Smith, I am just a patient.”
“That’s what he keeps telling me! I'll get him struck off. If that is what he is afraid of, I am sure I can arrange a service committee hearing for acute stupidity.”

Melanie just managed to suppress her laugh as she gazed upon the face of dismay, entwined with a hefty dose of anger. Melanie attempted to calm her with reassuring words, but unfortunately only served to increase the intensity of her emotions.
“Perhaps I could phone him on his mobile and tell him I've had a relapse?” Melanie said, in desperation.
The imagery it conjured up in the elderly lady's mind was enough to bring her out of her blighted mood.
“Good idea that Melanie. I'll go round there myself in a minute. That'll sort them both out.”
The older woman paused, sensing that her disappointment had got the better of her. Melanie recognised the effort she applied to restore calm, something that Smith had obviously learned from her.

“I never really liked her. Not from the moment we met. You know Melanie, we come from a humble background. I got the impression that we were never really good enough for her. It was only the fact that he was a doctor that she was interested in. He was besotted by her. You may think that it’s just a jealous mother talking, but he was oblivious to everything I said. She took up all his free time. He spent all his money on her. Not that I have a right to complain about that, you understand,” as she broke off, to aim a quick nod in Melanie's direction. Melanie nodded empathically. “Then of course she took a shine to Peter, his best friend. They'd been at school together and had been very close. She played one off against the other. It was almost as though it was an auction and she was going to settle for the highest bid.”
Melanie did manage a laugh at this point.
“Anyway James couldn't compete, and she married Peter. He was tipped to be a consultant and she didn't want to settle for a hard-up GP, who was supporting his old mother. Truth is, James was always a better doctor anyway, and I know he could have made consultant if he'd stayed in hospital. He had to become a GP to earn enough to settle the bills my care was clocking up. I have

never seen him look so troubled. He hasn't spoken of those months. I don't suppose he's mentioned it to you?"
The empathic response this time was a firm shake of the head, which Melanie quickly supplied.
"He was devastated by what had happened. To tell you the truth, I was delighted to see the wretched woman out of his life. I don't know what she is doing back after so long, but I tell you Melanie, no good will come of it, you'll see."

Melanie continued to listen attentively. The night staff came on and received the report from the day staff. The night Sister then came into the room to ask her politely if she would leave, as they were hoping to close the ward up for the evening. Melanie rose to go.
"Melanie, I want to apologise. Please forgive me, for going on so much."
Melanie's astute mind was scarcely needed to gauge the depth of the older woman's concern.
"I don't think he'll be very pleased if he thinks that I was the one who told you."
"Don't worry, he knows I can read him like a book. It wasn't your fault. You know, Melanie you may be the only person who can save him from this terrible woman."
Melanie smiled politely and did her best to look puzzled. She stood as she prepared to leave. Deep inside she rather hoped that she would be given a chance. She would certainly welcome the opportunity of meeting this woman who had had such an impact on the usually impassive and carefully controlled, young doctor. She wondered just what looks and skills she had, in order to evoke such a response, and what tactics she had employed to fire his emotions in this way. She left the older lady, deep in thought as she wondered if her son would see what was in front of him, in time to avert disaster.

Smith drove quickly to the restaurant. He wanted to be a little early so that she would not have the embarrassment of waiting for him

alone. As it was, she was even earlier, and she quietly sipped a sweet Martini spritzer as he approached. His gut was telling him that it was time to rekindle an old flame, still glowing in the depths, but definitely not extinguished: his head was advising caution. His heart had not been heard from, and would no doubt tip the balance one way or another. He sat down facing her. A waiter quickly presented and then disappeared in search of a fruit juice and another Martini.
"Long time no see, Annabelle."
"It was good of you to come."
"I am intrigued."
"Why so?"
"Why me and why now?"
She smiled. She was every bit as attractive as he remembered. The eyes, just a hint off pure ebony, reflected the light like polished crystal. Her hair was short, just as he had remembered, and beautifully cut. The earrings fell to her neck to accentuate the lovely sharp lines of her face of porcelain. The lips were shining with passion, again just as he remembered.

His gut was settling with familiarity, his head had gone quiet and he could feel his heart stirring restlessly.

"I needed someone to talk to."
The waiter came with the drinks and she quickly moved ground, almost as if she was playing for time and more evidence to arrive, before she presented her case.
"I was sorry to hear about your Mum, how is she?"
"She seems to be recovering well, thanks. It was a nasty pneumonia by all accounts, and as you may recall, she isn't in the best of health."
Another waiter appeared with the starters.
"I hope you don't mind I ordered your favourite. Prawn pil pil," she offered with a casual lack of concern.
"Anyway, she seems a lot better than she was, though it's too soon to say. What are you doing with yourself now, Annabelle?"

"I left nursing soon after we got married. I decided to become a pharmaceutical representative, I work for Glaxo in their respiratory division."

"Funny, I haven't seen you in surgery."

"Actually, I was promoted pretty quickly to the hospital accounts. I cover the hospitals and most of my territory lies to the North around Manchester and Preston."

"Do you enjoy your work?"

"It pays well, nice car, flexible working, private health, - the works. It can be a bit frustrating, as most doctors these days ask you how much, long before they ask you how good. The consultants don't have the same concerns, as they know the GPs have to pick up the tab from their budgets, so we usually lavish a bit more care and attention on the consultants, who soak it all up. Usually after ten or fifteen minutes they're eating out of my hand. As you know, generic drugs are eroding our sales but we're fighting back with new products and of course the new devices."

"Ah yes. Wondered where I'd heard those words before," he said as he realised for the first time just how calculating she could be, and how she welcomed the chance to manipulate others.

"OK so it's the company line, but it also happens to be true. Well, my figures have been increasing nicely and I should be due for promotion soon, moving on to the really big accounts like the teaching hospitals and having reps. under my wing. I'm taking delivery of a new Mercedes next week."

"I'm pleased it has gone so well for you," he offered sincerely, but an alarm bell was ringing deep within almost as if a ship's Captain were being alerted to treacherous waters.

"From a professional sense, yes."

Her pause signalled that she was ready for a return to the questions that he really wanted to ask, the long acrylic nails with the dark finish tapping expectantly upon the table. She delayed a little longer by asking him politely about his work and telling him how she had heard that he was now a full partner.

She paused again, waiting for him to come to the business in hand. She wanted to get things underway.

He obliged, this time, right on cue. “Now then where was I? Ah yes, why me and why now?”
She looked just a little obsequiously at him, as she leant in toward him. “Why you, is the easy one to answer. You do know that I've never loved anyone else.”
“And Peter?”
She produced a sorrowful look for his inspection. “We gave the marriage a really good try. I thought that it was Peter I loved, but I realised four years into our marriage that I was wrong. I haven’t missed a day thinking of you," she offered by way of complete reassurance of any doubts he may still have had. “I simply made a mistake. At first, I thought that I could pretend. Then I realised that I couldn't live a lie all my life. I deserve a life too. Eventually Peter realised what was beneath the pretence, and I just had to be honest with him and with myself.”

The ebony sparkled in the candlelight. His heart was waking to the gentle tones that had been absent for years, but still remembered, as if it were yesterday. She reached forward to touch his hand. Her touch still electrified him as the fingers closed around his palm firmly. He told himself later, that the only thing that could have been responsible for saving him was the waiter as he set down the main course. The hand was withdrawn to make way for the plates. Suddenly, the gentle mesmerism was shattered and his head insisted on one last line.
“So you simply made a mistake?”
“Yes, it’s that easy.”

Ultimately, the thing that really saved Smith that night was not some cool calculation, much beloved by Annabelle, but the fact that he was able to put himself in another person’s shoes and see things from their perspective.
“How has Peter taken all this?”
“You know Jim, he's married to his work. He's spent so long aiming for his consultant’s post that I think he has forgotten I'm here.”

"I can't believe that Annabelle, I think he has always loved you. Though it might not have been what I wanted to see, I couldn't deny what you had was real. Or so I thought. Have the three of us been wrong these past five years?"

There it was: the words that he spoke offered much more than a summary of the relationships that existed between the three of them, as clarity presented for the first time in five years. He realised that he had always been an outsider looking in at another's marriage, and this, unequivocally was where he should remain. Replacing Peter was the last thing that he should consider. He realised, in that moment, that he could not, and would not, attempt to turn the clock back.
"What happens if you wake up tomorrow and realise that it's me that's been the mistake?"
"I love you James."
"What happens to Peter?"
"I've been completely honest with him. I have not suddenly done this on a whim," she offered hastily, as she realised that this held more truth than she could admit, even to herself. "I made a mistake. Are you to punish me, and yourself, for all time because of that? We can be happy."

How he had longed to hear the words that flowed easily now, just like the wine. His heart was ready to accept her words, forgive and forget the past five years, but his head had awakened from its uncertainty and was issuing a warning that could not be ignored.
"Annabelle. You knew how I felt about you." The words he spoke had seemed so clear and so obvious, but at their first utterance in five years, he realised that such thoughts had long expired and he had been clinging to them more out of habit than genuine emotion.
"Can you not forgive me now? Anyone can make a mistake Jim?"

A mistake it may be, but this one was loaded with wreckage. He realised in those moments that he could not do to Peter, what Peter and Annabelle had done to him.

"Forgive me, Annabelle. You know I loved you more than life. You know I would have given anything to have you Annabelle, but things have moved on for me, and it's too late now to simply walk back into my life, as if the past five years aren't there."
"Are you punishing me?"
"No, how could I ever do a thing like that to someone I loved so much? I am saving you from possibly your second hasty decision."
"What do you mean?"
"I'm simply saying that time has moved on, and what seems right for you now, is no longer right for me. I am sorry. Five years has been a long time. I'm a very different person now, and to simply take up where we left off, just won't work."
"I know it will."
"I know that I would be lying to you and to myself. I am sorry, but you know that this particular bridge must come from both sides, if it's ever to meet."
"We can make it meet. Come back with me now and I will show you." Her eyes glowed now with unmistakeable sensual intent. His heart raced along with a passion that was now almost palpable in the space between them.
"I am sorry."

She realised, at that moment, that his mind was made up. She was used to changing men's minds: it just needed the right stimulus.
"Is there someone else?"
"There hasn't been anyone else since the day you left."
She paused as she rapidly gauged whether that could possibly be true; she knew that then, as always, he had no reason to lie.
"We can give it a try. You have nothing to lose"
"No," Smith realised at that moment that he had everything to lose, "what we had, belongs firmly in the past, and I won't go back, just to see if we have something or not. I am sorry."

Voices had risen to such a degree that they were well within the involuntary eavesdropping range. He did his best to whisper. "You must decide what is right for you and for Peter, as of this moment.

I can only say that I am not part of that equation. Forgive me. The person who loved you ever so much, started to be someone else five years ago and he has kept on changing since then."
"You are the man I now know I fell in love with all those years ago, and I realise I have not changed."
"Forgive me Annabelle."

As always the simple words spoken sincerely, as those chestnut eyes looked steadily toward her, conveyed more meaning than sentences could. She knew them to be true and unequivocal. She continued to appeal to his heart, but the head was now firmly in control. At last she accepted that there was no future for them. The ebony still sparkled in the ambient light, but was strangely distant. His heart protested deep from within, but his head would not be dissuaded. They finished their meal in near silence, with just the occasional polite word. Though they left the restaurant together, they had never been so far apart. Each knew that their parting hug would be the last they would ever see of each other. As he sat in his car, he felt as if a spell had been lifted from him. He felt tired and deflated, yet he knew, finally, that the irksome doubt and feeling of loss had been expunged at last.

As he drove home, even his heart lay ready to accept that he had done the right thing. He left the car, as usual, on the drive. As he entered his small but well-kept house, he noticed a message blinking on the answerphone with its usual annoying frequency, which seemed to make it harder to ignore. He pressed the button and was surprised to hear Melanie's voice. He remembered that he had given her his home number for use only in an emergency. Her improving condition rendered this possibility remote, but nevertheless, he listened attentively.

"Hi, it's Melanie here. Please forgive me for disturbing you at home. It's just that the meeting has been put back until 12:30. I hope you will be able to come. I'm sure you are very busy, as usual, so I will understand if you can't make it."

Though it was late, he knew that she would still be up. He hesitated for a few seconds then tapped out her number, which had somehow stuck in his memory though he could not think why.

"Hello?"
"Hi, it's James here. Thanks for the message. I hope you don't mind me phoning you at home? I thought that you would still be up."
"You know me, still working on my speech for tomorrow."
"So, how is it coming together? I have some good naval speeches I could pass by you?"
"No, I don't believe that England will be expecting me to do my duty, just yet; but keep them handy in case I get thrown out and need a new direction."
"Do you think there is the chance of that?"
"Always, James, always that possibility. Newman has been working on all of them, promising them anything, to get them to side with him. I hope that some revelation will appear, between now and the dawn. I've been trying to write this for days. I think that I'm just going to have to fly by the seat of my pants and hope that it will be enough."
"After what I have seen in the past few weeks I'm sure that it will be more than enough."
"That is so kind of you to say that, Doctor."

Her mind was working furiously on a difficult dilemma. How to ask the one question that was of overriding importance, yet so that it appeared only as a polite enquiry or a throw-away remark. In a way it was even harder to place via the telephone than at a face-to-face conversation. Only the tone of her words and of course her breathing could give her away. She controlled the urge to take a deep inspiration, and instead made sure that the breaths were slow and shallow, yet not so as to interrupt the words that she hoped would appear devoid of any moment at all. Eventually she settled for a simple, uncomplicated strategy.
"Nice evening?"

He hesitated for a few moments, almost as if not quite certain what to say, in case he was about to realise he had made a terrible error with Annabelle and that he should phone her at once. However, in that split second, he knew that second thoughts did not apply.
"Yes, in a way: I think I may have laid a ghost to rest."

Her next problem was not to appear too delighted. Once again she wrestled with breath and with tone. Her instinct was to give out a shout of delight and then rush round to inform his mother, but both actions would have to be firmly repressed. Again, the more simple the better, she decided.
"Oh Really. How do you mean?"
"You remember the girl in the photo?"
She hesitated deliberately. "Oh, Oh yes at the surgery?"
"I had a rendezvous with an old flame that I think had been refusing to go out for all this time. It's funny, just when the chance comes to kindle that flame, I decide that it's much too late and no longer what I want. Fickle we men aren't we?"
"More than you realise," she interjected, with feeling.
"Anyway, I was pleased that I went, and it was certainly nice to see her again, but I think that this will be the last. It's funny how things can come into sharp relief at a moment's notice and without the slightest hint of the trigger that will bring it about."
Again she chose her words with care.
"Well, if you're pleased at the outcome, then so am I."
"I'd better let you get back to your speech. Sorry to bend your ear, Melanie."
"Come now, bend *my* ear Doctor? After all you've been through with me. Don't give it another thought."
"Goodnight. And if I don't catch you before the meeting, good luck for tomorrow."
"Thanks, I will do my best."

She replaced the handset and permitted herself that quick skip round the room like a little girl being told that she really would be getting a pony for Christmas. She wondered whether it would be too late to phone the ward. Midnight – yes, perhaps, that would be unwise. Never mind, she was sure she could get a message through first thing, or better still, she would visit as soon as possible, even before her denouement with Newman.

As Smith sat down, he was only aware of an inner peace, which seemed to complement his tiredness. Neither party had realised that the responses, so delicately teased out, had been ones that he was most happy to divulge. His head rested on the back of the armchair as he put his feet up. Melanie was now far too excited for sleep. Her mind was racing, but none of her thoughts seemed to be compatible with her need to write the speech of her life. Mrs Perkins too, would have been incapable of sleep, had she known. For the first time in many months, Melanie could not wait for the dawn light to infiltrate her study window as she made herself comfortable on the settee. As each slept in typical, yet uncomfortable situations they could have been forgiven for forgetting completely about the prophecy that they were now determined with confidence to beat. Each should have realised that confidence was a fragile thing, especially when preceded by complacency.

Mrs Perkins slipped in with new-found silence. Of late, she had found Melanie asleep in a number of different places, only one of which was her bedroom. She had therefore grown accustomed to a game of hide-and-seek, to locate her somnolent employer so that she could prepare breakfast and get on with her daily routines without disturbing her totally unpredictable sleep pattern. As she entered the kitchen slowly and quietly, Melanie was already pouring her second cup of coffee.
"Morning Mrs P. Have I got something to tell you! Let me get you a cup of coffee." She sat her down, the excitement clearly in evidence and told her quickly of the events of the previous evening. Mrs Perkins listened thoughtfully and carefully. She tried her best to introduce a note of caution, rather than a bucket of cold water.
"Just be careful, Miss. You know these men don't seem to know their own minds when it comes to women. All their resolutions

and definite 'it's all overs' seem to evaporate, at the first hint of a short skirt and low neckline."
Melanie was almost surprised at the penetrating insight into the average male's behaviour, but she found herself nodding in agreement, before incredulity could gain a foothold. Obviously men hadn't changed in the least since Mrs Perkins's time!
"That gives me a good idea Mrs P. Thanks."

Without further comment, Melanie disappeared upstairs. It was going to be an important day. Her first stop was the hospital. Melanie knew that Mrs Smith would be interested to know the outcome of the date the night before and the old lady was delighted to hear the news. Of far more importance, however, was the fact that Melanie did not seem able to hide her delight also. Such a double delight, she had not realised she would witness.
"He's seeing sense at last. After what she did to him, then to have the audacity to phone him up and then tell him it was all a mistake. It takes the biscuit."
Melanie was always surprised to see this elderly woman with such a frail body unleash such powerful emotions from a brain that had obviously not deteriorated at all over the past years.
"Melanie he needs someone better than that. These recent years he has been living in the past. You told me he found a photo of her and put it in his surgery. I bet it had been there all along and may be had just been moved for dusting or reframing or something equally horrible."
Melanie smiled as she wondered just what that might be, but nodded along as the elderly lady was in full flow.
"Melanie, are there no friends of yours who you could introduce him to. Don't tell him of course and certainly don't say it was my idea."
"Well I don't know. I'm sure I could think of one or two who would jump at him. What's his type?"
"Someone a bit like you."

Years of careful study of people's reactions, their emotions as well as one's own, had been needed just to deliver that one tiny sentence. If a less skilled person had brought it forward, it would have sounded clumsy and contrived. As it was, it was delivered perfectly. The face was kept completely neutral, the voice very matter of fact and her eyes unwavering without any hint of a hidden meaning. The younger woman was a little taken aback by the directness and the clinical nature of the words, but she recovered quickly.

"Thank you for that, at least it gives me an idea of who to look for, Edith."

"Now that he's settled, he needs someone in his life. Has he mentioned his naval history yet?"

"No, only something about naval speeches."

"When he's not at work he's either reading about or constructing models of famous British warships. I think he'd marry his model of HMS Victory, if they'd let him."

"Fascinating," was the only word that sprang to Melanie's mind. "I didn't know that was his main hobby."

"He needs a bit more in his life, not those dust collectors and bygone triumphs that this country will never see again, I expect."

"Leave it to me Mrs Smith. I'll do my very best to introduce him to someone who will be suitable. I will be discreet, have no fear on that score," she interjected with new-found solemnity. As she walked down the corridor both women permitted themselves a girlish smile. Mrs Smith was delighted with the meeting, and could only repeat to herself what a lovely girl she was, and that she would do nicely for her son any day of the week. For her part, Melanie was assembling ideas very quickly, and each day brought fresh insight into the man; a surprise each day.

She was going to have to hurry, if she was to reach the airport in time.

CHAPTER XI

"MEETING"

Donald McDonald, non-executive chairman, stood at the head of the table. Newman had been there early, anxious to get on with things. He could see no reason for the delay. Melanie had still not put in an appearance. No doubt she was simply putting off the inevitable. Perhaps she was not even going to bother to attend. Rich, bitch, what did she need it for anyway: his plans had come together nicely, much better than he had dared hope. For all those years he had been on a pittance, a measly one hundred and fifty thousand pounds per annum, and all the work he'd put in, while these rich bastards had lived off his endeavours and the sweat of his brow, with their high minded ideas and posh look-down-one's-nose-at-you manner. It was time for all this to change, and time for him to reap the rewards that were now his for the taking. Twenty-five million dollars should be more than enough, but only what he was worth. The Americans had seen it, and he was going to make sure he delivered it to them lock stock and barrel, and to hell with everyone else. Funny how that conniving little bitch had guessed that they would close it all, and ship it Stateside as soon as she was out of the way. Her illness had given him the perfect opportunity to finish her, and she had played into his hands nicely, by asking for this meeting. How she would wish she had never come back.

Just as McDonald looked at his watch, Melanie's car came to a stop in her usual space, the front end dipping with a slight squeal from the tyres as they halted such a weight in so short a distance. McDonald looked as Melanie and Stella got out of the car. Melanie had diverted to collect Stella, who had flown in so that she could lend Melanie her support. Newman was surprised to see her, especially as he had deliberately tried to exclude her from the meeting. In any event it would make little difference to the outcome. Newman looked at Smith, with his stupid smile, his cheap shoes and even cheaper suit, as he wondered just why he had been invited. As a non-shareholder he had no authority to be at the meeting, but Newman had dismissed him as an irrelevance and certainly a lightweight; so typical of one of Melanie's friends, a nonentity, like her, and thus he did not lodge an objection with the chairman.

Smith sat impassively watching the people slowly arrive. He wondered how so many could have been duped by Newman. None of them looked especially gullible, and he could only wonder what they had been promised. Newman had certainly had many months to work on them, and from what he had seen in the past few weeks, he had used this time purely for his own advantage. Smith recognised a determined, yet aggressive personality, he had seen precisely this type before, and he had learned to recognise such a person's *modus operandi.* A little shiver ran down his spine as he remembered, from his own experience, that such people resorted, readily, to violence and destruction, especially when they did not get their own way, and that they were prepared to use any method, and sacrifice anyone in order to secure victory.

McDonald began, his gruff Scottish burr resonating around the room.

"As we are now all here. I hereby convene this extraordinary meeting. We have two motions to consider today, ladies and gentlemen. The first from Mr Newman, is to remove Melanie Jardine as director, and for the company to purchase her shares at par value. The second, also from Mr Newman is for the subsequent sale of majority shareholding to Warner Deville of Atlanta, whose offer, I understand is ten pounds per share."

An excited chatter ran round the room as the true value of the offer from Warners was disclosed to the assembly. Newman looked triumphant, and Melanie looked anxiously at Smith and Stella, perhaps the only two other people in the room who had not been impressed by the offer.

"Firstly I would like to call upon Brian Newman to speak, and then Miss Jardine would like to present her views."

Newman stood up.
"Thanks for coming everyone. I want to make this brief and to the point. As you know it's now well over twelve months since Melanie's father, Douglas, and her elder sister, Patricia, were tragically killed. I would like to extend my condolences to Melanie for her loss, which I am sure must have affected her terribly."
The unaccustomed words from Newman had an oleaginous, insincere tone to Melanie and to Stella. The others nodded in unison, but Melanie could see through the thin veil of polite preamble, which had been placed there only as a foil for what she knew would be coming next.

"Since then this company has been marking time. We have exciting new products coming out, but we will fail if we don't get them to market with sufficient backing. The company needs to move forward, not remain stuck in the past. Warners are prepared to buy into our company in a big way, and provide the investment we need to progress and to get our products in the market place. We are all aware, Melanie, that we cannot force you to give up your shares, and allow them to be purchased for the good of the company and, not forgetting, all its hard-working employees, who have given selflessly to this business during your protracted and, of course, sad absence. I know that I am now speaking for many who feel that the ship has been rudderless for too long, with no clear purpose and no true direction. I know, too, that I speak for many who would rather walk out now, than have the present situation continue. We therefore ask for a majority vote for the two recommendations put before you by Mr Chairman."

Newman sat down in triumph. Many clapped, some cheered, whilst others simply nodded. Only three were silent. Even the chairman seemed to be with the Newman camp. Melanie thought quickly and assessed the situation without making a move. So that was it. They could not force her to sell her shares to anyone. She still controlled more than any other person. Newman had offered them the carrot of untold riches if they sold out to Warners. Some of them would become very wealthy overnight, one or two millionaires. The thinly veiled threat presented by Newman was now obvious. If she did not accept the buy-back of her shares, key personnel would withdraw their services. No doubt there would be a mass resignation. Newman had timed things well. A little later, and the production lines would be rolling. Any earlier, would have given Melanie a chance to bring others in, but a delay of this magnitude, at this stage, would be catastrophic, and Newman was fully aware of this. This is why he had done his best to disable Ward. The company still owned the patents, but it would be in the hands of the receiver within weeks and especially so, with no other significant products to fall back on. The question of who then owned those patents, would be academic as far as the receiver would be concerned. They would be sold to the highest bidder, and Warners would almost certainly pick them up. She could attempt to stop them, even at that late stage, but any victory would be more pyrrhic than otherwise, and would cost a fortune.

Newman had judged correctly, but for entirely the wrong reasons, that Melanie would not stand in the way of the views of the majority and nor would she want to commit her own personal funds to a risky, face-saving venture simply in order to salvage her own pride. There were one or two holes in his delicate web of deceit, and she was going to have to drive a wedge right through them, if she were to have any chance of success. Melanie smiled to herself and risked a quick glance in Smith's direction. It was perhaps opportune that she had been unable to concentrate for long enough to complete the address that she had planned to make: as this is where she would have had to tear it up and simply tell them something of her thoughts. She stood as an unbowed warrior, who was prepared to fight to the finish for just cause, determined to look each and every one firmly in the eye.

As always she remained tall and erect, but on that day something else, something that was hard to quantify, would flow strongly with the young woman, and whether they would later refer to it as gravitas, charisma, allure or even simple plain, common-sense, all in the room would be aware of it, and the effect it would have on each of them.

The momentary pause became almost as a gap in time, so aware and so curious the people she faced. They waited, hardly daring even to breathe, or so it seemed, as she was about to start speaking. Each person in her audience shared the heightened sense of awareness, rather like that final moment of tension in the atmosphere just before a tropical storm breaks with devastating effect: the room was hushed almost to the point of precipitation, water into ice, cloud into rain, as she started to speak.

"Many thanks for giving me an opportunity to explain my point of view. Brian has raised a couple of points, and I would like to take a look at those, but I would like to begin by clarifying exactly where the company is at this point in time, so that there can be no mistake in anyone's mind."

A few seconds later, images from her laptop were in focus on the large screen.
"These are our sales predictions for the 3D Video card."
A line graph appeared on screen as it was fed from the computer.
"Figures show sales for the next twelve months. I'm now going to superimpose a bar graph showing sales revenue for the chips for the same period. You can see that projected sales are looking very healthy. Despite our competitive price, we are still able to maintain a generous margin. As we are, perhaps, the first manufacturer to contemplate production in such large numbers, we should corner the market if we can stick to a prompt delivery. Please note that I have deliberately chosen conservative estimates. I expect that actual sales under more realistic market conditions would increase these figures by at least a factor of two."
The intense silence remained unbroken as she continued. The key personnel had known about the new products for some months, but not the likely scale of their success.
"Let me now turn to the solid state disc, the SSD, we know by the name of 'Lightdrive'. I will show equivalent sales in numbers on

the line graph for the next twelve months, and the bar will show equivalent sales revenues. Again, these figures have been deliberately kept on the pessimistic side. I would expect a similar increase under actual market conditions. Let me now combine the two into one bar graph."
The two graphs were instantly summed as she clicked her laser pointer. An involuntary gasp came from the audience as they realised the true moment of sales within their grasp.

"No matter how good our products, they are doomed to fail if we cannot guarantee compatibility with existing, so-called industry-standard hardware and software. Several months ago we placed samples of our new products with giants in the industry; our new SSD is placed perfectly. Conformance testing went very well and they are now prepared to endorse our products as being one hundred percent compatible. Cooling is not an issue as heat output is negligible."

Melanie knew that modern demand for the storage and retrieval of vast amounts of data had brought about the need for huge arrays of file-serving computers, stacked row upon row and column against column and each and every one of these would produce enough heat to damage the one next to it, if significant cooling was not provided and allowed for.

"The 3D video card has been tested by some of the larger games suppliers and we have had it tested against some industry standards such as 'Crysis 3' and so on. Even though we are optimised for 3D performance, we are still beating the industry giants, with frame rates that our competitors cannot match. Several hardware manufacturers want the option of including our drives and chips into their products. Once widely accepted, the vastly improved specification of computers with our bits in them will allow a cut in price, an increase in performance, yet an increase in manufacturers' margins. "All in all, the future is looking pretty bright, provided you make the right decisions today."

A carefully judged pause followed, so that the full impact of her words could fall upon her audience, who were still spellbound in a quiet rapture.
"Let's now take a look at Warner Deville. I am sure that you all know that we are talking of a very big company in comparison with ours. If you would permit me to show you what happened after their two most recent takeovers. Firstly SG Laupin of Toulouse. They were swallowed up last summer. The patents which they filed in respect of the quad speed drives were taken over by Warners. Production was transferred to the States and today Laupin is nothing more than a bridgehead and assembly plant for American-made drives. A very similar thing happened last year to IG Teknick of Wilhelmshaven. Again Warners bought in, patents were stripped out, and the place was closed a month ago with the loss of one thousand jobs. I am not sure what guarantees you have secured, Brian, from Warners, but I would be grateful if you would explain them to these good people."

Silence followed as Newman stared at her, the black eyes darker than usual as he seethed with malign intent.

"Brian has put Warners' offer to you all, but if you could look at some of my sales projections, those of you in this room with equity in our business will be very, very wealthy, without selling to Warners, and we can continue to employ local people and give them much needed jobs."

More silence, as Newman looked at her with a view to doing serious harm to her, if he could just get her hands on her when alone. She used that silence to underline her point.
"I see; perhaps, there are personal guarantees then, that you have been able to secure?"

He remained capable of a sham of pleasantry only when things were going his way. As soon as things began moving away from him, his core of hatred and menace would be quickly exposed like thick rust hastily painted over. His expression of sheer hatred was now plainly visible on the face that had simple reverted to type.

"I would venture that the patents we do have, are the real reason why Warners want us so badly. I am not sure whether interest runs any further than that, and if they remain true to form we will all be retiring richer but somewhat sooner than we had anticipated. As for the workforce; they will retire to a dole queue from secure, interesting, and worthwhile employment. From taking on the world with a genuinely innovative British product, they will be taking on a UB40."

Anger that she couldn't quite master now rose within her as the normally warm glow in her eyes turned to steel as she looked directly at him.

"Just how much did it take, Brian for you to sell them out?"

Psychologists often talk of the constructive use of anger, to clarify a situation, to illuminate, for all to see, the correct path that lay ahead, and also to allow exposure of a mountebank as his true self. All these forces came into being with that flush of unrestrained anger that she now managed to confront and control. A ripple ran round the room as her normal composure returned, as they finally saw Newman in his true colours, and Melanie in hers.

"Let me now transport you twelve months hence if we remain independent. Warners and others will have done their best to create products similar to ours. We hope that it will take them longer than this, but we do not know what advantages they have gained."

Once again, the look fired at Newman was one of unbridled distaste. A slight pause followed to make sure that her audience had heard and understood the points she placed before them, and grasped the facts that flowed with her eloquent, relaxed and fluent delivery.

"What new developments do we anticipate over the next twelve months?"

This time she looked expectantly in the direction of Alastair Jones and Tony Newton. “Could you give us some idea of what we have in store?”
Both men stood, with equal measure of embarrassment and dejection.
“Nothing I am afraid Melanie,” came from Jones, and, “Nothing we could market,” came from Newton.

She smiled re-assuringly. The gathering was now her orchestra and she had become the conductor, her timing, perfection itself.
“Sunrise companies like ours survive on new products. You don't need me to tell you that if we do not bring these forward on a regular basis, then we do not survive. Please don't misunderstand me. Our planned releases will make every one of us very rich. If that is all that interests you, then we might as well sell to Warners and retire to the Bahamas. Those of you who are looking forward to a greater challenge then please remain seated.

“I have invited ten investors, who wish to advance one hundred thousand pounds, each to our company as part of the Enterprise Investment scheme. Their interest will be pure capital gain, linked to a tax-free investment. They will charge no interest and receive no equity whatsoever. The million pounds so raised should be injected purely into R&D and assist our two boffins to improve and bring on new products over the next twelve to twenty-four months.”

Jones and Newton were roused from their dejected state into a firm nodding approval.
She switched off the projector, restored the erect posture as she straightened and moved to the front, eclipsing the screen. The chairman slowly drew back the curtains to let the brilliant sunshine return.

“This is your company; you could say that I have no part of it. I can see that to many of you I must come across, almost, as a stranger, and that most of you have not had the chance to work with me and perhaps get to know me; and the reason for this is entirely of my making. I realise that the trust that I am asking that you now place in me, normally takes years to build and to justify. If it is your wish that I walk from here, today, without ever returning, then that is exactly what will happen. My father and Trish and you, have cared for this company with passion and flair; they and you have made it what it is today. I am not going to attempt to tell you that I know that I can do as well as they, in managing this firm, but I am going to ask for a chance to try. This company is capable of a great many things. We are on the verge of a breakthrough that will rank along with many other great British inventions. All I ask is that you give due consideration to what you have heard, and if you would like to hear more, then you have a chance to vote accordingly. If you prefer Brian's scenario, then I am prepared to throw in my shares at par, and I will walk away with good grace."

As she sat down, her confidence and composure suddenly gave way to an inner, uncontrollable nervousness. She struggled to control her legs lest they start flapping beneath her chair, and her eyes darted quickly round the room from face to face. She looked at Smith. He mouthed the word, "wow" in her direction and smiled, not that caring smile that she had seen on numerous occasions, but a smile that revealed much more from that calm façade. She wondered if he realised how his skills, his words and his very presence had catalysed the change within her, and how he had helped her to navigate through waters that she had previously regarded as impassable, even before her illness.

Some looked surprised, some relieved, others betrayed, as if the faulty promises expounded by Newman had been exposed for the cruel deception they really were. Two were beaming at her. Stella suddenly got to her feet and started clapping with gusto, followed an instant later by Smith. Others joined in until the wave reverberated round the room. Stella managed a quick wink as she glanced, and Smith a mixture of pride and sheer delight. Newman looked as if the Angel of Death had found him and now sat squarely upon his shoulders. The chairman rose.

"Thank you for that, Melanie. We have two motions before us. Perhaps we could have a simple show of hands and then move on to a ballot if required. Firstly for motion one, to remove Melanie Jardine as director of Jectronics."

Melanie was afraid to look round the room. Something told her that she must do so, and words beloved by her father and appropriate for moments like these came to her at that instant. 'Face the fear, or it will overwhelm you.' As she nervously looked up she could see that no hands had been raised. She could not bring herself to look at Newman who sat impassively at the corner of her vision. Had she looked in his direction she would have witnessed him seething with anger and malice. After a few moments delay the chairman asked for a show of hands for the second motion. Hands remained firmly by people's sides. The room was silent. Newman hung his head as he contemplated his shattered dreams that had come to nought.

"Have you anything to say?" McDonald looked expectantly in Melanie’s direction and then at Newman. Newman remained almost catatonic, as if all power of movement had been used up, alongside the unravelling of his corrupt and evil plans. Melanie rose slowly but her confidence already showing through.

“Brian has already indicated that he no longer wishes to work with me. I would ask you to consider two amendments. Firstly that Mr Newman be removed as director of this company, that his shares be bought back at par and retained for the good of the company, and secondly that I be appointed as Managing Director, CEO."

McDonald, sensing the mood in the assembled personnel, lost no time in asking for a show of hands for each of the two amendments. Solemnly, but firmly, a forest of hands appeared for each. Melanie beamed triumphantly. People at last sought a break in the sober proceedings, and clapped and rushed up to congratulate Melanie. Only Newman remained seated, still frozen as his mind feverishly sought a means of redressing the balance even at this late stage. A sense of loss turned into frustration and soon to anger, which in turn brought out the violence, to which he resorted readily to settle matters that had gone against him. Without warning he shot out of his chair, with the anger fuelling his threat of unrestrained madness.

As he rose, Melanie sensed the impending danger. She reached for the phone and asked for security to escort Newman from the building. Newman's wild frenzy intensified even as she replaced the handset. His eyes glared with unchecked ferment as he screamed at her.

" You conniving little bitch, it should have been your car that went off the road. If I can't have it, then there won't be anything worth having. I'll see you in hell!"

Newman charged out of the room, his brain finally unhinged by the events. He pushed people out of his way with new-found strength, arising from his mania. He disappeared into the fileserver room and barricaded the door. Like all the rooms which faced the stairwell, its walls were made of armoured glass to allow entry of natural light and create a bright, open space around the large spiral staircase.

They could only look impotently at his every move. Smith had managed to work his way round to Melanie's side of the table in the commotion.

"Melanie, what's the significance of the fileserver?"

"Unfortunately the file server has a download of all the production schematics for our two new products. We finalise them on the computer and then pass them over to production: without those we will be weeks behind."

"Do you not keep backups?"

"Oh yes, indeed we do, but unfortunately they are locked in a fireproof safe in the same room. Guess who has a key?"

Newman started with the fileserver by throwing it round the room and jumping up and down on its metal casing. The delicate hard discs inside were comprehensively disrupted. Then came the even more fragile back-up tapes, which Newman ripped apart with his hands. His mounting frenzy disturbing but strangely compelling, as they continued to watch.
Smith looked at Melanie with open mouthed horror. "It looks really bad then."
"Well that depends. Did you keep those little plastic boxes that I gave you, safe?"
"Ah those. You told me that they were really valuable and I only managed to sell them on e-bay for five pounds, for the two. Hardly covered my postage."

"You know, Doctor Smith, that the tabloids are always looking for juicy 'human interest' stories, though they do prefer a good bout of violence, I think. How about," as she scribed the air with her hand as if reading a headline, "'*Family doctor slain by crazed businesswoman.*'"
"Well, now that you put it in that way I'll just have to see if I can fish them out of the postbox at the end of my road?"

Stella arrived and gave Melanie a hug.
"I knew that you would do it. Melanie I am proud of you."
"Thanks Stella, I wasn't sure until the final show of hands."
"You were magnificent. You really showed them. Talk about a chip off the old block. I just knew you had it in you."
Melanie went silent as she considered the heartfelt words.
"Thanks for that," as she squeezed Stella.

Eventually the security men managed to extract Newman from the fileserver room. The floor was strewn with a twisted mass of metal, of plastic and tape. He had done his best to destroy everything he could lay hands on. They led him away to await the arrival of the Police. His frenzied efforts had left him temporarily exhausted, the security men relaxed their grasp momentarily. It was enough for him to break free and take a mad lunge in

Melanie's direction. Smith blocked the move quickly and firmly. As he screamed forward, Smith aimed a sharp blow to his larynx. He collapsed on the floor gasping for air, and now completely disabled. Smith ushered Melanie away with Stella, as Newman continued to choke and splutter. "You haven't seen the last of me, you stupid bitch."

Melanie looked up at Smith, stunned by the speed of his reaction and the thoroughness of his reply. Smith looked a little embarrassed.
"Sorry about that Melanie, I thought that there was no telling what he might do. It will only disable him for a few minutes and I didn't hit him very hard."
"Not at all Doctor, please don't apologise, we all know how you spent your youth," as she wondered, and not for the first time, exactly what sort of youth that was.
He looked more embarrassed than ever and the blush spread outwards from his ears and over his face.
"It must have been just a lucky punch."
"One that I am so grateful that you made. I don't know what he would have done to me had he reached me."

Stella changed the subject quickly. "How about a celebration tonight? Dinner for three at Delphinos?"
"I'd rather not at Delphinos, if that's OK? How about Fuscardi's," he suggested.
"My favourite," said Stella with her most alluring tones, as she almost purred in Smith's direction.
"I'll pick you both up. You at 7:45 Stella, and you at 8:00. Is that OK?" Melanie suggested, both nodded in agreement. Smith looked at his watch.
"I'd better dash. I've got more visits to do. See you later madam MD," he interposed.
The two women looked on as he dashed off down the stairs and out to the car park. "Did you see that, Melanie, Smith moved like lightening."

"Wow, yes, I don't think Newman knew what had happened to him."
Melanie linked Stella, as she often did when wanting to put something by her. "When you get back off your holiday we need to have a long chat. It seems that courtesy of Mr Newman, who I hope will be taking up a completely different set of pastimes, we have a pretty important and senior vacancy. I wonder if you'd care to step into his shoes, Stella? Everyone likes you, everyone trusts you, and I'm sure they can't think more highly of you; and neither could I. I know, too, that you are more than capable," she confirmed, before Stella's first reaction caused her to reject the upwards move.
"I won't have to go creeping round the place, making secret deals and undermining my boss will I?"
"Not unless you really want to! Please think about it, and we'll talk when you get back off holiday. The other good news I have for you, is that I managed to get you a return flight today. If we leave now we will catch it nicely."

Stella looked carefully at Melanie, as she attempted to detect any flicker of emotion.
She could not help but test her friend. "You just wanted him to yourself. Melanie, you're getting too good at all this underhand dealing."
Melanie's smile said more than words as she squeezed Stella's arm even more enthusiastically.
Eventually she said. "Come now, we can't have Tony waiting for you."
Stella's eyes twinkled with their usual vitality.
A hint of seriousness crept into Melanie's voice.
"I want to thank you for coming off your holiday like this. Your support has meant a lot to me over these past weeks. I couldn't have done it without you."
The twinkle gave way to her beaming smile.
"I wouldn't have missed it for the world, even if you are sending me back a little early."

They both giggled as they made their way out to the car park and found the Jaguar, which had just been returned to Melanie from the body shop. The car started with a quick flick of the key and made its usual steady progress to the airport.

“Thanks once again Stella. I'll see you in a week, and have a think about what I said?”

The mischievous glow returned as Stella said, "I'll be much too busy to think about that. You just concentrate on getting Dr. Smith struck off."

Both laughed again; a quick hug was offered from Stella as she acknowledged the return of her boss and her friend, just before walking through the gate with a hurried wave as her flight was called for the last time.

CHAPTER XII

"EDGE of PASSION"

The Jaguar stopped at his gate. He had been watching through his lounge window and saw the large door slowly open as she carefully swung her legs out, before pulling herself out of the car. It was all executed with smooth precision, bordering on sheer elegance, so typical of her. There was quite an art in getting out of a car, especially one that sat a little low on the road. He couldn't help but wonder if she had had to work at such manoeuvres or if, as it seemed, it all came naturally. He came to the door before she could reach for the bell, which had been broken for some months. He hesitated for a second as his eyes insisted on absorbing the vision in front of him before all else.

To describe it as a quintessential black dress would have been accurate but would not have conveyed the stunning looks, nor the effect it would have on all who would gaze upon her that evening. Like all success stories, it was not isolated excellence in one direction, but carefully struck compromises in different areas that came together to achieve the devastating result. The length was above the knee but not too revealing. It hugged the figure without appearing too tight. The neck was set low so as to enhance the elegance of her bosom, neck and fine-featured face, without appearing meretricious. The design looked expensive, but had an air of simplicity. The cut was sharp and well tailored but softly feminine. The pure, midnight black, with just a shimmer of obsydian seemed to complement perfectly her own colouring. The shoes were a little higher than usual and accentuated, still further, the long, shapely legs, the patent leather shining in the available light. She was without other adornment except for the Omega, as always, on the left wrist, and a breathtaking necklace of emerald-cut diamonds arranged radially, each scintillating, even in the subdued light. Earlier he had seen power-dressing at its best, but now the picture was that of a radiant, sexy and alluring woman, who was at the same time demure. Her confidence shone like the necklace in the evening sun, potentiating her subtle but unmissable poise.

As his brain was engulfed by the vision in front of him, he felt his heart thumping, his mouth drying, and he was now frightened to speak as he could swear that his whole body had begun to tremble, while he could only pray that it was not visible as he anxiously tried to tighten his entire frame. Eventually he did manage words and desperately chose ones that would divert her discerning gaze away from him. “Melanie you look stunning: killer legs,” as he did his best to ensure that an appreciative complimentary look did not transgress to a stare which might also reveal more of his nervousness.

“Why, thank you doctor. I bet you say that to all your patients,” she offered with just a hint of tease, as always modulated by the compelling smile, that was seen so readily these days.
“Not quite Melanie,” he returned, as she gave him a moment whilst embarrassment joined his surging thoughts.
“Actually it’s surprising what a bit of spray-on tan can do to even ordinary legs like mine.”
A word more like ‘extraordinary’ was in his mind. She stood next to him.
“I told you, in my Laboutins I’d be as tall as you.”
“This is only because I'm not wearing my fluffy socks.”
“Nice tie!” she said, as she noticed that he was wearing the tie that she had offered him, in place of the Mini.
“Oh it’s from some old patient of mine. You know we doctors, get given such things all the time.” The simple words of bravado hid the fact that it was one of the nicest things he owned. Indeed, it was one of the nicest things that he had ever owned.
“Spray Tan?”
“Yes, it’s probably safer than the real thing. You doctors are always going on about too much sunbathing. So I have a young chap call round with his airbrush and spray me all over.”
“Wow, some people have such hard jobs.”

“Well, let's just say that his partner, Nigel, doesn’t mind!”
He was aware of the delicate hint of her perfume, which seemed to intoxicate, as he found himself inhaling deeply in an attempt to prolong the experience. He closed the door behind him and walked alongside to the car.

He had seen beautiful women, from afar, but had never seen one in action at such close quarters. He had hitherto been the observer looking in at the chap accompanying the stunning woman, wondering just who he was. On this occasion he was to be in that spotlight. That evening his eyes were to be opened as he witnessed, first-hand, the effect that such a person could have. Like many men, he had never plucked up enough courage to ask a girl he considered unattainable, for a date at school or at University. He had never considered himself handsome enough or wealthy enough or interesting enough, to make such a leap. Annabelle was attractive, but words such as 'gorgeous' and 'ravishing' seemed to exceed an accurate description of her looks. Melanie’s attractiveness had not gone unnoticed, but further analysis had always been blocked by the professional environment under which they met. In addition, his first duty was to her as his patient, as someone in danger of taking her own life, and he accepted fully that he was charged with getting her better, not looking at her hem line. Meeting her in this way, for a purely social occasion, seemed to strip away his professional insulation, leaving him open to the intoxicating spell cast by a truly beguiling woman. Nothing of his previous experience could prepare him for what he was feeling now. He realised that, in comparison, his feelings for Annabelle had been nothing more than a schoolboy crush, as he struggled with surging emotion that would have mastered him had he not clung to the escape strategy, what Psychologists would call ‘displacement’, of reminding himself on more than one occasion that evening that she was a patient and nothing more.

"Could Stella not make it?" he asked curiously.

"No, she forgot that she'd booked a plane straight back. She has a week left, and I think she was keen to rejoin her current boyfriend."
"Current boyfriend. Is she a bit of a man-eater?"
"She does seem to go through them at a fair rate. I suppose she will find someone she wants to settle down with, or he with her, but she's young yet."
"Unlike you, Melanie?" His curiosity deepening all the while, as he endeavoured to gain insight into her thinking.
"I feel as if I have had the weight of the world on my shoulders, and that it's starting to show."
"No, I can't see that person these days, Melanie."
The long fingers played with the CD auto-changer in a familiar pattern so that she had to avert her eyes for only a few seconds while she selected the CD and the track she wanted. He noted that music meant a lot to her, and the tracks she played often reflected the mood she was in, or were even used to convey a message about how she felt. He wondered what tracks she had played in the depths of her depression, and toyed with the idea of asking but thought better of it, rather than disturb one of her favourite tracks.
"I haven't been here in years," he said.
"Not one of your haunts then, James?"
"No, not really: as a junior doctor I was either on call, recovering from being on call or skint. It did wonders for my social life."

The door opened and they stood for a few seconds on the threshold of the restaurant, noting the packed room. The head waiter came up to her and greeted her like a long lost relative, his effusiveness more genuine than contrived, telling her how nice it was to see her again, as he escorted them to the reserved table in the corner. Heads turned as they entered. Some could not help but look, once, twice; some stared and others stopped conversations as they were ushered into the corner table. Smith noted that interest was not only confined to her, but also directed at him. The very act of accompanying her had, in some way, elevated his status, as people were curious to discover which qualities a man would need, to have even a chance of being with such a person. The fact that she was largely oblivious to the turning heads and the curious, seemed only to heighten his own experience.

Guiseppe accompanied them to the table as the flicker running around the room settled, apart from one or two who would be unable to stop themselves from glancing at regular intervals for the whole evening. More heads turned as Luigi, the restaurant owner, insisted on the rare step of coming up to a customer's table to greet a special guest. He too was captivated by the spell, as he laughed and joked with his guests. To Melanie he was ebullient, to Smith there was that mixture of curiosity and envy that he had seen several times that night already. The proprietor could no more have resisted kissing Melanie, once, twice, three times, than gaze at a fireball that had suddenly lit the heavens. He shook them both warmly by the hand, lingered only for as long as was polite, before returning to the kitchen to personally instruct the staff, who were to serve them that evening.

Eventually Smith's curiosity overflowed. "Melanie, do you come here a lot? It's just that you've had such a warm welcome."
"No, not really. Luigi is always polite. We come here occasionally from work and we did have a Christmas 'do' here on one occasion."
Smith's curiosity remained. Waiters came to fuss with menus, drinks and napkins, but soon melted into the background. Smith moved the glass lantern so that its radiated light did not come between them. Once again, subdued lighting seemed to grant dispensation for all that might be asked or stated, and even more importantly, would allow for more than the usual fleeting contact of their eyes.
"So, Melanie, how do you feel now that you have encouraged Newman to take up strawberry picking after all."
"I think the Police will want to feel his collar first. Destruction of the server for a start, the hastily foiled lunge at me, and hopefully a few questions about the two joyriders-with-menace. I think he'll be out of circulation for some time."

"Let's hope so," Smith agreed. "Can they tie him to the two thugs who came after you?"
"I don't suppose they can, definitely. He was, as you could see, angry, so angry, he could argue that he was just lashing out at me but I suspect that when he said, 'it should have been you who went over the edge,' he really had planned for it to be so. The car was stolen and the police are still working on dental records. I'm afraid there was not a lot left of my two pursuers, after being engulfed by the flames."
Sensing deeper waters, "are you okay about this, Melanie?"
"Your intervention helped me so much. Just talking it through, as we did, seemed to calm the whole thing down. I was a nervous wreck. If it hadn't been for you I don't think I would have been able to get back behind the wheel."
"I think that Newman was rather hoping you would not."
"I don't think he had anticipated your expert input. Your timely intervention and counselling skills kept me up and batting. Have you had special counselling training?"
"Not really, but it is an interest of mine. So many people, these days, are under so much stress. It forms a large part of our work, one way or another. Many of the physical illnesses have been conquered. If it wasn't for stress and smoking, I think I'd have my feet up on the desk all day."
"I don't think so, you'd be too busy patrolling the Seabridge estate looking out for needy patients and other deserving causes."
"Talk about deserving causes: your playground is coming on really well. They have got on with it and they've started work on Foden Lodge as well."
"I drive past every few days in my disguise, just to take a look."
"What disguise is that then Melanie?"
"You know my depressive, verge of suicide look."
"I haven't seen that person, for a long time, Melanie."
"I'm told she moved out of town and won't be returning."
"I 'm sure that you're right," he concluded.

Eye contact was held steady under the protection of the subdued lighting. Smith perceived only two deep pools of darkest hazel, which seemed to magnify his nervousness and the battle he faced with his feelings, that he recognised were having more of an impact upon him than he would want to admit even to himself. The eyes were unwavering and seemed to draw strength from the amber flame which flickered between them, as he was aware only of being sucked deeper and deeper under her charming spell. As they continued to talk his eyes too, seemed transfixed by the vision in front of him. Her beauty was not a static artificial image that simply registered upon him, but a vital, fluid thing that impacted on every nerve fibre in his consciousness. Those sparkling eyes that seemed to study his every move, the white even teeth, the soft lustrous lips which looked so sensual and inviting. The delicate fragrance drifting over with her every move, so subtle yet so stimulating. The long delicate fingers that would be used to gently frame her own face as if she were studying each reaction; and the voice with its velvety, rich timbre that was as unmistakeable as it was appealing. Of most significance was the relaxed easy going way in which her qualities flowed with an unrehearsed natural rhythm. This contrasted sharply with Annabelle who had almost deliberately cultivated what qualities she had, in order to use them to bend and shape others to her will. He realised that she had not made a mistake with Peter, she had simply grown tired and wished to move on to other conquests.

As he continued to look at Melanie, just one vital tenet allowed him to retain his sanity in the intoxicating mix that would otherwise have overwhelmed him. She was his patient, the person who in the depths of despair had committed to a sad, uninviting and painful death because of the absolute dominance of despair within her. He had used every ounce of skill, of training and, yes, instinct to rescue her from this unappealing pathway, and the result almost shimmered before him. The vital point, that he had not even dared admit to himself, was how his own presence, his personality and absolute interest in his patient had catalysed that reaction, to make its effect so overwhelming. He told himself that he asked the questions of her simply because he was still keen to distract her from more damaging thoughts, though more dispassionate analysis would conclude that his delight came as much from watching that joyous smile on those pink sparkling lips, as they continued to frame her words with such a delightful voice, as from his heightened awareness of every nuance of emotion as it crossed her face.

"So, then Melanie, you seem to have come so far; all in all, how do you feel?"
"Is this a Truth or Dare?" she asked as the glimmer refused to depart from her face for even a second. She continued, leaving her query hanging, "how do I look, Doctor?"
"You look great, and to answer your question, I suppose it's part truth and part dare!"

Any man would have been forgiven for uttering completely different words at the slight pause that opened, words that might have proclaimed for the whole restaurant to hear about the beguiling woman, in whose company he found himself. It was only by reminding himself again and again of his commitment to his training and to his profession, that he managed to subjugate understandable but dangerous feelings of a more venal nature that surged within him throughout the entire evening. He recognised, as a shiver ran down his spine, that any newspaper from any week would contain at least one story of a doctor who had failed in this regard - and he was determined not to be amongst them.
"You have come a long way, Melanie, in a short space of time. Nasty depressions can take months. I'm not pouring cold water on your circuit board, but please take your time, and don't take on too much stress."
"I promise. This sounds like your 'time to leave speech'."
"No, not at all; you don't get rid of me so quickly. I will expect to see you in my surgery at regular intervals, so that I can keep my beady eye on you. Besides Mrs Farnell has become quite attached to you. She doesn't even bother putting your notes away, so you'd better not disappoint her."

"Try keeping me away. I haven't finished showing you up in front of your patients. There must be still one or two who haven't seen me run out in floods of tears."
"Actually, one or two."

The eyes averted for a few seconds, as she too relied on simple reflexes to cover more difficult ground and provide even more protection than the subdued lighting afforded.
"I do want you to know how grateful I am for all that you have done for me."
"I suppose, in a way, if the appendicitis hadn't deflected you, things might have been very different."
"I did my best to dissuade Mrs Perkins from phoning the surgery, but I was in too much pain to argue."
"I am pleased that you didn't manage to stop her, as I'm certain that death from raging peritonitis would have been very unpleasant."
"Do you doctors often weigh up what are pleasant and unpleasant ways to exit from this world?"
"Unfortunately we often deal with people who are suffering from either a terminal illness or a terminal phase of an illness. Given that we can often do no more than keep the patient comfortable, we can at least make sure that he or she is kept pain free, and if there are unpalatable options, we do our best to select the least unattractive one. No patient should die in pain, for instance, with modern therapeutics being what they are. We also come across people who have made attempts, with varying degrees of intent, to end their own lives. I saw a teenager brought in through casualty who had taken what you were thinking about. She had a horrible death when her heart stopped working properly. We tried everything we knew to stabilise her heart, but it eventually just gave up. I will always remember a little old lady of eighty, who decided to swallow all her sleeping tablets and take a nice hot bath. She knew that the sleeping tablets were not strong enough to kill her, but she also knew that by the time she woke up, hypothermia would have long claimed her. She was actually found in time and

made a good recovery. I am told that she is still alive and well, in a nursing home."
"It must be quite depressing dealing with all this death."
"Strangely, no. A life is always worth fighting for, and even if you are dealing with a terminal case, you can often fight a good rearguard action to make sure that the patient dies with dignity."
"Surely it must affect you."
"I don't think anyone can do it well, unless they have reached some accommodation with the fact that their own life will end some day. I don't think doctors get depressed over dealing with dying patients, it's usually the fear of litigation and stress at work that gets most of them. Suicide, alcoholism and divorce rates are higher than in any other profession."
"So are you doctors not a good bet for marriage then?"
He was aware of a slightly brighter spark from the hazel eyes. He hesitated only for an instant, "I suppose it depends on who we marry."

She decided to seize the moment and ask the question that had been burning in her mind.
"Last night, you said that you had laid a ghost to rest?"
"I seem to have been pining all these years for nothing more than a memory. I would have given anything to hear the words I heard from Annabelle just a few hours ago, but I realised as soon as the words were released, that it was no longer what I wanted. Its a funny thing, life: when you get what you think you want, you realise that you were wrong all along. I seem to have wasted the past five years."
"Really ?"
"Well, that is a bit of an exaggeration. I have done a lot with the past five years, and I am both delighted and grateful to be where I am now. I always wanted to be a doctor, and I feel very pleased to be staying on at Lorne Street. I think Dr Michaels and I will make a good team. I grew up round here, but till now I've had to move every six months to different specialties in different hospitals. You just get to know a place and the people, and it's time to move on. My Mum is always encouraging me to settle in one place: I think

she'll be delighted to have me nearby. She's always trying to marry me off with someone or other. I think she's just trying to keep Annabelle out of the picture."
"Perhaps you're right," Melanie said thoughtfully.

Waiters seemed to come and go with different courses, but were ignored apart from polite nods and thanks as the plates were removed and replaced, and wine was poured. Time seemed to disengage completely from their conversation. They were oblivious as the restaurant slowly cleared, and waiters began to strip the tables. Guiseppe was his usual polite self and made no attempt to hurry them. He did, however, dutifully return at regular intervals with refills of hot coffee. Slowly the realisation dawned that the restaurant was quite empty. Guiseppe, still at his most polite, brought the bill with carefully disguised relief on his face. They left after thanking him for his cuisine, his patience and his kindness. He seemed genuine in his request that they should return soon.

The Jaguar stood alone in the dark car park. They walked in silence, once again each with their own thoughts and quiet counsel. As they walked side by side his hand gently brushed, only for an instant, against hers. In her hypersensitive state it felt more like an electric shock down that half of her body. Goose pimples shot up her arm as she gave a slight shiver. "Are you cold, Melanie? I have been known to lend my jacket in cases of hypothermia."
"I promise, I always take very hot baths and get out, long before they have gone cold."
"I want to thank you for coming tonight. For so many months, life hasn't been worth living. You have shown me that there is a point to it all, and I am so grateful."
"You were never alone with all this, Melanie. I knew you would come through, and you've done better than my wildest dreams could hope. I'm sure that you will continue to improve and put past events behind you."

It was not what was said, that was of significance: rather what was not said. Neither had dared to mention the gypsy, for fear that it might shatter what had been a wonderful evening for her, and one that Smith would find himself revisiting through the nights that lay ahead. He couldn't help but hope that her ordeal was now in the past. There remained only subconscious thoughts, which would remind both of them in their dreams, that they had been granted a pleasing but brief interlude from the forces which now faced them unequivocally. There was more that his heart and his head were telling him he wanted to say, that his sense of duty and a strict code of ethics refused to sanction. The fierce debate within was extinguished by the sudden appearance of his house in the powerful headlight beams, to bring to a close the small oasis that had been created temporarily, in the desert of those professional ethics. He hesitated as the door opened far enough to allow the courtesy lights to come on.

"Melanie, I haven't had such a good time since our graduation night and we stayed out drinking the whole night in Salford docks."

"I'm really pleased to hear it," she began "James.....," a long pause followed but hung frustratingly across the ether.

He hesitated expectantly. More restrained words, than those initially intended, followed, "thanks for coming."

"My pleasure. I'll see you in surgery as arranged," was all he could manage, as the desire to say and do more was overcome by training and duty. Only the eyes transmitted and received far more than words would be allowed to convey, and the courtesy lights that flared against the darkness were the only other witness that evening.

Chapter XIII

"Unchained Prophecy"

The following day, Smith arrived at the surgery a little earlier than usual. Had the ever-watchful Mrs Farnell been present, she would have noticed a man deep in thought, as a noiseless, but all-consuming, subroutine was running in his head. He sat at his desk in a vain attempt to read his post and sign a few repeat prescriptions from the day before. His mind was working furiously, but on other things. His mood was an uncertain mix of happiness and frustration, as once again the head and heart were locked in a battle for supremacy of thought and deed. He knew, deep within, that more focussed thoughts were forming, but at that point in time, all he had were nuances of emotions. He recognised the flush of happiness that was doing its best to overwhelm him and persuade him to leap around the room. He had not felt this way for some years.

The timid knock at the door was more than sufficient, in his heightened state of awareness, to scatter his thoughts. Janice entered in her usual calm, respectful way. She was carrying a set of notes.

"It's Mr Allenby, Dr Smith, he's brought his three year old daughter, and wonders if you would be prepared to see her now."

"That's fine Janice, ask them to come straight in, if you will."

"Many thanks Doctor Smith," she smiled, as she bowed her head, ever so slightly.

Jack Allenby was the village postman and a very infrequent visitor, as a patient, to Lorne Street. He ushered his little girl in, before him as he gently touched her left shoulder, his right hand carrying his rolled-up cap.

"It's very good of you to see Sophie like this, doctor. We didn't have an appointment, but the wife said I should bring her straight over."

"What seems to be the problem then, Jack?"

"My wife says that Sophie has been acting a bit strange of late."
"How do you mean?"
"She's been losing her balance quite a bit, and falling, even in the house."
"How long has this been happening?" Smith asked, as he focussed initially on the postman.
"Past couple of months, Doctor, but it seems to be getting more frequent."
Dr Smith got down to the level of his patient as he knelt on his carpet.
"How old is Sophie now?"
"She'll be four in eight weeks," calculated the postman, quickly.
"Could I see her walk?"
Allenby did his best to encourage the nervous patient to walk across the small surgery. She was old enough to be frightened, but too young to co-operate, nevertheless Smith applied himself to a very careful examination of his patient.
"The walking seems fine now, Jack."
"That's the problem Doctor it's not all the time. She had a 'do' this morning, but she seems OK now."
"Is she eating well?
"Oh yes, never better. I hope I'm not wasting your time, doctor. It was the missus who said I should come."
"Not at all Jack. You did the right thing, and please say that to Mrs Allenby as well.
"I'd like to examine young Sophie, if that's OK with you? Perhaps we could sit her on your knee."
Smith was as patient as he was thorough. His examination was faultless. He had learned the lesson years ago, that the diagnosis always eluded those who made rush judgements, didn't examine their patients or listen to what they had to say. Fifteen minutes later he stood up.
"I need to have a look in Sophie's eyes. It's often difficult at this age. I'm just going to darken the room slightly."
"I thought it might just be the weather, doctor. It hasn't rained for weeks and it isn't any cooler."

"Look, Jack. I have to tell you that I can't find anything obviously wrong, but these symptoms should not be ignored. How do you feel about me sending Sophie off to see a doctor who specialises in children?"
"Do you think that's necessary, could it be just the heat doctor?"
"I don't think so, and whilst I can't find anything seriously amiss, I think it advisable given what you've told me, if I arrange for a second opinion."
"I'd better discuss it with the missus doc. if that's Ok?"
"I'll ask my secretary to get an appointment as soon as we can, and I would advise that it is in Sophie's best interest. We'll contact you when the appointment comes through. In the meantime if Mrs Allenby is not happy with that, why not have her call me so that we can discuss it?"

Mr. Allenby left with Sophie, relieved that Dr Smith had not found anything untoward, but worried about having to go to the hospital. Smith stayed at his desk for a few moments, writing out a referral letter to the Paediatric Neurologists at the Royal Manchester Children's Hospital. He came out of his room and found Janice.
"Janice, I know that Mrs Farnell is away this week, but I wonder if you would do me a favour?"
Janice's eyes lit up. She was always delighted to help in any way, especially when the young Doctor Smith was the one making the request. Her eyes and her body posture indicated that no reasonable request would be denied.
"I'd like you to phone Robin Williams' secretary at RMCH and ask her for an urgent appointment for this child. You can fax my referral letter through to him."

Janice was young, bright and efficient. Smith knew that his instructions would be carried out to the letter. Her inexperience, however, meant that she would not ask the one question that he would forget to clarify. Which of them would notify the family of the appointment? As it hung unspoken, neither could be aware that its omission would be the first step along a pathway that would lead to despair for all those concerned. Janice smiled as she eagerly accepted the notes. She decided to attend to his request immediately, rather than put it to one side for later. Her efficiency and innocence could not divert the sequence of events that would crystallise the gypsy's terrible vision into all-consuming reality.

Smith finished his surgery. His worry over Sophie had refused to die down despite the busy morning. He had nothing to go off, yet his instinct, his 'spider sense', as he would refer to it, was tingling. Neurological assessment of a patient so young was almost impossible for anyone but a specialist, and even they would rely heavily on high-tech investigative techniques. He saw that Janice had placed Sophie's notes in his tray with the appointment time and date attached. What he could not know was that Janice, being less experienced in the secretarial work of the practice, would not realise that it was also her task to phone Sophie's parents with the details. The date of ten days hence was not bad for Paediatric Neurologists. Getting an appointment could often be difficult, and an urgent one, even more so. He thanked Janice for her prompt action, but still did not think to clarify whether she had notified the parents.

He had been hoping to pop round to see Melanie, as he was sure that he'd left his mobile phone in her car. He phoned her at work and agreed to meet her at Shiplake, eagerly accepting her offer of some lunch. He noted that Melanie's car was not alone on the circular courtyard. Next to the Jaguar was a magnificent Bentley, gleaming in the sunshine. Mrs Perkins came to the door.
"Morning, Dr Smith. Miss is expecting you. She's in the conservatory."
"Thank you Mrs. Perkins: are you well?"
"Never better doctor, thanks to you," she said with her wry grin.
Melanie stood as he entered.
"James, I'd like you to meet someone. This is Rupert Hartington-Bell."

He hadn't noticed the figure who had been sitting facing Melanie as he walked in. Rupert stood up and held out his hand. As often with double-barrelled names, Smith was unsure whether to make the effort of trotting the whole lot out, or adopt the less formal but infinitely easier method.

"Pleased to meet you, Rupert: James Smith."

Despite the weak and watery handshake, that made Smith feel like attempting to dry his palm on his trousers, Rupert had obviously long held the view that he was just that bit superior to just about everyone else. The high cheek bones would have assured their owner handsome looks, but his face was a little too narrow, and the nose a little too long, to support such an attribute: the sandy hair, a little greasy, as it seemed to bunch to one side above his right eye.

"Pleased to meet you, Smith. Jolly fine job you've done with old Melanie here."

Smith wondered from the intonation whether he was talking more about a well-bred racehorse than a person, but decided that in Rupert's eyes the two would probably be of equal significance! The tweed jacket, gold-rimmed spectacles and unlit pipe, seemed to go happily with the image that he obviously liked to project to the outside world. Smith couldn't help but wonder just what Melanie was doing with such a person. He would not have to wait long to find out.

"She's done very well: my star patient; though I must confess that she's done all the hard work and I just helped her through."

"Come now Smith, you're being a bit coy there, old chap: that's not what Melanie tells me. What do you say Moopy, my love?"

It was good that he turned in Melanie's direction at this point, as otherwise Smith would have been unsure who 'Moopy' was.

"Rupert has just driven up from London and come all this way to see me," she interjected quickly, fearing that Rupert would not let her get another word in.

"And wouldn't you come all this way then, Smith, to see such a beautiful woman? What a fiancée! I'll be the luckiest man in London, what do you say Smith?"

"Are congratulations in order, then?" came the reply.

"No, not exactly, James. Rupert has been asking me to marry him since my days in London."
Rupert decided to cut in. "My God, Melanie you can't stay here, in this big place, all alone. Why not sell this mausoleum and come with me?"

Smith realised that tact was not one of his strong points. In fact Rupert's entire persona had something of grandiloquence about it. Every gesture, as the arms flounced from his side, was used to draw attention to each word. The more Smith looked, however, the more he realised that emptiness lay behind those gestures, like a Ringmaster about to announce the start of the greatest show on earth, not having realised that his animals had long since returned to the wild.

Rupert continued, "you come and marry me. You'll want for nothing, and you won't be stuck out here in the sticks, miles from anything or anyone civilised."
Rupert was so far wrapped up in himself that he either did not notice, or did not care what others thought. Smith wondered which was the worse of the two. He decided to excuse himself and beat a hasty retreat.
"Forgive me for interrupting, but I wonder, Melanie, if I left my phone here when I visited yesterday."
Melanie realised that he was attempting to spare her any embarrassment with unnecessary explanations as to how she had come by his phone.
"Here it is, James. Lunch won't be a minute?"
"Actually an urgent visit came through just before I left, and I must decline, but thank-you anyway."

Melanie had come to recognise his look when an expedient lie was thrown in casually, so as to avoid any undue discomfort either to himself or third parties. She decided to go along with it, rather than attempt to make him stay in a situation in which he was uncomfortable. Rupert was oblivious to the interplay between the two, as he continued to extol the virtues of a move to London and

marriage to him. Smith shook Rupert's hand with an almost imperceptible hesitation.
"Nice meeting you, old chap, you must come and visit me in Kensington. We could do with a few good chappies like you."
Smith forced a smile, as best he could, and prayed that his car would start with minimal delay so that he could be on his way, and certainly well away from this insufferable egoist. Melanie saw him to the door and squeezed his hand as if she knew exactly what he was thinking.
"He's not that bad really, at least when you get to know him. He is very kind, and he means well."
Smith felt a little exposed by the accuracy of her mind-reading. He did his best to assume a featureless smile as he departed with more haste than politeness would have dictated, but he could only conclude that she had read his mind, that was churning with countless thoughts as she continued to study him with her concerned but deliberative gaze.

He sat behind the wheel, the interior of the car granting asylum from that scrutiny, and allowing him to attempt to calm his thoughts, as eventually the engine started. His mood that morning had been reflective and more peaceful than the unhappy turmoil now struggling to find expression. His ability to define things more succinctly was limited to a simple comparison; that morning he had been unsure, but happy: and now he was only certain that unhappiness had somehow crept in. His mind had not yet finished assessing all the information, and would no doubt return to the subject countless times over the next few hours: of that, too, he was certain.

He decided to take a quick lunch before returning to the surgery. Eating had a calming influence as he managed to bring his restless thoughts into a more disciplined line. Why had Melanie not mentioned this Rupert chap before, and where had he been when, as she had hinted at on more than one occasion, she had needed friends and confidants? Melanie had deflected his talk of engagement, but it had obviously been an item between them for some time. He could obviously offer Melanie everything that a material heart could desire, even though the GP had never seen such a facet in her character. Surely, no-one could despise her for opting for security and comfort, especially with all that she had been through. Ultimately, Smith clung to the view that his objection to Rupert's presence was not that he disliked him in any way, but that he and Melanie seemed oddly mismatched. Perhaps Smith had not seen the side of her personality that would interact more favourably with Rupert's; perhaps he had not been looking for it. Smith was from an entirely different social set and background, and he had never experienced the kind of lifestyle that both Melanie and Rupert took for granted; such common ground that assured their compatibility with regard to class and breeding and other criteria that he would never understand. When all was said and done, if she were happy with Rupert, no-one had a right to interfere in any way.

He reminded himself that he could play no part in her life other than as a GP, an adviser, a supporter and at the furthest point of latitude that a professional relationship would allow, a friend possibly, but certainly never more than that. The duty he held toward a patient, as always, created some semblance of working truth in his restless and poorly focussed thoughts, and by clinging to this the GP would be able to continue his role. More insightful thoughts might have clarified this last thought as a piece of driftwood that would keep him afloat, barely, in the flood tide that otherwise would have inundated him. He could only hope that when his duty to his patient was at its end, his professional ethics would be there, to assure him that at all times he had behaved with entirely appropriate conduct. Surely there was nothing more to consider about the matter. Why he still felt restless and unhappy, he was at a loss to explain.

At the end of a busy afternoon surgery, rather than go straight home for dinner, he decided to visit his mother in hospital. Though he was to stay chatting for nearly an hour, his ever-watchful mother noticed immediately that he was preoccupied. She managed to ask him if he was well, but knew that she could take things no further when he replied in a simple affirmative without any more detail. Though he offered his usual bright and animated chatter, he could not hide from his mother something of what lay behind it. Just as he bent to kiss his mother goodbye, Melanie popped her head round the corner.

He turned towards her. "Hi there Melanie, I was just leaving, please pull up a chair." He offered the chair and skirted round the bed, as she entered. "Nice to see you Melanie, See you tomorrow, Mum."
"Thanks for coming James. Don't work too hard in that surgery now will you."

Mrs Smith was delighted that he had gone. Having Melanie all to herself was a much easier way of gathering information, especially about her son, who had long since stopped telling her anything too important, in case she worried.
"Now Melanie, come and sit down." She had that sparkle in her eye, as she patted the chair, her excitement like that of a little girl waiting to open a birthday present. Melanie complied and smiled, recognising similar emotions that she had seen in Smith. The strength of the bond between them came from the fact that neither had to pretend or to resort to subterfuge. Their relationship had grown stronger, and a mutual respect and genuine liking had forged that link.
"James is a bit glum tonight. He seems very preoccupied and not his usual sunny self. Any ideas, Melanie?"
"I'm not sure, Edith," Melanie still felt a little awkward calling her by her first name, 'Mrs Smith' seemed so much more natural, but she had insisted. "I don't think he hit it off with a friend of mine today."
"That's not like him. I don't think something like that would upset him," she replied confidently.
"This friend keeps asking me to marry him."

Melanie had learned to notice the slight nuances in her expression that even those who had known the older lady for many years would not spot, and which gave vital clues to the feelings deep below. The slight pause, now, allowed Edith to quickly realign such thoughts.

"Oh Melanie, I am so pleased for you. I had no idea you had a fiancé."

"He would make me secure and would look after me. I would never have to want for anything."

"I am sure that James will be so pleased for you too," the old lady offered as sincerely as she could.

"I wouldn't want for anything, not even have to lift a finger."

Edith noted the repetition as if the young woman was doing her utmost to convince herself of the attraction in the offer made to her. Edith now did her best to distract Melanie.

"So, is there to be a wedding at that beautiful Manor house?"

"That's the trouble, Edith, Rupert wants me, expects me, to move to London to be with him."

"Melanie, are you sure? You're still young, my dear. I do so want you to be happy and making compromises now in order to feel less lonely, or more secure, or with the hope of things somehow, working out, just isn't right. It won't do for you. I can't tell you what to do. No-one has a right to do that. Forgive me, I sound as if I'm an interfering old busybody. A hasty decision is unwise. All I ask you to do, is think carefully and don't accept what might not be in your best interests."

Mrs Smith sensed that she had perhaps said a little too much and managed, by using more self-control than she realised she possessed, to stop there. Paradoxically, Melanie's thoughts seemed to awaken from a trance.

"Edith, you know I welcome your opinion. I would not want to leave Shiplake, and I would not want to desert the business. Not after the backing I've just received. It would be a real stab in the back to them all. Rupert would want me to sell everything to be with him. His father owns the merchant bank where I once worked, he doesn't believe in women having their own careers."

Mrs Smith couldn't believe the words she was hearing. The saying 'bite one's tongue' was heavily in play now. She knew that if she were to attempt speech its tone would instantly betray her. She could barely manage a nod as she did her best to avert her gaze, before her eyes revealed more than was wise. The delicate cover up was not lost on Melanie. A silence opened, as each reflected on their own thoughts. The elderly woman managed speech first.

"I'm sure the past months have been desperately lonely for you. I know that you're so much better now than you were. No-one else could possibly understand how desolate it must have been for you, Melanie, and I can see that you would not want to risk such isolation again. Why not play for time, and see how you feel in a month or two?"

A tear glistened in Melanie's eye as Mrs Smith spoke.

"You know how grateful I am to James, don't you. I would not be here now if it hadn't been for him."

"I know that Melanie and so does he. He too would only want what makes you happy."

"He'll never see me as more than a patient."

"Melanie, you know that his sense of duty makes him what he is. If he hadn't been able to look at things objectively, he would not have been able to help you. Give him time, Melanie. I know him better than he knows himself." The older lady looked grave and her speech was careful and well considered, yet something shone in those short sentences. Melanie's composure returned as the words sank in. She smiled once again.

"Please forgive me for bringing all this to you. Here you are, in here to get well, and here am I, weeping on your shoulder."

"Not a bit of it. I rely on you to bring me all the gossip. That son of mine thinks it's a sin to have a good gossip. He doesn't know how stimulating it can be."

"How are you, Edith?"

"I'm better by the day. They say I'll be going home soon. Just a bit of physio. to get me back on my feet and they'll kick me out, I expect."

“That is good news. You wouldn't consider convalescence at Shiplake would you? I would get some nurses in and a physio. to help you.”

“Melanie, that is so kind of you, and I'm really touched, but I have to get back to my old routine again or I'll end up unable to care for myself. It’s bad enough having carers coming in so many times a day. I don’t know how James managed to afford it. His wages have never been that high. I'm so grateful to him; without his help I would have ended up in a care home. It’s my fault that he hasn’t had time to think about his own life or even make friends of his own. I am hoping that now he's more settled he will have time to think of more important things than me – like a social life. I think with just a little more time we'll both see a less formal side to him. It will do him good, Melanie, and I for one can’t wait!"

Melanie rose and kissed her.

“Edith, you are a remarkable woman. Thank you.”

“Don’t thank me. I want to thank you for coming and for sharing a little piece of your life with me.”

“I must dash now. Rupert is going back to London tonight and I think I owe him my honesty.”

Melanie arrived home and found Rupert where she had left him, still in front of the television, totally absorbed. She sat down beside him and took his hand in hers, so that he would focus on what she had to say. “Rupert, I do appreciate you coming all this way, and you know how flattered I am by your offer of marriage. But this is where I belong, Rupert: my life in London is now over, and this is where I intend to remain. I can’t desert the business, the people who've put faith in me, and Shiplake. I know your motives are of the highest order, and I really thank you for that, but to go with you, just isn't right.”

“Look here Melanie. My motive is simply that I love you and want to remove you from all this. Come with me, and I will make you happy.”

“I am happy, Rupert. This is where I belong.”

"Look, old gal, you're tired and you seem upset. I'll be leaving for Cape Town in two weeks on a business trip for the bank. If you want to come with me, then you know where to find me. Why not think things through, and I 'm sure you'll see things my way.
"You are a sweet person, Rupert. I think that I have made the right decision for both of us. Please don't hate me."
"I could never do that, old girl. If you change your mind?"
He walked into the hall. She made no attempt to follow him, nor he to look back. He could not think for the life of him why she was so keen to stay in that old place with so many tortured memories, when she could take up residence with him, as his wife in London, and want for nothing for the rest of her days. How stupid women were becoming, these days, with all this talk of careers and independence. He was convinced that allowing them to have the vote was the first step down that pathway!

Mrs Perkins had by coincidence decided that the china stores needed a complete spring clean and had set about the task. She appeared from the kitchen as soon as she heard the door close.
"Can I get you a cup of tea Miss?"
"Mrs P, you should have been home hours ago."
"You know Miss, since my Bill died there isn't a lot to go home to. I would much rather stay and finish the china."
"Come on then Mrs P. sit down, I'll make you a cup of tea, for a change."
Melanie placed a steaming mug in front of her and sat facing. Mrs Perkins had been anticipating such a move.
"I sent Rupert back to London. Do you think I've done the right thing?"
Mrs Perkins couldn't stand the arrogant, affected man and she hated the way he treated her boss, and the way he ignored her as if she were nothing. Paid servant she might be, but nothing, she was not, and she had stayed at her post caring for the young woman in any way that she could, whilst people like him swanned in and out again, when all along she had needed someone to stick with her, come what may. She remembered the many occasions when Rupert had arrived to spend the night with Miss Melanie. On more

than one occasion the poor girl had been sobbing in the depths of night and had simply needed the warmth of a caring person next to her, rather than one who saw the whole enterprise as a means of dissipating his sexual urges as he had groaned and gasped whilst Miss sobbed quietly. He would then eat his fill at breakfast, and be on his way with a quick slap on the young woman's back for her trouble. She realised that her opinion was not what was needed, and if the happiness of her boss was now in play, she needed to give her as dispassionate advice as she could. Ultimately she knew it would come down to something quite simple. Simple but crucial.
"Are you in love with him my dear?"
"No."
"Perhaps then, you have done the right thing?"
"I could grow to love him."
"I don't hold with such views myself, Miss. I often think that's a bit of an excuse, and perhaps that wouldn't be fair to either of you. When I met my Bill, I'd fallen off my bike over by the old farm, cut my knee really badly, I had. He came over and picked me up off the floor and set me down on a bale of hay he'd got from the field. I knew then that he was the one, it sort of hit me it did, and I knew right then and there, I'd just met my husband."

Melanie tried to smile but nervousness was firmly in charge of her emotions. It was almost as if the housekeeper's view of things had come straight from a children's story with an assured happy ending, or perhaps such things were a more regular occurrence when Mrs Perkins was Melanie's age. But they surely could not be reliably applied in today's troubled times, where people were more shallow and happiness much more elusive.
"He would make me secure. I would want for nothing."
"I don't think that would be enough for you, Miss."
"Maybe I won't meet anyone else; perhaps this will be the only time I'll ever be asked. Perhaps I'll end up lonely and alone."
Mrs Perkins smiled as she reflected on her own uncertainties when she was Melanie's age; the passing years had provided a little wisdom that she wanted to share now with the young woman.

"I can't see that happening, Miss. Have you seen that nice young doctor?"
"He's married to his work. He would never view me as being anything other than a patient. He's frightened of being struck off, and what people would think of him."
"Perhaps he needs a bit more time. Only a short time ago he was doing his best to…. get you well again." Mrs Perkins hesitated as she selected the most tactful words.
"Honestly, he'll never see me as anything more than a patient. He has this sense of duty which blots out all other impulses."
"I'm not sure about all this, but I do know that if he really cares for you, then sooner or later he will find a way of showing that. Whatever happens, Miss, I'm sure it will be for the best, and these things tend to have a habit of sorting themselves, to my mind anyhow."
"I don't know why I'm going on like a love-sick teenager. I'll be so busy with this company, I'll have no time for any sort of relationship. I sent Rupert back to London, so I could get on with things here, and I don't want anything or anyone to get in the way of that."
Once again Mrs Perkins smiled to herself. She knew that Melanie believed all that she had said - almost.
"I know that you'll do very well, Miss; and I'm sure you'll be busy, as you say. There's no harm in having a social life too."
Melanie nodded, "you always say the right thing Mrs Perkins. Where would I be without you?"
Mrs Perkins smiled once again but rose to get on with her china.
"I was wondering if it would be all right if I slept in tonight, Miss, so that I can make an early start and finish off this china."
"Of course, Mrs Perkins, you know that. Come on, why not call it a day and I'll give you a hand before I go to work tomorrow."

Melanie had an appointment with Dr Smith later that morning. True to her word, she rose early to help Mrs Perkins with the china, and managed to spend two hours in work before arriving just in time for her appointment. Mrs Farnell was still on holiday and once again Janice had managed to position herself on the desk

so that she could manage Dr Smith's surgery. She looked crestfallen as she saw Melanie arrive. Her good looks, the poise, the bright smile, the face that exuded warmth from every angle and the easy going grace that seemed to flow with her like a cool breeze on a hot summer's day.
"Dr Smith will be with you shortly, Miss Jardine. Please take a seat and I'll tell him that you're here."

Melanie sat down as Janice continued to study the long legs and the slim figure, the smart suit, the unassuming friendly manner that was not at all conceited or vain even though she had every right to be. How could any man, anyone, fail to notice her charms. Her presence shone like a beacon on a dull day and lit a dark room. Dr Smith arrived and shook her hand as usual. He guided her into his surgery.
"Melanie, nice to see you. How are you?"
"I'm fine thanks; I'm getting better by the day. I hope that Rupert didn't upset you yesterday."
"Not at all Melanie. I could see that the two of you had a lot to talk about, and I thought it best if I made a polite excuse."
"You were most welcome to have some lunch with us."
"I know that, Melanie, it's just that I could see that the two of you had some catching up to do. How is Rupert?"
"He's gone back to London. I think they had a Board meeting this morning and he had to be there."
"Do you want to talk about things?"
He deliberately phrased the question as openly as possible to encourage her to talk about her feelings and gauge some idea of her mental state.
"Rupert has been asking me to marry him for months, but I honestly don't think that I'm ready for marriage. He wants me to sell the business move to London, sell Shiplake. Can you imagine such a thing?"
"Only if it's what you really want."
"No-one at Jectronics would ever never forgive me. They would all be rich people now if they hadn't backed me."

"They backed you because they thought you were right. You mustn't allow guilt to get in the way of something if you feel it's right for you."
"It isn't."
"Ok, then Melanie, that seems like a decision of sorts?"

He sensed her frustration and decided to approach from a different direction.
"I know that you'll always consider other people and I know that it's unwise of me to say that you should consider yourself more, because it's simply not in your nature. You have done your best for these people, you genuinely believe that the package you put together is best for the shareholders, the workers and even the country. Sometimes, Melanie, you have to consider your wants, your needs and your wishes. I'm sorry if I sound as if I'm preaching to you."
"James, I need that factory, I need those people, I need my life here in Little Dunham," ...... the pause hung almost painfully in the air as she struggled with words that she wanted to add, yet could not.

Smith, too was struggling: he desperately wanted to hear the sentence completed and desperately wanted to be included. As the pause opened up, he reacted quickly to close it with semblance of normality, even though both knew that there was so much more that they wanted to convey and receive.
"...and Rupert?" he managed to attach as fast as his racing mind would allow.
"He's not right for me. I have too much to do here and I won't be able to do that if I'm chained to his kitchen sink."
"Is it that bad?"
"No, forgive me; it's just that I'll have to be something that I'm not. His ideas of women are a little traditional, shall we say. We women stay at home, have the babies and wait for our man's arrival from a hard day providing for us. That, as you know is not how I've been brought up, and Dad would see it as being put back half a century."

“I understand Melanie,” Smith offered, but Melanie was not sure that he did. Once again however, he tried switching the direction of his words.
“How do you feel?”

Smith had somehow regained his professional composure and had once again projected the empathic yet carefully shielded image that did not dare reveal too much of his inner self. He knew that his own thoughts had no place within effective counselling, as they burdened rather than relieved the patient, and that emotional interplay would destroy his own objectivity and once again risk hurting his patient more, as well as damage his own credibility.
“Apart from this feeling that I have hurt Rupert, I feel fine. I haven't felt as well as this for eighteen months.”
“Do you think that by being honest with Rupert you have in fact hurt him, or simply disappointed him?”
“I suppose I need to be honest with myself and reveal some of my true feelings.”
“How is your sleep?” he asked by way of a desperate strategy to change the conversation to more familiar ground
“I'm not sure that I'll ever sleep again.”
“Have the tablets not helped with your sleep?”
“I feel more alert during the day, and calmer, but I am still disturbed by the image of the gypsy." She touched the silver necklace reflexly, almost like rosary beads.
“What is that round your neck, Melanie?”
“The gypsy gave it to me.”
She undid the clasp and handed it over for his closer inspection. He looked surprised.
“Do you know what this is?”
“No, please tell.”
“This is a Scarab. The ancient Egyptians revered the humble dung beetle, as they believed that it held a special relationship with the passage of the sun across the sky, and the rising sun each morning would be equated with rebirth of the soul. She must have given this to you as a talisman, to protect you.”

Smith looked at it for a few moments and rubbed its surface gently with his thumb as it lay in his palm. He could not know that he was correct in almost all details, except the one that was to be the most critical of all. He handed the necklace back to her.

"The gypsy's mood seemed to change as she gave this to me. She told me that the hand of fate would reach out to me, and that if I ignored it, nothing could save me."
Smith considered her words for a few moments. "All seems quiet now, Melanie; I wonder if it's the calm before the storm?"
"I was rather hoping that we had escaped: that the prophecy had been in some way diverted by the very fact that I knew of it. I suppose that is silly, especially as it failed to save my family."
"Melanie, you need to be positive and confident. Defeatism can only harm you. You are in control of your own destiny, and you must shape it." He continued to fashion an eclectic mix of several strategies and viewpoints that he hoped would alter the as- yet-unfulfilled prophecy. They continued to talk. Immersion in their conversation seemed to decouple them from the concept of the linear passage of time. Eventually it was the quiet knock on the door that interrupted their flow. Janice entered.
"Excuse me Dr Smith, Miss Jardine. As your afternoon surgery is due to start in about half an hour, would you like me to send out for sandwiches?"
"Thank you Janice, that would be very kind."

Janice smiled. The mask of efficiency slipped only briefly but it was enough to reveal the adoring eyes to Melanie's deliberative gaze. Janice closed the door quietly.
"Dr Smith, I can't bear it. Another one holding a torch for you. That poor young girl is all starry eyed just when she looks at you."
Smith held up his hands defensively.
"Innocent of all charges. I never touched her, guv."
"These poor young girls!"
"Melanie, she's not that young. You make me out to be a cradle snatcher."

He looked at Melanie; the gleeful fascination now coursing across her face like a spark of electricity as she homed in on Smith's self-inflicted need to somehow justify himself, where no such clarification had been needed. Obviously enjoying herself she continued, "these poor young girls, getting all steamed up about that nice Dr Smith. You need a stable girlfriend or a wife, or tell them that you're gay or something."

"I am working on it, Melanie - the girlfriend I mean. I promise. Now that I'm settled I'll turn my attention to it with urgency. I thought that maybe, Annabelle, but I know that it's all in the past."

"Perhaps *you* need to look forward, not backwards"

He studied her fleetingly: not for the first time had he been amazed by the transformation in his patient.

"Melanie, it is so good to see you looking so, so,"

"So..?" she prompted.

"so well," he finally offered.

She rose. "I must go. If I stay here any longer, Janice will let my tyres down."

"Actually I saw her carving through your brake pipes with a kitchen knife."

She smiled.

"Thank you for coming Melanie. Do you want to come again?"

"Yes please. Someone has to keep an eye on you. Make sure that you don't run off with an ex, cheap floozy, half the women in this practice. Tick all that apply," she suggested.

He rose to shake her hand. "See you next week, Melanie, if I don't see you at the hospital," which he realised now, was more likely than not.

"I'm going before they arrest me for aiding and abetting a child molester."

Janice's relief at her departure was thinly veiled.

"Good afternoon, Janice."

"Good afternoon, Miss Jardine."

CHAPTER XIV

"LUCID INTERVAL"

Smith's afternoon surgery ran as smoothly as usual, and he was on his very last patient when the call came through. Janice interrupted him with her usual politeness.

"Excuse me Dr Smith but I have a doctor White on the phone: she says that it's important that she speaks with you."

"Thank you Janice, please put her through. Kim, everything all right?"

"No James, I am afraid it's your mum."

Smith knew that she only ever called him James when there was a serious problem.

Kim continued, "I'm afraid she started with haemoptysis this afternoon. We will be sending her for a VQ scan as soon as we can organise one. It sounds like bad news, though, James."

Smith knew that coughing up blood could be due to a blood clot that had travelled to the lungs. Though the special scan that Kim talked about would reveal a definite diagnosis, it could not improve the prognosis, especially in one as frail as his mum. He knew that such events were often fatal.

"Thanks for letting me know, Kim. I'll come over as soon as I've finished my surgery."

Later, Smith would have no recollection of that last consultation, nor of driving to the hospital. Kim was waiting for him in the office.

"It's not looking too good James. We suspect a pulmonary embolus. We haven't done the scan yet, but we have started clot busters and intravenous Heparin."

Smith knew that immobile patients were at risk of developing blood clots in the deep veins of the legs. These clots could easily travel through the heart and become deposited in the lungs, forming the so called pulmonary embolus. Despite modern

therapeutic agents to dissolve the clot, and other agents to thin the blood, he knew that it was often all too late.
“You know that we will do all that we can." She tapped his shoulder as if to reaffirm that was her intention.
Smith nodded. He had been here with his own patients many times before. Only the very young, the very fit, or the very lucky, lived. He went into the side ward. His mother lay on the bed, her face ashen and sweaty. The mask hissed oxygen continuously. The infusion pumps with their attendant plastic tubes and lines together with a syringe driver were slowly propelling small quantities of Heparin into one of the cannulas in her arm.
She looked up as he entered. Somehow she managed a few words.
"Not dragging you away from another surgery are they. You must be too busy."
“Not at all, I had nothing else to do, so I thought I might as well come and see what you're up to.”

The smile triumphed fleetingly over the breathlessness and exhaustion. Smith knew only too well about the immense strain that would now be exerted upon his frail mother’s heart and lungs, and knew that, inevitably, exhaustion would be victorious over one or both. He sat quietly in the chair. Each breath seemed a struggle. To give in to the sweet seduction of tiredness grew more tempting with each inhalation. The nurse brought him a cup of tea as he began his lonely vigil in a scene that he knew could have only one conclusion. Darkness came forward as if marking the closing scenes from a tragic play. A little while later Melanie arrived, stopping short as the scene of unabridged distress met her as she turned into the room. She rushed forward and squeezed Mrs Smith’s hand in a desperate attempt to lend some support to the patient’s desperate fight to make one breath follow the next. Mrs Smith tried but failed in summoning a smile, but she did manage a few gasping words as the tubing continued to hiss with more oxygen.
“Melanie, not you too. Have you both not got better things to do than hang round here?”
"No, sorry, looks like you're stuck with us.”

Smith rose to allow Melanie to sit. The nurse brought another chair and tea. Melanie sat down and leaned forward to squeeze the hand once again, willing her to breathe.
“James, you look all in, why not pop home for an hour or two. I'll hold the fort.”
He rose slowly, kissed his mother and squeezed Melanie’s shoulder.
“I'll pop home for a sandwich and a shower. Can I bring you anything?”
“No thanks, James. I'll be here when you get back.”
Smith's departure seemed to give life back to the patient.

She struggled to remove the mask as if the words she wished to impart were now more important than whether she lived or died. She held Melanie’s hand as tightly as the twisted claw would allow.
“I'm finished Melanie.”
Melanie started to demur but Mrs Smith continued.
“I want to thank you for your friendship. I also want to apologise about James. You look so good together, and I know that he really cares for you, it’s just that he could never admit it even to himself. I didn't know that you were contemplating engagement to your young man from London.”
Melanie struggled to interpose corrective words, but the elderly lady knew that time was running out, and she would not have long to finish.
“The estate he took you to, Melanie. James grew up on that estate. He played on the playground you've just rebuilt. His father was a no-good, womanising drunk who took his inadequacies out on me and James. I'll never know where he got the strength from to endure it all and lift himself clear. Once the house went quiet as his father slept it off, out would come the books and he'd try to get through his homework and studies. He was desperate to succeed. It sounds so cruel of me to say, but we were glad when it was all over for the two of us. We were both relieved and delighted.”

Tears had filled the old lady's eyes and began to overflow onto her cheeks.

“Things were hard, but in truth, he'd already drunk away all our savings and most of what he'd earned. James worked like a demon. Days at school and college, nights part-time to raise money. I was also able to work at first. James was like a man driven, determined to get to medical school. Every fibre of his being seemed focussed to that end. It was either to atone for the behaviour of his father or to prove that he was better. He didn’t ever want ‘like father like son’ to apply to him. As my health began to deteriorate I was unable to work full-time, and then not at all. Fortunately James was in his final year by that time, and we had managed to build up savings to carry him through. All he ever wanted to be, was what he is. Without his work he has nothing. It was the only thing that kept him going through those horrible times when he was little. He never really had a childhood. He seems to have carried the weight of the world on his shoulders ever since. You're a good influence on him Melanie, I am sorry if I implied anything else before I realised you were engaged.”

Exhaustion took its eventual toll. She leaned back into the pillows, the force that had driven her, now spent. Her eyes closed as all energy was diverted to the heart and the lungs. Her grasp became weak and also icy cold as the circulation began to fail.

Melanie sat quietly in semi-darkness illuminated by regular flashes from the infusion pump and a fluorescent green glow from the heart monitor. The tears beaded and then flowed as she sat gazing at this woman whose life seemed so sad.

Her understanding had advanced one more step but she could not understand why this information had been imparted at that moment. She realised that the elderly lady saw that she would probably never have another opportunity, but its significance must be very great indeed, for her to use what little remained of her strength to deliver it. Mrs Smith knew the vital importance of the information, yet Melanie was not to see its relevance until it was too late. As she continued to toil with the problem, Smith returned looking far more refreshed. The suit had been exchanged for a

more comfortable pair of trousers and a thin jumper to take the chill off the autumn air. Melanie looked very tired, almost as if she were about to drift off to sleep. He touched her hand gently. “Melanie why don't you get home. I'll call you if there are any developments.”
“James, I'd like to stay if that's OK with you?”
He nodded and squeezed her hand a little more tightly.
“Yes of course.”

The seconds ticked into minutes and the minutes into hours. The sands of life itself began to trickle steadily through the hourglass. Both had drifted off to sleep in their chairs, positioned next to each other. Mrs Smith awoke as if by some unknown signal. She sat upright in bed and removed the oxygen mask. Smith too, awoke followed by Melanie. Even the slightest noise was discernible in their heightened and anxious state. Smith had seen these lucid intervals in patients before. Those in a deep coma or after a severe stroke had been known to seemingly but fleetingly recover, before death had supervened. Relatives were often grateful for the opportunity to say goodbye to loved ones. Smith knew this would be his.

The pain had gone as had the breathlessness. She spoke clearly and without hesitation.
“James, thank you for being so good to me all those years. No-one could ever wish for a kinder, more caring son. I want you to know how proud of you I am, and always will be.” She knew that time was running out, and the short reprieve was from death itself. “Melanie, I feel as if I've known you all my life, how I wish that I had. I'm so lucky to have known you these last days. I love you both.”

The eyes closed for the last time as she sank gently into the pillows, and was embraced by the arms of a dignified death. Pain had gone, as had suffering. Her face remained in death, but in peace, and the twisted body too, seemed, at last, to be devoid of spasm that had racked it for years. Death had granted its last reprieve from pain and suffering. Smith rose slowly to squeeze the lifeless hand, and kissed her gently. He could see that suffering had passed with life. Melanie did her best to wipe away the tears, but did not manage to stem the flood which began welling up from within. Smith turned to her and rubbed her arm reassuringly. “Melanie, I want to thank you for being with me. You meant an awful lot to her and I do appreciate it.”

“She was a wonderful person. James I am so sorry.”

The gloom in the cubicle hid something of his acute discomfort and the panoply of emotion he was now experiencing: there was a mixture of gratitude that her suffering was over, and guilt for needing to feel loss. Even at that moment of despair, his professional instincts dictated that he hold within himself much of what should have been allowed to flow. Sensing his unease, and the turmoil that he struggled to master, she touched his hand gently.

“I suppose I've been preparing for this day for years. Now that it has arrived it doesn't seem any easier.”

“Come on, I'll make you a cup of tea.” She rose and waited in the corridor for him to say his last good-bye. They drove back to Shiplake where they sat facing each other at the kitchen table. The harsh light seemed much too bright, so she activated the under-lighting beneath the chrome and glass shelving. Smith found refuge in his mug, being unable to meet her concerned gaze, for once the situation reversed. She knew from her own experience and the very counselling that he had painstakingly provided, that listening was the best plan as she sat glancing up at him from her own drink.

"We had quite a humble background. Mum and I seemed to cling together. My father was a difficult man who liked no-one and would often subject my mum to a lot of suffering. We were always short of money as he was not good at providing for us. My mum had to work to support me.”

Melanie did her best to appear as if she were hearing the words, he slowly released, for the first time. She made no attempt to interrupt him, nor reveal that his mother had given her the even more brutal truth some hours before. She could not help but stand amazed at the man before her. The disadvantages he had faced, and the success he had wrought from such a terrible situation. She sensed it was nothing short of a miracle that a kind, gentle, well-balanced individual could have emerged at all, let alone making it through five years at medical school followed by GP. training. She continued to listen without interruption, finding herself leaning ever so slowly closer toward him as he spoke. Suddenly as he finished speaking, the irresistible impulse was translated into movement. Without hesitation, that more considered thoughts would have introduced, she leant forward and kissed him on the side of the cheek. How he restrained himself at this point, as her lips lingered fleetingly in such close contact with his, he would never know.

She spoke even before embarrassment could supervene. “Thanks for sharing that with me, I don’t know what would have happened to me if it had not been for you.” She was aware of an urgency in that there were more words she wanted to impart and she could only feel a little glimmer of relief that the circumstances granted dispensation to allow her to show something of the mood within her. Before either could frame another thought or utter a word, Smith's phone rang. Its shrill tone shattered the mood and the words that hung unsaid, irrevocably, he gave a little jump as it went off. He mouthed an apology as he reflexly withdrew the device from his pocket.

“Ah Smith - Michaels here. Just heard the terrible news. Forgive me I just wanted to tell you that I have cancelled your surgeries. Please take as much time as you need for compassionate leave won’t you, and please accept my deepest condolences.” Though the short staccato style remained, the words were conveyed with genuine sadness, the uncharacteristic nature of which could only magnify the emotional charge that, in that moment, existed between them.

"Thank you Dr Michaels, if I could phone in a day or two when I have made some arrangements."
"Yes, yes of course Smith; just take your time my boy."
As he clicked the phone to terminate the call, he desperately wanted to return to those vital few seconds, now gone, and to hear the words that she had been about to relay across the tiniest of gaps that had lain for a moment between them. The words and the moment had now evaporated like a speck of slaked lime hitting water.

Melanie rose very early the next morning and spent the time watching the sunrise over the lawns from her bedroom window. It had been weeks since her abortive suicide attempt. What a change James's presence had made, and how different she felt now, compared to back then. Without further hesitation she picked up the telephone and dialled his number.

"Melanie it's so kind of you to ring," he hesitated before framing his next words.
"Melanie I had better go and make some arrangements."
"Oh no, you don't get rid of me that easily. Come on, I'll pick you up in an hour."
" Melanie, I have to tell you it's only six a.m."
"OK then I'll pick you up, get the toast on; I'll be there as soon as I have washed this hair."
"I can see that you won't take 'no' for an answer, Melanie, so I'll get the kettle on and start slicing the bread."

Fortunately he had just finished his preparations as Melanie squeezed the Jag. onto the drive next to his Maestro. She breezed into his tiny kitchen and stretched her slim frame in order to squeeze herself behind the small table with two chairs. He placed a rack of wholemeal toast in front of her, together with low fat spread, marmalade and honey. He couldn't help but stare at her just a little. She had simply combed the hair through and left it to dry in the balmy day of late summer. How striking she looked first thing in the morning, in the most simple of circumstances, as the sunshine seemed to be reflected from within that head of glorious hair.

She laughed; the array of flashing white teeth, dazzling in the clear visage.
"You got ready quickly, I've have only just put the phone down."
"I've never been one to spend hours getting ready and I'm not one for much makeup and things like that. Mum and Dad were always too busy working, to make proper young ladies of us, I suppose."
He studied the lovely skin and the compelling hazel eyes, which seemed especially vital that morning
"I bet other women just hate you. Just a quick wash of the hair, pull some jeans on and a top and there you are, absolutely stunning."
"Well Doctor Smith, that is a compliment, thank *you*," she said. Her playful mood, simply at the thought of being given the chance to return some of the support he had given her, stifled any hint of embarrassment that otherwise would have existed on her face at such a moment. "I take it there is no secret surveillance in here from the Sunday tabloids or the GMS…"
"You mean the GMC. I've told you they do all the striking off, there is to be done."
He gazed at her for a second or two longer. She caught his appreciative eye, and once again the bright mood provided a counterbalance to his more fragile state.
"Now you're going to tell me that I've got toothpaste on my lip or a wart on my nose aren't you?"
"No, Melanie, I can say that those were not the words uppermost in my mind."
He sat facing her across the tiny table.
"Quite cosy this eh?" she suggested as she looked around.
"Well not quite as big as the palaces that some are fortunate to live in. Not that I'm jealous, mind, as I wouldn't fancy the Council tax. Do they go all the way down to Band Z?" he asked with sudden inspiration.
"Actually, I hate to disappoint, but they do not. Although they do find more inventive ways of getting you to cough up the cash."

"It must have been lonely, though Melanie," he said with sudden serious affect.
"You're telling me," she nodded with a mix of relief and a shiver of sadness that flashed upon her. "There was Mrs P. of course, who has been like a mother to me, but I guess I don't know what I'd have done without you," she glanced up from the mug of coffee as sadness existed, fleetingly, upon her face. A slight pause as more serious thoughts now intruded, he sighed, "come on, you, let's get this unpleasant business over with shall we. I bet some of these places will be open now.

She was now sharing, with some vigour, his ability to lighten a serious situation with a refreshing and light-hearted perspective, whilst at the same time acknowledging and supporting the more vulnerable person's position. The self same skills he had applied in her direction were now there to support him as the unspoken but clear message came through, that this was precisely her intention. In addition her buoyant stance alloyed, at each moment, with complementary sincerity, would prevent either party from the trap of sinking into more serious and more damaging loops of thought that neither could withstand at that point in time.

Hours later, as the undertaker stood to express his deepest sympathy one last time, and escort them through the door, she squeezed his hand as if she were transferring not just encouragement, but also the strength to continue, just as he had done for her those months before. She drove him back to the small but tidy home, where the worn carpet set the scene for much of the furniture. She was well aware that the stimulus of necessity had driven the need for quite humble surroundings, but as always, there was much more to the man who would, she realised, not know the price of things - but would be confident of their value. In the corner stood an old television that she had not realised would still work with modern services. He sat quietly in the morning room as she busied herself in the small kitchen, making a cup of tea. As she carried the tea through she noticed the wooden model of the Victory on the dining table. She smiled as Edith's words echoed in her head.

“So this is how you spend your time when you're not curing the sick and needy.”

“Yes, I'm afraid it is,” he said somewhat sheepishly. She gazed at the detailed model with genuine enthusiasm.

“This is magnificent, it must have taken you months and months to get it this far.”

“Well, I find that if I complete a step or two each day, at least it moves forward just a bit more, if you catch my meaning and, of course, it's not quite finished,” he interjected. “I find the slow construction a great stress reliever after a day of poorly patients.”

“I can see this is a real interest of yours,” as she noted the bookcase stuffed with books about the Royal Navy and especially Nelson.

She stayed until long after dark, neither really wishing even the sad day to come to an end. Eventually, noting the late hour she stood and motioned towards the door. He desperately wanted to hold her in his arms and ask her to stay; and the words he was struggling with were precisely the ones she longed to hear. She remained his patient, however, and he her doctor. He knew that despite the circumstances, the GMC would take a very dim view of any physical contact between them, and he knew only that the thoughts he struggled with would have to remain as thoughts, since the slightest suggestion of anything more than that, would be punished, quite correctly, without mercy. She sensed his unease and could only mitigate his turmoil and her own, by moving without hesitation into the cold night air. As he watched her go, his dilemma intensified with the distance opening between them. Only then did he realise that the methods he had used to save her had stripped away the professional veil of separation, insulation, objectivity, and dispassionate analysis behind which all doctors needed to operate, in order to protect themselves from the feelings that now consumed and threatened to overwhelm him. His instinct had told him that treating her conventionally and in maintaining a professional distance would not have won through. He had saved her precisely because of the attention and closeness of the relationship that he had engendered. This had provided the spark, the catalyst, to the subtle but powerful reaction. Could he now stop that reaction, or was the truth simply, that he needed her as much now as she needed him? The aching he felt deep within, unmatched in its intensity to anything he had experienced before, only widened the gulf between his current emotion, and the needs of the profession he loved so much. Even as her car started, he wanted to rush down the gravel drive and reveal some of his feelings towards her.

Another restless night awaited as his grief mixed with the turmoil of his feelings towards her, and the stark fact that professional conduct would be required at each and every future consultation. The early hours brought out this conclusion time and time again, yet his brain and body yearned for a solution that would not incur the wrath of the GMC. The dawn light simply brought exhaustion and hopelessness, rather than that sought-after solution that seemed more remote and less likely than ever. In that night of turmoil, that held a million thoughts all on endless loops, that continued to dispel any hint of sleep, he thought of Melanie many times, and wondered what lay within her thoughts and dreams.

Her night had closely mirrored his, with surging, recurrent thoughts that had expunged the need for sleep. On more than one occasion she had looked at the telephone by her bed and had even lifted it from its cradle so that she might dial his number and hear that smooth voice with its rich, reassuring timbre that seemed to have healing properties of its own. Though she sensed that he would be entirely receptive to such a call, ultimately she realised that she could neither appear to be so forward nor expose him to incautious distractions that could cause him significant harm.

Mrs Perkins arrived, her usual cheery self, to find Melanie sitting sipping coffee with a couple of pieces of toast in front of her.
"How is Dr Smith holding up Miss?"

“Well we got all the arrangements made yesterday. It’s such a shame; Mrs Smith was a remarkable woman and someone whom I really liked, despite not having known her for long. I know that Dr Smith told me that she had been living on borrowed time for a while, but I can imagine what he is going through, nonetheless.”
Mrs Perkins wrapped her own hands around Melanie’s, which were especially warm from holding the hot mug.
“I can only imagine what you have been through, you poor love. I don't know how you survived.”

“I don’t think I would have, Mrs P, without Dr Smith - and you, of course.”
“I know; he's done a marvellous job, and I'm so pleased to see you looking so much better these days. You're a changed woman and I know that he has helped a great deal in restoring you to your full health. We have to look after him now. Do you think we could ask him for tea, Miss ?”
Melanie hesitated, this would have been an ideal suggestion. She realised, too that the wily housekeeper had latched on to some tenets of the relationship that existed between them, but she knew that this would not help Smith in his need to maintain a business, rather than social, agenda.
“I'll perhaps phone him later, Mrs P. and let you know?” The young business woman was now uncharacteristically undecided. Her first thought, that surely nobody could object to a simple dinner invitation, had then to be modified, and catastrophically so, as she acknowledged the nascent private feelings that she suspected she and Smith now shared.

Melanie had much to do at work. The file-server was up and running and the network back on line without a hiccup. The engineers had restored the backup tapes that fortunately Smith had not sold on E-bay as he had teased. Suzy from switch, knocked at her door.
“Miss Jardine, I just wanted you to know how glad I am that you are back and in charge.”

"Thanks for that Suzy." Melanie sensed that there was more to say. She motioned towards one of the chairs in front of her desk.

"Miss, I want you to know that Newman made me spy on you. He told me that he would...." She broke down in tears at this point. Melanie popped round the desk and sat next to her, after closing the door to her office securely.

"Do you want to tell me about it?"

Suzy told Melanie all about the date she had had with Newman.

"He told me, Miss that he would double my salary, and as soon as he had got rid of Miss Stella I could be his PA. He insisted I should sleep with him to prove my commitment."

Melanie's stomach churned as unpalatable detail was given.

"Miss he took photos of us making love, and said that he would post them on the Internet if I didn't help him, by telling him where you were going and when. I am so sorry Miss, I never meant to harm you. I loved your dad and your sister. They were kind to me."

Melanie put her arm around her as she sobbed uncontrollably. It took some time for the young secretary to calm herself enough in order to hear what Melanie had to say.

"Please don't worry about your job here, it's safe; and I want to thank you for being honest with me. I really value that. Newman was wrong to do that to you, and you should know that to coerce you in that way is against the law. I think the Police will be very interested to know what you know, if you're strong enough to tell them what you told me. The Police will also make sure that they recover the digital tape or whatever. I can only guess what you have been going through and I wonder if some counselling would help you. How old are you Suzy?"

"Twenty in a few weeks, Miss."

"I am sure we'd be able to get some private counselling for you, if you feel that this would help you; and the firm will be responsible for any costs involved. I would very much want you to continue to work here. I know that you don't know me as well as you knew my father and my sister, but we can mend that as the months pass, if you are willing."

More tears flowed but these were of relief at the unburdening rather than the guilt and suffering that they had replaced.
“Miss, you are so kind. I'm so sorry if I let you down.”
“I don’t think it was your fault. I think Newman manipulated you, and it doesn't reflect on you at all. You've done a super job here, and I hope you'll continue to do so. I'm going to see if I can get some counselling for you at the Priory clinic, and if you so wish, when you are feeling stronger, we can think about contacting the Police. I believe Newman has been released by the Police pending his trial, so if he shows up, phone them straight away and also phone me day or night. Would you like to go home Suzy ? I can telephone you with the appointment later?”
“No Miss, I am here and I'm here to stay; I don’t want you to start worrying about me, I am not going to let you down again.”
These last few words provoked a further flush of tears, but the hastily applied tissue mopped them up rapidly.
“OK, give me a minute, and I'll speak with the Priory.”
“Miss this is so kind of you, it’s so expensive there.”
“Expense doesn't come into this, if they can help you get over these unfortunate events.”
Suzy swept quickly down the metal stairwell outside Melanie’s office before anyone could see her distressed state. Melanie decided to phone Smith for his opinion.

“What a man - eh Melanie, don’t you just love this man? I think strawberry picking would be unkind to strawberries, and the sooner they lock him up and superglue the lock the better. Speak with Beverly the Nurse administrator at the Priory, tell her that I told you to ask for her. She'll sort it for you. She and I go way back.”
“Oh no not another one, I can't bear it – don’t tell me she is just a friend.”
“And a very good friend too, though I think she will be retiring next year,” he said, deliberately placed the emphasis on the retirement.
“Are no ages safe from you! Oh and by the way, Mrs Perkins wonders if you would like to come for tea tonight?”

"With such a good offer from Mrs P., how could anyone refuse. Is she married, Melanie, and does she like younger men?"
"I'll be putting Bromide in your carrot juice if you're not careful."
"With an offer like that, just how could a red-blooded male decline. What time would you like me? How about seven pm. sharp, or any other time that suits."
"They all seem fine to me - I'll see you later."

Melanie made arrangements for Suzy to be seen that week. Beverly was very helpful, especially so, when Melanie had told her that Smith had suggested that she ask for her. "Oh give him my love," she went on. Melanie could only smile as she thought of yet another woman quietly holding a torch for him.
"How do you know James then?" came the inevitable question.
Melanie would not have hesitated, up to that point, in answering that she too was simply a patient. Yet now that seemed strangely inappropriate.
"Oh I'm just a friend," eventually she offered in tones that created as much puzzlement in the nurse as contemplation in Melanie. What was it that had effected such a transition, she could only wonder as she replaced the phone. Still preoccupied with this she went in search of Suzy who was almost back to her efficient self on reception. Melanie handed the appointment details over to her in an envelope.
"Oh Miss Jardine, I was just about to telephone you, Mr Ward is here."
As the ponderous black suit turned, she recognised Mr Ward.
"Sorry about barging in without an appointment, Melanie, but I wondered if you would peruse these final figures and I have some production grade prototypes here for you."
She popped into the lift with Ward, assuming that the task of climbing the stairs would be too cruel for him to contemplate.
"Many thanks for bringing these round Mr Ward. We're in full swing here."
"I am sorry that you had to doubt me, Melanie. I'm so pleased that Newman has met his match and received his just deserts. He put me through hell, Melanie; I should have been stronger, like you."

“I think that's all in the past now, and both our companies must look to the future.”
“I won't let you down again Melanie” He wanted to say much more, but the look on the rotund face, held more than his words could have conveyed and she simply nodded by way of acknowledgement.
“I know that. Can I offer you a coffee, Mr Ward?”
“No, thank you, Melanie I must be shooting along, I remember sitting here.....” he let the words trail off
“I know, I miss them too.”
“Yes, well, so sorry to have burst in like this, I'm sure you are very busy”
“No, no not at all.” She offered her hand by way of reassurance that she would not let recent events stand in the way of either business, nor forgiveness. The cool, precise but firm handshake locked briefly with his puffy and sweating palm, and they retraced the route back down the lift and through reception into the car park.
“I'll let you know how we get on. I'm meeting our two resident geniuses this afternoon,” Melanie said as she showed him through the large door that was barely wide enough for him to pass.

Melanie sat in the lab next to Newton and Jones.
“These lattices are excellent. We've just run them up against our conformance software and it’s looking very good. Just how much of this can we get our hands on?” asked Newton.
"Mr Ward has promised us first call on their entire output, and we've negotiated thirty days’ terms on everything. We can ask for the precise quantities we need and they will courier it to us, so we don't have to hold expensive stock.”
Both men wondered just how Melanie had managed to negotiate such favourable terms. Newman had promised them much, but they had long since realised the empty nature of his promises.
“We are so please to be working with you,” Jones said.
“I hope that as time passes I will earn your trust,” she said modestly.
“I think you already have, eh Tony?”

Tony Newton nodded enthusiastically, as he assessed the latest figures from the test rigs, which showed a performance from the solid state drive, that only their wildest dreams could have hinted at. He cooed with delight.

“At these figures we could get easily two Terrabytes per drive formatted, together with rapid access times that will blow the competition away.”

“Well if the production models are half as good as this we have a sure-fire winner here,” added Jones.

“Mr Ward assures me that they will be,” she said convincingly. “OK lads the next question is, how soon do you think we will be in full-scale production?”

“If we go for round the clock shift working we can be ready within the month,” offered Newton.

“OK, then let’s authorise that,” agreed Melanie.

“We'll need some extra bodies too,” cautioned Jones.

“Stella will be back from her holidays tomorrow; I'll ask her to start advertising straight away. For the moment if we put people on bonus incentives at least they will be paid for the extra they put in.”

The two scientists looked at her with fresh vision and glanced at each other. “The next few weeks will be very interesting,” she said.

“I'm hoping that's an understatement,” Jones said calmly.

Melanie left the engineers still doing some final testing. She decided to head for home and help Mrs P. with the preparations. Her heart skipped a couple of beats with delight at the thought of seeing Smith again. She detected his nervousness and apprehension, and ultimately realised that she could not allow her wants and needs to compromise his security and standing in a profession that was his life. There must be a way through this dilemma. The simple truth, she gravely reflected, was that she did not know how she could bear not having him in her life. She had dared to hope that it was the same for him too.

As she drove into Shiplake she noticed another car on the drive. She recognised the maroon Bentley as belonging to Rupert, long before the number plate was visible. She wondered what he was doing there; no doubt she would not have to wait long. Smith would be on his way, and the inner shiver reflected her worries over the two men meeting once again, and she realised with a certain prescience that it would be far from a relaxed evening. Simple common decency would dictate that Rupert be asked to remain having, no doubt, just driven up from London. She found Mrs Perkins in a state of distress, Rupert had created a steady stream of requests for cold drinks, hot drinks, wine and also something to eat, and had totally occupied the housekeeper. She would have to distract him while Mrs P was allowed to get on with things.

She led him quickly into the Conservatory.
“Rupert I thought you were planning your trip to South Africa?”
“I have put off my trip Melanie, to try, one last time, to talk you out of this madness. Melanie, what does one have to say to get you to change your mind? You know you can’t stay here all on your own. There is everything you need in London. With me you will have everything that you could ever want or dream of. Come with me now, and we can send for your things: close this place and leave it all behind.”
“Rupert you sound as if you are plucking me from an inner city slum. You have to realise that I am very happy here, and that there are a lot of people at work who are depending on me.”
“Oh no; not that little electronics firm. You must surely have someone to whom you could hand it over, or could you not sell it to the Americans, the Germans or the Japanese eh? Besides there aren’t that many employees, bugger them, sack the lot of them and you will be free. What are these people to you? Nothing that’s what they are."

She realised at that moment of sublime crystallisation what she had always suspected about Rupert. His perspective on everything was coloured by unalloyed self-centredness. He was not attempting to be hurtful or disparaging of other people's efforts - he simply did not see them, and therefore had no means of evaluating them. He had, in the past been very kind to her, and she did not doubt that he wanted what he considered to be the best for her. In making those assumptions, however, his mind negated any other possible viewpoint or the fact that others might well depend upon her presence, and that ultimately this was where her own happiness lay. In that moment, as clarity of thought intruded, she realised that she had simply accepted their relationship without question or scrutiny of any kind, as if its very existence was the only justification required for it to continue. One further thought, which refused to depart, was that belief that here was a man who conducted himself in a way that her father would never have contemplated.

She gave out a long sigh, but before she could speak; she was interrupted by Smith's arrival. He rushed in with his usual enthusiastic steps, only to check himself as he saw Rupert, who rose to shake his hand. Smith prepared himself to clasp the watery grasp once more.
“Oh Smith old chap, what are you doing here? A bit late for a house call eh? Oh, I forgot you poor buggers have to visit all times of night and day. Are you ill eh, Melanie? Looks fine to me, Smith old chap.”
Melanie cut in with difficulty. “Actually Rupert, I had invited Dr Smith round for tea. He has been so kind to me that I wanted to convey my gratitude,”
Smith looked a little nervous as Rupert assimilated this information. “And Dr. Smith, Rupert has just popped in to see how I was.”
“No, not actually, Melanie. Now tell the good doctor why I am really here.”
Patience was obviously not a strong streak within him, so he continued, "I want to take her away from all this, Smith. She would have a much better life with me. What do you say?”
“Rupert I don’t think....,” she began again.
“No, no Moopy, I am interested in what *your* doctor has to say.”

"Well, Rupert, where Melanie chooses to live is certainly not up to me, and I would have to advise her to live where she feels she would be most happy."
"Exactly! Just how I feel," Rupert crowed triumphantly.
Smith continued, "I'm not able to say whether that would be with you in London, or here at Shiplake, surely you need to ask her? Would you like me to leave so that the two of you can talk?"
"No, no Dr Smith," Melanie almost pleaded.
The speed of her reaction was not lost, even on Rupert who could neither see why this fellow, of very little account, was there in the first place, nor why the man should be persuaded to stay; especially when there were important things to discuss. Finally a thought occurred to him that he realised he could not discount and which led to conclusions that, he realised, he did not like one bit. Smith looked a little awkward, the charged atmosphere in the room reminded him of times long ago.

Mrs Perkins broke the gravid pause as she announced that dinner was ready. Melanie had planned to eat informally with Smith in the Conservatory, which regardless of time, weather or season remained her favourite room. Mrs Perkins had decided on a little more formality when Rupert had appeared unexpectedly. Smith had not previously seen the magnificent dining room with its majestic wooden table of solid Mahogany. He had never seen such an ornate and lavishly decorated room. The ceiling sported intricate plasterwork, and at its centre descended a magnificent chandelier of crystal with eighteen bulbs arranged in three tiers. Sensing Smith's thoughts Melanie offered, "Sorry this is a bit formal, but as Rupert is with us."

Melanie sat facing the two men. Smith observed, once again, how her eyes sparkled their deep hazel, even in the low lighting as the wavering candlelight on the table flickered mesmerisingly across the fine-featured face. He looked quickly away as the first course was set down. He hesitated only for a second as he looked at the array of cutlery in front of him, he knew only that you had to start from the outside and work your way in, but what seemed like a complete canteen before him caused him to pause. Smith had been used to snatching food on the run, first at home as a little boy for fear that his father would soon return, or in the hospital knowing the bleep could go off at any moment. In any event, food was eaten without ceremony at unrefined speed and with whatever accoutrements were to hand. Rupert's intervention in pointing out the correct choice only served to embarrass him. Melanie did her best to steer the conversation into the gap of awkwardness. Though Rupert was not the most sensitive of people, his powers of observation, such as they were, had been stimulated by the interaction between the two. He noted the fleeting glimpses, the emotion reined in with each eye contact: the way Melanie looked at him and the unexpected nervousness of Smith. Sensing a losing hand, he embarked upon a line of questioning as anger and suspicion welled from him.

The central facet of Rupert’s personality was predicated on the simple fact of never having lost anything. Everything he had ever wanted, had been given rather than earned; even in business his family had applied enough money, or petitioned powerful friends to ensure that no business deal was beyond reach, and would at all times be concluded in his favour. What he now observed between the two caused fear as he realised that that neither his position, his power nor that of his friends could alter it.
The sparkle in the eyes, the glances that were held just long enough, the smile that was mirrored from one to the other. His growing witness might, in another, have promoted learning and reflection, but in such a person, with such a background, its only product was that of seething anger. Smith was its target. His mind was racing with the ferocity that could only be engendered by denied love. Just what could Melanie see in this man of no breeding, who was nothing and who, by all evidence before him, had nothing, not even a decent suit. Surely she could not be bedazzled by such a person when, with him, she could have anything she wanted. He would have to demonstrate his point, just

as he would to errant shareholders who had the impertinence not to accept perfectly reasonable terms being offered to them.

"So, Smith just how can you bear to work in this NHS; surely it's about to collapse in turmoil despite the billions being pumped in."
"Well, it's true that the NHS needs a radical rethink, and there is a lot to be done."
"I was reading in the paper about a casualty department that reduced its trolley waits by removing the wheels off the trolleys. The poor patients still had to wait two days to get to the ward."
"I read that report too Rupert, and I am afraid it's probably true. The trouble with goal- and-initiative-led changes is that human nature tends to bend the measurement criteria so as to fit the target being measured."
"So they cheat, eh."
"Yes, I suppose they do."
"Don't you think they should just scrap it and replace the whole thing?"
"I can see why many would feel that way; the trouble is, what would they put in its place; and as always, the disadvantaged would suffer the most."
"You people get paid so little, surely it can't be worth your while. What are you on then Smith, sixty thousand, seventy, whatever it is it can't be enough?"
"Nearer forty actually, Rupert."
"My God man, only forty thousand, I earn that in a month!"
Melanie shifted nervously to display her displeasure. Rupert continued to glare at Smith unabashed.
"I know that GP's will never earn, for instance, what some people in the City earn, or a premier league footballer. I suppose, that I'd like to tell you that the job isn't about money, it's about satisfaction in that work and ..," began Smith.
"You're not going to tell me about a calling, are you?" He looked ceiling-wise as if Smith was now trying his patience.
"Well, I would argue that my sense of job satisfaction is strong. I wouldn't be interested in a higher paying job just for the money. I suppose I would say that when people become ill they realise just

what a prize good health is, and how much less important money is."
"You're trying to tell me that you're a visionary?"
"No, Rupert; I'm trying to tell you that I do my best to focus on what I think is important; and that remuneration, though nice, is not the main factor why people choose medicine, or say nursing, as a career."
"I move in circles where money, position and power count for everything."
"With respect, Rupert, I would have to say that is a million miles away from my world."
"There you are Melanie, see what this country existence does for people? You'd better come with me, before you start saying ridiculous things like that."

Melanie could see Smith struggling with rising anger. He obviously yearned to answer Rupert back. Rupert was certainly doing his best to bait him. She witnessed how Smith applied masterful restraint and even managed a defusing, "Perhaps you are right, Rupert."
"Actually, Rupert, I quite like what Doctor Smith says."
Her words of support toward Smith made him more angry still, Rupert wasn't finished. "My God, now old girl, you know so little about this. When did you last use the NHS?"
She tried to change Rupert's line of aggressive enquiry.
"Rupert, I should have told you that Dr Smith's mother has just passed away, and he is on compassionate leave."
There she was defending him again like some lovesick puppy following him round. This was simply not on, and he would have something to say about this as soon as he had got rid of Smith.
"Sorry about that old man."

Smith knew all about hostility, and he was acutely aware of a rising tide of it from Rupert. For much of his life he had borne witness to his father's temper and violence, and there were only two solutions in his experience; either react to it, or run from it. He would never become what he had seen his father become.

"My goodness is that the time? I must be going."

Melanie walked him to the door, whilst Rupert picked up a fat cigar and clipped the end with menace. His temper had whipped up into unrestrained frenzy that he needed to dissipate via thinly veiled threats directed at the young doctor who had spent much of his life under the roof of someone who had employed more physical means of achieving the same ends. As soon as Melanie returned, from showing Smith to the door, he began.
"Impudent fellow, do you see the way he looks at you? I'll have him struck off. He's displaying much more than a professional interest in you, my girl, and I do not think it is healthy."
Melanie's brain raced at the implications of his words as fear rose within her.
"Dr Smith is a good friend, Rupert, but he has at no time behaved improperly toward me."
"I'm not sure that the Medical Council would see it that way."
Melanie tried a different tack. "Just what is upsetting you Rupert?"
"I just don't like the way he looks at you, Moopy, my dear."

Melanie thought quickly. Neither Smith nor Melanie had subjected their relationship to the scrutiny that Rupert seemed determined to apply now. Rupert's agile but crafty mind had correctly guessed that the good doctor, in particular, had much to lose if he was seen to have overstepped the mark as regards a wealthy, attractive, vulnerable patient; especially one who was linked with a powerful man such as himself. Melanie quickly reasoned that her defence lay with honesty.
"You don't know Rupert, because you weren't here, just how lonely and how low I was."
Rupert motioned to speak but Melanie remained in control.
"I am not implying that you are in any way to blame for my illness. However I am sure that you will agree that I have much to thank Dr Smith, and the NHS, for."
Rupert detected that her words were a coy but foolish attempt to divert him from the measures that he now knew were necessary. Sometimes the only way to rescue a situation, was drastic action,

painful though that might be, and he knew that ultimately she would thank him for it.
"And Smith is now to abuse that gratitude?"
“Rupert, Dr Smith is abusing nothing. He is just a very good doctor as well as a good friend, for whom I have the highest regard.”
“Melanie, I am sure that Smith knows that you are a wealthy woman.”
Her placid face and bright, friendly, gleaming eyes now took on a completely different aspect, signifying that she was to accept no more. She stood.
“Rupert, I think it is time for you to go. I think we all need to calm down.”
“Very well, Melanie, but if he once puts a finger on you I'll make sure that being struck off is only the start of his problems.”

Melanie had seen a very different side to Rupert. She could not be sure whether jealousy, or loss of what he considered to be something of value, was its prime mover. She hated to part on such bad terms with anyone. Rupert had been kind to her in the past. She knew at an instinctive level, that it was a change in her that he could detect, that was unsettling him now. To attempt to placate him now would imply either that she agreed with him or that he had frightened her, or both.

Despite the late hour, Rupert found himself checking in to the village hotel, and could only reflect upon the magnificent master bedroom at the Manor, with those unequalled views and the occupant who would be all alone. Just as the thought came to him, he considered returning unannounced to Shiplake to see if she had been joined by Smith, but the late hour and one glass of wine too many advised him, even in his agitated state, against such a move. In any event he now held within his grasp far more powerful instruments with which to resolve his problem and ensure that the young woman didn’t do something foolish.

Smith's mind too was working feverishly. He had found that adding a few more components to the Victory was a calming influence, especially before bed. At that point Melanie had decided that another late night call was needed.
“I am sorry if Rupert was rude," she began.
“Rupert seemed upset, angry with me. Have I offended him in some way?”
She knew that the lie would be detected if she were face to face, and could only hope that the telephone and keeping her words as clipped as possible would suffice to mask it. She could say nothing except for, "I'm sure that's not the case, he hardly knows you.”
Smith’s pause reflected his deep thought also.
“Well, I just wanted to thank you for coming and to apologise once again if Rupert was rude to you.”
“Melanie,” - she tensed within herself almost as though by prescient vision she could anticipate the words that were then to follow.
“Melanie, you seem so much better now. I thought that may be we could release you from your review appointment. Perhaps come and see me in a month or two.”
Anticipation of the words did not allow for a more full response than, "OK, that’s fine"

Rupert’s strategy had hit home after all. Smith knew that Rupert had simply highlighted the inappropriateness of many of his own thoughts, as if he had looked through his mind with a magnifying lens. He knew that he was impotent against the wealthy and powerful financier, and knew, also, that his position as a GP was unlikely to survive if he should be foolish enough to even attempt to challenge him. Rupert had simply and unequivocally hinted at such a thing, and Smith knew that Melanie would be unable to protect him against such an onslaught, and nor should she be asked to try.

Melanie too had sensed that bright thoughts and fledgling hopes had been exposed to the clear light that had caused them to evaporate, and had left fear for each of them, and especially for

Smith, in their wake. Certainly Rupert held all the cards, and she now realised that he would not hesitate to use them in any way that he saw fit. Melanie had seen in the past that few businessmen were like her father. Enemies, or people who simply lacked money or influence were destroyed without a backward glance if they should get in the way, and to her shame, she realised that she had never stopped to contemplate what it would be like to be on the receiving end of such a casual misuse of such resources.

“OK, Doctor Smith." The emphasis on the Dr was unavoidable as she no longer had any power to divert the nuance in her voice. Each knew the other well enough for the separation that was opening between them to be detected.
“That’s fine, I'll see you, perhaps, in a couple of months. May I still come to the funeral? I was so fond of your mother.”
The fact that she had to ask and to remind, stung more than she had intended. It was his turn now for a passive agreement.
“Oh yes, of course Melanie, you are more than welcome, my mother would have wanted you there.”

She replaced the receiver, her thoughts in a whirl and knew only that in the troubled night that lay in prospect she would revisit all those words said, and those unsaid. over and over again.

CHAPTER XV

"RETRIBUTION and FEAR"

Melanie was in work early the following day, and waited patiently for Stella to arrive. She greeted her friend, who looked tanned and relaxed, with a mixture of enthusiasm and relief, doing her best to listen attentively as Stella discussed the holiday, and Tony. In due course she was able to steer the conversation round to some of the issues that had been burning in her mind since the small hours.
"Stella, have you had a chance to think about taking up Newman's job here?"
"Well someone has to keep an eye on you, I suppose it had better be me."
Melanie hugged her for the second time. Stella knew her boss well enough to know that there was more to come, and anticipated the more serious tone. They chatted for some time about Melanie's plans for the business. Stella listened for the most part as she was keen to gauge her boss's views.
"So how is the Dishy Doc?"
"Oh, he's OK."
"What do you mean OK? That doesn't sound OK to me, sounds a bit like a damp lettuce leaf to me!"
"Stella, he is my Doctor," she began and then a little more uncertainly, "besides Rupert is very much on the scene at the moment."
"Oh no, not old Rupe!"
Melanie hated it when she called him by that name.
"Rupert has been kind to me, and he intends to carry on in that vein."

Stella couldn't bear the man; and she hated the way he looked at her as if she were dirt, yet did not seem to be able to stop staring at her décolletage at each available opportunity. Worse though, was the way he looked at Melanie as if he were gazing at a prize pig that he had secured in the local livestock show, and not a young,

sexy woman who could, Stella knew, stand comparison with anything on two legs!
"Sorry Melanie I just don't think he is right for you – unlike the 'DD' of course."
"Stella!"

She knew that Melanie did not want to be drawn into consideration of either man at the moment, so she deftly changed the conversation back to work. The two women spent the rest of the day in Melanie's office discussing and poring over ideas for the future of the business. Stella was bursting with enthusiasm and this was partly due to the fact that she had been thinking about her work and her new role whilst she was away, and partly the result of the change in Melanie that had taken place in a relatively short span of time, which was a delight to behold. Neither woman could fail to spot the fact that the company was poised on the edge of something momentous if they could just keep everyone motivated after the damage inflicted by Newman.

Melanie drove home a little later than usual. Mrs Perkins had deliberately stayed, just to make sure that Melanie had something to eat before she left her. Mrs Perkins left her with a tray of food and had secured a promise from her boss that she would begin to eat it before it had cooled. "I'll be off then, Miss. and I'll look forward to seeing you tomorrow," she said, with her usual simple and sincere approach. It was only when she had vacated the house, through the back door, in order to find her bicycle that Mrs Perkins became aware that she had missed something of vital significance. The back door had been open as she left the kitchen. She knew that she had closed that very same door not half an hour before. Old she might be, but stupid she wasn't. She repositioned her bicycle against the wall and gently opened the heavy kitchen door with frustrating care so as not to make a sound. She could hear a man's voice coming from the conservatory.

He had been sitting in the gathering darkness as Melanie had entered. He rose quickly, before she had fully registered his presence. He grabbed both her hands using unequivocal force that hurt her, as he crushed them together and secured them with one of his own. The other hand held a large roll of tape. Melanie cried out, but she knew that now Mrs Perkins had gone there was no-one to hear the cry. Her assailant knew this too as he laughed, the cruel smirk lingering on his face as he enjoyed the terror now coursing across hers. She struggled as she recognised him and his intention, but he was too strong and had been given the advantage of surprise. He took full advantage of that surprise and seemed to delight in watching her struggle against his overwhelming strength.

"I told you I would be seeing you again, Melanie. Our final meeting, I fear," he offered, with mocking obsequiousness. He rapidly bound her wrists together, using multiple loops of tape around them. She struggled against him with vehemence. He raised the flat of his hand and smacked it violently against her cheek without restraint. She involuntarily howled with pain as he motioned to hit her again. Intense pain was propagated with explosive force, as the tissues stung viciously, causing her to gasp for breath and her eyes to stream under its ferocity. A look of triumph crossed his face as he took the opportunity, relished so long, of causing her pain, not only to dissuade her from a hopeless struggle, but also giving him the chance to show how much he hated her and to treat her with undiluted disdain and do with her whatever he wanted. She stopped struggling. He produced a pair of scissors to cut the tape, and now that her hands were restrained, he pushed her, using both hands, palms poised as a battering ram so that she fell backwards onto the chair. He quickly lifted both ankles. Once again she moved to resist him, and he raised his wide palm again as if to strike her, with even more violence in his eyes. Once again unequivocal force was used to crush her ankles together so that he could apply more tape. Lastly, he cut a small rectangle to push over the lips, that were now gasping for air. For some strange reason a spurious thought came to her as she remembered a debate in the paper as to whether such tape should be called "duct" tape or "duck" tape, followed quickly by the more relevant one, that she now recognised herself to be in great danger.

Only then did an entirely different look cross Newman's face as he realised that he now held complete dominance over her. He looked at the shapely legs, the skirt having ridden up just a little.
"Shame I've bound those ankles."
He roughly inserted his hand between her knees and stroked casually up between her thighs as she writhed with detestation. Enjoying her discomfiture, he bent more closely as if to whisper in her ear, his smoky breath having its usual nauseating effect on her, but now magnified by the pain in her face, the aching from muscles that had struggled against him, and the fear over exactly what his intentions were.
"Shame, I didn't do you, like I did your sister. She wasn't a bad screw, just like you I bet," as he continued to stroke ever higher between her thighs. "She used to like a bit of smacking, liked having a good slap, used to really get her in the mood." He laughed as she lay helpless before him and continued to writhe within his disgusting embrace. Only her eyes could convey her total outrage. Suddenly, he became aware that time was pressing.
"Shame I haven't got more time," he declared as he removed his hand and her skirt was allowed to fall to a more modest length.
"Shall we go for a drive Melanie? Your car I think; they tell me posh cars, like yours, can easily catch fire, and their occupants, especially when doused in petrol." His face became a sneer as he laughed, the ghastly image now confronting his terrified prisoner. Triumph replaced the lust upon his face which in turn had replaced the menace. She didn't yet know just how clever he had been. A mocking sycophantic voice was effected.

"Fools, you fools. Did you think you could escape me? That company was mine. I put all the work in while the old man strutted round the place, and your posh bitch of a sister lauded it over me like some paid skivvy, there just to do her bidding and service her when she felt like it. I showed them, tried to get rid of me, I don't think so." He wiped the corner of his sneering mouth, now salivating at its edge, with the pressure of his words and his desire to demonstrate some of the bile that consumed him, as he shouted at her.

"Bentley leaves the road, clear as day. I wonder if they ever knew what hit them? Sadly you will, Melanie, you will know a great deal about what's about to hit you. Please take my new SatNav, Sir, and try it for me? Poor old Newman can't afford a proper one, in the Bentley, like yours. Would you make sure its working for me Sir? What, that wire? It's just some modifications, and that battery? Oh that's nothing too, let me place it in your car for you. Please Sir. Fools didn't know it was rigged to go off as soon as they hit the motorway.

"Boom," he said as he smashed his hands together, as if he was going to hit her again.

"Boom, off they went, those Fentanyl ampoules.

"Boom, off they went, and off the road *they* went.

"Boom, you'll soon be joining them my dear."

He tried but failed, utterly, in manufacturing a mocking look of concern on his cruel face once again, as her eyes stared wide with the recognition of the devastating truth that had eluded her for over eighteen months. He grinned like a gargoyle, his grisly expression taking even the permanent cruel sneer, that his face carried, to a new level. Paradoxically it was the intensity of the malign expression that saved her, as she knew that she had to keep staring straight at him, if she were to stand any chance at all.

"I might not get my hands on your company, but the last thing you'll see is the inside of a burning wreck."

Too late, far too late, he was aware of the slight sound behind him.

"Boom! I don't think so Mr Newman, not tonight thank you."

Mrs Perkins was neither strong nor tall. Upon hearing the commotion, she slowly crept up behind Newman, who was totally preoccupied with tormenting his victim. She swung the cast iron skillet she had brought from the kitchen, as one might a tennis racquet, and smashed it, using all the force she could muster. His antics facilitating the summoning of extraordinary force, Newman went down with a sharp, satisfying clang as the metal resonated on violent contact with his skull. The force not enough to knock him out, but more than enough to stun him. He went down at the apogee of his triumph. As he fell to the tiled floor Mrs Perkins grabbed thc scissors to cut Melanie's hands free. She did her best to wrap the tape round Newman's wrists. She sat down heavily upon his dazed form, gaining more time, as Melanie cut the tape from her ankles. Melanie then helped Mrs Perkins to bind him, in exactly the way that he had bound her.

Melanie was not aware that she could hate anyone as much as she hated Newman at this point. He had killed her father and sister, purely for material gain. He had intended to do the same to her, simply out of spite. Mrs Perkins moved to the telephone to contact the Police. Melanie knew that if she stayed in the same room as him, she would not be able to control the anger that was welling up. She tied more tape round his ankles for good measure and knelt beside him, as she slapped a rectangle of the tape forcefully on his thin lips. She slid her hands between his thighs.
"Sorry Newman, I'm used to a real man, not some weak excuse for humanity."

She turned to Mrs Perkins. "What a wonderful woman you are. Just what could I ever have done without you? You surprise me more by the day." Melanie picked up the heavy skillet and at that moment considered lunging at Newman with it. In those closing seconds, it was thoughts of Smith and his careful, measured response at all times that calmed her. He would behave with restraint at a time like this, and she knew he would have defeated his anger, just as she must now.
"Miss, it's my pleasure," came from a delighted Mrs Perkins who had clearly enjoyed her exertions.

Whilst waiting for the Police to arrive, Melanie searched the Internet for Fentanyl. She discovered its true nature, that its fumes would be deadly in the confines of a car, especially if the ampoules were broken in the heating matrix or air-conditioning unit. Fast-acting, untraceable as it vapourised, and deadly. She also found a tiny article that conjectured how the Russians had ended a siege in a cinema with what was thought to be Fentanyl pumped in through the windows. Half the hostages had died, owing to its toxic nature, said to be one hundred times more powerful than Morphine. Fragments of glass had been found in the footwell of the car, no doubt this was from the ampoules of Fentanyl, and the battery was probably to power some sort of tiny detonator to fracture them.

She sat with the housekeeper in the kitchen to wait for the Police. Neither woman could bear to remain in the same room as Newman, now immobilised on the floor of the conservatory. Mrs Perkins was now shaking with the after shock. Melanie made her a cup of tea as they waited. Melanie was surprisingly calm; grateful for the fact that at last some of the pieces were falling into place for her. This was more than enough to expunge the personal terror that she had experienced, once again, at the hands of another. The Police soon arrived and Newman, still a little dazed, was led away. Melanie could not bear to look at him. A policewoman took their statements and informed them that Newman would be held in custody. Eventually the two women were alone again.

"Come on Mrs P. how about a brandy? And then I'm going to make up a bed for you, it's too late for you to cycle home." Once again, both women took to their beds with much to think about. Only when Melanie got to bed did the tears form. As she sat gently sobbing, she thought much about wishing there were someone with whom she could share some of her innermost thoughts. In the darkest of nights, however, she realised that at last some of those tears held something of a relief; and inevitably again her thoughts turned to Smith: it was as if his calm demeanour now resonated within her; he had made her a better person, and this was the thought that presented just before sleep claimed her.

Melanie did not see Smith again until the day of the funeral. She sent flowers, and also tried to call on a number of occasions, she texted and even phoned the surgery. Even the ever-efficient Mrs. Farnell, could not supply more detail. It was as if he had disappeared. Eventually she decided simply to turn up at the funeral knowing that he would definitely be there.

Very few were in attendance. She recognised Kim, the consultant from the hospital, and she surmised that some of the other women present had been Mrs Smith's carers, from the gratitude and warmth that Smith extended in their direction with every word and his body language. Melanie hated funerals, and she had already attended more than most in her relatively short life. After speaking with the carers, he had become unusually quiet as he became immersed, no doubt in thoughts of his own. He asked Melanie if she was OK, having detected immediately the shiver. She did her best to nod and smile reassuringly, even though she herself was in a far from a calm state. Ultimately the thought that prevented her from sinking into unrestrained emotion was the fact that she was here to lend support to him, at least as a friend, and also to a delightful old lady for whom she had felt sincere friendship, despite the short time they had known each other.

A solitary grave had been opened in the village churchyard. The vicar conducted a short, but moving ceremony as the coffin was lowered into the baked and brittle earth. Melanie did her best to stem the tears that were appearing in her eyes, still trying desperately to be strong for him but ultimately failing. The funeral over, Smith dropped a solitary rose onto the coffin and Melanie did the same. He turned to her, his face pale and deathly like an inert mask that had never known life. He thanked her for coming, she wanted to hug him at this point and to continue to hold him until the grassy banks had long since worn to dust, and the seas had risen to obscure the earth in the last dying days of the planet. She knew that hugging and kissing him, as her instinct directed, would embarrass him, so she gripped his hand firmly and prayed that her touch could reveal some of the thoughts that she desperately wanted to express. He in turn raised that hand, with the long elegant fingers, the beautiful nails and the sweet smell that seemed to intoxicate from each pore of her skin and kissed it lightly, as might a pilgrim on sensing that his lifelong journey had not been in vain.

Though, as usual, he was never less than polite to the few who had paid their respects, the only person he could see was Melanie, and he knew that his inner feelings would have mastered him had he not spent a lifetime in denying himself anything that might be responsible for triggering his father's unfailingly cruel attention, whilst doing his utmost to protect his mother. How his kiss electrified her, she moved to hold on with every ounce of her strength, just as he let go and turned away. His slightly wide-based gait, like that of a sailor on a pitching deck, covered the distance to the car park as she wished she could scream at him to stay, whilst she rushed over to hold him. She watched as more tears stung her eyes while she waited for the usual delay in his starting his car.

Over the following days she tried repeatedly to contact him. He returned some of the calls and seemed his usual polite self. She knew that the polite overtones could not hide from her the fact that he needed to be alone. Her surging feelings toward him meant that her usual acute instinct and insight had deserted her just at the most crucial moment. He could not begin to frame how much he needed her company, and for much of this time he was a little boy desperately hiding from his father, whilst at the same time needing his love, example and guidance that any small boy had a right to expect. She told herself that her instinct to be with him in his grief had to be resisted. The only way that she could help was to give him the space he needed. Anything else would be sheer selfishness on her part.

Whilst having lunch with Stella a few days later she caught sight of him on the far bank of the river. Stella noticed the focus and intensity of her gaze. She nodded in his direction. "Why not take a walk down, Melanie?"
"No, Stella I think he wants to be on his own right now."
"Nonsense, Melanie," with a little more force than she had intended. "these men don't know what they want, at times like

these. He wants you to go down there, grab his hand in your own and tell him, tell him, girl what you want him to know and what I know he wants to hear."

Melanie knew Stella to be a good friend, sincere and loyal. Sadly Melanie knew her to be man mad and rather than see the merit of each word that she spoke, she allowed herself to lapse into a tangential track that would depart irrevocably from the correct circle of thought.

"I'm not sure you do, Stella. I think he is either grieving, worried about what people would say or he has been put off by Rupert's appearance last week."

"I think it's about time you sent old Rupe packing."

Melanie cringed once again as she heard Stella called him by that name and by latching onto the inconsequential, she missed the most vital message in that simple sentence. Stella's impetuosity did not assist.

"I think I should go down there and straighten this out." She moved to push back in her chair.

There was an urgency in Melanie's voice, almost a pleading. "No, Stella, please."

Stella could see the emotions cross her friend's face, emotions that were wholly new. She remained for a second or two as each woman reflected on their own thoughts. Eventually Stella stood up.

"Come on, I've got to get back to work. I have a terrible boss who watches the clock."

"Oh I've heard about her, isn't she the one who makes you work nights and weekends and pulls you off nice holidays with hunky boyfriends."

"I'll say; I don't even get time to feed my cat. Good job *I* have friends," with just a slight emphasis on the 'I' to create a slight tease. They found the car in the car park and drove back to work.

If Smith had looked up, even for a moment, he might have noticed them. His head was bowed, however, noting only the path in front of his feet as he walked, his mind bursting with a million things, each demanding attention and yet none of them made much sense. Thoughts with regard to his mother were more defined. He looked back upon her difficult life with him, the father he had loathed for what he had done to both of them. Yet his mother's passing had paradoxically triggered the occasional happy memory of his childhood, though he immediately recognised that such reminiscences were few and far between, and heavily outweighed by the catalogue of abuse that had rained down upon them. Inevitably his thoughts drifted in Melanie's direction. He was delighted with her progress. He knew that his intervention, with just a little luck thrown in, had saved her. She had come back from the brink, and was so much better that he realised that she probably no longer needed his input, and he would probably raise this with her at their next consultation. He wondered if she could be happy with Rupert. Like would marry like, which is the way that it had always been among the upper classes, and other factors would surely not be given even fleeting consideration when things like, success, money and family connections were in play. He thought about his conduct with regard to Melanie: why such thoughts intruded now he was uncertain, and in any case he knew his behaviour toward her had surely, always been professional and proper. Just one tiny thought held sway against all that had gone before; she had made him a better person than he would have been had he never met her. This fact and her restoration to the strong, intelligent attractive woman that she was always destined to be, was enough for him; and all else was insane wandering.

Dr Michaels had been very kind and removed as much pressure as he could from his shoulders, but he realised now it was time for him to get back to work, and start to develop the practice along more contemporary lines. In any event he understood, as more focus came to him, that this is where his thoughts, efforts and future direction lay, and not with wild thoughts about the personal relationships of a patient.

The following day he returned to work. Mrs Farnell had returned from her annual trip to Scarborough and her refreshed presence was firmly in charge of the surgery once again. The usual impassive expression softened more than a little when she saw him, and he was surprised when she entered his room to express her condolences, and even more remarkably to say that she was pleased to see him back. Hardly a day passed when Mrs Farnell did not reveal another tiny facet of her character. As always, she was sincere and discreet in any comment she passed, and he knew that the practice was lucky to have her; he could also see just how Dr Michaels had come to rely upon her. It was then that he realised that her absence invariably brought about a negative change in the senior partner. On more than one occasion Michaels had booked the same days as annual leave, and Smith then realised that this was by no means co-incidental.

Mrs Farnell had booked a light surgery for him, and his confidence soon returned as he became immersed in his work, his patients' problems, and the task of filtering the common, easily remedied problems, from the more serious ones that patients presented with. As there were no visits he popped upstairs to the common room to join Dr Michaels for a light lunch. Dr Michaels was exceptionally friendly and spoke to him with almost fatherly concern. "How are you, my boy? Glad to see you back. Take your time over the next week or two."
"Thanks for all your help Dr Michaels, I hope that I haven't inconvenienced you too much?"
Michaels gave a rare chuckle as the sentiments hit him.
"Not at all. Quite enjoyed myself. One or two decided to wait for you to come back."
He reflected that Smith's popularity had grown steadily in the time he had been there, but there was life in the old dog yet, and he had been pleasantly surprised by his own performance. Typical of young Smith to think of him at a time like this.

"What time is my surgery starting Mrs F?"
"You're booked from two-thirty Dr Smith. Miss Jardine is your first patient," she offered, without the slightest nuance of emotion crossing her face. She watched carefully as his expression changed

so subtly, as a floating cloud of unhappiness, perhaps even regret, came over, followed by a rapid brightening. None but the most skilled observer of men and their moods would have noticed anything at all, but at this and so many other things, Mrs Farnell was unequalled. They both watched as the silver Jaguar swept into the small car park.

He waited by the reception window as she entered. Only Mrs Farnell was aware of the degree of tension that existed between the two, and this was reflected by the poor eye contact. A palpable distance had formed between these two young people. Perhaps Dr Michaels had taken him to one side to warn him of becoming too friendly with a patient. She thought this was unlikely. If this had been the case he would have sought her opinion, or at the very least informed her. No, she concluded, this rift was even deeper and she wondered just how it had come about. Smith shook Melanie's hand, as usual, smiled in his polite courteous way, as usual, ushered her into his office as usual, but there was no mistaking, by Mrs Farnell at least, that a certain distance had opened between the two of them.

Melanie desperately wanted to tell him about Rupert and something of her feelings, but she realised, just before such words came forth, that it would be the height of selfishness to burden him at this point in time with any of them. She could not fail to detect the slight coolness that had crept in as soon as Smith had heard Rupert talk so proprietorially about her and marriage.

"Melanie, you do look so well."
"I do?"
"Are you still taking the tablets?"
"I am. Each morning, as instructed by 'Superdoc'."
"How is your appetite?"
"Wonderful, did you not see me eat everything put in front of me?"
"And your sleep?"

"Not so good. I get two or three 'good' hours, but I suppose that is better than it has been." She wondered whether she was going to get a full night's sleep ever again.

"You're not going to ask for knockout drops again are you?"

"What and miss this? No, not for the world. I am back and I intend to stay the course."

He asked about Newman and was amazed at her resilience in coping with yet another attack. He smiled and nodded. He was constantly impressed by the woman. She had been through so much and yet remained so strong. For sure, some of this had been due to his efforts, but he had never discounted how she had fought against her dire predicament.

"Melanie, sounds good, it all sounds good. I am going to have to elevate you to my star patient."

"What will the other two patients say!"

"Well, they can still be in the top three. And how is work?"

"We're all set. The test production lines have been run and we have been testing and testing, until we can think of nothing else to test, and hopefully we are ready to launch. Enquiries are very high and a number of orders have come in. We just have to deliver what we say we will."

"I am sure you will," he offered in earnest. "So I take it you will be sticking with the business?"

"Yes, you bet."

Here was her chance to tell him about her plans, about Rupert, about everything.

He desperately wanted to ask about Rupert and whether he had expressed his views when Melanie had revealed her intention to remain with the firm. He spoke just as she was about to reveal something of her thoughts.

"We'll, Melanie you do seem so much better, so, perhaps, finish off the tablets you have and then take no more. We'll see you in a month or before if there are problems."

She knew that he was correct, and she knew that his professional side was firmly in charge, now, of all he said and all he did. How she regretted those words and how they made her feel. She stood, the erect poise, present as ever: but lacking, like sunshine after an arctic winter, was the serene smile that would brighten any room, including his. She looked at him hard, as if even now hoping for more words that would make it right. A hint of sadness formed in his eyes just as in hers, as he realised that his duty, as a doctor to her was coming to an end, and any attempt to prolong it would be unwise, unforgivable and unprofessional. He stood after a slight pause, as if he realised he was seeing her for the last time. He extended his hand to hers and the firm shake interlocked all too briefly. How he wanted to say, and do, much more. How she wanted to hear and feel much more. As always the eye contact conveyed more than the medium of speech ever could. She struggled for words that died a lonely death on her face, and squeezed the hand more tightly than ever. She smiled, briefly, turned and was gone. So many thoughts of hers and of his had failed to find a voice, and now would simply not be revealed.

He sat down heavily in his chair, suddenly feeling tired and alone. His mother's passing had brought into sharp focus some of the things that he now knew his life lacked. He knew that the brightest thing in his life had just departed, would be unlikely to return, and there was nothing he could do about it. Mrs Farnell had sensed the mood in each of them, as might an old seer reading palms as easily as the minds of men. She brought in the notes for the rest of the surgery and was her usual, cool, efficient self. In his deep melancholia he did not witness her gentle concern, knowing nods and kind smile as she offered to assuage some of his feelings.

Melanie sat in the car for a few moments. She had wanted to say so much, surely she should have screamed at him to shut up whilst she told him some of the thoughts she had restrained. Yet how could she visit this upon him, in the middle of his surgery, at a time like this? And surely she had embarrassed him already more times than kind patience could forgive. She felt like a traveller whose recently- boarded a train was slowly drawing away from the place she wanted to be, with each beat from the mighty engine pulling with an unalterable momentum, building by the second.

She knew too that she could not suddenly reveal her true feelings without the risk of alienating him forever. He was obviously acutely aware of his professional role and his responsibilities, and equally the conduct that was demanded of anyone held fit to practise medicine. She would have to make the first move, as he could not. She hammered her fist into the steering wheel as frustration came over her. Both were caught in a cruel impasse and neither could take steps to bypass it. The cruellest thing of all was the hint, deep within, that he wanted, so much, to hear the words she desperately wanted to say.

Smith waded, wearily through his surgery. The caseload seemed to contain far more of the mundane than usual. He would normally accept that this was the nature of general practice, but such thoughts would require a much lighter perspective than he was capable of at this point.

He was unaware of the events unfolding in the office. Mrs Farnell had taken a call from the teaching hospital. She was informed that Dr Smith had made an urgent appointment for a young patient called Sophie Allenby in the paediatric Neurology clinic. The family had failed to appear, with no word being given. Could Dr Smith review the patient since no further appointment would be sent until they had heard from the GP. Mrs Farnell took down all the details and asked Janice to retrieve the notes from the filing carousels. Janice immediately recognised the name.
"Dr Smith asked me to book an urgent appointment for the little girl about ten days ago."
Mrs Farnell looked at the copy of the referral letter in the case notes. She immediately asked the one question that would clarify the situation and the problem.
"Janice did you notify the Allenby's of their appointment, or did Dr Smith do that?"
Janice hesitated in an agony of enlightenment.

"I, I assumed that Dr Smith was going to do that."
"No matter, Janice, we will straighten things out and please do not distress yourself," sensing that this was exactly the emotion now in the ascendant in the young woman's thoughts.

As always Mrs Farnell now took charge of the situation. She waited, outside the consulting room door, for the next opportunity to slip in between Smith's patients. She showed him the notes.
"Forgive the interruption, Dr Smith, but Manchester Royal have just telephoned about this little girl defaulting on her urgent appointment. I assumed you would want to know as soon as possible."
Smith looked aghast. "This is all my fault. I had assumed that Janice had informed them," as he realised ultimately that two mutually incompatible assumptions were now in force. Smith knew only too well that ultimately the GP bore full responsibility for any failure of communication, and that excuses would not change that state of affairs. Like all good clinicians, however, he acted quickly to limit the damage.
"Mrs Farnell, I was just a little concerned about this little girl. Would you telephone appointments and ask them if we could have another urgent appointment, please, owing to an administrative error, entirely of my making."

The more she saw of this young doctor, the more impressed Mrs Farnell became. There were no excuses, no attempts to blame others, or to avoid responsibility. He looked squarely down each and every barrel that was aimed in his direction, and would go on doing his utmost until, one day, that trigger was pulled. Mrs Farnell departed and returned a few minutes later. "Dr Smith I have been on to Dr Williams' secretary at the MRI and he is unhappy at releasing another urgent appointment as the clinic is over-subscribed and the next available, 'routine' is thirty days' away."
"Please reserve that one then, Mrs Farnell and we could perhaps ask the Allenbys to come in with Sophie for a review?" Mrs Farnell tried to phone the parents at once, but received no reply,

nor was she able to locate a mobile or leave a message. Something was troubling Smith and it continued to do so throughout his surgery. Concern was tinged with panic as unaccustomed fear intruded. A simple mistakc and yet the patient would now wait another month. He had no firm diagnosis, yet he knew that he had been concerned about her presentation. If he could review the patient, either further clarifying features may have appeared, or indeed, she might even be so much better. Only the chill that cascaded down his spine gave a hint as to what was to come about. He knew that Sophie had not been ill enough to admit as an urgency, yet his instinct about her refused to allow him to be complacent.

Mrs Farnell tried to contact the Allenbys all afternoon, and Smith tried again later as he finished his surgery. He thought about calling on his way home but then realised there would be little point in this, since they were clearly not at home. He would try again first thing. He decided to go home, cook an evening meal and do his best to get a night's sleep, as he recognised a weariness building within. He stifled the urge to phone Melanie, but did not wish to dwell on why such a thought had occurred to him. In any event he concluded she might well be out and about with Rupert, and had possibly have taken him up on his offer to visit him in London. In point of fact, Melanie was going through a very similar dilemma. She was aching to phone him, so much so she wondered if she could feign illness, or perhaps something acute like another appendicitis, before she realised that you could only have it removed once!

As always, Mrs Perkins was not far away to intercede in a moment when she detected such turmoil within her boss. She began by humming within close proximity as she tidied and dusted, no doubt something that had already been moved and dusted half a dozen times. When this did not provoke a suitable response, she decided to go for the direct approach. "Is there anything I can do for you Miss?"

"Oh Mrs Perkins, what am I to do? If only I could sit and talk to him. I really miss his company"
"How do you think he feels, Miss?"
"I just don't know. He has never given any indication that his interest in me is anything other than professional."
Mrs Perkins nearly laughed out loud with the words she had just heard and could not believe that someone who was normally as perceptive as Miss Melanie could have uttered them. Mrs Perkins decided to start with some simple yet obvious evidence and to lay it before the young woman.
"What do his eyes tell you?"
Melanie paused as if the very question was reaching for information that had somehow been imparted to her in strict confidence. The housekeeper decided that she was going to have to be more direct.
"He's interested Miss."
"How do you know?" Melanie asked, as if she were searching for confirmation of the existence of Dark Matter.
"I know." Mrs Perkins was about to divulge confidential information that was in fact known by all those who had seen the two together, but apparently not by the two young people in question. She paused for a deep breath and averted her eyes, so acute had become the young woman's distress.
"I loved my Bill more than words can say, and I do believe that he loved me with every ounce of his body. We were together for nearly forty years, until he was taken from me. In truth, I never saw him so much as look at another woman. I know that he could not have loved me more, and yet I never saw him look at me the way that the nice young doctor looks at you."

Melanie stared for a moment, as if having discovered the secret of Dark Matter after all, but for that second, neither woman could speak. Mrs Perkins, however was not quite finished.
"There are indeed many things in this life that I am not certain of, but I am certain of this. He loves you from the top of his head down to the bottom of his woolly socks, I see it in his eyes, in the way he looks at you, the way he speaks to you, the way he speaks

about you when you are not there. In fact if I were a betting woman and had any money I would bet every penny on that being as fact. Forgive me for being candid like, Miss"

Melanie had managed, just, to get over the shock of the words she had just heard. She decided that Mrs Perkins was on a roll and no doubt having clarified Dark Matter could continue in the same vein and now explain the secrets of the Universe, itself.

"So what should I do?"

Mrs Perkins sensed that she had said enough, but she knew of one who would love to get started on the problem.

"Now, Miss, that I cannot say, but have you thought of having a word with Miss Stella?"

"She's not the most discreet."

Mrs Perkins ignored the caution that had crept in and she was, once again, in full flow.

"No, Miss, beggin' your pardon, but I think if you were to have a quiet word with her and explain your situation, I am sure she is the person for this tricky situation."

"Mrs Perkins, you are a marvel."

She hugged the mature lady with enthusiasm. Mrs Perkins beamed by way of reply.

"The young Doctor Smith has made such a difference to your life. That day he walked in to your bedroom I hoped beyond my wildest dreams that he could get you better."

Mrs Perkins looked at the clock.

"My goodness me, I had better be getting home."

CHAPTER XVI

"NEXUS of PAIN"

Weathermen were already talking of drought records being broken as the hot summer extended into the dry autumn. The gardeners had had to stop pumping water from the mere as its level was falling rapidly. The once magnificent lawns had long since changed to dry, brown thatch, and even that was wearing back to a bed of baked and cracked earth.

Melanie read for a short while, then decided on a long, self-pampering, soak in the bath. She felt more than a little guilty as she remembered, only when she had filled the bath, the prevailing water shortages, and having no-one present to witness her excess made her feel even more remorseful. However, there followed the most restful night's sleep she had had in a long time. Some of her thoughts were coming into focus now, and she was grateful for Mrs Perkins' frank discussion. What a wonderful person she had been, and what an insightful person she was. With such logic on tap, Melanie could forgive her the inquisitive streak that accompanied it.

Smith's night was turning out to be the opposite. He felt so tired as he turned in that he was certain that sleep would arrive, only to be still disappointed as he saw the clock click round, some two hours later. He continued in this restless frame of mind for the rest of the night, until the dawn light signalled the coming of daylight to re-establish itself in command of another day. He decided to shower, get dressed and make an early start in work.

Melanie, too, was in work early. She waited patiently for Stella to arrive, having drunk three mugs of tea before her sports car flashed into the car park. Her friend's eagerness to discuss something was readily apparent and Stella did not have to think too hard or too long to guess just what or whom it was about.

"Stella can I ask your opinion?"

"About anyone in particular?"

"I'm not sure what's going on, but I do know that I'm so happy when I'm with him and unhappy when I'm not."

"Well I know exactly what's going on," she said with certainty that belied her young age. "My diagnosis is simple. A bad case of 'lurve' if ever I saw one."

Melanie's inability to respond as though some unutterable spell had suddenly been voiced, only confirmed Stella in her belief. She used the pause to continue quickly. "Well, now that we've got that out of the way, how does he feel?"

Melanie's voice returned. "Now that, is the tricky one. I just don't know, or at least I'm not sure. He is so married to his work you know?"

"Well, I'm sure that he looks at his work, the way I've seen him look at you!"

"OK then, I think he's frightened."

"Of what, might I ask?"

"Of being struck off, of failing in his duty as a doctor."

"Well, now you're talking, what have the two of you been up to whilst I've been away; tell the juicy bits first, then fill in the rest of the detail later. Is it a case of take your clothes off and put them next to mine, like I read in the Sunday Tabloids each week?"

Stella had never seen Melanie blush before, even when Newman had been screaming at her.

"Absolutely nothing," she offered quickly, sensing that Stella was in full flight, and doing her best to generate an indignant tone in an attempt to calm her friend's flow of words.

"It's just that," there was a pause.

"Just what?"

"You know? Fraternising with patients is frowned upon, and anything more, you get struck off."

"So who's going to know or care what the two of you get up to, and who's going to make a complaint to the GMC? It's not that you're promised to anyone else, despite what that old fart thinks."

"Stella, don't talk about Rupert that way."

Stella almost laughed, when she realised that her friend knew immediately whom she had in mind.
"He has been kind to me, and always has my best interests at heart."
"He wants to own you. He's a bit like Newman without the smoky breath and of course, with loads more dosh. He looks at you like some thoroughbred filly in his stable. A prize Geranium to put in his hot house, besides I don't remember him ever being that kind to you?"
"Thanks for that Stella," Melanie replied, initially a little hurt, but then she realised that the words, spoken by an honest and true friend, contained the unabridged truth.

She then remembered the times that Rupert had visited, times when she was desperately low and also very lonely. On each of these occasions he had stayed the night, availed himself of sex, when she needed company more than anything, and was on his way the following morning: leaving her in the same vulnerable state in which he had found her. Those simple words contained more than truth, they had forced Melanie to look beyond the superficial thoughts, with which she had run her life these past months, and to confront some of the more painful knowledge that had lain submerged throughout this time. Smith had set in motion this change, in order to bring about her recovery, and she now recognised that such a process, once begun, could not be halted.
"You know its true. So what has he got to do with the dishy doc?" Stella clarified, sensing that Melanie had drifted for a second.
"Rupert tells me that he doesn't like the way James looks at me."
"Was his face all green at the time? Of course he doesn't like the way Smith looks at you, most women would kill for a man like that, to look at them in that way!"
Melanie smiled. Stella always had the knack of setting things right: somehow, no matter how dark and grey the sky, she could always find that ray of light hidden behind the thickest cloud. She did not disappoint; her best was still to come.

"Melanie, I don't see what all the fuss is about."

Melanie gazed at her friend in wide-eyed disbelief, Stella had obviously not been listening to her; had she not heard about the difficulties that she and Smith faced. Stella was just warming up, however, and logic was about to flow with the precision of a beam focussed to split an atom.

"You've not done anything? Correct? You mad fool, just let me get my hands on him, woman."

"Correct, no nothing, I mean."

"You are over eighteen, and therefore a consenting adult?"

"No, I mean yes, well I mean, I would be, if I got the chance."

"You will girl, you will, just listen."

Melanie stared at her friend as if the sermon, upon which she had chanced, was about to reveal the meaning of life as well as the proof of Resurrection, all in one simple statement. Her friend did not disappoint.

"He can't touch you, cause he'll get struck off; but you think that he could be persuaded by the odd low-cut blouse, short skirt, wink in the right direction; that sort of thing?"

"Stella!" She feigned shock, but in truth such advice was only what Mrs Perkins had imparted, though she had hoped that Stella hadn't noticed that she had been following that advice for a week or two now.

"He can't touch you because you are a patient? What," she said triumphantly, "if you were not his patient?"

"I would lose a good doctor."

Stella had lost count of the number of positive attributes that one could bestow upon Melanie, with no hint of exaggeration or bias. She was, clever, honest, a good friend, loyal, stunning to look at and a whole host of other things too numerous to list; it seemed however that simple observation and common sense had deserted her in her moment of greatest need.

"Now, tell me what you could gain; a boyfriend, lover, soul-mate, someone to share a cold bed with, a warm piece of toast or a hot cup of coffee, someone to snuggle in front of the telly with. Tick all that apply."

Stella was in full flow and in such mood, as always, simply unstoppable; she beamed with self-satisfied delight that was as compelling as it was infectious. As always, the most effective solution was the simplest. Leaving Smith's list would allow for an unencumbered relationship that was free from external scrutiny by Smith's peers. Melanie's face lit up, in direct response to her friend's conclusion.

"Stella, I like it, so good, so good." She put her arms round her and hugged her, the relief palpable. "My only worry is that if I change doctor will I ever see him?"

"I can't believe what I am hearing here. You cannot be serious." She gesticulated, as if waving a tennis racket around. "I take it he does have one of these new fangled mobile phones," she emphasised the words as if she were crossing unfamiliar territory with a child. Stella continued to delight in the situation. Melanie suspected that her usual stance of requiring every last detail to be fully dissected and examined, was part of that enjoyment.

"Let's just recap shall we, whilst we take a look in the mirror eh, gal? He's a man, got at least one good eye, and a pulse." She counted off on her fingers. "Anything else we require here - oh yes, and that as well, so that's four things. I take it he has got four things?"

Melanie blushed again, "Well, yes I assume so. I think his mother would have told me if there were only three."

"Believe me there are four, I've seen how he looks when he's been a passenger in your car, when you're wearing one of those skirts that's just a bit narrower than a scarf!"

"Stella !"

"Well a girl's gotta know these things."

"Right," Stella said with a finality, as the last conclusions had been drawn. "Suppose you go off and register with that practice over the hill, I mean round the bend, you know, Oak Lane? Just be careful of old McGill: he's notorious for touching up all his female patients and listening to their chests - whatever they present with!"

"Sounds like fun," offered Melanie, finally synchronising with her friend's mood.

“Yes, I've been in there four times and never been touched, I feel quite insulted! You could always go and get him struck off, instead of Smith, you know.”
“Stella !”
“Only joking.” ‘Gosh,’ she thought to herself, ‘this girl has it bad, can’t even see the joke!’ “I make an appointment with ‘DD’ and put your cards on his table, so to speak. He rushes from the building, past a waiting room full of patients, and you both ride off into the sunset together, or at least Tatton Park festival, which is on next week!”
“Sounds simple,” Melanie said, as more foreboding crept in than enthusiasm. Just what could go wrong? The churning feeling in the pit of her stomach gave a hint that things would be far from simple.

Melanie kept herself busy all day; Stella’s words kept recurring as she just had to run through them again and again as if doing so would guarantee a favourable outcome. Stella made plans to call in to the surgery the following day and obtain an appointment with Dr Smith as soon as possible.

Another restless night brought Smith into work early, once again. He went through his post, signed some prescriptions and read through some discharge letters from the hospital as he drank a cup of coffee, which stimulated his heart into palpitations, but was unable to dispel some of the weariness from another restless night. It was only when he heard a commotion downstairs in reception that the surge of adrenaline brought his senses to life with a sharp jolt. Mrs Farnell appeared in the stairwell.
“Is there anything I can do Mrs Farnell?”
“It’s Mr Allenby. He's brought Sophie in, saying that he wants to see Dr Michaels urgently.”
“I can see her now.”

Just at this point Stella entered the waiting room and sat down. She had decided that the best plan was for her to attend in person in order to book an appointment with Smith. The waiting room was small but comfortable. The slightest sound could be heard wherever one sat, and certainly by less inquisitive people than she.

Mrs Farnell hesitated, itself a very unusual occurrence and one that had been seen infrequently over the previous thirty years, but its presence was unmistakeable now, as she faced a difficult dilemma. “He says he will only see Dr Michaels.”
Smith suddenly became aware of a thump from his heart, and a corresponding throbbing of the blood vessels in his neck; and that awful leaden feeling in his stomach, which was replaced with nausea and even faster palpitations. His eyes stared wide, as if he had been granted prescient vision of the events that were now unfolding in the small surgery. Events that were about to engulf him. Dr Michaels’ car had appeared and Mrs Farnell, was still struggling with unaccustomed emotions, as she left Smith frozen at the top of the stairs while she met the senior partner.

The small space seemed to magnify the events. Smith could only continue to stare. Michaels was greeted by rapidly escalating chaos, that he too had seen infrequently over the years. Allenby was carrying his daughter and refusing to sit down or to depart, until she had been seen. He had refused to see Dr Smith. Mrs Farnell had abandoned her usual serene efficiency, and damage-limitation had replaced it, whilst she attempted to placate the angry father, with anxiety now written to her usual calm visage. Patients were slowly arriving for the day’s surgeries. Stella could only watch, with her own wide-eyed horror, as she gripped the plastic seat, frightened that her legs would start shaking if she were to relax for a moment her nail splitting grip, her mouth, now, as dry as an Egyptian tomb.

It had been many years since a case had presented that had deflected Michaels from removing his coat. Mrs Farnell had not wasted those vital seconds that Dr Michaels had granted her as he crossed the threshold into the surgery, all eyes on him and on Allenby.

"Mr Allenby wonders if you would be so kind as to see his daughter, Sophie, before you start Dr Michaels?" Though her porcelain, steady exterior of tranquillity was rapidly returning, the two had known each other for so long that he could immediately see the effort she was applying to maintain that image. This in turn allowed him enough time to calm his own feelings of alarm, at the sight and posture of the male patient before him. He smiled gently in her direction as if acknowledging her turmoil and her attempts to master it. In a moment he turned to Allenby and his little girl, now lying limp in his arms.

"Come with me Jack." The slight nod was directed simultaneously in two directions with two messages that speech could not render, as he led the way to his consulting room. To Mrs Farrell it signified that he thanked her most sincerely, but that now he would handle it, and to the agitated postman it signified that he would grant his entirely reasonable request without delay. Allenby followed with only a slight hesitation, as if he had expected more discussion before action was taken.

Mrs Farnell quickly re-established control of the situation, making sure that each of the reception staff were given duties to perform, that telephones were manned and that patients, like Stella, who had attended in person, were processed without further delay. Smith appeared at the office door. He wanted to ask several questions but Mrs Farnell was by now firmly in command. "Dr Smith, I have placed your notes in your room. Two patients have arrived already and are sitting in the waiting room."

Mrs Farnell was correct as usual. His questions would have to wait and the open reception area was never the best of places to ask them. The surgery went quickly enough, but he was anxious to catch Dr Michaels. He did not have to wait for long after his surgery finished, in order to have at least some of his questions answered.

Michaels came in to his room soon after his last patient had departed. His expression and voice filled with an almost fatherly concern.

"It's a bad do with the Allenby girl, Smith. I saw that you referred her urgently. It's a shame about the mix-up with the appointment." Michaels averted his gaze at this point as if he was about to cross into even more uncomfortable territory. It was unusual for even serious events to overwhelm him, but Smith observed it now. Michaels continued, but was now gazing at a point on the desk, not at Smith directly.

"Something nasty afoot there, Smith. The girl's been fitting today. I sent her straight to hospital."

Dr Michaels looked up, and it was now Smith's turn to avert his gaze. His eyes widened with fear as the sickening thump hit from deep within his stomach once again.

"Maybe I should have sent her in the first time I saw her."

"Your notes, as always, are exemplary. From your examination there wasn't a lot to go on," opined Michaels, in unusual conciliatory tones. Smith continued to stare into the distance. Once again he sensed a deeper crisis of events that were about to envelop him.

"I'm not at all sure what's wrong with her, but she seems to be deteriorating rapidly," was Michaels' unfortunate but accurate conclusion. "I'll phone the hospital later and find out what the devil's going on."

Smith nodded. Racing thoughts in his brain precluded utterance of words. Dr Michaels sensed the disarray and sickening worry at the thought that someone's life lay in the balance, because of a misdiagnosis or a simple delay that would ultimately be seen as the GP's responsibility. Michaels rose to go.

"Thanks for coming in to tell me what's going on," Smith offered with his usual politeness, despite feeling on the far side of wretched.

Michaels was never one to reveal too much of his inner thoughts. Their utterance now, far from slaking Smith's worry, increased it.

"You have no need to worry Smith: you're not only one of the best doctors that I've ever had the pleasure of working with, but almost certainly the best GP."

"Thank-you for that, Dr Michaels."

Michaels phoned the admitting team later that day, to see if there was any news. They informed the GP that they weren't at all certain what was going on, but that they were hoping to do a CT scan that night. Lumbar puncture had ruled out meningitis, but there was a hint of raised pressure inside the brain.

Another night of turmoil lay in wait for Smith. The doctor's curse of assessing and revisiting events and diagnoses and misdiagnoses, ran in a continuous loop through his mind for much of the night. Eventually he pulled some clothes on, and decided to go for a drive: travelling along the quiet roads as the dawn began to flood night into day with unremitting sunshine. As he passed Shiplake he resisted the temptation to drive between its magnificent stone pillars through the heavy ironworks of the gates, usually left open. He viewed with some fear his developing insight into his own emotions. His need to see Melanie as a patient had started to decline, yet his need to see her as a friend and a confidante had risen in equal part. How he had failed as a doctor, failed as a man! It seemed as if despair itself had locked on to his very soul.

He reached work a little later. He had had to wait for the petrol station to open so that he could fill the Maestro and then spent an age trying to get it started, much to the bemusement of other drivers used to more reliable, modern cars. He was sorting through his post in the upstairs office when the call from the Paediatric Neurologist came through from the hospital. He had urgent news about Sophie.

"Hi James, its Paul Serenghotti here; Sophie was transferred to my care here at the MRI last night. We managed to get her into the scanner. I'm afraid it's not looking good. It looks like an Astrocytoma and it's perched in the worst possible place just over the brainstem. We haven't got any histology, of course, but from how quickly the poor girl seems to be deteriorating, it's probably a Glioblastoma. Rare as hens' teeth, but deadly. Radiotherapy and surgery are out of the question. We'll have a word with the Christie to see about chemotherapy, but I'm not hopeful. The family are gutted as you'd expect. I've had a word with Mr and Mrs Allenby. I'm afraid he is very angry. One of my juniors shot his mouth off, and Mr Allenby's taken onboard what was said. I'll try to straighten things out."

Smith knew that an Astrocytoma was a rare, but deadly tumour, especially when it occurred at the base of the brain; the part that controlled swallowing and breathing. Smith also knew that the only form of treatment, chemotherapy, was often ineffective, and after that, it was a waiting game. In some parts of the brain, operations could be carried out to debulk the tumour, a word that always caused a shiver to run down Smith's spine when he thought of it. He doubted that Sophie would be amenable to surgery. He also knew that of all the brilliant Neurosurgeons at Manchester Royal, Paul Serenghotti was *the* most brilliant. Smith thanked the Neurosurgeon and went downstairs to inform Dr Michaels. The rest of the week seemed to pass like a blur, as Smith did his best to remain focused on his patients and eagerly awaited more news about Sophie, daring to hope, even now, that the Neurosurgeon's predictions were wrong.

Friday dawned bright but cloudy. Smith arrived at the surgery just before Stella who had arrived for her appointment with him in order to 'finally sort things out', as she had put it, with much bemusement and more than a hint of tease to her boss, who had been patiently waiting for this day to arrive. "Leave him to me, Melanie," she had announced confidently. "I'll have the two of you closer than two robins on a snowy branch in winter, in no time."

Once again, an early call came through on the bypass number that hospitals and emergency services used. Mrs Farnell took the call with a grave expression. She voiced the desperately sad news that she was compelled to relay, that Sophie had died in the early hours of the morning. Smith was present in the office when she released the words that went off in his psyche like explosions hitting him with physical force.

Stella had just entered and was about to give her name in to reception. Allenby rushed in, pushing past her in his haste. He looked dreadful, and was unshaven and unkempt as if he had been sitting by the little girl's bed for days.

"There he is, that's him," he shouted, pointing at Smith. The sight of the young doctor in the office seemed to infuriate him. He shouted aloud. "He's killed my little girl. That doctor told me, if only they'd had her a bit sooner, there was much more they could have done; told me it was a disgrace the GP hadn't done something sooner. Might even have been able to save her."

Allenby's desolate mix of grief and anger had caused him to act erratically as he assessed the glass panels and the louvres of glass on the reception windows to see if he could get through. So intent, was he on reaching Smith that Mrs Farnell and the receptionists feared for their safety, and wondered what he would do next.

"That's the bastard there. He killed my girl. You wait Smith, I'll have you. You wait till my solicitor gets hold of you." His agitated state would have whipped up into more of a frenzy had Mrs Allenby not come running in after her husband.

"Please forgive him doctor, he's tired and upset. He don't mean none of those words, we both know what a kind and caring young doctor you have been to all of us."

The tears continued to flow down her red and sore cheeks in little rivulets.

"That specialist, Paul 'Slotty', told us they couldn't 'ave done no more for our Sophie even if they'd seen her months ago. He told us it wasn't your fault n'all."

Jack Allenby turned to his wife and hugged her as both dissolved into pillars of tears, that appeared without end. Michaels appeared at this point, but Mrs Farnell was, as usual, anticipating his every word.

"Janice, two teas please," and continued, "shall I put the Allenbys in your room Dr Michaels?" The distraught parents were led into Dr Michaels' consulting room. Mrs Farnell was still firmly in command. She strode into the waiting room and apologised for any inconvenience; she asked if those whose appointments were routine, would please book for a few days' hence.

Stella knew that she had better leave, and that her mission and her message lay in tatters at the hand of despair that now permeated the quiet little surgery. Just before she left, she saw Smith, his ashen face frozen between the trident of fear, torment and wretchedness. The words, though coming from a grieving parent who needed someone to blame, were out and could not be recovered. Several patients were muttering between themselves, and Smith was their object. One patient asked if he could cancel his appointment with Dr Smith and book with Dr Michaels instead. Others formed a quiet queue.

Stella sat in the car and phoned Melanie; her hands were shaking as she desperately tried to target the touch screen. How must Smith be feeling at the sight of the Allenbys in the midst of the torture of grief. Melanie's excited voice appeared in Stella's handset as if she had been anticipating her call any moment.
"How'd it go Stel ?"
"Badly Melanie, very badly I'm afraid."
"Oh no what did he say?"
"Nothing, poor soul was poleaxed," she relayed to Melanie the events of the morning. Melanie's mood changed from expectation, to disappointment, to despair at the thought of the two parents. She thought, too, of Smith, and knew, whether it was his fault or not, he would take it all on, and blame himself vehemently. His desire to help his patients, and to do right by them all, would be crushed under the tide of grief that had been unleashed, and Melanie understood all this as if she had been there in person.
"Stel, what should we do?"
"Not a lot I suspect, Melanie. Smith is on leave now for a few days, so I won't be able to get back to see him."
Such thoughts were far away from Melanie's mind as concern for all the protagonists was now uppermost.
"Dr Michaels has grabbed the reins and that Practice Manager was stupendous, we need someone like her Melanie!"

"Stella, are you coming back to the office?"
"Yes, Melanie I'm on my way now."
"OK, I'll get the coffee on and we'll talk some more."

Smith was upstairs as Dr Michaels finished his surgery. He looked up from the murky mug of coffee that had long since cooled, as other thoughts had swept in, and subjugated any thoughts of thirst or hunger.
"I am sorry about all this Dr Michaels."
The older GP gave an unaccustomed smile. Here was this young GP in the midst of horrors of his own and he was the one apologising.
"Allenby is in the middle of his grief, Smith. He's not a bad man. He's still looking to place blame on someone, and that young Neurology doctor had no right to say that they could have saved her; shooting his mouth off like that, should be sacked." Several thoughts were obviously queuing sequentially and as was his wont, Michaels gave vent to them all in short bursts.
"Allenby has gone home to cool off. Better phone your defence union to put them in the picture, but I suspect they won't need to get involved, Smith. I doubt Jack will take it any further, and his wife is very level headed. I delivered June Allenby myself, few years ago now! You have some days off now, Smith; so get going and don't worry about things here. It's been a bad time for you, my boy. Can't get any worse."
The simple words were not meant as any sort of challenge, but unfortunately held no predictive value whatsoever in the events that were now set to test Smith to destruction.

Smith walked into the car park. The cold wind caused a shiver to course through his entire frame. So many thoughts were stampeding through his mind, that his head had long since started hurting with the stress that seemed to beset him from all sides. Most of all he felt isolated and alone. That poor child lay cold in the hospital mortuary, and her parents had been led to believe that it had been directly as a result of the delay in her being referred. Though the view had been triggered by the incautious words of a junior doctor, before more senior and more balanced views had been offered, Smith knew that such words once out, were difficult to discount. As always, such opinions, held enormous destructive power, whether true or otherwise. Grief reactions were often accompanied by the need to blame. The death of their only child was an enormous loss to bear, and as grief unfolded, many painful emotions would be unleashed. The remote possibility that Smith's unwitting delay had led to the little girl's death, refused to be dislodged by more informed logic. It lay restlessly on his mind and continued to gain ascendancy as weariness began to subdue his more discriminative powers. Worse, much worse was the thought that crept in and refused to be dislodged, by simple reference to the facts, that the attention and time he had devoted to Melanie had caused him to be distracted, and somehow miss something that would indeed have saved that little girl. He drove straight to his mother's house. He had a lot of clearing up to do. The estate agent was to meet him there next week with a view to putting the house on the market.

Stella poured Melanie another coffee.
"I tell you Melanie, if you had been there you couldn't have done anything. The father whose little girl had died came charging in, all set to swing for poor Smith. Just what could he do? He was shouting and screaming and obviously very upset. Smith just stood there transfixed. That practice manager was pretty quick and soon siphoned him off. Dr Michaels came in to calm him down and they all went into his consulting room. Poor Smith was absolutely banjaxed. They said I could wait, but after what had happened I didn't think it right.'
"No of course not Stella."
"Any other ideas Melanie?"
Melanie shrugged as if acknowledging her impotence over events.
"Melanie, have you tried phoning him at home."
"Yes Stel, thought of that, the mobile is off and the answer machine is on. I have left messages."
"Well Melanie, you've nothing to lose now. Drive round and see him. If he is going to get struck off," she paused as she realised

that her words were more in prospect now than ever before. “Sorry Melanie, I didn’t mean.”
Melanie hugged her. “Don’t worry Stella, the same thoughts are going through my mind. You're such a good friend, thank you for all your help.”

Melanie decided to drive straight round to Smith’s house. Unfortunately all was quiet, only an oily patch on the drive marked the spot that would normally reveal the Maestro's position. She quickly pushed a note through and drove home.

Mrs Perkins had already heard the news via village gossip. Less charitable sources held that the little girl had died as a result of negligence by Dr Smith, though most held a more balanced view. “What will you do now Miss?”
“Wait I suppose, Mrs P. I have changed doctors, the paperwork will go through in the next few days. He obviously has a lot on his mind right now and I don’t want to intrude.”
“I'm sure you won’t be doing that, Miss. I'm sure he would always want to see you, however bad things are.”
“He might even have gone away for the week,” as Melanie drifted into parallel thoughts with those of the housekeeper.
She went to sit in the conservatory. Thoughts in this bright airy room always seemed a little easier. She shivered with a mixture of cold, anxiety for Smith, and tiredness. Mrs Perkins arrived with a tray of tea and snacks. Her instinct, as always at a time like this, was to feed her boss with as many tasty things as her mind could compass. Melanie looked up as she entered, Mrs Perkins could see that she had been crying.
“I can’t just sit back. I have a terrible premonition. He's in danger Mrs P. and it’s all my fault. Ever since he set eyes on me, things have gone downhill for him. First his Mum dies and now this.”
Mrs Perkins sat next to her and rubbed her knee as one might a child’s who has just fallen from a swing. “Now then Miss, don’t you be thinking such things. That young doctor is not finished yet, and besides, I've never seen him so happy as when he's talking to you. I just wish you could see the way he looks at you. Those

events have nothing at all to do with you, and what's more he'll face those better than if you were not here."
Melanie looked away quickly as if needing to hide the concern that crossed her face. In that moment she recognised that an oppressive atmosphere hung over her, an atmosphere that she had hoped lay in her past and not her future. Her tear-swollen eyes looked outside to the parched gardens and the ground that remained dry and burnt, as she reflected that the Spring and life-giving rains seemed an eternity away. Both women could not help but wonder what further casualties would follow over the coming barren winter.
"I must help him."
"I'm sure you will, Miss."
"My intervention hasn't changed the outcome before, Mrs P."
"That was a long time ago now, Miss and you are a very different person than all those months ago – thanks to him. Was there anything you could have done to change things?"
"You are right of course, Mrs P."
Each woman managed to create a smile purely for the other's comfort, each held private thoughts that were very different than those suggested by the uncertain smiles.

Smith had spent the day at his mother's house. He was grateful for the fact that there was much to be done. By keeping busy he could stem the relentless flow of thought through his tortured brain. The phone rang, but he did not answer it. As night descended his mood spiralled down with it. His isolation and loneliness seemed to be increased still further by the cold lifeless house, which had once been warm and welcoming. He continued with the grim task of clearing away personal belongings. So many of these objects triggered memories that he had to stop at regular intervals, and work through those memories as they arose; and most were painful ones centred around the misery of their lives under constant fear from his father. Auctioneers had agreed to remove the larger items, though in truth there was little of any value and he wondered if they would cover their costs. One or two paltry items held more happy memories and he placed these carefully so that they could be transferred to his own home.

Eventually deepening darkness suggested that he should return home and finish the job on another day. His own house was only slightly more welcoming. Having no mother to protect, triggered a gulf within him, a void that was hard to contemplate let alone fill. He realised that he had no-one, not a soul with whom he could talk and utter just a few of those things now queuing with urgency in his mind. He put on all the lights in his tiny sitting room in an attempt to dispel the gloom there. He found the note that Melanie had pushed through and also the two messages on the answerphone, now blinking as it sought attention. Michaels had left one of the messages, informing him that Sophie's body had been released to the undertakers and the funeral was scheduled for Monday. He picked up the telephone. His urge to phone Melanie was as a deep-sea diver needing oxygen. He knew that it would be unfair to burden her at this time with his own worries, and almost certainly unethical in any event. He could not know that she thirsted for that call, as the parched lawns gasped for life-giving water. His heart was screaming for a very different action, but his tired and tormented brain still held sway as he replaced the handset within its cradle, its little charging light coming on as he did so.

He thought of extracting a frozen meal from his small freezer, but could generate no enthusiasm for such an action. He decided to shower and attempt to retire early. Another restless night lay before him. He had forgotten the last time he had snatched more than an hour or two of unbroken sleep. Weariness was no protection against his need to go through events just one more time; as if revisiting them would somehow change them and make them right, or deliver some sense to light the gloom. As tiredness and exhaustion rose in him, insight into his own condition fell in tandem. His awareness of his own state of health was rapidly diminishing. He had informed depressed patients, like Melanie, on more than one occasion that insight into one's own condition, and objectivity, would be the first and most vital senses to be lost in a deteriorating patient. He paid no attention to his own words. His instinct, that he needed to be alone in order to serve some penance for his sins, was the one that would be the main driving force on the route to his own destruction. The display on his alarm clock advanced to almost midnight.

The phone rang, and years of being on call triggered the automatic movement to reach for the handset. Only then did he hesitate. It continued to ring and he had forgotten to reactivate the answerphone.

"James is that you?"

"Melanie! You are late."

"Sorry, I've been thinking of you all day. Are you all right?"

"Never better Melanie."

She knew this to be a reflex reply; an answer that one might give as one brushed past a stranger. She switched ground quickly in order to elicit a more accurate answer as to his true condition.

"I heard what happened about the little girl."

How he ached to tell her, to unburden some of his emotion and decouple those punishing thoughts from his raging brain. How could he, the patient's doctor do such a thing? His performance was already being called into question by half the village, a little girl lay dead because of him and here he was, wanting to pour his heart out to someone who had been through enough problems of her own. He knew then that he had to arrest his own decline, and moved precisely away from the strategy that might have saved him.

"These things happen, unfortunately, from time to time. It's very sad, but we are dealing with human life, and sometime bad things happen."

She tried desperately to approach via a different route. "Is there anything, anything at all I can do for you?"

"No, not really Melanie, thanks for asking. I have a few days off and I'm planning to clear Mum's house so the estate agent can put it on the market."

Once again she tried, "I have strong muscles, if you need a hand."

"I am sure you have Melanie, but it's nearly done now, and won't take much longer."

Having hit a brick wall again, she realised that direct speaking was the only option still open.
“James, I need to see you. I need to talk to you. I need to tell you so much.”
He realised that this he could not block, but he could deflect. “Righto, Melanie as soon as I've finished a few things. How about that?”

Melanie realised this was the best deal she would be able to negotiate. She toyed for some time with an urge to drive round to his house and bang on the door until it opened. Ultimately she realised that he had put himself behind that door for a reason and perhaps she should just trust him. He had demonstrated on many occasions, in treating her, that his instinct was rarely wrong. She had failed to grasp that such instinct had been disabled, and fatally so, by the more telling emotions of tiredness and despair that were now in force.
“OK,” she signalled defeat, “will you call me when you have a moment, and perhaps we cold meet up?”
“I certainly will,” he managed with a slight hint of unaccustomed formality.
“Sorry to phone you so late.”

These simple words nearly caused the dam wall that had been erected against her, to fail. A cascade of words queued in his brain: he wanted to say that she could phone him for as long as time existed to measure the call, and could stay on the line until decay caused the copper in the wire that connected them, to turn to disparate atoms. He would remain listening to her beautiful, bright, friendly voice, that seemed to announce a sunny day or a perfect spring with every word she spoke, until he was unable to listen any more. He did manage a perfunctory, “it’s kind of you to ring”, as the handset was replaced, before the words could gush out; and once again it was his sense of duty as a GP that kept that dam intact.

Monday morning came, clouds blotted the sun, but still could deliver no rain. The whole village lined the streets as Sophie's tiny coffin was borne by a single hearse, filled with flowers and followed by another, also crammed with flowers. Everyone stood in silent respect, their heads bent as if the grief had weighed them down with physical as well as emotional force. The procession made its slow, respectful, but agonising, way through the village. The Allenbys had elected to walk in front of the hearse, their faces hollow and ghost-like as if grief had stripped their life away from them, along with any trace of hope or happiness. Some wept as they passed, others stared at the ground in numbed disbelief. Still more waited patiently at the small churchyard. A congregation of family and close friends filled the church. Most shops had closed out of respect, and Dr Michaels had cancelled the morning surgery so that they too could show their support. Those with faith, clung to it, those without, had their atheist views reinforced, and the agnostics, their sense of a possible deity made less tangible. The vicar gave his address via loudspeakers inside and outside the tiny church. Many recognised that the reading was from the Bible, a few knew that it was from Romans VI, "What will separate us from the love of God," even fewer remembered that it was the reading at the service at the time of the Aberfan disaster in Wales, that had claimed the lives of many schoolchildren: regardless of what they believed or remembered – all wept unceasingly.

Smith kept a discreet distance. He had no wish to remind the parents of more negative thoughts than the poor souls were already dealing with. He managed to catch a glimpse of Melanie standing erect outside the Post-Office. Just as she turned, almost as if she had detected his presence, he shrank back away from the line of sight. He had parked his car out of the way in the deserted side streets.

Later, he sat in his sitting room. The door knocker chattered urgently as the Postman leapt out of a large red van with a slim envelope that had to be signed for. It looked official and Smith could see that it was marked 'Special Delivery' and it had various bar codes and ciphers applied to it, which enhanced its air of formality. Smith opened it reflexly, with little further thought.

Doctor James Smith.

Smylie, Arbuthnot and Williams.
Solicitors
Kensington Rd
Kensington
Greater London

We act as solicitors to Mr Rupert Hartington-Bell.

We have been instructed by Mr Hartington-Bell, who is intending to lodge a formal complaint against you. We have notified the General Medical Council, Professional Conduct Committee of what we regard as a serious breach of professional standards with regards to a patient registered with you; in that you are alleged to have entered into an improper relationship with Miss Melanie Jardine of Shiplake Manor, Little Dunham on or between the beginning of May 2011 and today's date. We are preparing papers that will serve as a restraining order upon you, and you are instructed to make no attempt whatsoever to contact or approach Miss Jardine. As soon as the restraining order has been effected it will be served upon you, and we intend for it to remain in force at least until such time as the GMC has conducted an enquiry, the time and date of which you will be notified; and you are hereby given notice that your attendance at such enquiry will be compulsory.

In addition we have begun enquiries into the death of your father Mr Jules Smith, formerly of 15 Anson Way. Our assertion is that on or around the night of 23rd June 1994 he was unlawfully killed at the above address. A file of further information will be passed to the Police with the recommendation that further enquiries are made.

You are required to remain available for questioning upon receipt of this letter and you are further required to remain within the jurisdiction of the United Kingdom authorities until such time as the information has been investigated.

As with all solicitors' letters, no name was at the foot of the letter and just an anonymous swirl above the name of the solicitors.

He stood stupefied as he read: it was almost as if the words and their meaning had stunned his already dangerously overtaxed brain. He remained motionless, for several minutes as he attempted to digest the contents of the letter. There was no decipherable signature at the foot of the letter: it was almost as though he was not worthy of any direct contact with the exalted person who had written it, who no doubt viewed him as undeserving of any kind of personal recognition whatsoever. Rupert was obviously determined that he should have no contact with Melanie ever again, and had also had him investigated, probably by private detectives. Smith could have sworn in the past few days that he had been followed.

Smith had often told his patients that human flesh could bear only so much pain, so much torment. Something had to give, as once these limits had been exceeded then, such flesh would fail. This moment came as he realised he could no longer see a way through. What point was there in continuing, when the exit was blocked? Today was his thirtieth birthday, no other post had arrived for him, there was not another soul, still alive, who would know that fact. He thought briefly of the number of occasions that his mother had sneaked a hastily assembled card or small present to him, whilst his father snored in his large armchair, occupying most of the front room of their tiny and chaotic house.

It was then that he first caught a glimpse of the black void that called from within. At first he refused to acknowledge its presence, as he sat and tried to make sense of his life that was now imploding. However, simply remembering that it had been there, was more than enough to secure its return.

Rupert arrived at Melanie's house in his beautiful new Bentley. He had always chosen this marque, as did his father, though this was the first time he had selected a green one. Someone had told him that green cars were unlucky, though he could think of no reason why this should be so, as 'unlucky' was the last thing he associated with himself.

"Moopy, dear Moopy, please sit down next to me and hear what I have to tell you." He patted the cushion on the settee in an enthusiastic boyish manner. "That awful man will trouble you no more."

Melanie had to think for long moments before she realised just who Rupert was referring to. It was only by recalling the detestation on his face, the last time the men had met, and by contrasting it now with his self-satisfied grin that she was able to guess who he was referring to.

"Smith is history. I have sorted that interloper, once and for all. I'm sure he was after your money, you know Moops, darling, well, worry about him no more."

There were so many assumptions in those sentences that she just had to correct; but she decided to start with the one uppermost in her mind.

"In what way have you sorted him Rupert?"

"Thought he could cross me. I don't know who he thinks he is. Doesn't even know which fork to pick up. How dare he cross me." Rambling sentiments emerged before he was able to calm down enough to bring some focus to the words he wished to convey. "Well, my solicitors have contacted the GMC and are about to present them with a formal complaint from me as to his conduct and his improper relationship with you."

"And what improper relationship is that, exactly Rupert?"

Melanie's gathering recovery had assured liberation from many of the negative thought processes that had beset her and threatened her for the past eighteen months. Both she and her agile, free flowing mind had been set free by a good man's perseverance and consummate skill. She had shown herself to be capable of so much in the last twelve months, and Smith had shown her how to hone the skills that, she now knew, she held in abundance. She called now for just some of the skills he had bestowed upon her, the ability to assess, maintain calm and do the right thing in terrifying situations where others would have crumbled; and at all times to stand apart from the tawdry manoeuvres espoused by others. Such skills flowed seamlessly now, as she clarified the situation, calmly but avid for more information.

"Good grief, my girl you can see the way he looks at you, the way he hangs on each of your words like some love sick puppy. I won't have it. He's after your money, my girl."

How she hated the way he said 'money' – he placed an undue emphasis on that simple inoffensive word, as if he were debasing it in some way.

"Let him try to get round the GMC. Thank goodness we still have some good old institutions like these, they'll keep the cheerful chappie at bay at the very least. That's if they don't strike him orf of course! Just who does he think he is, trying to take me on? He is nothing."

Rupert continued for a while in the offended tone, that had obviously been whipped up by the thought of the young doctor trying to challenge him in some ill-defined way. Rupert had such little insight; he had never needed it, for he had always been right. Had he been able to summon just a little self-awareness he would have realised that his contempt for Smith was fuelled by jealousy, that most dangerous of all emotions; the only thing that could debase love, and turn it into hatred. The reason why he handled jealousy so poorly was because he had never had to confront it. Any time he had come across a situation that may have engendered such a feeling, his parents immediately acted so that any comparison, whether it be a new toy, a holiday, a new car, a career or earnings were immediately changed, by their intervention, in his favour.

"I also have a private investigator on him." He nodded to her, as he knew that his next revelation would be the knockout blow that would sweep Smith from her life forever and into the gutter, which is where he belonged.

"Moopy, has he told you that he was involved in his father's death and it certainly was not an accident?"

Rupert saw the horror coursing across her face. He smiled, the smile of a fool. He could not grasp that the emotion now coming to the fore was unabridged concern with regard to what he had released upon the unsuspecting Smith, just at his most vulnerable point.

"Didn't tell you about that did he, eh, old girl," as he totally misread her expression. "The Police were involved. Only the fact that he was fourteen caused them to suspend their enquiries, that and pleading from his mother, of all people. I suspect she should have dealt with him there and then. It looks as though he has always been a bad one. Good job I have saved you from him, eh old girl. Now Moopy, shall we talk some more about our future, now that detestable man has been given, or is about to be given, his just deserts." His tone becoming more self-congratulatory, as he sought to sweep her away, with his industry and sheer brilliance in exposing a charlatan as his true self.

"Can't see him showing his face round here again, any time soon. I've really sorted him, I can tell you, old girl."

Melanie stood up briskly, causing Rupert's hand, with which he had been patting her left thigh as one might the hide of a prized racehorse, to fall away. Truth was, she could bear to hear his vicious ramblings no more, and certainly could bear no contact with him. Whilst sitting she was, at all times, impressive, when standing, she unleashed the formidable person within.

"I don't think you will, old man," was delivered quietly, but unmistakably. A more perceptive person than Rupert would be needed to identify the faint mocking tone she had adopted and to detect that the calm lay temporarily, as before a storm.

"No, Moops, I have, I can tell you for a fact he is 'history'," he affirmed with a slight sibilant tone to the 's'.

"No Rupert I don't think he is."
Rupert eventually saw something of her thoughts and her mood, but much too late. He had finally detected that before him stood an immensely strong, talented woman who was about to reveal a facet of her character that even he could no longer miss, and would be unable to discount. Her voice was calm, she spoke slowly and clearly so that he could not miss the importance or the implications of the words she was about to unleash.

"Some years ago, Rupert, my father intervened to save a young investment banker. Some say that the trade he authorised that day was a simple mistake, others say that it was illegal, even fraudulent. In any event, if the trade had been discovered then sadly, that person would have been ruined. He would never have been employed in the City again, despite his many and varied connections. If he had been summarily dismissed in disgrace, then, as you may know Rupert, he would never have been able to rise within Gatkins and Eatby, the merchant bank, I believe, your father now owns, is that correct Rupert? And he certainly would never have been able to take on his son, whose advancement in what to others, would be a very competitive environment owes everything to the father's forceful influence. My father covered that trade with a massive tranche of cash, that he had to move heaven and Earth to provide in a hurry, in order to close out that position before it could be detected, and he took that secret, almost, to his grave. He was a gentleman and certainly would never have spoken of it. It was, in fact, known only to a very few and possibly not even revealed to that son who benefited so much from the influence that his reprieve could then provide.

"Don't you believe that honest, decent people should be granted freedom from things being dug up from their past that should have no bearing on events today, Rupert?" She placed emphasis on his name to make absolutely certain that he understood all that she had to say. "I think such folk who have done no harm, and have done no harm to me, certainly, should be allowed to live their lives without tawdry threats don't you? It would certainly be a great shame if they were to be treated in the way that they were hoping to treat others, do you agree, Rupert?"

Rupert finally saw what a formidable person she was; he learned, too late, the meaning of friendship and of loyalty and what a person was prepared to do in order to protect those, they cared about. He nearly learned that jealousy had to be confronted, not bought out by money and influence; and that power had to be used responsibly. He realised that ashes rather than triumph lay before him and his only recourse now was to comply with what came next.

"I am certain that any decent person would want to call off their threats, and any damaging investigation for such a person, aren't you Rupert? "Why don't you," was delivered almost as if such a thought had occurred to her for the first time, "do that decent thing Rupert? You can do it, I am certain, from your car phone whilst you drive down to London. I know that we will not be meeting again Rupert, and I do want to thank you for your co-operation in this matter. Please instruct your solicitor to inform me in writing within twenty four hours of your change of heart."

Rupert was stunned: he attempted speech, but for once nothing would come. His mouth, with those thin lips, dropped open as if he were now so distracted he could no longer support them against gravity, and still no words came forth. Mrs Perkins, who had spotted a spec of dust just on the marble bust in the hallway, just outside the conservatory, had to cover her own mouth to hide the cry of delight that she otherwise would not have been able to stop.

Rupert stood up. His face pale and his eyes staring wide, as he realised he was staring at defeat.

"I'll be off then, in that case, Melanie."

"Goodbye Rupert, thank you for calling - and for your co-operation." A hand of steel gripped his as she turned.

Their meeting was over.

Rupert was over.

Mrs Perkins gave her a beaming smile as she walked past, a smile in part of sheer delight but also of unabridged admiration for this young woman who now shone with so many desirable attributes and was also so attractive to look at.

As Rupert drove away, still in a state of numbed disbelief, Melanie suddenly began to hurry. Her mind was racing with thoughts as to just what the vainglorious Rupert, who had acted purely out of spite and self-serving vanity, that she realised she could tolerate in no-one, had visited upon the kind and gentle GP whose sole aim had been to help her. She gunned the Jaguar into life and swept down the drive. She headed straight for the Seabridge estate, and stopped to ask several pedestrians for directions to the local library, which after some time she was able to find. She realised that she had all the information that would now assist with her search. The local paper, prior to the last five years, had been placed on microfiche. She asked the librarian for the relevant spools over fifteen years old. She knew from Edith that they had lived on the Seabridge estate. The Seabridge Advertiser must have reported the events of that day. She rapidly scanned the front pages of each and every issue. In due course she found exactly what she had been looking for.

"*Father killed in freak accident.*"
"A young father was killed today when he stumbled and fell through a glazed door panel. Mr Jules Smith was believed to have been drinking heavily. His fall against the glazed panel, which unfortunately had been replaced after a previous fall, with ordinary glass rather than safety glass, caused him to sever the main artery in his neck. The Police Surgeon was called and ascertained that death would have been practically instantaneous. Mrs Edith Smith was interviewed by the Police. In her statement, she informed the Police that her husband stumbled and fell head-first through the glass panel which shattered with jagged edges which badly cut his neck.
The Police interviewed the widow and son, but decided to take no further action.

Our source from the Police was quoted as saying 'This is nothing more than a tragic accident. This gentleman, who we understand had a problem with drink, simply lost his footing and severed the carotid artery, in the neck when he fell through the glass door. We have statements from neighbours who heard and saw, something of the events and won't be taking it further.'"

Just at that point Melanie realised that she was not alone, the librarian stood next to her. "I remember that day. We lived just over the road. He was always coming home drunk at all times of night and day. We could hear him down the street. First he would start on his wife and then that poor boy. Never had a thing, not a toy, not a bike, no new clothes, nothing. His Mum bought him a toy train one Christmas, it was thrown through the window the following day by that vicious man. The lad was lucky to get fed. He was lucky to get out alive, the leathering that old fella used to dole out to him. We didn't have much, but I can tell you, we were rich by their standards. Nobody intervened in those days, not the neighbours, not the police, no-one. People forget: in those days, men almost owned their wives and what went on behind closed doors was nobody's business. People kept quiet, they turned a blind eye to suffering, and that little lad suffered more than anyone, I can tell you. He took it all out on that boy, it's a wonder he's not covered in bruises to this day, the beatings he had to endure. The father came home that day, blind drunk as usual; we could see him ranting and raving. We were hiding behind this bush in their garden. He made a rush for her as he was going to hit her. That boy stood in front of his mother and pushed him away. Then he really went berserk and charged at both of them. The boy pulled his mum out of the way just in time."

Tears formed in Melanie's eyes as she thought about that little boy, very frightened and very alone. Whilst he worried about whether he would get any tea or just a good hiding, Melanie's family were wondering whether to spend Christmas in Zermatt or perhaps Meribel. Whilst Melanie's dad deliberated on a goose or a turkey for Christmas dinner, or most likely both, he would be lucky to catch a stale sandwich, sneaked to him as his father slept it off. One thing was for sure; he had never had a pet rabbit.

“He carried on straight through that window. Of course, he’d patched it up with ordinary glass from the last time he’d kicked it in, in a drunken rage. The glass must have cut his neck. She screamed for towels but I didn’t see anyone rush to help him. Most had been on the end of his behaviour at some time, and nobody lifted a finger. It was all over in seconds anyway, so the Police said to my dad. Blood was everywhere. They closed the place up and moved them, smartish.”

Only then did the librarian stop to ask a question. “Did you know the family Miss?”
“Oh no, not me; my daughter is doing a project for school about notable events in our local history but this seems a bit too violent, so I think it's back to the drawing board.”
“I’m told he's a doctor now and a good one, so I've heard,” offered the Librarian.
“Is that a fact? Well, good for him,” Melanie said, as she switched down the machine with a mixture of relief and also overwhelming sadness for the little boy, who had never known a childhood, only fear.

As Melanie drove away, her thoughts were only about Smith, of the suffering he had endured, and how that little boy somehow had turned it around. He had told her once that suffering was a relative, not an absolute, term and she wondered how he viewed his childhood as compared to some of those who were more fortunate. Would each night bring restless thoughts of pure envy toward those who had had happy, well balanced lives, or was his work and his manner a continuous celebration that he was grateful for his deliverance and that of his mother too, from their own personal hell. Having observed Smith at close quarters for some weeks now, she knew the answer without much deliberation, and her admiration for him and what he had become grew stepwise.

Once again Smith noticed the black void, that appeared, at first, almost fleetingly as he reflected on despair. A Mathematician would have recognised that it represented nothing rather than zero. He refused to acknowledge its influence or even to consider it, but by then it was too late, as it made its presence felt more and more. A nexus of pain and suffering greeted him at every turn. The void promised not a diminution of that suffering, but an elimination, which became more and more compelling, the more he suffered. He had cleared the house, which was now in the hands of the estate agent. He didn't have the concentration to read nor to finish off his wooden scale model of 'The Victory'. The quiet periods where he just sat and thought were a fertile breeding ground for low thoughts, that under ordinary circumstances he would not have countenanced; but these were far from ordinary circumstances. Once he had glimpsed that void, he realised that it offered a break from the turmoil, an end to the pain and to the suffering that was with him for much of the day and nearly all of his nights. As the slow seduction continued, he found himself increasingly less able to tear himself away. Gradually eating, sleeping and even thinking were supplanted by its calming influence. It was a simple next step to consider that being part of that expanse, by letting it envelop him completely, was a way that would lead to freedom from the pain and suffering that now beset him. As the week continued this course of action became more and more attractive.

Friday would be the day. The day he planned to leave. He spent Thursday tidying his affairs and he wrote two letters to seemingly the only two people he knew on earth. One to Dr Michaels and one to Melanie. A tiny flicker of emotions presented as he wrote Melanie's letter, but it too was accompanied by painful feelings in equal measure and his course of action was now re-affirmed as just thinking of her had caused such agony. Agony, from which the numb void had promised to deliver him.

Celestial bodies that had been in constant movement since their formation in the swirling dusts of space, billions of years before, fell into the alignment, at precisely this moment, dictated since time began. Mrs Smith had forseen that this point would arrive but had been unable to see beyond it. Had she been here, she would have wanted to tell him that no mother could love a son more and that there was nothing he could do that would lessen the pride in him that she would hold forever.

Melanie's father would have wanted her to know that he was deeply sorry if she had ever felt that she was loved any less than her sister; he had been bedazzled by a very bright light, but he should never have lost sight of the fact that there were others in close proximity who were no less worthy.

Only the gypsy had seen past this conjunction and the tears that she shed now, were all for Smith.

CHAPTER XVII

"SWIRL of DEATH"

Friday, he rose early, took a shower, shaved and got dressed. Leaving his breakfast untouched, he arrived at the surgery. When asked later, nobody there had noticed any change in him except, perhaps that he had been a little smarter than usual, wearing his best suit; but other than that he was his usual self; bright, friendly and interested in all those he spoke with that morning. The thing that puzzled all the staff was why he was there at all: there were no surgeries booked and he wasn't expected until the following week. Mrs Farnell caught a brief glimpse of him and stood still in her tracks as she gazed at him, her perceptive antenna raised, as always, but for once, unable to register what was on his horizon. Before he left the surgery he gave Janice two envelopes and asked that they be put in the post. She explained that the post had already been taken that morning but she would attend to his request personally. Janice was a dutiful soul, especially when faced with a request, any request from Dr Smith. She had bought a new skirt, had had her hair cut, and sported a more feminine blouse than Mrs Farnell would have liked. Janice had decided that it was now or never and even the beguiling Miss Jardine was not able to spend as much time with Dr Smith as she could. Janice put her coat on as soon as her break arrived and walked down to the centre of the village to attend to his request. She looked down at the new shoes, which were killing her feet.

It was only when she reached the village that she noticed that the uppermost envelope was addressed to Dr Michaels. Why had Dr Smith asked her to post it? She could only assume some confusion on his part. She shrugged her shoulders and decided to slot Dr Michael's letter into the post-box. Curiosity had made her temporarily retain the second, more substantial letter. Only as an immaculate silver Jaguar came to a sure-footed halt over the road, did she notice that the letter was for Miss Jardine, who had just left

the car and was about to enter the Newsagent.
"Miss Jardine?"
Janice looked at Melanie with the usual nexus of surging emotion, centred on envy, admiration and awe. Just how could she look so good, how could any woman look that good with such a casual disregard for anything other than the bare minimum of makeup; although as usual she wore a beautiful suit that enhanced her slim, taut figure and gorgeous shoes that looked perfectly at home on her feet, unlike those now tormenting Janice herself.
"Miss Jardine, forgive me, Dr Smith gave me this letter to post and I couldn't help but notice it was addressed to you." Janice offered the letter with an outstretched left arm and as it extended it gave prominence to the pretty bracelet.
"Oh, Janice, what a lovely bracelet."

Melanie's kindness and ability to notice what many would see as insignificant, as always, served to stifle any hint of jealousy even in those less forgiving than Janice. Janice blushed, as if she could sense that Melanie had read her thoughts.
"Oh thank you, Miss Jardine it was my twenty-first yesterday, and this was a present from my Mum and Dad."
Melanie extended her upturned palm to support, the delicate bracelet as she conveyed her sincere congratulations that melted any trace of ice in Janice's heart. Had she been able to read Melanie's mind, she would have encountered thoughts as to whether it was too late to send a present to the young receptionist to mark such an important event. Melanie rotated the links slowly round the offered wrist as she viewed the unusual charms. Suddenly, she noticed the unmistakeable shape of a silver Scarab, similar to the one she wore round her own neck. The gypsy's penultimate words echoed once again, with inescapable moment. The unexpected development foreshortened her next words, but not her politeness.
"That is beautiful Janice, many congratulations again."

Melanie knew that she had to return home in order to read the letter. She bid 'goodbye' to Janice and hoped that the surge of curiosity it caused had not made her appear rude. Smith had intended the letter to go in the post-box. He had assumed that she would not view its contents before tomorrow morning, at the earliest.

"*The hand of fate will reach out to you; and you will ignore it. Nothing can save you then.*"

This was it, Janice had been that 'hand' and Melanie was about to drive home, using time that she realised events had already moved to deny her. She ripped open the envelope: it contained a handwritten note. She was aware of her heart missing beats as she read quickly with mounting panic, words that became as a Tsunami of fear hitting a theretofore wide, sunlit beach.

Melanie ,

I hope you will be able to forgive me sending you this little note rather than putting in a personal appearance, which I would have preferred.
I can see now what a mess I have made of just about everything, and I am grateful to Rupert for clarifying things for me and I can, at last, see how foolish I must have appeared in his and, most likely, your eyes too.
I feel so ashamed and so stupid, and I know that only by leaving now, will I ever be able to begin to set things right.
The past days have taught me so much about some of the things that are so important, and I do hope that you can forgive me if you feel I ever overstepped the mark as a doctor whose main aim at all times was to see you get better. I do know that now Rupert is back in your life, your progress will be maintained, and I hope that at least in some small way I have been able to assist you, at least a little, in your recovery. I can only hope that you will be able to see that my efforts were meant to help you and in no way to hinder; and I want you to know that I am unable to forgive myself if this, at any time, was the case.

I can see, at last, that by leaving now, in this way, I can begin to underline my apology to you, and it also gives me an opportunity to atone for my confusion and my unprofessional attitude toward you. I have seen, first hand, what a kind and caring person you are and I do hope that you can see a way to forgive me in due course.

With every best wish for your future health and happiness,
Also please find enclosed a CD – that I somehow managed to burn, my first ever! -it contains a track with the words I would have wanted to say to you but now I realise that I never could.

Yours, James.

She slotted the CD into the aperture. She wasn't sure at first of the significance of Smith's letter: an uneasy feeling intruded that gave a strong clue to the events now in progress. As the song came up she recognised the artist as the Bee Gees, but had never heard the track before – 'Secret Love' Now the words resonated inside causing mounting distress as, at last, she could see the danger ahead.

When do I cry
This breakin' heart
Just hurts me more
When we're apart
And there are two of us
With our secret love
Sleep pretty baby while you wait so long
Livin' with a love that's not just make believe

How stupid she had been. The seconds ticked by relentlessly, seconds that she now recognised were measuring the end of Smith's life. He was to be the last victim that would see the end of the heartbreaking sequence of events.

The Melanie of old would have done nothing more than recognise the impact that events would have on her life: how she had changed. Now, however, her sole thought was whether she still had time to save him. She started the car, she knew where to find him, as her mind started to race with a torrent of thought and images, verging on the counterproductive side of panic. The car raced through the village at a speed that reflected her distress. She wept with unrestrained emotion as she now understood the emotion that was engraved on the gypsy's face. Melanie thought that she had seen casual dismissal, but she now realised that it was unabridged sadness as the gypsy had foreseen the outcome.

Smith had driven straight home after leaving the surgery. For the first time in many weeks things seemed very clear. His mind had finally deciphered the riddle that had been running like a subroutine in his overworked brain. How to find peace? How to avoid further torment? How to gain rest, and how to make amends to Melanie, finally and irrevocably? He acknowledged, at last, the all-encompassing answer that had come to him in the night. Like a primeval puzzle, set at the dawn of time, that an ancient mechanical apparatus had been directed to work on, the last cog had clicked into place and here, at last, was the ultimate panorama stretching before him as if he could see clearly, for the very first time.

Where do parallel lines meet? Where in the Galaxy are stars born? Where does time begin and end? Where do suns spin down and die? He now knew not only the answer to these questions, but also how to travel there. The black void, that nothingness, had supplied all the answers and more. There, he would wait for her.

He turned the key, the engine started at first bidding, without hesitation of any kind. He could not recall a time when it had started so quickly. He laughed as he carefully closed the garage doors and got into his car.

The Jaguar charged into Smith's drive. His car was not there. She panicked as she wondered just where he might be. She knew that he always left the car on the gravel drive, having joked with her many times that it made no difference to whether it started or not. The oily patch, as always, marked the position it usually occupied. Where was he? She flew from the car and rushed to the bay window leaving the driver's door open and the engine ticking vigorously with its unusual exertion. She gazed through the window, uncertain as to what she might find. Her heart could beat no faster as it pumped violently within her chest, almost forcing her gullet back into her mouth with its ferocity. She swallowed hard in an attempt to induce more calm than she could feel, but the heart continued its exertions to make its presence felt with each and every beat. Smith was not in the morning room, but the sight of the 'Victory' lying smashed beyond repair on the floor intensified her alarm, as fear, that she had known all too well in her relatively young life, broke in. It seemed that Smith had destroyed his pride and joy, the product of all those hours and hours of leisure activity in a whim that mirrored the destructive forces imploding in him.

She raced back to the car and wondered where to go next. Later, she would not recall what made her switch off the engine. She could only conclude that its rhythmic, quiet pulsation was somehow at variance with the emotions raging through her brain. Silencing the engine at that point, whilst she collected her thoughts, would crystallise the grim discovery she was about to make. As the engine quietened, she became aware that another engine was running. By cruel irony, only her past experiences could prepare her for the sight, she had hoped she would never witness again. She almost shrieked as she realised that the sound was coming from within the garage. A mixture of rage, coupled with utmost despair, hit her in the pit of her stomach and succeeded in replacing her pounding heart as the organ most demanding of her attention. Her head was now pulsating too, in time with the unabridged panic coursing though her. She flicked the key quickly and slammed the control in drive as soon as the engine caught. She was not prepared to give in passively to another grim discovery without a fight, and if that fight was already lost, then she would die with him: the decision immutable as the gypsy's prophecy.

So this was it, as foretold, Smith was to be the next victim and the "hand" that she was about to ignore could only be Janice's bracelet as if the charm itself was there only to mock her as Smith died; she could have acted no more quickly, surely it could not be too late? The only calming thought, was her determination to be with him at whatever price, and whatever lay beyond those doors.

The bonnet crumpled only slightly, as it struck the rotting doors, with a deafening thud, as the planking splintered. Airbags went off with explosive force and the car fell silent as protective mechanisms came into effect. She pressed the reset button to bring power back to the car as the airbags now lay limp across the dashboard, and restarted the engine. She turned the control, throwing the powerful bulk of the car into reverse without delay. The doors parted and fell away as she reversed. The fumes billowed out as a cruel reminder of her mother's fate. On that occasion she had held back, too terrified to effect discovery, this time every fibre demanded to see exactly what lay inside. She called now for the last great gift that Smith had bestowed on her. Hope was the gift that he had reinvigorated, and she knew instinctively that, with hope, she could vanquish fear. Fear that otherwise would have prevented her from going into such a noxious environment and crossing the small but lethal gap from the garage opening to the car door. Fear that would have warned that approaching the wrong side of the car and remaining within the fumes' toxic embrace for a few seconds more would, surely, claim her too. Still more vitally, in a sublime moment, she realised that she had been freed from the fear that had stalked her, like a vulture following a stumbling traveller, since her fateful visit to the gypsy. Fear of death, fear of loneliness and ultimately fear of life. She knew then that Smith, and her recent experiences, had delivered her from such a cruel companion and that she would never take up with it again.

Observers would also ponder the fact that Smith's car was so old: it had no catalytic converter which would have destroyed most of the noxious fumes that were now killing him. She knew about that sweet, bright pink colouration of the victim's lips, she had seen it before. This was their kiss: this was the seal of their work. She didn't know why Carbon Monoxide was such an able killer, but she knew that Smith would know. She'd never read of its triple-poisoning effect on the blood and the oxygen it was supposed to carry, but she knew that Smith would know. She didn't know how long it took to die in such an atmosphere, but she realised, now, that Smith would know that too.

People would ask just why had she instinctively gone down the passenger's side? The door was unlocked as she wrenched it open with a violence she'd not believed herself capable of. Melanie would never know just where the strength came from to get him out of that car. The fumes of death were embracing him as split seconds passed into infinity itself. She wanted to shriek to the heavens themselves, as her own strength began to fade, if only they could intervene on her behalf, rather than play mute witness to the brutal, cruel events unfolding with a foretold precision. She thought, perhaps, of sitting in the car beside him and letting the prophecy devour the two of them in an all- consuming haze; this is why she had chosen the passenger door. Alongside hope existed determination, and this came into force, perhaps most simply, to deny those fumes his lifeless body. Perhaps she recognised that by pulling him from the car she would have one last chance to gaze at the handsome lines, the firm jaw and imagine one last time the playful smile that had crossed those lips, now so pink. Ultimately, determination – all that courage would allow, was now in control and surely only this was responsible for the massive reserves of strength, which were found and applied, as she dragged his limp body from its rusting tomb.

He was to die, so that she might live. Desolation consumed her as she realised that, she could neither sanction nor live with such a thought. She staggered the short, but almost insurmountable distance to the opening and fresh air. She coughed uncontrollably as her lungs tried to dispel the noxious fumes and gasped still further when they discovered this toxic air was the only one being offered. Her eyes watered as they struggled to guide her in the swirls of death. She pulled him onto the drive. She failed to register the pain as the gravel bit into her knees as she cradled his head on her lap. Forces that had been building within her since the day her mother died, in another fume-filled garage, were given vent, and there came forth a heart-rending shriek as she wondered how fate could have dealt her such cards, followed by interminable sobbing, which once again was her only answer.

As the tears fell in unrestrained cascade, the heavens opened to pay homage to the most perfect of torments in which the young woman found herself. The rain, that had been absent for most of the year, decided at that moment to prepare its own backdrop, almost like a deluge of tears falling from the heavens themselves. She caressed his limp head on her lap, and as she did so, she could see that frightened little boy, the one who had hidden from his father's raging temper. The boy who had spent much of his young life too terrified, time and time again, to intervene, even to save his mother. The boy, who had never known peace, who had been beaten to within an inch of his life, just for bearing witness. She saw too, that older boy who had stepped in, to save his mother, that fateful day, only for that act of bravery to visit more torment upon him. Well, he knew peace now. As he lay dying, now, within her warm embrace, she cradled his head and kissed his handsome face. Defiance rose within her.

“Don't you dare die on me! Don't leave me here all alone,” she cried more to the gods than to Smith's limp form. With one final act of sheer rebellion, she was not prepared to admit defeat, just yet. She carefully placed his head on the ground and breathed into his open mouth as she tilted the head back. She thudded her fists on the chest just as she had seen them do at the hospital, arms straight and press, press, press on that breast bone until one could do it no longer. She continued with mouth to mouth as best she could - those firm lips that she had wanted to kiss a million times, framed her stuttering attempts to make life cling to a dying body. She remembered the oxygen in Smith's boot and quickly applied the mask to his mouth and then continued to thrust down on his chest. She listened above the hiss of the oxygen to the centre of his chest. She was not sure whether she could feel a heart beating above the pounding of her own heart, but she was not going to stop now, she would continue until exhaustion claimed her. She reached for her mobile, fortunately nestling in her suit pocket and dialled 999. An Ambulance was despatched with urgency. Only when they had arrived on the scene, did she phone Michaels.

Smith had told her about the symbol of the humble dung beetle, the Scarab. He had not known that it was a sign of resurrection into the afterlife, for those who had departed this mortal life. The ancient Egyptians would have been able to supply much of the missing detail. The industrious, little beetle in moving tiny spheres of dung was believed to equate with one's rebirth, across the sky and into the dawn of the hereafter. However, it was also believed that only the most worthy, signified by the purity and hence the lightness of one's heart, would achieve this goal. The dead person's heart would be weighed against a feather. "Heart, do not stand as a witness against me," was often the last exhortation as the heart was placed in the balance opposite the feather, to decide a man's fate. The Egyptians believed that Khepri, "He who is coming into Being" was the creator god and the Scarab was his servant, creating that rebirth, only if the heart did not outbalance the feather. Perhaps Khepri recognised his servant around the woman's neck, as she fought relentlessly for the man with the heart so pure, and smiled; the feather fluttered as it then bowed to the forces now upon it.

The Ambulance was in a headlong rush to get Smith to the hospital.
"Melanie, no, not to the hospital, it's too far, there isn't time, to the Multiple Sclerosis charity, it's nearer, tell the men they have hyperbaric oxygen," implored Dr Michaels. The Paramedics

understood instantly. “Righto Miss,” they said, “we'll divert there on Dr. Michaels' authority.” The Paramedics continued with pure oxygen and compressions on his chest throughout the journey. Melanie grasped his hand, now terrified to let go, and willed him to breathe, to somehow absorb that oxygen over the much sweeter poison of Carbon Monoxide.

Michaels had phoned ahead to the MS foundation. Eager arms lifted Smith from the stretcher and placed him within the Hyperbaric oxygen chamber. The deathly, sweet pink was still present, but Melanie was convinced that she had seen a tiny flicker on the face that she had stared at intently throughout this time.
“Can I go in with him?” she begged.
“OK Miss, but we will have to raise the pressure very quickly, so keep swallowing hard.”
Only Melanie’s ears could feel the rising pressure. She was not quite sure what purpose the chamber would serve, but she knew that Oxygen was held under very high pressure. Only later would Michaels explain that at high pressures the tissues could receive oxygen directly without relying on the poisoned blood, which would take too long to return to its vital role.

Slowly, as the hour passed, a thousand prayers were answered; from Dr Michaels, Mrs Farnell, the staff, from Molly Fay, from Ruby Jones and from the thousand patients that Smith had served selflessly, from Mrs Perkins, from Stella and ultimately from Melanie who knew only, now, that she would align herself with him, come what may. Smith stirred, he tried to sit up but his aching, dizzy head forbade any such movement. She hastily dried the last of a million tears, not wanting his waking vision to be anything other than her joy. She leant over him and framed his face gently with her delicate hands and the slim, elegant fingers. She kissed him, taking the opportunity, just as he began to come round from what, without her, would have been certain death.

“Dr Smith, you aren't going to get rid of me that easily. That’s the last time I let you do any car maintenance,” she began, “go out to

top up the oil and this is the mess I find you in. I have a lovely new car, a beautiful Mini Cooper, still in my garage which would not need any fettling under the bonnet for many a month, and then perhaps we could leave it to the dealer."
"I might have known you'd still have that car, have you not thought of anyone else you could give it to?"
"No-one quite so deserving, I'm afraid, so it looks as though you're just going to have to shut up for a change."
There was that winning smile again, the one that had been slowly developing for many months, with that conflagration of pure amber within those eyes of clear hazel. The narrow confines of the chamber meant that the two were already in close proximity, but now she moved even closer, enhancing the intimacy that she could not help but delight in, that he could deflect no longer. Her voice changing to a lower register as she almost whispered, "I am so sorry about Rupert. I found out what he had done to you."

He smiled, "Rupert, says I cannot speak to you ever again, just being near you will incur his wrath, you'd better move back. His solicitor will appear any minute, put the cuffs on and cart me away."
"Oh I wouldn't worry about Rupert, if I were you. I have suggested to him that he needs a new perspective on not only his own life but also his relationship with others, and the suggestions that I have put to him, I think, will occupy him for quite some time."
"He's not going to let my tyres down is he?"
"No, I don't think either of us will be hearing from him any time soon, if at all."
"Wow, just what did you say to him?"
"Come now, you know us businesswomen, ruthless to the core."
"Melanie, I just have to say ...."

The technician who had been monitoring the patient in the chamber thought he had better interrupt at this point.
"Excuse me, but it's time to reduce the pressure. Keep swallowing hard."

Slowly the pressure returned to normal levels. Smith was extracted from the machine. His head was a lot clearer and now with something vital that he just had to say.
"Melanie, I just have to tell you ....."

"We'll just take you over to the blood lab to measure your Carbon Monoxide levels, he'll be back in ten minutes," suggested the technician.
"Melanie I have something to tell you, could you wait here for ten minutes and they'll have me back.
She looked at him, the amber flecks now emerging with their effulgent glow, like sunshine breaking through a foggy day as they homed in upon their target.
"No, I'm not sure I can wait that long," she offered with an impish grin, now refusing to be displaced from the beautiful face, that seemed locked only on him.

The technician did not need any clairvoyance to detect that it would be a good time for him to pop out and check the calibration of his machines.
"I'll be back for you in a moment Dr Smith."
"Dr Smith you were saying?"
"Melanie, thank you for saving me. I am so sorry, I feel as if I have let you down. Can you possibly forgive me?"
She thought for a moment: how typical of this man, the person, the doctor who had been stretched to breaking point. He had witnessed horrors first-hand that would have claimed many others including her; and only had thoughts, at that moment, for her, his patient.
"I'm just not sure," a feigned serious expression now on her pretty face, "let's see, I suppose you did save me from misery, loneliness and a horrible death. I'll think about it, but even *so* I suspect it will take a long, long time."

Suddenly the expression changed. Crystal tears formed in the corner of her eyes and threatened to overflow.
"Just what do you think I could do without you?"

"I'm sorry Melanie; there just didn't seem to be a way through. It seemed the only way out. I just wanted it all to go away. It seemed that sleep was the only relief."

Only then did the serious face return as he finally formulated the words from thoughts that had been building since the day he had set eyes upon her. "Melanie, there's something else, something really important, and I can't put it off any longer," he began.

"Truth or Dare?" she interrupted, as she smiled at him enigmatically.

"I want to tell you the truth, of course," he said, as he began again.

She smiled; he hadn't quite got the hang of things. "No, you have to say 'Truth or Dare', then I have to comply. So go on then, 'Truth'," she waited and looked at him intently. "Now you have to say something true."

"That's going to be difficult, just what would you suggest?" as he finally registered her mood.

"Well you might have to say something true but personal like, 'I love Admiral Nelson'."

"No, Melanie what I want to say is," he began again, as he acknowledged the playful smile now in charge on her face.

Suddenly she pressed a delicate long finger to his lips.

"Not another word: the GMC might just hear you and strike you off after all," she paused as the surge of emotion built within each of them; she realised that the moment was now at hand. "Go on then doctor, you were saying." He formed his lips to kiss that finger before gently removing it.

He smiled; two hearts, which had been beating in perfect synchrony, could stay silent no longer.

He sat up slowly, his soft, gentle hands now held the pretty face, the face of the one he had gazed at, supported, commiserated with and brought back from almost certain destruction, now the object of his unwavering attention. He spoke, knowing that neither he nor she could deflect those words any longer. Just before he spoke she recognised that this, not hope, was the last great gift, the one that he had created in her and exactly the one she had created in him.

"I love you Melanie: I think I always have, I know I always will and I want to say it now, out loud and I don't care what the GMP say about it."
"GMC," she said, acknowledging his tease. "Shh, say no more, it's our secret, our secret love," she whispered conspiratorially in his ear. The enticing smell of her perfume now filled his lungs and held the promise of life over the toxic fumes that had only offered death.

She paused, as the weight of her stare, could for that instant, support no words.
"OK: I have decided I'll forgive you, but only, only if you tell me what you have just said, in painstaking detail, each day for the rest of our lives, and of course kiss me like this." She held him firmly, as if escape was no longer possible; she kissed him, finally, as if forces that had been building within each of them since the day they had met were unequivocally given vent. A kiss that both knew would be every bit as passionate at the end of time as it was now at the first.

Perhaps they told each other that they could indeed keep a 'secret love' known only to the two of them. However, not even the unsighted could miss the passion and affection that each held for the other, and so it would be, that the 'secret' love was, in fact, a very open secret, open to all who had knowledge of them.

The technician returned, sensing that his need to check his calibrations was an opportune moment to have left the two of them alone. Dr Michaels was waiting for them as they brought Smith back to the laboratory. Smith was too embarrassed to speak.

Michaels spoke up in his usual clear, but truncated style. "I told you to get that damned gas boiler fixed Smith and it nearly goes and kills you."
Smith was placed in a wheelchair and wheeled out to Michaels' car.

"We're off to the Alex to get some more tests done and just make sure things are returning to normal."
The bright cherry pink had long since been replaced by a more vital shade as the remnants of the Carbon Monoxide had been flushed from his blood. Melanie looked at her phone. An urgent text had been received. She looked at the screen incredulously, but said nothing. Even more important events were still unfolding, than the words that she had just read.

Michaels spoke steadily as he drove. "I've had a word with Paul Serenghotti, he has reprimanded his junior. He tells me that Sophie's tumour was so advanced that nobody could have done anything. It was wrong for the SHO to give Allenby any other impression. Allenby called round today to tender his apologies. Funny thing grief."

Melanie looked at Smith: sadness over the little girl's fate passed through her as a shadow crossing her own grave. Smith instantly detected her thoughts, but it was Michaels who spoke, tears forming in all their eyes as he did so.
"You know, Smith, that poor little girl was dead long before she walked into your surgery. Admitting her there and then, at that second, would only have robbed her, and her parents, of two weeks of normal life at home for which they will always be grateful. You can blame yourself forever, for a delay that otherwise changed nothing, or you can be perhaps the best doctor I've seen in a long time and go on to be a brilliant General Practitioner."
Both Smith and Melanie were stunned not only by the words but also their unusual length from the senior partner. Michaels, however, was not quite finished.
"I also spoke with the Medical Defence Union, who feel there is no case to answer, as the delay would have caused no more progression in poor Sophie's case. They tell me they do not think the GMC would be particularly interested, even in today's troubled times, even if Allenby wanted to take things further, which he does

not. I don't think I had anything else to say to the GMC did I Melanie?"
"I can't think of anything in particular Dr Michaels," she advised mysteriously.
"Allenby, has asked me if the family can rejoin our list. How do you feel about that Smith?" Smith nodded into the rear-view mirror. He still did not trust himself to speak. "The PCT have been informed about your accident. I told them all about your gas boiler. A friend of mine is condemning it as we speak, and will make sure it is replaced when you get back from your holiday."
Smith shook his head quickly, as if the Carbon Monoxide poisoning was causing him to hallucinate.
"Dr Michaels, that is so kind of you to fix the heater," he said, as Michaels' strategy became clear and he did his best to nod as if he had been aware of this fact all along. No-one would ever need to know that Smith had attempted to take his own life. Anticipating his next question Michaels continued, "and he will also replace those rotten doors. Melanie you must be more careful when you are driving onto Smith's drive in future." He did his best to look sternly in her direction.
"I know Dr Michaels, women drivers, you know how we can't control these big cars, I will be more careful in future!"
"Just one more thing Dr Michaels, I don't have any holidays planned," remembered Smith.
"The PCT have agreed to a sickness locum for you for three weeks. Don't worry Smith, it'll be coming out of your profit share, which has shot up beyond all measure since you joined me. I thought you were overdue a break, especially now that Jardine woman has left our list, our workload should be much reduced and we can settle down to some peace and quiet."

The gathering darkness meant that Smith could no longer see his face in the rear-view mirror. Melanie was stifling a giggle.
"You actually left my list, Melanie, how could you, after all we did for you?"

"Come now, James I don't think the GMC would take kindly to you taking one of your patients on holiday to Nelson's Dockyard, Antigua, now would they?"
"Is that Truth or Dare?"
"Oh I'll think of lots of 'dares' for you whilst we are away," her eyes aglow with sensual intent.
"Dr Michaels, I don't know what to say."
"Well, Smith I expect you back in one piece in three weeks and ready for work, we have a surgery to run here. Now what do you say?"
"I want to say thank you. Will you be alright Dr Michaels, with me gone for so long?"
"I've run this practice for thirty years and I don't think another few weeks will make much difference," he paused in a moment of epiphany, "besides, it's about time I had a long talk with Anne."
"Who is Anne, Dr Michaels?" they both asked in unison.
Dr Michaels laughed out loud. "Oh that's Mrs Farnell to you two!"
They both looked at each other. Suddenly things became very clear.

Michaels had never had any children of his own. He reflected to himself that a son, like Smith, would have made him very proud and a moment's sadness came over him, as he reflected on opportunities lost. The interior light came on as he stopped at the Alexander hospital and as the door opened slowly, he gazed intently once again in the rear-view mirror. He could at least make sure that Smith did not allow his work to replace his life, and consume that life as Michaels had allowed it to consume his own. He looked over at Melanie who, for once, also seemed lost for words. What a fine couple they would make. It was, surely, also time for him to ask the question of Anne Farnell that he had been meaning to ask her for thirty years. Michaels was going to make sure that no more opportunity was lost.

The nursing staff waited at reception with another wheelchair to convey the young GP to the ward, so that monitoring could be performed overnight. They whisked him away. Melanie held back just a little, she wanted to catch Dr Michaels on his own. There were so many things she wanted to tell him and the sentence started without a hitch, "Dr Michaels ...," the words ultimately failing as she couldn't hold back the hug that she now realised was so much more important than any words as she threw her arms around him. He stiffened, then yielded to the irresistible charm of the ravishing woman.

"Do you think Smith would still want me if I were poor?"

"I think the state of your finances would be the last thing that someone like Smith would worry about."

She showed him the text. "Our main product has developed a serious flaw, they are not sure they can fix it. It looks as if I am ruined. I'll have to sell Shiplake, everything, just to keep the staff in their jobs."

"I think that Smith is a very lucky young man," he ventured, "I can't see anything you have just said changing that view."

"No, Dr Michaels I think I am the lucky one."

"After all you have been through, Miss Jardine, I hope you will be very happy."

The beatific smile shone with full intensity, almost as if the sun's setting had been delayed by that brilliant, amber afterglow residing within her eyes. "Don't worry Dr Michaels, I'll have him back in one piece in three week's time, ready for some serious doctoring, besides he is going to have to keep me, I think."

Michaels smiled enigmatically. "Good job he's the best doctor I have seen in many a year."

She hesitated only long enough to plant a peck on his cheek before rushing ahead to catch up with Smith.

Dr Michaels felt the blood rush to areas of his body that it had not reached for some years. No doubt about it, Smith was a very lucky man. He blushed intensely, as he steadied his nerves and suddenly rejected the idea of phoning Anne Farnell. Something told him that at a time like this, a personal visit was more appropriate. He knew with newly discovered certainty, that she would still be awake, and prepared for any eventuality.

THE END